HERE LIES OUR SOVEREIGN LORD

Due to illness, Jean Plaidy was unable to go to school regularly and so taught herself to read. Very early on, she developed a passion for the 'past'. After doing a shorthand and typing course, she spent a couple of years doing various jobs, including sorting gems in Hatton Garden and translating for foreigners in a City café. She began writing in earnest following marriage and now has a large number of historical novels to her name. Inspiration for her books is drawn from odd sources – a picture gallery, a line from a book, Shakespeare's inconsistencies. She lives in London and loves music, secondhand book shops and ancient buildings. Jean Plaidy also writes under the pseudonym of Victoria Holt.

The Charles II Trilogy

HERE LIES OUR SOVEREIGN LORD

JEAN PLAIDY

Pan Books London and Sydney

First published 1957 by Robert Hale and Co
This edition published 1969 by Pan Books Ltd,
Cavaye Place, London, sw10 9pg
9 8 7
© Jean Plaidy 1957
ISBN 0 330 02326 8
Printed in Great Britain by
Richard Clay Ltd, Bungay, Suffolk

For
VIVIAN STUART
with love

'Here lies our Sovereign Lord the King,
Whose word no man relies on;
He never said a foolish thing,
And never did a wise one.'

Thus wrote Rochester. The King, amused, replied:
'The matter is easily accounted for—my discourse is my own, my actions are my ministry's.'

AUTHOR'S NOTE

IT is so generally believed that Charles died a Catholic that I feel I must explain why I do not hold that belief. The deathbed scene has always worried me a great deal because I have felt it to be out of line with Charles' character. Therefore I was anxious to find a convincing explanation.

It is true that Father Huddleston came to him on the night before he died, and that Charles made no protest when it was suggested that he be received into the Catholic Church; but when all the facts are considered I think there is a viewpoint, other than the accepted one, which serves to explain his acquiescence.

On that Sunday, the 1st February, 1685, he ate little all day; he passed a restless night and next morning, while he was being shaved, fell down 'all of a sudden in a fit like apoplexy'. He never fully recovered, although he had periods of consciousness during the next five days which were spent in great pain aggravated by the attention of his physicians who, not knowing what remedies to use, applied most of those of which they had ever heard. During those five days, hot irons were applied to the King's head, pans of hot coals to all parts of his body, and warm cupping glasses to his shoulders while he was bled. Emetics, clysters, purgatives, blistering agents, foul-tasting drugs, and even distillations from human skulls, were given to him – not once but continually. Spirit of sal ammoniac was put under his nose that he might have vigorous sneezing fits, and when he slipped into unconsciousness cauteries were applied to revive him. So that in addition to the pain of his illness he had these tortures to endure.

He knew that he was dying on the Monday, yet he made no effort to see a priest. When Bishop Ken begged him to receive the rites of the Church of England he turned away; but this was a natural gesture, for he was suffering great pain and discomfort, and he had never been a religious man. All through Monday, Tuesday, Wednesday, and Thursday he had been, as he said, 'an unconscionable time a-dying', and on Thursday night the Duke of York and the Duchess of Portsmouth (who both had their reasons) brought Huddleston to his bedside; and at this late hour, according to those few people who were present, Charles joyfully received Huddleston's ministrations.

I believe that Charles was too ill to resist the importunings of his brother and his mistress. I believe that in that easygoing manner which had characterized his entire life he gave way as he had so often before. That is if, after four days of acute agony, discomfort, and intermittent unconsciousness, he was even aware of what he was doing.

According to Burnet, Ken pronounced the absolution of his sins over the King's bed, and in his last hours Charles said that he hoped he should climb to Heaven's gate; 'which', goes on Burnet, 'is the only word savouring of religion that he was heard to speak'.

Charles' attitude to religion had always been constant. He had modelled himself on his maternal grandfather, Henri Quatre, who had ended religious strife in France when he changed from Huguenot to Catholic, declaring that Paris was worth a Mass. Charles believed that religious toleration was the way to peace. He was tolerant to Catholics, not because he was a Catholic, but because they were being persecuted. He had said of Presbyterianism: ''Tis no religion for gentlemen.' This was during his stay in Scotland when he had been forced to hear long prayers and sermons every day, and repent of so many sins that he said: 'I think I must repent that I was ever born.' He had declared: 'I want every man to live under his own vine and figtree.' But this did not mean he was a Catholic.

His attitude to the Church was often frivolous. He had in his youth been hit on the head by his father for smiling at the ladies in church; and as Cunningham says, 'he had learned to look upon the clergy as a body of men who had compounded a religion for their own advantage'.

To his sister Henriette he wrote: 'We have the same

8

disease of sermons that you complain of. But I hope you have the same convenience that the rest of the family has, of sleeping most of the time, which is a great ease to those who are bound to hear them.' He greatly regretted that he had not been awake to hear delivered to Lauderdale a reproof from the pulpit: 'My lord, my lord, you snore so loud you will wake the King.' Burnet, who was a large and vehement man, had once when preaching thumped his pulpit cushion crying: 'Who dares deny it?' to which Charles answered audibly: 'Nobody within reach of that devilish great fist.'

It was Charles' belief that God would never damn a man for a little irregular pleasure; and he had declared his conviction that the greatest sins were malice and unkindness. Such a man would, in my opinion, never 'play safe' at the eleventh hour. He had borne great pain with immense courage and patience which astonished all who beheld it. He was not afraid of death. If he believed that malice and unkindness were the greatest sins he must also have believed that he had sinned less than most men of his age.

I list below some of the books which have been of great help to me:

Bishop Burnet's History of his Own Times, with notes by the Earls of Dartmouth and Hardwicke and Speaker Onslow, to which are added The Cursory Remarks of Swift.
Diary of John Evelyn. Edited by William Bray.
Diary and Correspondence of Samuel Pepys.
A History of English Drama. (Restoration Drama 1660–1700.) Allardyce Nicoll.
The Private Life of Charles II. Arthur Irwin Dasent.
Royal Charles – Ruler and Rake. David Loth.
King Charles II. Arthur Bryant.
The Court Wits of the Restoration. John Harold Wilson.
The Story of Nell Gwyn. Peter Cunningham.
Nell Gwynne, 1650–1687. Her Life Story from St Giles's to St James's with some account of Whitehall and Windsor in the Reign of Charles II. Arthur Irwin Dasent.
Nell Gwyn. Royal Mistress. John Harold Wilson.

Great Villiers. Hester W. Chapman.
Louise de Kéroualle. H. Forneron.
*Rival Sultanas: Nell Gwyn, Louise de Kéroualle and Hortense
    Mancini*. H. Noel Williams.
Lives of the Queens of England. Agnes Strickland.
British History. John Wade.
History of England. William Hickman Smith Aubrey.

J.P.

ONE

ALL through the spring of that year there had been growing tension in the streets of London. It had communicated itself to aged and young alike. The old woman with her tray of herrings on the corner of Cole-yard where it turned off Drury Lane, watched passers-by with eagerness as she called: 'Good herrings! Come buy my good herrings.' If any paused, she would demand: 'Is there news? What news?' The children, ragged, barefoot and filthy, playing in the gutters or trying to earn a coin or two by selling turnips and apples or helping the old woman dispose of her herrings, were alert for news. If any stranger rode by they would run after him, fighting each other for the privilege of holding his horse, demanding with their own brand of Cockney impudence: 'What news, sir? Now Old Noll's departed, what news?'

Every day there were rumours. The observant noticed changes in the London they had known for the last ten years and more – small changes, but nevertheless changes. The brothels had flourished all through the Commonwealth, but discreetly; now, passing through Dog-and-Bitch Lane, it was possible to see the women at the windows, negligent in their dress, beckoning to passers-by and calling to them in their harsh London voices to come inside and see what pleasures they might enjoy. Blood-sports were gradually coming back to London once again.

'We are getting back to the good old days,' people said to one another.

On the cobbles outside one of the hovels in Cole-yard, three children sprawled. They were unusually good-looking, and none of them was marked by the pox or any deformity. The two elder children – a girl and a boy – were about twelve years old, the younger, a girl, aged ten; and it was this ten-year-old who was the most attractive of the three.

Her bones were small and she was delicately formed; her hair fell in a tangle of matted curls about her shoulders; it was of a bright chestnut colour; her hazel eyes were full of mischief; her nose, being small and *retroussé*, added a look of impudence to her face. For all that she was the youngest and so much smaller than the others, she dominated the group.

Beside the boy lay a torch. As soon as it was dark he would be at work, lighting ladies and gentlemen across the roads. The elder of the two girls was casting anxious glances over her shoulder at the hovel behind her, and the young girl was laughing at the elder because of the latter's fear.

'She'll not be out for a while, Rose,' she cried. 'She's got her gin, so what'll she want with her daughters?'

Rose rubbed her hand along her back reminiscently.

Her young sister jeered. 'You should be smarter on your feet, girl. Shame on you! You an active wench, to be caught and pasted by an old woman full of gin!'

The child had leaped up; she found it hard to remain still for any length of time. 'Why,' she cried, 'when old Ma turned to me with her stick I ran straight in to her . . . thus . . . caught her by the petticoat and swung her round till she was so giddy with the turning and the gin that she clutched me for support and begged me stop her from falling, calling me her good girl. And what said I? "Now, Ma! Now Ma . . . You take less of the gin and be more ready with a kiss and a good word for your girls than with the stick. That's the way to have good and loving daughters." She sat flat on the floor to get her breath, and it was not till she was fully recovered that she thought of the stick again. Then 'twas too late to use it, for her anger against me had sped away. That's the way to treat a drunken sot, Rosy girl, be she who she may.'

As the girl had talked she had changed from the role of drink-sodden old woman to sprightly mischievous child, and each she had performed with an adroitness that set the others laughing.

'Give over, Nelly,' said Rose. 'You'll have us die of laughter.'

'Well, we all have to die one day, whether it be of laughter or gin.'

'But not yet, not yet,' said the boy.

'Mayhap twelve years is a little too young, cousin Will. So I'll have mercy on you, and you shall not die of laughing yet.'

'Come, sit down and be quiet awhile,' said Rose. 'I heard tales in Longacre Street this day. They say the King is coming home.'

'If he comes,' said Will, 'I shall be a soldier in his Army.'

'Bah!' said Nell. 'A soldier to fight the battles of others? Even a link-boy fights his own.'

'I'd have a grand uniform,' said Will. 'A beaver hat with a feather to curl over my shoulder. I'd have a silver chain about my neck, riding boots to the knee, and a red velvet cloak. I'd be a handsome gallant roaming the streets of London.'

Nell cried: 'Why not be the King himself, Will?' Will looked crestfallen and she went on kindly: 'Well, Will, who knows, mayhap you shall have your beaver hat and feather. Mayhap when the King comes home 'twill be the custom for every link-boy, from Aldgate Pump to Temple Bar, to have his beaver hat and feather.'

'Nelly jokes,' said Rose. 'My girl, one day your jokes will land you into trouble.'

'Better be landed in trouble by jokes than felony.'

'You are too smart for your years, Nell.'

There was a clatter of horse's hoofs as a man came riding by. All three children got to their feet and ran after the man on horseback who was pulling up at a house in Drury Lane.

'Hold your horse, sir?' said Will.

The man leaped down and threw the reins to Will.

Then he looked at the two girls.

'What news, sir?' asked Nell.

'News! What news should such as I have to give to a drab like you?'

Nell dropped a curtsy. 'Drabs who would be ladies, and serving men aping their lords all have a right to news, sir.'

'Impudent beggar's whore!' said the man.

13

Nell stood poised for flight.

'I am too young for the title, sir. Mayhap if you pass this way a few years later I shall have earned it.'

The man laughed; then feeling in his pocket flung a coin at her. Expertly Nell caught it before it fell to the ground. The man passed on. Will was left holding his horse, while Nell and Rose studied the coin. It was as much as Will would earn for his labour, and Rose remarked on this.

'The tongue is as useful as a pair of hands,' cried Nell.

'What will you do with the money?' asked Rose.

Nell considered. 'A pie, a slice of beef mayhap. Mayhap. As yet I have decided on one thing only: It shall not buy gin for Ma.'

As they strolled back to Cole-yard, their mother appeared suddenly at the door of the hovel.

'Rosy! Nelly!' she screeched. 'You lazy sluts, where are you? I'll wallop you till you're black and blue, you lazy good-for-nothings, both of you. Come here at once . . . if you want to live another hour. Rosy! Nelly! Was ever a good woman cursed with such sluts?' Suddenly she saw them. 'Come here, you two. You, Rosy! You, Nelly! You come here and listen to your own mother.'

'Something has happened to excite her,' said Rose.

'And for once it is not the gin,' added Nell.

They followed Madam Eleanor Gwyn into the dark hovel which was their home.

*   *   *

Their mother sat down panting on a three-legged stool. She was very fat, and the effort of coming to the door and calling them had tired her.

Rose pulled another stool up to her mother's; Nell spread herself on the floor, her legs and tiny feet swaying above her recumbent body, her vital heart-shaped face supported by her hands.

'There are you two, roaming the streets,' scolded Mrs Gwyn, 'never giving a thought to the good days ahead.'

'We were waiting for you to come out of your gin-sleep, Ma,' said Nell.

Mrs Gwyn half rose as though to cuff the girl, but thought better of it.

'Give over with your teasing, Nell,' she said, 'and listen to me. There's good days coming, and shouldn't we all share in them?'

'The King's coming home,' said Rose.

'You two don't remember the old days,' said Madam Gwyn, lapsing into one of the sentimental moods which often came to her after consuming a certain quantity of gin. Nell found them less tolerable than her other phases, preferring a fighter any day to a maudlin drunkard. But now her keen eyes saw that this mood was a passing one. Her mother was excited. 'No, you don't remember the good old days,' she went on. 'You don't remember the shops in the Royal Exchange, and all the merry girls selling their wares there. You don't remember seeing the young cavaliers about the streets. There was a sight for you – in their silks and velvets and feathers and swords! There was a life for a girl. When I was your age there was good sport to be had in this old city. Many's the time I've stood at a pillar in St Paul's and met a kind and generous gentleman.' She spat. 'Kind and generous gentlemen – they went out with the King. They all followed him abroad. But things is different now – or going to be.'

'The King's coming home!' cried Nell. She was on her feet, waving her arms and bowing. 'Welcome, Your Majesty. And what difference are you going to make to two skinny girls and their gin-sodden bawd of a mother?'

'Be silent, Nell, be silent,' warned Rose. 'This is not the time.'

'Any time's the time for the truth,' said Nell. She eyed her mother cautiously. Madam Gwyn returned her stare. Nell was too saucy by half, Madam Gwyn was thinking; but the girl was too spry to be caught and beaten, and in any case she wanted Nell as an ally now; she herself was the one who had to be careful.

And to think she's but ten years old, pondered Nell's mother. Her tongue's twice that age for all her small body and her child's face.

Madam Gwyn was filled with self-pity that she, a loving mother, always thinking of her girls, should be so treated by them; with cupidity, in assessing the value of these two girls in her proposed venture; and with admiration for herself because of the livelihood with which she was going to provide them.

'Nelly's right,' she said placatingly. 'It's always best to have the truth.'

'When the King comes home,' said Rose, 'London will change. It'll be like the old London Ma knew as a girl. And if things change for London, they change for us. But it's a long time since Noll Cromwell died, and the King is still not home. I can remember, when he died, everybody said, "Now the Black Boy will be home." But he didn't come.'

'The Black Boy!' cried Nell. 'How black is he? And is he such a boy?'

'It's his swarthy skin and his way with women. He's as dark as a blackamoor and always a boy where the girls are concerned,' said Madam Gwyn. She began to laugh. 'And Kings set fashions,' she added significantly.

'Let's wait till he's here before we line the streets to welcome him,' said Rose.

'No,' said Nell. 'Let's welcome him now. Then if he does not come we've had the fun of welcome all the same.'

'Put a stop to those clacking tongues,' said Madam Gwyn, 'and listen to me. I'm going to make this place into a nice house for gentlemen . . . There's the cellar below, where we'll put a few chairs and tables, and the gentlemen will come in to take their fill.'

'Their fill . . . of what?' said Nell sharply.

'Of pleasure,' said Madam Gwyn, 'for which they'll pay right well. I'll let some of the girls hereabouts come in and help me build up a nice little house, and it'll all be for the sake of my girls.'

'And a little extra gin,' murmured Nell.

Rose was silent and Nell, who knew her sister well, sensed the alarm in her. Even Nell fell silent. And after a while Madam Gwyn dozed, and Nell and Rose went to the old herring-woman on the corner to help sell some of her wares.

*   *   *

They lay side by side on their pallet. Close to them, on hers, lay their mother. She was fast asleep, but Rose could not sleep; she was afraid; and Nell sensed Rose's fear.

Nell's tongue was sharper than Rose's and Nell was bright enough to know that there were some things about which Rose must be – on account of her two years' seniority – better informed than herself.

Rose was alarmed at the prospect of the 'house' which her mother was planning; and Nell knew that Rose was thinking of the part she would be called upon to play in it. This meant entertaining men. Nell knew something of this. She was so small that she appeared to be younger than she was, but that had not protected her from the attentions of certain men. Her pert face, framed by abundant curls, had not passed unnoticed. On more than one occasion she had been beckoned into quiet places and had gone, hoping to earn a groat or two, for Nell was often hungry and the smell of roasting flesh and hot pies which filled certain streets was at such times very tantalizing; but she had quickly retreated after inflicting kicks and a bite or two, and there had been a great terror within her which she had hidden by her indignant protestations.

'Rose,' she whispered consolingly, 'mayhap it won't come.'

Rose did not answer. She knew Nell's way of not believing anything she thought might be unpleasant. Nell would play at the pageants and the excitement of the King's return over and over again, but of these plans of her mother's which might prove unpleasant she would declare – and believe – they would come to nothing.

Nell went on, for Nell found it difficult to hold her tongue: 'Nay, Ma's house will come to naught. 'Tis many years since there has been this talk of the King's return. And is he here? Nay! Do you remember, Rose, the night of the storm? That was years and years ago. We lay here clinging one to

17

the other in the very fear that the end of the world had come. Do you remember, Rosy? It had been a stifling hot day. Ugh! And the smell of the gutters! Then the darkness came and the thunder and the wind seemed as though it would tear down the houses. And all said: "This is a sign! God's angry with England. God's angry with the Puritans." Do you remember, Rosy?'

'Aye,' said Rose. 'I remember.'

'And then just after that old Noll died and everybody said: "God is angry. He sent the storm and now He's taken old Noll. The Black Boy will be home." But that was long, long ago, Rose, and he's not here yet.'

'It was two years ago.'

'That's a long time.'

'When you're ten it's a long time. When you're as old as I am . . . it's not so long.'

'You're only two years older than I am, Rose.'

'It's a great deal. A lot can happen to a girl in two years.'

Nell was silent for a while; then she said: 'You remember when the General came riding to London?'

'That was General Monk,' said Rose.

'General Monk,' repeated Nell. 'I remember it well. It was the day after my birthday. It was a cold day. There was ice on the cobbles. "A cold February," everyone was saying. "But a hard winter can mean a good summer, and this summer will surely bring the Black Boy home."'

'And it looks as though it will,' said Rose.

'What excitement, Rosy, when the General rode through London! Do you remember how they roasted rumps of beef in the street? Oh, Rosy, don't you love the smell of roasting rumps of beef? And there's one thing I like better. The *taste* of it.' Nell began to laugh.

'Oh, what a time that was, Rosy,' she went on. 'I remember the bonfires – a line of them from St Paul's to the Stocks Market. I thought London town was burning down, I did indeed. There were thirty-one at Strand Bridge. I counted them. But best of all were the butchers and the roasting rumps. That was a day, that was. I always thought, Rose, that it was for my birthday . . . coming so soon after it, you see. All those fires and good beef! I went with the crowd that marched to the house of Praise-God Barebone. I threw some of those stones that broke his windows, I did. And someone in the crowd said to a companion: "What's it all about, do you know?" and I answered up and said: "'Tis Nelly's birthday, that's what it is, though a bit late; but Nelly's birthday all the same." And they laughed in my face and someone said: "Well, at least this child knows what it's all about." And they laughed more and they jeered and were for picking me up and carrying me nearer to the bonfire. But I was scared, thinking they might take it into their heads to roast me in place of a rump . . . so I took to my heels and ran to the next bonfire.'

'Your tongue again, Nell. Guard it well. That was the end of the Rump Parliament, and the General was for the King.'

'It was not so long ago, Rose, and this time he'll be home. Then there'll be fun in the streets; there'll be games in Covent Garden, Rose, and there'll be fairs and dancing in the streets to the tunes of a fiddler. Oh, Rose, I want to dance so much I could get up now and do so.'

'Lie still.'

Nell was silent for a while. Then she said: 'Rose, you're afraid, are you not? You're afraid of Ma's new "house".' Nell threw herself into her sister's arms. 'Why, Rose?' she demanded passionately. 'Why?'

This was one of those rare moments when Nell realized she was the younger sister and begged to be comforted. Once they had been more frequent.

Rose said: 'We have to make a living, Nell. There are not many ways for girls like us.'

Nell nodded fiercely; and a silence fell between them.

Then she said: 'What shall I have to do in Ma's house, Rose?'

'You? Oh, you're young yet. And you're small for your age. Why, you don't look above eight. Keep your tongue quiet and none would think you were the age you are. But your tongue betrays you, Nell. Keep a fast hold on it.'

Nell put out her tongue and held it firmly in her fingers, a habit of her very young days.

'You'll be well enough, Nell. Just at first you'll be called upon to do nothing but serve strong waters to the gentlemen.'

The two sisters clung together in silence, rejoicing that whatever the future held for them, the other would be there to share it.

*   *   *

Nell was there in the streets when the King came home. Never in all her life had she witnessed such pageantry. She had climbed on to a roof – urging Rose and her cousin Will to climb with her – the better to see all that was to be seen.

Nell's eyes shone with excitement as others, following her example, climbed the roof to stand beside the three children; Nell jostled to keep her place and let out such streams of invective that those about her were first incensed, then amused. She snapped her fingers in their faces; she was used to such treatment; she knew the power of her tongue which always made people smile in the end.

From where she stood she could see St Paul's rising high on Ludgate Hill and dominating the dirty city, the hovels of which clustered about the fine buildings like beggars about the skirts of fine ladies. Even the wide roads were so much in need of repair that they were full of potholes; the small streets and alleys were covered in mud and filth. The smells from the breweries, soap-makers and tanneries filled the air, but Nell did not notice this; these were the familiar smells. On the river were boats of all descriptions – barges, wherries, skiffs, anything which could float. Music came from them, and shouting and laughter filled the air. Everyone seemed to want to talk of his pleasure in this day so loudly as to shout his neighbour down.

The bells were ringing from every church in the city; the roughness of the roads was hidden by flowers which had been strewn along the way the King would come; tapestry was hung across the streets and from the windows. The fountains were running with wine. All the people seemed to be congratulating each other that they had lived to see this day.

Over London Bridge and through the streets the procession came on its way to the Palace of Whitehall. There were all the fine ladies and gentlemen, all the noblemen and women who surrounded the King.

Nell leaped with excitement and was warned by Rose and Will that if she did not take greater care she would fall from the roof.

She paid no heed, for at that moment the cheering and shouting of the people had become so loud that she could no longer hear the pealing of the bells. Then she saw the King ride by, tall, and very dark – a veritable Black Boy – bareheaded with his black curls falling over his shoulders, his feathered hat in his hand as he bowed and smiled to the crowds who were shouting themselves hoarse in their welcome.

The dark eyes seemed to miss no one. All about her Nell heard the whisper: 'He smiled at me. I swear it. He looked straight at *me* . . . and smiled. Oh, what a day is this! The King has come home, and England will be merry again.'

Behind the King came all those who had followed him from Rochester, determined to accompany him into his capital, determined to drink his health in the wine flowing from London fountains, determined to show that not only in London did people welcome the King to his own.

Nell was quiet as she watched the rest of the procession. She was wishing she was one of the fine ladies she saw riding there. Those little feet of hers would look well in silver slippers. She longed for a velvet gown to replace her coarse petticoat; she would have liked to comb the tangles out of her hair and wear it in sleek curls as those ladies did.

Rose was wistful too. Rose had changed lately – grown secretive. Rose was now working in her mother's house, and Rose was reconciled. She was pretty and many men who came to the house asked for Mrs Rose. Nell, hurrying from one table to another serving strong waters, eluded those hands stretched out to catch her; she could not curb her tongue and she knew how to use it to advantage – not to charm those men with the ugly lustful faces who gathered in her mother's cellar, but to anger them, so that they felt more inclined to cuff that slut Nelly than to caress her.

It was seven of the clock by the time the procession had passed and they could fight their way back to Cole-yard, where Madam Gwyn was waiting for them. There was free wine in the fountains that day, but all the same she anticipated good business in her cellar.

*   *   *

It was early morning and there were still sounds of revelry in the streets.

Rose was not in the house in Cole-yard. She had gone off with a lover. 'A fine and gallant gentleman,' mused Madam Gwyn. 'Ah, what I do for my girls!'

It was not easy to sleep. Nell lay on her pallet and looked at that mountain of flesh which was her mother. She had never loved her. How was it possible to love one who had cuffed and abused for as long as one could remember? What did Ma want now but a life of ease for herself – ease and gin, of course. She was meant to keep a bawdy-house. Sugary words came easily to her tongue when she talked to the gentlemen, just as abuse came when she scolded her daughters. All her hopes were in Rose – pretty Rose who already had found a lover from the casual callers at the house.

And, mused Nell, what else was there for a girl to do? Sell herrings, apples, turnips?

Rose had a fine gown given her by her lover, and she looked very pretty when she sauntered out into Drury Lane. The other girls were envious of Rose. Yet Nell did not want that life. Nell was going to remain a child – too young for anything but to serve strong drinks – for as long as she could.

'Ma,' she said softly, 'are you asleep?'

'There's too much noise outside for sleep.'

'It's good noise, Ma. It means the King's home and things will change.'

'Things will change,' wheezed Madam Gwyn. Then she said: 'Nell . . . there's nothing left in this bottle. Get me another.'

22

Nell leaped up and obeyed.

'You'll kill yourself, Ma,' she said.

Madam Gwyn spat, and snatched the bottle roughly. Nell watched her, wondering whether when she was young she had ever looked as pretty as Rose.

'I deserve my fancies,' said Madam Gwyn. ''Twas a goodly night. If all nights were as good as this one I'd be rich.'

'Mayhap they will be, Ma, now the King's come home.'

'Mayhap. Mayhap I'll have a true brothel. There's more to be made in a brothel than a bawdy-house. Mayhap ere long I'll have a place in Moorfields or Whetstone Park. Why should such as Madam Cresswell, Mother Temple, and Lady Bennet do so well, while I have my cold cellar and just a few sluts from the Cole-yard?'

'Well, Ma, you've done well. You've got the whole of this place now, and the rooms above this bring much profit to you.'

'You're growing up, Nell.'

'I'm not very old yet, Ma.'

'I once thought you'd be every bit as good as your sister. I'm not so sure now. Don't none of the gentlemen ever have a word with you?'

'They don't like me, Ma.' Madam Gwyn sighed, and Nell went on quickly: 'You've got to have someone to serve the brandy, Ma. You couldn't get round quick enough with it yourself. And would you trust any but me with that fine Nantes brandy?'

Madam Gwyn was silent, and after a while she began to cry. This was the maudlin mood, and for once Nell was glad of it. 'I'd have liked something better for my girls,' mused Madam Gwyn. 'Why, when you were born . . .'

'Tell me about our father,' said Nell soothingly.

And her mother told of the captain who had lost all his money fighting the King's battles. Nell smiled wryly. All poor men in these days had lost their money fighting the King's battles; and she did not believe this story of the handsome captain, for what handsome captain would have married her mother?

'And he would give me this and that,' mourned Madam Gwyn. 'He spent all he had as soon as he got it. That was why he died – blessing me and his two girls – in a debtors' prison in Oxford town.'

Madam Gwyn was crying noisily; outside in the streets the merry-making continued, and Nell lay wide-eyed yet dreaming – dreaming that some miraculous fate took her from her mother's bawdy-house in Cole-yard and she became a lady in a gown of scarlet velvet and silver lace.

*   *   *

Nell stood watching the builders on that plot of land between Drury Lane and Bridge Street.

Will was with her. Will knew most things that went on in the city.

'You know what they're building here, Nelly?' he said. 'A theatre.'

'A theatre!' Nell's eyes sparkled. She had been to the play once in Gibbon's Tennis Court in Vere Street. It had been an experience she had never forgotten, and swore she never would. When she had left the place the enchantment had lingered and, having memorized most of the attractive roles, she had continued to play them out ever since, partly for the benefit of any who would listen and watch, chiefly for her own satisfaction.

What more exciting than to prance on a stage, to have all the people in the theatre watching you, to hear them laugh at your wit, always knowing that their amusement might as easily turn to scorn. Yes, those laughs, those tender languishing glances from young gallants, might easily be replaced by bad eggs or offal, filth picked up in the streets. Nell's eyes sparkled still more as she thought of what she'd have to say to any who dared insult *her*.

And now they were building a new theatre. Because, said Will, the King cared greatly for the theatre and actors; he liked men who could make him laugh, and actors who could divert him with their play.

Gibbon's Tennis Court were no longer considered good enough for a King's Theatre, and this was to be built. So

24

Will had heard two gentlemen say, when he had lighted them across the road. It was going to cost the vast and almost unbelievable sum of one thousand five hundred pounds. 'Mr Killigrew is making all arrangements,' added Will.

'Mr Killigrew!' said Nell, and she laughed loudly. Rose had a new lover. He was a gentleman of high degree and his name was Killigrew – Henry Killigrew. He was employed by the Duke of York, the King's brother; but, more important still, he was the son of the great Thomas Killigrew, friend of the King, Groom of the King's Bechamber and Master of the King's Theatre. It was this great Thomas Killigrew who was responsible for the building of the new theatre, and the fact that Rose's lover was his son gave Rose added lustre in Nell's eyes.

She could scarcely wait to reach home and tell Rose what she had discovered, so bade a hasty farewell to Will, who looked hurt. Poor Will, he should be accustomed to her by now. Will was fond of her; he was afraid that one day her mother would succeed in making her work in the house as Rose worked, even though Nell was determined not to. Nell had her eyes on another life. It was not like her to be secretive, but this she kept to herself. She had started to dream ever since she had watched the King ride into his capital and had seen the fine ladies in their silks and velvets. She had wanted to be as they were and, perhaps because she knew that the nearest she could get to being a lady of quality was to act the part – and this she believed she could do so that none would know her home was a bawdy-house in Cole-yard – she had made up her mind to be an actress.

When she arrived at the house she realized with dismay that soon the gentlemen would be crowding into the cellar, and she would be running from table to table serving brandy, wine or ale, avoiding the hands that now and then sought to catch her, making use of her nimble feet either to kick or to run, and scowling – squinting too – to distort her pretty face.

She went to the room where the girls sat when they were not in the cellar. Rose was there alone.

Nell cried: 'Rose, they're building a theatre by Drury Lane and Bridge Street.'

'I know,' said Rose, smiling secretly. He told her, thought Nell.

'It's Henry's father, who is the King's Theatre Master,' said Nell. 'He is having this done.'

''Tis so,' said Rose.

'Does he talk to you of the theatre, Rose?'

Rose shook her head. 'We don't have time for talking much,' she said demurely.

Nell began to jig round the room. Rose looked at her intently. 'Nelly,' she said, 'you're growing up.' Nell stood still, some of the colour drained from her face. 'And . . . in your way . . .' said Rose, 'you're a pretty wench.'

The horror had frozen on Nell's face. 'Mayhap,' went on Rose, 'you would miss my luck. 'Tis not every girl from Cole-yard who could find herself a gentleman.'

'That's so,' agreed Nell.

'You love the theatre, do you not? You would like to go often. Why, I'll never forget the way you were when you came home after seeing the players – nearly driving us all crazy and making us die of laughing. Nell, how would you like to be in the theatre while the players act?'

'Rose . . . what do you mean? Rosy, Rosy, tell me. . . . Tell me quickly or I'll *die* of despair.'

'That's one thing you'd never die of. Listen to me: I know this, for Henry told me. The King's company have granted to Mrs Mary Meggs the right to sell oranges, lemons, fruit, sweetmeats, and all manner of fruiterers' and confectioners' wares. That will be when the new theatre opens. Oh, it's going to be such a place, Nelly!'

'Tell me . . . tell me about Mary Meggs.'

'Well, she will need girls to help her sell her wares, that is all, Nelly.'

'And you mean . . . that I . . .'

Rose nodded. 'I told Harry about you. He laughed fit to die when I told him how you squinted for fear the gentlemen should be after you. He said he had a mind to try you himself. But he did not mean that,' added Rose complacently. 'I told him how you wanted to be in the playhouse all the time, and he said, "Why, she'd make one of Orange Moll's girls." Then he told me about Mary Meggs and how she wanted three or four girls to stand there in the pit and chivy the gentlemen into buying China oranges.'

Nell clasped her hands together and smiled ecstatically at her sister. 'And I am to do this?'

'I know not. You go too fast. Did you not always? If Mary Meggs makes up her mind that you will suit her, and if she has not already found her girls . . . well then, doubtless you will serve.'

'Take me to her. Take me to her now. I must see Mary Meggs. I must! I must!'

'There is one thing you must not do – and that is squint. Mary Meggs wants pretty girls in the pit. No gentleman would pay sixpence for a China orange to a girl who squints.'

'I shall smile . . . and smile . . . and smile . . .'

'Nell, Nell, don't smile so downstairs, or you'll look too pretty.'

'Nay,' said Nell. 'I shall look like this as I serve the waters.' She made a hideous grimace, squinting diabolically, pulling down her lids with her fingers, and drawing her mouth into a snarl.

Rose doubled up with laughter. Rose laughed easily nowadays. That was because she was thinking of her lover, Harry Killigrew. Life was wonderful, Nell decided; one never knew what was coming. Poor Rose had been frightened of the cellar and the gentlemen, and now that work had brought her Harry Killigrew; and his connection with the King's players was to give Nell an introduction to Orange Moll Meggs and bring her near to her heart's desire.

Rose was sober suddenly. 'There is no need for you to hurry to Mary Meggs. Harry will say: "Mrs Nelly is to sell oranges in the King's Theatre because Mrs Nelly is the sister of my Rose."'

Nell flung herself into her sister's arms, and they laughed together as they had often laughed in the past, laughed for

27

happiness and relief, which, Nell had said, were so much more worth laughing for than a witty word.

*　　　*　　　*

Henry Killigrew did not come to the cellar that night. Rose was always anxious when he did not come. Nell was anxious now. What if he never came again? What if he forgot all about Rose and her sister Nell? What if he did not realize how vitally important it was that Nell Gwyn should become one of Mary Meggs' orange-girls?

Nell moved among the gentlemen with an abstracted look, but she was ever ready to elude their straying hands. She was sorry for poor Rose; for if her lover did not come, Rose would be forced to take another, provided he would pay the price her mother demanded.

Rose was no longer indifferent, because Rose was in love. It was as important now for Rose to elude those straying hands as it was for Nell to do so.

Nell felt sudden anger against a world which had nothing better than this to offer a girl, when others – such as those ladies in velvet and cloth of gold and silver – whom she had seen about the King on his triumphal entry into his Capital, had so much. But almost immediately she was resigned. Rose had her lover, and those ladies riding with the King had not seemed more radiant than Rose when she had been going to meet Henry Killigrew; and when she, Nell, was one of Mary Meggs' orange-girls she would know greater happiness than any of those women could possibly know.

Now her eyes went to Rose. A fat man with grease on his clothes – doubtless a flesh-merchant from East Cheap – was beckoning to her, and Rose must perforce go and sit at his table.

Nell watched. She saw the big hands touching Rose, saw Rose recoiling with horror, her eyes piteously fixed on the door, waiting for the entry of her lover.

Nell heard her say: 'No . . . No. It is not possible. I have a gentleman waiting for me.'

The flesh-merchant from East Cheap stood up and kicked the stool on which he had been sitting across the cellar.

Others watched, eyes alert with interest. This was what they liked – a brawl in a bawdy-house when they could throw bottles at one another, wreck the place, and enjoy good sport.

Madam Gwyn had come from her corner like an angry spider. She raised her slurring gin-cracked voice. 'What ails you, my fine gentleman? What do you find in my house not to your liking?'

'This slut!' shouted the flesh-merchant.

'Why, that's Mrs Rose . . . the prettiest of my girls . . . Now, Mrs Rose, what has gone wrong here? You drop a curtsy to the fine gentleman and tell him you await his pleasure.'

The flesh-merchant watched Rose and his little eyes were cruel.

'He's planning to hurt her,' shouted Nell in panic.

Rose cried: 'I cannot. I am ill. Let me go. There is a gentleman waiting for me.'

Rose's mother took her by the arm and pushed her towards the flesh-merchant, who gripped her and held her to him for a few seconds; then he was roaring with rage, shouting at the top of his voice. 'I see it now. She has my purse, the slut!'

He was holding a purse above his head. Rose had stepped back, staring at the purse with fascinated eyes.

'Where did you . . . find that?' she asked.

'Inside your bodice, girl. Where you put it.'

''Tis a lie,' said Rose. 'I never saw it before.'

He had caught at the drapery at Rose's neck, cut low to show her pretty bosom. He tore the charming dress which was a present from her lover.

'Lying slut!' cried the merchant. 'Thieving whore!' He appealed to others sitting at the tables. 'Must we endure this treatment? 'Tis time we taught these bawds a lesson.'

He kicked the table; it was cheap and fragile, and it was smashed against the wall.

'I pray you, good sir,' soothed Madam Gwyn, 'I pray you curb your anger against Mrs Rose. Mrs Rose is ready to make amends. . . .'

'I never saw the purse,' cried Rose. 'I did not take the purse.'

The merchant paused and ceremoniously opened the purse. 'There's ten shillings missing from it,' he said. 'Come, give me what you've taken, slut.'

'I have not had your money,' protested Rose.

The man took her by the shoulders. 'Give it me, you slut, or I'll bring a charge against you.' His little pig's eyes were glistening. His face, thought Nell, was like a boar's head which had been pickled for several days. She hated him; if she had not grown accustomed to keeping herself under control in the cellar, she would have rushed at once to Rose's defence. But she was afraid; for that which she saw in the man's eyes was lust as well as the desire for revenge; and she was afraid of lust.

He had turned now to the company. He shouted: 'Look to your own pockets. They lure you here; they drug their waters; how many of you have left this place poorer men than when you entered it? How many of you have paid too dear for what you've had? Come! Shall we allow these bawds to rob us?'

One of the men shouted: 'What will you do, friend?'

'What will I do!' he screamed. He had caught Rose by the shoulder. 'I'll take this whore and make an example of her, that I will.'

Madam Gwyn was beside him, rubbing her fat hands together. 'Mrs Rose is my prettiest girl, sir. Mrs Rose is longing for a chance to be kind to you.'

'I doubt it not!' roared the man. 'But she comes to her senses too late. I came here for a good honest whore, not a jailbird.'

'I'm no jailbird!' cried Rose.

'Is that so, Miss?' snarled the man. 'Then you soon will be. Come, my friends.'

And with that he dragged Rose to the door. The men who were sitting about the tables rose and formed a bodyguard about him. 'Take the thief to jail!' they chanted. 'That's the way to treat a thief.'

Rose was pale with horror.

Everyone was leaving the cellar. They could visit a bawdy-house at any time; but it was not so often that they could see one of the patrons drag a girl to jail.

'I've been robbed here more than once, I swear it,' declared a little man.

'And I!' 'And I!' the cry went up.

Nell moved then; she ran after the group who were pushing their way into the street. Already down in Coleyard the flesh-merchant was calling out where he intended taking Rose, and crowds were gathering.

'A pickpocket whore!' Nell heard the words. 'Caught stealing money.'

''Tis a lie. 'Tis a lie!' cried Nell.

Nobody looked at her. She fought her way to Rose. Poor Rose, bedraggled and weeping so bitterly, her pretty gown ruined, her pretty lips begging, pleading, swearing that she was innocent.

Nell caught at the flesh-merchant's arm. 'Let her go. Let my sister go!'

He saw her, and as she clung to his arm he raised it and swung her off her feet.

'It's the imp who serves strong waters. I'll warrant she's as quick with her fingers as the other. We'll take her along with us, eh, my friends?'

'Aye, take her along. Take the whole lot along. Have them searched, and have them hanged by the neck, as all thieves should be.'

Nell caught one glimpse of Rose's anguished face. Nell's own was distorted with rage. She dug her teeth into the flesh-merchant's hand, gave him a kick on the shin, and so startled him that, letting out a cry of pain, he relaxed his hold on her.

She screamed: 'Run, Rose. Run!' as she herself darted through the crowd. But Rose could not so easily make her escape; the crowd saw to that; and in a few seconds the flesh-merchant had regained his hold upon her, and the shouting crowd carried Rose Gwyn to Newgate.

*   *   *

Nell had never known such fear as now was hers. Rose was in jail. She was a thief, the flesh-merchant had declared; he had discovered his purse on her, and ten shillings were missing from it. There were even men to come forward and say they had seen Rose take the purse.

Rose had a fine dress, it was remarked. By what means had she, a poor girl in a low bawdy-house, come by such a garment? She had stolen the money to pay for it, of course.

Those who were found guilty of theft suffered the extreme penalty.

Nell walked the streets in her misery, not knowing which way to turn for comfort. Her mother drank more and more gin, and sat weeping through the day and night, for few people came to the cellar during those days. The rumour had spread that if you went into Mother Gwyn's house you might lose your purse. There had been many lost purses, and now Mother Gwyn as a result was going to lose her daughter

Rose . . . in prison. It was terrible to think of her there – Rose who such a short while ago had been so happy with her lover, the man who thought so highly of her that he had promised to make her sister one of Orange Moll Meggs' girls.

There was only one person who could offer Nell comfort, and that was her cousin Will. They sat on the cobbles in the yard and talked of Rose.

'There's nothing can be done,' said Will. 'They've declared her a thief, and they'll hang her by the neck.'

'Not Rose!' cried Nell, with the tears running down her face. 'Not my sister Rose!'

'They don't care whose sister she is, Nelly. They only care that they hang her.'

'Rose never stole anything.'

Will nodded. 'It matters not whether she stole or not, Nelly. They say she stole, and they'll hang her for that.'

'They shall not,' cried Nell. 'They *shall* not.'

'But how will you stop them?'

'I know not.' Nell covered her face with her hands and burst into loud sobs. 'If I were older and wiser I would know. There is a way, Will. There must be a way.'

'If Mr Killigrew had been there it would not have happened,' said Will.

'If he had been there, he could have stopped it. Will, mayhap he could stop it now.'

'How so?' said Will.

'We must find him. We must tell him what happened. Will, where can we find him?'

'He is Groom of the Bedchamber to the Duke.'

'I will go to the Duke.'

'Nay, Nelly. You could not do that. The Duke would never see *you*!'

'I would *make* him see me . . . *make* him listen.'

'You would never reach him.' Will scratched his head. Nell watched him eagerly. 'I saw him last night,' added Will.

'You saw him? The Duke?'

'Nay, Henry Killigrew.'

'Did you tell him about Rose?'

'*I* tell *him*? Nay, I did not. I was holding a torch for a gentleman close by Lady Bennet's, and he came out. He was as close to me as you are now.'

'Oh, Will, you should have told him. You should have asked his help.'

'He has not been to Cole-yard since, has he, Nelly? He's forgotten Rose.'

'I'll not believe it,' declared Nell passionately.

'Rose used to say you only believed what you wanted to.'

'I like believing what I want to. Then I can make it happen mayhap. Does he go often to Lady Bennet's?'

'I heard it said that he is mighty interested in one of the girls there.'

'That cannot be. He is interested in Rose.'

'Such as he can be interested in many at a time.'

'Then I will go to Lady Bennet's, and I will see him and tell him he must save Rose.'

Will shook his head.

Nell was the wildest thing he had ever seen. He never knew what she would do next. There was one thing he did know: it was folly to dissuade her once she had set her mind on something.

* * *

So the small raggedly clad girl waited in the shadows of Lady Bennet's house. None of the gentlemen passing in and out gave her a second glance. She looked much younger than her thirteen years.

She knew that she would find Henry Killigrew there. She must find him there, and she must find him quickly, for Rose was in acute danger. If she could not find him at Lady Bennet's, then she would at Damaris Page's. She could be sure that it would be possible to find such a profligate as Rose's Henry undoubtedly was, at one of the notorious brothels in London.

Nell felt that she had grown up in these last days of her grief. She was no longer a child but a woman of under-standing. Nothing she discovered of Henry Killigrew would surprise her as much as the fact that he had ever come to Cole-yard.

And it was outside Lady Bennet's that she came face to face with him. She ran to him, fell on her knees before him, and took his hand in hers. There was another gentleman with him who raised his eyebrows and looked askance at his companion.

'What means this, Henry?' he asked. 'Who is the infant?'

'God's Body! I swear I've seen the child somewhere ere this?'

'You keep strange company, Henry.'

'I'm Nell,' cried Nell. 'Mrs Rose's sister.'

'Why, now I know. And how fares Mrs Rose?'

'Badly!' cried Nell in sudden rage. 'And that seems small concern of yours.'

'And should it concern me?' he asked flippantly.

His companion was smiling cynically.

'If you are not knave it should,' retorted Nell.

Henry Killigrew turned to his companion. 'This is the child who serves strong waters at Mother Gwyn's bawdy-house.'

'And strong words with it, I'll warrant,' said the other.

'A sharp-tongued vixen,' said Henry.

Nell cried suddenly: 'My sister is in prison. They will hang her.'

'What?' said Henry's companion languidly. 'Do they then hang whores? It will not do.'

'Indeed it will not do,' cried Henry. 'Shall they hang all the women of London and leave us desolate?'

'God preserve the whores of London!' cried the other.

'They will hang her for what she has not done,' said Nell. 'You must save her. You must take her out of prison. It is on your account that she is there.'

'On my account?'

'Indeed yes, sir. She was hoping you would come; you did not, but another did. She refused him and so he accused her of this crime. He was a flesh-merchant of East Cheap. Rose could not endure him . . . after your lordship.'

'The vixen sets a drop of honey in the vinegar, Henry,' murmured his friend, flicking at the lace of his sleeve.

'Do not mock,' said Henry, serious suddenly. 'Poor Rose! So this flesh-merchant had her sent to prison, eh . . . ?' He turned to his friend. 'Why, Browne, we'll not endure this. Rose is a lovely girl. I meant to call on her this very night.'

'Then call on her in jail, sir,' begged Nell. 'Call on her – and you, being such a noble gentleman, can of a certainty procure her release.'

'The little vixen hath a good opinion of you,' said Browne.

'And it shall not be misplaced.'

'Where go you, Henry?'

'I'm going to see Mrs Rose. I'm fond of Rose. I anticipate many happy hours with her.'

'God will reward you, sir,' said Nell.

'And Rose also, I pray,' murmured Browne.

They walked away from Lady Bennet's while Nell ran beside them.

*   *   *

Life was truly wonderful.

There was no longer need to hide her prettiness. Now she

washed and combed her hair; it hung down her back in a cloud of ringlets. There was no longer need to squint and frown; she could laugh as often as she liked – an occupation which suited her mood more readily than any other.

On the day she walked into the King's Theatre, she was the proudest girl in London. Lady Castlemaine, for all that she was the King's pampered mistress, could not have been happier than little Nell Gwyn in her smock, stays, and petti-coat, her coarse gown and her kerchief about her neck; and she was actually wearing shoes on her feet. The chestnut curls hung over her bare shoulders; she looked her age now. She was thirteen, and even if it was a very small thirteen it was a very dainty one.

The men could look as much as they liked now, for, as Nell would be the first to admit, looks were free and any man who was prepared to pay his sixpence for one of her oranges could take his fill of looking.

If any tried to take liberties they would meet a torrent of abuse which seemed startling coming from one so small and so enchanting to the eye. It was said in the pit and the middle and upper galleries that the prettiest of all Moll Meggs' orange-girls was little Nelly Gwyn.

Nell was filled with happiness, for Rose was home now. She had been saved by the two gallants whom Nell had called in to help her. What a wonderful thing it was to have friends at Court!

A word from Henry Killigrew, Groom of the Bed-chamber, to the Duke, a word from Mr Browne who, it appeared, was Cup-bearer to the same Duke, and Rose was granted a pardon, and had merely walked out of her jail.

Moreover Mr Browne and Henry Killigrew had been somewhat impressed by the wit and resource of Rose's young sister whom they addressed with mock ceremony as Mrs Nelly; and Henry had been only too ready to see that Mrs Nelly became one of Orange Moll's girls, for, as he said, it was such girls as Mrs Nelly for whom Orange Moll was looking – and not only Orange Moll. He intimated that when he strolled into His Majesty's Theatre he also would not be averse to taking a glance at Mrs Nelly.

Nell shook her curls. She felt that she would know how to deal with Henry Killigrew, should the need arise.

In the meantime her dearest wish had been granted. Six days of the week she was in the theatre – the King's Theatre – and it seemed to her that, in that wooden building, the pageant of life at its most exciting passed before her eyes. She did not know which delighted her more, the play or the audience.

It was true that the King's Theatre was a draughty place; its glazed cupola let in a certain amount of daylight which in bad weather could make it somewhat uncomfortable for the occupants of the pit; sometimes it was cold, for there was no artificial heating; sometimes it was stiflingly hot from the press of bodies, and this heat was augmented by the candles on the walls and over the stage.

These were trifling matters. Gazing at the stage it was possible to forget that her home was still the bawdy-house in Cole-yard; here she could live in a different world by aping the actors and actresses; she could see the nobility, for often the King himself came to the playhouse. Was he not its chief patron, and did not all the actors and actresses of the King's house call themselves His Majesty's Servants? So, it was natural that he should often be there, sometimes with the Queen, sometimes with the notorious Lady Castlemaine, sometimes with others. She would see the Court wits – my lord Buckingham, my lord Rochester, Sir Charles Sedley, Lord Buckhurst. They all came to the play, and with them came the ladies who interested them at the time.

She had heard wild stories concerning them all, and to these she listened with relish. She had seen the Queen sail up London river with the King after his marriage; she had been with the crowd which had witnessed their arrival at Whitehall Bridge, while the Queen Mother, who was on a visit to her son, waited to receive the royal pair on the pier which had been erected for the occasion; and all were so gorgeously clad that the spectators had gaped with wonder.

She knew, too, that the King had forced the Queen to accept Lady Castlemaine as one of the women of her bedchamber. All London talked of it – the resentment of the

Queen, the flaming arrogance of Lady Castlemaine, and the stubbornness of the King. She was sorry for the dark-eyed Queen, who looked a little sad at times and seemed to be trying so hard to understand what the play was about, laughing a little too late at the jokes, at which, poor lady, she might have blushed instead of laughed had she understood them.

Then there was the arrogant Lady Castlemaine, sitting with the King or in the next box and speaking to him in her loud imperious voice so that the audience in the pit craned their heads upwards to see and hear what she was at, and the galleries looked down for the same reason; for when Lady Castlemaine was in the playhouse few paid attention to the players.

There was often to be seen in their boxes those two rakes, Lord Buckhurst and Sir Charles Sedley. Lord Buckhurst was a good-natured man, a poet and a lover of wit, whose high spirits very often drew him into prominence. Sir Charles Sedley was a poet and a playwright as well. He was so slight in stature that he was nicknamed Little Sid. These two were watched with alert interest by the house. With Sir Thomas Ogle they had recently behaved with reckless devilry at the Cock Tavern, where, having eaten well and drunk still better, they had gone to the balcony of the tavern, taken off all their clothes, and lectured the passers-by in an obscene and offensive manner. There had been a riot and as a result Little Sid was taken to court, heavily fined, and bound over to keep the peace for a year. So the audience watched and waited, no doubt hoping that these three rakes would repeat here in the theatre the performance they had given at the Cock Tavern.

Here was Nell's first glimpse at the high life of the Court. And, in addition to watching at close quarters the highest in the land, she could practise her repartee on the gay young men in the pit. All those with a strain of puritanism, left over from the fifties, stayed away from the theatre which, they declared, was nothing more than a meeting place for courtesans and those who sought them; and indeed the noblemen in the pit and the boxes, and women from the

38

Court together with the prostitutes, made up the greater part of the audience. The women wore vizard masks (which were supposed to hide their blushes when the dialogue on the stage was too outspoken) and the lowest aped the highest; they chatted with each other, noisily sucked China oranges, threw the peel at each other and the players, showered abuse on the actors and actresses if they did not like the way the play was going, fought one another, and added to the general clamour. Courtiers, and apprentices aping courtiers, made assignations with the vizard masks. The side boxes, which cost four shillings, were filled with ladies and gentlemen of the Court and were only slightly raised above the pit, where the price of a seat was two shillings and sixpence. In the middle gallery where a seat cost a modest eighteen pence sat the quieter folk who wished to hear the play; and in the shilling gallery were the poorest section of the audience, and here coachmen and footmen, whose masters and mistresses were in the theatre, were allowed to enter without charge towards the end of the play.

Each day Nell found full of incident. Never could one guess what would happen next at the playhouse, what great scandal would be talked of, or what great personage would quarrel with another during the course of the performance.

She could listen to the loud and often lewd conversation between courtiers in their boxes and vizard masks in the pit, conversation in which the rest of the audience would often join as they combed their hair or drank noisily from the bottles they brought in with them; some stood on the benches and jeered at the players, quarrelled with the sentiments of the play, or even climbed on to the stage and attempted to fight an actor for his dastardly conduct in the play or mayhap on account of some real grievance.

It was all clamour, and colour, and Nell loved it. Nor was this the sum of her excitement; for her, by no means least of the theatre's attractions was the play itself.

And when the handsomest actor of them all, who was considered by many to be the company's leading man, played his parts he could often quieten the noisiest of the

39

audience. He would strut the stage, not as himself, handsome Charles Hart, but as the character he played; and if that character were a king it would seem that Charles Hart was as much a king as that other Charles who sat in his box, alert and appreciative of one who aped his royalty with such success.

Nell thought Charles Hart godlike as he came from the back stage and stepped on to the apron stage, and by his magnetic presence demanded attention. She would stand very still watching him, forgetting her load of oranges, not caring if Orange Moll should see her staring at the stage instead of doing all in her power to persuade someone in the audience to buy a fine China orange. Nell had spoken to the great man once or twice. He had bought an orange from her. He had noted her dainty looks with appreciation, for Charles Hart was appreciative of beauty. He had never yet been made aware of the agility of Nell's tongue, for she had been reduced to unaccustomed silence in the presence of the great man. Yet he must have known that she had a ready gift of repartee since no orange-girl could have survived long without it.

This day he was playing the part of Michael Perez in *Rule a Wife and Have a Wife*, and many from the Court had come to see him. Nell was in a daze of admiration as she went into the tiring room to see if she could sell an orange or two to the actresses.

Several gallants were already there, for they were admitted to the tiring room on payment of an extra half-crown, and there it was possible for them to have intimate conversation with the actresses, perhaps make love to them there or make assignations for such love-making in more private places.

Nell was greatly attracted by the tiring room; she had heard that actresses were paid as much as twenty to fifty shillings a week – a fabulous sum to a poor orange-girl; they looked quite splendid off the stage as well as on it, for they had beautiful clothes which were given by courtiers – and even the King himself – for use in their plays. The gentlemen fawned on them, pressed gifts on them, implored them to accept their invitations; and the actresses gave answers as pert as any they used to their stage lovers.

'A China orange, Mrs Corey?' cooed Nell. 'So soothing, so cooling to the throat.'

'Not for me, wench. Go along to Mrs Marshall. Mayhap she'll get one of her gentlemen friends to buy her a China orange.'

'I doubt she'll get much more from him!' cried Mary Knepp.

And Mrs Uphill and Mrs Hughes went into peals of laughter at Mrs Marshall's expense.

'Here, wench,' called Mrs Eastland, 'run out and buy me a green riband. There'll be a groat or two for your pains when you return.'

This was typical of life in the green tiring room. Nell ran errands, augmenting her small income, and very soon took to wondering what Peg Hughes and Mary Knepp had that she lacked.

It was when she had returned with the riband and was making her way backstage, where Mary Meggs kept her wares under the stairs, that she came face to face with the great Charles Hart himself.

She curtsied and said: 'A merry good day to Mr Perez.'

He paused and, leaning towards her, said: 'Why, 'tis little Nell the orange-girl. And you liked Michael Perez, eh?'

'So much, sir,' said Nell, 'that I had forgot till this moment that he was an even greater gentleman – Mr Charles Hart.'

Charles Hart was not indifferent to flattery. He knew that he – with perhaps Michael Mohun as his only rival – was the best player among the King's Servants. All the same, praise from any quarter was acceptable, even from a little orange-girl, and he had noticed before that this orange-girl was uncommonly pretty.

He took her face in his hands and kissed her lightly. 'Why,' he said, 'you're pretty enough to grace a stage yourself.'

'One day I shall,' said Nell; and in that moment she knew she would. Why should she not give as good an account of herself as any of the screaming wenches in the green room?

'Oh,' he said, 'so the girl hath ambition!'

'I want to play on the stage,' she said.

He looked at her again. Her eyes were brilliant with excitement. There was a vitality which was rare. God's Body! he thought. This child has quality. He said: 'Come with me, girl.'

Nell hesitated. She had had similar invitations before this. Charles Hart saw her hesitation and laughed. 'Nay,' he said, 'have no fear. I do not force little girls.' He drew himself up to his full height and spoke the words as though he were delivering them to an audience. 'There has never been any need for me to force any. They come ... they come with the utmost willingness.'

His fluency fascinated her. He spoke to her – Nell – as though she were one of those gorgeous creatures on the stage. He made her feel important, dramatic, already an actress, playing her part with him.

She said: 'Willingly will I listen to what you have to say to me, sir.'

'Then follow me.'

He turned and led the way through a narrow passage to a very small compartment in which were hanging the clothes which he wore for his parts.

He turned to her then, ponderously. 'Your name, wench?' he asked.

'Nell . . . Nell Gwyn.'

'I have observed you,' he said. 'You have a sharp tongue and a very ready wit. Methinks your talents are wasted with Orange Moll.'

'Could I act a part on the stage?'

'How would you learn a part?'

'I would learn. I *would* learn. I would only have to hear it once and I would know it.' She put down her basket of oranges and began to repeat one of the parts she had seen played that afternoon. She put into it the utmost comedy, and the fine lips of Mr Charles Hart began to twitch as he watched her.

He lifted a hand to stop her exuberance. 'How would you learn your parts?' he said. Nell was bewildered. 'Can you read?' She shook her head. 'Then how would you learn them?'

'I would,' she cried. 'I would.'

'The will is not enough, my child. You would be obliged to learn to read.'

'Then I would learn to read.'

He came to her and laid his hands on her shoulders. 'And what would you say if I told you that I might have room for a small-part player in the company?'

Nell dropped on her knees, took his hand, and kissed it.

He looked at her curly head with pleasure. 'Od's Fish!' he said, using the King's oath, for he played the part of kings now and then and had come to believe that in the world of the theatre he was one, 'You're a pretty child, Mrs Nelly.'

And when she rose he lifted her in his arms and held her so that her animated face was on a level with his.

'And as light as a feather,' he said. 'Are you as wayward?'

Then he kissed her lips; and Nell understood what he would require in payment for all that he was about to do for her.

Nell knew that she would not consider anything he demanded as payment. She had already learned to adore him from the pit; she was ready to continue in that adoration from a more intimate position. She laughed, signifying her pleasure, and he was satisfied.

'Come,' he said, 'I will go with you to Mary Meggs, for it may be she will by now be too ready to scold you, and it is my wish that you should not be scolded.'

When Mary Meggs caught sight of Nell she screamed at her: 'So there you are, you jade! What have you been at? I've been waiting here for you this last quarter-hour. Let me tell you that if you behave thus you will not long remain one of Orange Moll's young women.'

Charles drew himself up to his full height. Nell found herself laughing, as she was to laugh so often in times to come at this actor's dignity. In everything he did it was as though he played a part.

'Save your breath, woman,' he cried in that voice of thunder with which he had so often silenced a recalcitrant audience. 'Save your breath. Mrs Nelly here shall certainly not remain one of your orange-girls. She ceased to do so some little time ago. Nelly the orange-girl is now Nelly the King's Servant.'

Then he strode off and left them. Nell set down her basket and danced a jig before the astonished woman's eyes. Orange Moll – none too pleased at the prospect of losing one of her best girls – shook her head and her finger at the dancing figure.

'Dance, Nelly, dance!' she said. 'Mr Charles Hart don't make actresses of all his women – and he don't keep them long either. Mayhap you'll be wanting your basket back when the great Charles Hart grows Nelly-sick.'

But Nell continued to dance.

*   *   *

Now Nell was indeed an actress. She quickly left her mother's house in Cole-yard and most joyfully set up in lodgings of her own; she took a small house next to the Cock and Pye Tavern in Drury Lane opposite Wych Street. Here she was only a step or two away from the theatre, which was convenient indeed, for the life of an actress was a more strenuous one than that of an orange-girl. Charles Hart was teaching her to read; William Lacy was teaching her to dance; and both, with Michael Mohun, were teaching her to act. Mornings were spent in rehearsing, and the afternoons in acting plays which started at three o'clock and went on until five or later. Most of Nell's evenings were spent with the great Charles Hart who, delighted with his protégée, initiated her into the art of making love, when he was not teaching her to read.

Rose was delighted with her sister's success and she became a frequent visitor at the lodgings in Drury Lane. Nell would have liked to ask her to come and live with her; but Nell's small wages just kept herself – and as an actress it was necessary for her to spend a great deal of her income on fine clothes. Moreover Rose had her own life to lead and often a devoted lover would take her away from her mother's house for a while.

Harry Killigrew was one of these, as was Mr Browne; and in the company of these gentlemen Rose met others of their rank. She was as eager to avoid flesh-merchants from East Cheap as she ever was, and continuously grateful to Nell who, she declared, had saved her from a felon's death.

Nell played her parts in the theatre – small ones as yet, for she had her apprenticeship to live through. Charles Hart proved to be a devoted lover, for Nell was an undemanding mistress, never a complaining one; her spirits were invariably high; and she quickly learned to share Charles Hart's passion for the stage.

There were times when he forgot to act before her and would talk of his aspirations and his jealousies, and beg her to tell him without reserve whether she believed Michael Mohun or Edward Kynaston to be greater actors than he was. He often talked of Thomas Betterton, one of that rival group of players who called themselves The Duke's Men, and who performed in the Duke's Theatre. It was said that Betterton, more than any man living, could hold an audience. 'Better than Hart?' demanded Charles Hart. 'I want the truth from you, Nell.'

Then Nell would soothe him and say that Betterton was a strolling player compared with the great Charles Hart; and Charles would say that it was meet and fitting that *he*, Hart, should be the greatest actor London had ever known, because his grandmother was a sister of the dramatist, Will Shakespeare – a man who loved the theatre and whose plays were often acted by the companies, and which, some declared, had never yet been bettered, surpassing even those of Ben Jonson or Beaumont and Fletcher.

Sometimes he would tell her how he had been brought up at Blackfriars and, with Clun, one of the other members of the company, had, as a boy, acted women's parts. He would strut about the apartment playing the Duchess in Shirley's tragedy *The Cardinal*, and Nell would clap her hands and assure him that he was the veriest Duchess she had ever seen.

He liked to pour his reminiscences of the past into Nell's sympathetic ears. And Nell, who loved him, listened and applauded, for she thought him the most wonderful person she had ever known, godlike in his ability to raise the orange-girl to the green room, a tender yet passionate lover to introduce her into a milieu where, she was aware, she would wish to play a leading part.

She allowed him to tell his stories again and again; she would demand to hear them. 'Tell me of the time you were carried off and imprisoned by Roundhead soldiers – taken while you were actually playing, and in your costume, too!'

So he would throw back his head and adjust his magnificent voice to the drama or comedy of the occasion. 'I was playing Otto in *The Bloody Brother*. . . . A fine play. I'll swear Beaumont and Fletcher never wrote a better. . . .'

Then he would forget the story of the capture and play Otto for her; he would even take the part of Rollo, the Bloody Brother himself, and it was all vastly entertaining, as was life.

And in the boxes at the theatre there appeared at this time the loveliest woman Nell had ever seen: Mrs Frances Stuart, maid of honour to the Queen. The King gazed at her during the whole of the play so that his attention strayed from Charles Hart, Michael Mohun, and Edward Kynaston; and, what was more remarkable, neither tall and handsome Ann Marshall, nor any of the actresses could hold his gaze. The King saw no one but Mrs Stuart, sitting there so childishly pretty with her fair hair, great blue eyes, and Roman nose, so that my lady Castlemaine was in such a high temper that she shouted insults to the actors and actresses – and even spoke churlishly to the King himself, to his great displeasure.

It all seemed remote to Nell; she had her own life to lead; and if it was less grand than those of these Court folk in their dazzling jewels and sumptuous garments, it was lively, colourful, and completely satisfying to Nell; for one of her great gifts was to be able to enjoy contentment with her lot.

And there came a day when she thought her joy was complete.

Charles Hart came to her lodging and, when she had let him in and he had kissed her, declaring that she was a mighty pretty creature in her smock sleeves and bodice, he held her at arms' length and said in his loud booming voice: 'News, Nelly! At last you are to be an actress.'

'You are insolent, sir!' she cried in mock anger, her eyes flashing. 'Would you insult me? What am I indeed, if I am not an actress!'

'You are my mistress, for one thing.'

She caught his hand and kissed it. 'And that is the best part I have yet been called upon to play.'

'Sweet Nelly,' he murmured as though in an aside. 'How this wench delights me!'

'As yet!' she answered promptly. 'I beg of you to tell me quickly. What part is this?'

But Charles Hart never spoilt his effects. 'You must first know,' he said, 'that we are to play Dryden's *Indian Emperor*, and I am to take the part of Cortes.'

She knelt and kissed his hand in half-mocking reverence. 'Welcome to the conquering hero,' she said. Then she leaped to her feet. 'And what part for Nelly?'

He folded his arms and stood smiling at her. 'The chief female role,' he said slowly, 'is Almeria. Montezuma will sigh for her favours; Mohun will play Montezuma. She however longs for Cortes.'

'She cannot help that, poor girl,' said Nell. 'And right heartily will she love her Cortes. I will show the King and the Duke, and all present, that never was man loved as my Cortes.'

'Ann Marshall is to play Almeria. Nay, 'tis not the part for you. You are young yet to take it. Oh, you are learning . . . learning . . . but an orange-girl does not become an actress in a matter of weeks. Nay, there is another part – a beautiful part for a beautiful girl – that of Cydaria. I have said Nelly shall play Cydaria, and I have made Tom Killigrew, Mohun, Lacy, and the rest agree that you shall do this.'

'And this Cydaria – she is of small account beside that other, played by Mrs Ann Marshall?'

'Hers is the sympathetic part, Nelly. There is a pink dress come from the Court – a present from one of the ladies. You will well become it and, as you are the Emperor's daughter,

47

you shall wear plumes in your hair. There is something else, Nelly. Cydaria wins Cortes in the end.'

'Then,' declaimed Nell, dropping a curtsy, 'must I be content with Cortes-Hart and revel in this minor part.'

*   *   *

She was dressed in the flowery gown, her chestnut curls arranged over her shoulders. In the tiring room the others looked at her with envy.

'An orange-girl not long ago,' whispered Peg Hughes. 'Now, fa la, she is given the best parts. She'll be putting Mrs Marshall's nose out of joint ere long, I'll warrant.'

'You know the way to success on the stage surely,' said Mary Knepp. 'No matter whether you be actress or orange-girl – the way's the same. You go to bed with one who can give you what you want, and in the dead of night you ask for it.'

Nell overheard that. 'I thank you for telling me, Mrs Knepp,' she cried. 'For the life of me I could not understand how you ever came to get a part.'

'Am I a player's whore?' demanded Mrs Knepp.

'Ask me not,' said Nell. 'Though I have seen you acting in such a manner with Master Pepys from the Navy Office as to lead me to believe you may be his.'

Ann Marshall said: 'Stop shouting, Nelly. You're not an orange-girl now. Keep your voice for your part. You'll need it.'

Nell for once was glad to subside. She was sure that she would acquit herself well in her part, but she was experiencing a strange fluttering within her stomach which she had rarely known before.

She turned from Mrs Knepp and whispered her lines to herself:

> '*Thick breath, quick pulse and beating of my heart,*
> *All sign of some unwonted change appear;*
> *I find myself unwilling to depart,*
> *And yet I know not why I should be here.*
> *Stranger, you raise such torments in my breast . . .*'

48

These were her words on her first meeting with Cortes when she falls in love with him at first sight. She thought then of the first time she had seen Charles Hart. Had she felt thus then? Indeed she had not. She did not believe she would ever feel as Cydaria felt; Cydaria is beside herself with passion; wretched and unhappy in her love for the handsome stranger, fearing her love will not be returned, jealous of those whom he has loved before. There was no jealousy in Nell; love for her was a joyous thing.

She could wish for a merry part, one in which she could strut about the stage in breeches, make saucy quips to the audience, dance and sing.

But she must go on to the stage and play Cydaria.

*   *   *

The audience was dazzling that day. The King was present, and with him the most brilliant of his courtiers.

Nell came on the stage in her Court dress, and there was a gasp of admiration as she did so. She glimpsed her companions with whom she had once sold oranges, and saw the envy in their faces.

She knew that Mary Knepp and the rest of them would be waiting, eagerly hoping that she would be laughed off the stage. They would, backstage, be aware of the silence which had fallen on the audience as she entered. There was one thing they had forgotten; orange-girl she may have been a short while ago, but now she was the prettiest creature who ever graced a stage, and in her Court dress she could vie with any of the ladies who sat in the boxes.

She went through her lines, giving them her own inimitable flavour which robbed them of their tragedy and made a more comic part of the Princess than was intended; but it was no less acceptable for all that.

She enjoyed the scenes with Charles Hart. He looked handsome indeed as the Spanish adventurer, and she spoke her lines with fervour. When he sought to seduce her and she resisted him, she did so with a charming regret which was not in the part. It called forth one or two ribald

49

comments in the pit from those of the audience who followed the course of actors' and actresses' lives with zest.

'Nay, Nelly,' called one bright fellow. 'Don't refuse him now. You did not last night, so why this afternoon?'

Nell's impulse was to go the front of the stage and retort that it was no wish of hers to refuse such a handsome fellow and she would never have thought of doing it. The fellow in the pit must blame Master Dryden for that.

But Cortes' stern eyes were on her. My dearest Cortes-Charles, thought Nell; he lives in the play; it is this story of Princes that is real to him, not the playhouse.

'"Our greatest honour is in loving well,"' he was saying.

And she smiled at him and came back with:

'Strange ways you practise there to win a heart
Here love is nature, but with you, 'tis art.'

No one had taken any notice of the interruption. There was nothing unusual in such comments on the actors and their private lives, and the play went on until that last scene when Almeria (Ann Marshall) brought out her dagger and, for love of Cortes, prepares to stab Cydaria.

There were cries of horror from the pit, cries of warning: 'Nelly, take care! That whore is going to stab thee.'

Nell reeled, placed the sponge filled with blood which she had concealed in her hand on her bosom, and squeezed it; she was about to fall to the floor when Cortes rescued her. There was a sigh of relief throughout the house, which told Nell all she wished to know; she had succeeded in her first big part.

When Almeria stabbed herself, and Charles Hart and Nell Gwyn left the stage arm-in-arm, the applause broke out.

Now the actors and actresses must come back and make their bows.

'Nelly!' cried the pit. 'Come, Nelly! Take a bow, Nelly!'

And so she came to the apron stage, flushed in her triumph; and if her acting was not equal to that of Mrs Ann Marshall, her dainty beauty found an immediate response.

Nell lifted her eyes and met those which belonged to a

man who leaned forward in his box. His dark luxuriant curls had fallen forward slightly. It was impossible to read the look in the sardonic eyes.

But for those few moments this man and Nell looked at each other appraisingly. Then she smiled her impudent orange-girl smile. There was the faintest pause before the sensuous lips curled. Others in the theatre noticed. They said: 'The King liked Nelly in her new part.'

* * *

Now Nell was well known throughout London. When people came to the King's Theatre they expected to see Mrs Nelly, and, if she did not appear, were apt to ask the reason why. They liked to see her dance and show her pretty legs; they liked to listen to her repartee when someone in the pit attacked her acting or her private life. They declared that to hear Mrs Nelly giving a member of the audience a rating was as good as any play; for Nell's wit was sparkling and never malicious except in self-defence.

There were many who believed she was well on the way to becoming the leading actress at the King's Theatre.

Often she thought of the King and the smile he had given her. She listened avidly to all news of him. It was a great thing, she told herself, to perform before the King.

Elizabeth Weaver, one of the actresses, had a tale to tell of the King. Elizabeth held herself aloof, living in a state of expectancy, for once the King had sent for her. Nell had heard her tell the tale many times, for it was a tale Elizabeth Weaver loved to tell. Nell had scarcely listened before; now she wished to hear it in detail.

'I shall never forget the day as long as I live,' Elizabeth told her. 'My part was a good one, and a beautiful dress I wore. You reminded me of myself when you played Cydaria. Such a dress I had. . . .'

'Yes, yes,' said Nell. 'Have done with the dress. It's what happened to the wearer that interests me.'

'The dress was important. Mayhap if I had another dress like that he would send for me again. I'd played my part; I'd taken my applause; and then one of the footmen

51

came backstage and said to me: "The King sends for you."'

'"The King sends for you." Just like that?'

'Just like that. "For what?" I said. "For what should the King send for poor Elizabeth Weaver?" "He would have you entertain him at the Palace of Whitehall," I was told. So I put on a cloak – a velvet one, one of the company's cloaks; but Mr Hart said to use it since it was to Whitehall I was to go.'

'Have done with the cloak,' said Nell. 'I'll warrant you weren't sent for to show a cloak!'

'Indeed not. I was taken to a grand apartment where there were many great ladies and gentlemen. My lord Buckingham himself was there, and I'll swear 'twas my lady Shrewsbury with him and . . .'

'And His Majesty the King?' said Nell.

'He was kind to me . . . kinder than the others. He is kind, Nell. His great dark eyes were telling me all the time not to be afraid of them and the things they might say to me. He said nothing that was not kind. He bade me dance and sing, and he bade the others applaud me. And after a while the others went away and I was alone with His Majesty. Then I was no longer afraid.'

Elizabeth Weaver's eyes grew misty. She was looking back, not to the glories of Whitehall, not to the honour of being selected by the King, but to that night when she was alone with him and he was just a man like any other.

'Just a man like any other,' she murmured. 'And yet unlike any that I have ever known. He gave me a jewel,' she went on. 'I could sell it for much, I doubt not. But I never shall. I shall always keep it.'

Nell was unusually quiet.

She is waiting, she thought, waiting and hoping that the King will send for her again. He never will. Poor Bessie Weaver, she is no longer as pretty as she must have once been. And what has she ever had but her youthful prettiness? There are many youthful pretty women to surround His Majesty. So poor Elizabeth Weaver will go on waiting all her life to be sent for by the King.

'A sorry fate,' said Nell to herself. 'Give me a merry one.'

But she often found her thoughts going back and back again to the King who had smiled at her; and in spite of herself she caught her breath when she asked herself: 'Will there ever come a day when the King will send for Nelly?'

* * *

In the days following her success as Cydaria, Nell revelled in her fame. She would wander through the streets smiling and calling a witty greeting to those who spoke to her; she liked to stand at the door of her lodgings, watching the passers-by; she would stroll in St James' Park and watch the King and his courtiers at the game of *pelmel*, in which none threw as the King did; she would watch him sauntering with his courtiers, feeding the ducks in the ponds, his spaniels at his heels. He did not see her. If he had would he have remembered the actress he had seen at his playhouse? There were many to watch the King as he walked in his park or rode through his Capital. Why, Nell asked herself, should he notice one young actress?

But each day she hoped that he would come to see her perform.

Fate was against Nell then. She was ready to rise to the top of her profession, and suddenly the happy life was no more.

During the weeks which followed the production of *The Indian Emperor* there were rumours in the streets. The Dutch were challenging England's power on the high seas. That seemed far away, but it proved capable of altering the course of a rising young actress's life. When Nell saw a Dutchman whipped through the streets for declaring that the Dutch had destroyed the English factories on the coast of Guinea, she was sorry for him. Poor fellow, it seemed harsh punishment for repeating a tale which proved to be false. But a few days later England declared war on the Dutch, and then she began to realize how these matters could affect her life. The theatres were half empty. So many of the gallants who had sat in the pit and the boxes had gone to fight the Dutch on the high seas; the King came rarely to the theatre, having matters of state with which to deal; and since the

53

King did not come, neither did all the fine ladies and gentlemen. Thomas Killigrew, Michael Mohun, and Charles Hart, who had shares in the theatrical venture, began to look worried. Charles Hart recalled the days of the Commonwealth when it had been an offence to act, and actors had been deprived of their livelihood. Those were grim days, and even Nell's naturally high spirits were quelled by acting to half-empty houses and by a lover turned melancholy. Yet, ever ebullient, she prophesied a quick defeat of the Dutch and a return to prosperity. But that April there occurred an even more disastrous event than the Dutch war. Like the Dutch war it had broken gradually upon the people of London, for even towards the end of the year 1664 there had been rumours of deaths in the Capital which were suspected of being caused by the dreaded plague. With the coming of the warm spring and summer this fearful scourge broke out afresh. The gutters choked with filth, the stench of decay which filled the air and hung like a cloud over the city, were the best possible breeding conditions for the terror; it increased rapidly, and soon all the business of the town was brought to a standstill. A short while ago Nell and her companions had played to half-filled houses; now they had no audiences at all. None would dare enter a public place for fear that someone present might be infected. The theatres were the first places to close and Nell was deprived of her livelihood. Charles Hart was plunged into melancholy, more at the prospect of being unable to act than because of the danger of disease. He declared that they must leave London and go farther afield. In the sweeter country air it might be possible to escape infection.

'There are my mother and sister,' said Nell. 'We must take them with us.'

Charles Hart had seen her mother; he shuddered at the prospect of even five minutes spent in her company.

''Tis quite impossible,' he said.

'Then what will become of her?'

'Doubtless she will drown her sorrow at losing you, in the gin bottle.'

'What if she takes the plague?'

'Then, my little Nell, she will take the plague.'

'Who would care for her?'

'Your sister doubtless.'

'What if she also took the plague?'

'You waste precious time. I wish to leave at once. Every unnecessary minute spent in this polluted place is courting danger.'

Nell planted her small feet on the floor and, placing her hands on her hips, struck what he called her fish-wife attitude, since it was doubtless picked up when she sold fresh herrings at ten a groat.

'When I go,' she said, 'my family goes with me.'

'So you choose your family instead of me?' said Hart. 'Very well, Madam. You have made your choice.'

Then he left her, and when he had gone she was sad, because she loved him well enough, and she knew that being unable to act he was a melancholy man. And she was a fool. What, she asked herself, did she owe to the gin-sodden old woman who had beaten and bullied her when she was able, and whined to her when she was not?

She went to Cole-yard; and as she passed into that alley Nell's heart was merry no longer, for on many of the doors were painted large red crosses beneath which were written the words 'Lord have mercy upon us'.

*   *   *

Nell stayed in the cellar, with Rose and her mother, for several days and nights. Occasionally either Nell or her sister went out into the streets to see if they could find food. There was scarcely anyone about now, and grass was growing between the cobbles. Sometimes in their wanderings they would see sufferers by the roadside, struck down as they walked through the streets, displaying the fatal signs of shivering, nausea, delirium. Once Nell approached an old woman, because she felt she could not pass her by without offering help, but the woman had opened her eyes and stared at Nell, shouting: 'You're Mrs Nelly. Stay away from me.' Then she tore open her bodice and showed the terrible macula on her breast.

Nell hurried away, feeling sick and afraid, aware that she could do nothing to help the old woman.

They lived this cellar-existence for some weeks, occasionally venturing out and returning, feeling desolate and melancholy to see a great city so stricken. During the night they heard the gloomy notes of the bell which told them that the pest-cart was passing that way. They heard the sepulchral cry echoing through the deserted streets: 'Bring out your dead.' Nell had seen the naked bodies passed out of windows and tumbled into the cart just as they were, body upon body since there was no time to provide coffins; there were no mourners to follow the dead to their graves; the cart went its dismal way to the burial ground on the outskirts of the city where the bodies were thrown into a pit.

Then one day Nell cried: 'We can no longer stay here. If we do we shall die of melancholy if not of the plague.'

'Let us to Oxford,' said her mother. 'Your father has relations there. Mayhap they would take us in till this scourge be gone.'

And so they made their way out of the stricken city. That night they slept in the shelter of a hedge; and Nell felt her spirits lifted in the sweet country air.

TWO

IT was nearly two years later when Nell came back to London. Life was not easy in Oxford. She had gone back to selling fruit and fish when she could lay her hands on it. Rose worked with her, and the two girls from London, so sprightly and so pretty, were able to keep themselves and their mother alive during those two years.

News came from London – terrible news which set them all wondering whether they would ever return there. Travellers brought it to Oxford during the month of September, a year after Nell and her family had arrived there. Nell, eager for news of what was happening in Drury Lane and whether the players were back, heard instead of the disastrous fire which had broken out at a baker's shop in Pudding Lane and quickly spread until half the city was ablaze. The wild rumours reaching Oxford were numerous. Many declared that this was the end of London, and that not a house was left standing; that the King and all his Court had been burned to death.

Nell for once was speechless. She stood still, thinking of Drury Lane and that squalid alley where she had spent most of her life, the old Cole-yard; she thought of Covent Garden, the Hop Garden and St Martin's Lane. She thought of the playhouse – that which she thought of as her own – and that rival house, both furiously burning.

''Tis the judgement of God on a wicked city,' some people declared.

Rose cast down her eyes, but Nell was shrilly indignant. London had not been wicked, she cried; it was merry and full of pleasure, and she for one refused to believe that it was a sin to laugh and enjoy life.

But she was too wretched to retort with her wonted spirit.

Each day there came fresh rumours. They heard that the people had thrown the furniture from their houses and packed it into barges; that the flames had spanned the river; how the wooden houses on London Bridge had blazed; how the King and his brother the Duke had worked together to prevent the fire from spreading; that it had been necessary to use gunpowder and blow gaps in the rows of highly inflammable wooden houses.

And at length came good news.

It came from a gentleman riding through Oxford from London, a prelate who mourned the restoration of the King and looked yearningly back at the puritanism of the Protectorate.

Riding to Banbury, he stopped at Oxford and, seeing that he was a traveller who had doubtless come from London, Nell approached him, not to ask him to buy her herrings, but for news.

He looked at her with disapproval. No woman of virtue, he was sure, could look like this one. That luxuriant hair allowed to flow in riotous disorder, those hazel eyes adorned with the darkest of lashes and brows – such a contrast to the reddish tints in her hair – those plump cheeks and pretty teeth, those dimples and, above all, that pert nose, could not belong to a virtuous woman.

Nell dipped in a charming curtsy which would have become a lady of high rank and which Charles Hart had taught her.

'I see, fair sir, that you hie from London,' she addressed him. 'I would fain have news of that town.'

'Ask me not for news of Babylon!' cried the good man.

'Nay, sir, I will not,' answered Nell. ''Tis of London I ask.'

'They are one and the same.'

Nell dropped her eyes demurely. 'I hie from London, fair sir. Is it in your opinion a fit place for a poor woman to go home to?'

'I tell ye, 'tis Babylon itself. 'Tis full of whores and cut-throats.'

'More so than Oxford, sir . . . or Banbury?'

He looked at her suspiciously. 'You mock me, woman,'

58

he said. 'You should go to London. Clearly 'tis where you belong. In that cesspool everywhere one looks one sees rubble in the streets – the evidence of God's vengeance . . . and these people of London, what do they do? They make merry with their taverns and their playhouses. . . .'

'You said playhouses!' cried Nell.

'God forgive them, I did.'

'And may He preserve you, sir, for such good news.'

A few days later she, with Rose and her mother, caught the stage-wagon and, after a slow and tedious journey travelling two miles to the hour and sitting uncomfortably on the floor of the wagon as the wagoner led the horses over the rough roads, they were jolted to London.

Nell could scarcely help weeping when she saw the old city again. She had heard that old St Paul's, the Guildhall, and the Exchange, among many other well-known land-marks, had gone; she had heard that more than thirteen thousand dwelling-houses and four hundred streets had been destroyed, and that two-thirds of the city lay in ruins – from the Tower, all along the river to the Temple Church, and from the northeast gate along the city wall to Holborn Bridge. Nevertheless she was not prepared for the sight which met her eyes.

But she was by nature an optimist and when she remem-bered her last sight of the city, with the grass growing between the cobbles, with its red crosses on the doors and its pest-carts in the streets, she cried: 'Well, 'tis a better sight than we left.'

Moreover the King's Servants were back at the play-house.

Nell lost no time in presenting herself at the playhouse, miraculously preserved; and indeed Thomas Killigrew had, during the time it had not been used, enlarged his stage.

*   *   *

London was glad to see Nell back. She had changed in her two years' absence. She was no longer a child. At seventeen she was a poised young woman; her charms had by no means diminished; she was as slender and as dainty as ever; her tongue was as quick; but all who saw her declared that her beauty was more striking than ever.

She scored an immediate success as Lady Wealthy in James Howard's *The English Monsieur*, and later she played Celia in Fletcher's *Humorous Lieutenant*.

There was still great anxiety throughout the country; the plague and the fire had crippled trade, and the Dutch were threatening. In her lodgings in Drury Lane which she had taken again Nell thought little of these things. She gave supper parties and entertained her friends with her singing and dancing. These friends talked of the scandals of the Court, of the theatre, and the roles they had played; it never occurred to them to give a thought to state affairs or to imagine that such matters could concern them.

To these parties came men and women of the Court; even the great Duke of Buckingham came. He was something of a mimic, and he declared he wished to pit his skill against Mrs Nelly's. With him came Lady Castlemaine, who was graciously pleased to commend the little comedienne on her playing. She asked questions about Charles Hart, her great blue eyes rapaciously aglitter. Charles Hart was a very handsome man, and Nell had heard of the lady's insatiable hunger for handsome men.

One of the lampoons which was being quoted throughout the city concerned the King's chief mistress. It was:

> '*Full forty men a day provided for the whore*
> *Yet like a bitch she wags her tail for more.*'

This was said to have been composed by the Earl of Rochester – who was Lady Castlemaine's own cousin and one of the wildest rakes at Court. He had recently been imprisoned for abducting an heiress; he was so daring that he cared not what he said even to the King; yet he remained in favour.

Henry Killigrew was there; he had been her friend since the days when she had begged him to help her obtain a pardon for Rose. Now she knew that he had been Lady Castlemaine's lover as well as Rose's and was the greatest liar in England. There was Sir George Etherege, lazy and good humoured, known to them all as 'Gentle George'. Another who came to her rooms was John Dryden, a fresh-complexioned little poet who had written several plays and promised to write another especially for Nell.

This he did and, very soon after her return to London, Nell was playing in *Secret Love, or the Maiden Queen*, and the part of Florimel, which had been specially written for her, was the greatest success of her career.

All the town was going to see Mrs Nelly as Florimel, for in Florimel Dryden had created a madcap creature, witty, pretty, full of mischief, expert in mimicry; in other words Florimel was Nell, and Florimel enchanted all London.

She could now forget the terrible time of plague; she could forget poverty in Oxford, just as in the beginning she had forgotten the bawdy-house in Cole-yard and her life as orange-girl in the pit. Nell knew how to live gloriously in the joyous moment, and to remember from the past only that which made pleasant remembering.

She had lost Charles Hart. He had never forgiven her for choosing her family instead of him. Nell shrugged elegant shoulders. She had loved him when she had known little of love; her love had been trusting, experimental. She was grateful to Mr Charles Hart, and she did not grudge him the pleasure he was said to be taking with my lady Castlemaine.

What she enjoyed now was swaggering across the stage, wearing an enormous periwig which made her seem smaller than ever – a grotesque yet enchanting figure, full of vitality, full of love of life, full of gamin charm which set the pit bouncing in its seats, and every little vizard mask trying to ape Nell Gwyn.

And at the end of the play she danced her jig.

'You must dance a jig,' Lacy had said. 'Moll Davies is drawing them at the Duke's with her dancing. By God, Nelly, she's a pretty creature, Moll Davies; but you're a prettier.'

Nell turned away from his flattering glances; she did not want to seem ungrateful to one who had done so much for her, but she wanted no more lovers at this time.

She wanted no man unless she loved him, and there was so much else in life to love apart from men. She might have reminded him that Thomas Killigrew paid a woman twenty shillings a week to remain at the theatre and keep his actors happy in their amorous moments. But being grateful to Lacy, she turned away as she had learned to turn away from so many who sought her.

And there were many seeking her. She was the most discussed actress of the day. There might have been better actresses on the stage but none was possessed of Nell's charm; though some admitted that that mighty pretty creature, Moll Davies, at the Duke's Theatre, was the better dancer.

In the town they were quoting Flecknoe's verses to a very pretty person:

> *'She is pretty and she knows it;*
> *She is witty and she shows it;*
> *And besides that she's so witty,*
> *And so little and so pretty,*
> *Sh'has a hundred other parts*
> *For to take and conquer hearts . . .'*

The gallants quoted it to her; in the pit they chanted it. And they roared the last two lines:

> *'But for that, suffice to tell ye,*
> *'Tis the little pretty Nelly.'*

And, although the times were bad and it was hard to fill a theatre, those who could tear themselves from state matters came to see Nell Gwyn play Florimel and dance her jig.

*   *   *

The King was melancholy. Frances Stuart, whom he had been pursuing for so long, had run away with the Duke of Richmond; and matters of greater moment gave him cause for anxiety. His kingdom, well-nigh ruined by the disastrous events of the last two years, was facing a serious threat from the Dutch. He had no money to refit his ships, so he negotiated for a secret peace; the French were joining the Dutch against him; but the Dutch, who had suffered no such hardships, had no wish for peace.

The King rarely came to the play; he did not even come for John Howard's new piece *All Mistaken or The Mad Couple*, in which Nelly had a comic part.

As Mirida she had two suitors – one fat, one thin – and she promised to marry the one if he could grow fatter, the other if he could lose his bulk. This gave her many opportunities for the sort of buffoonery in which she revelled. Lacy, stuffed with cushions, was the fat lover, and Nell and he had the audience hysterical with laughter. An additional attraction was Nell's parody of Moll Davies in her role in *The Rivals* at The Duke's; and with her fat lover she rolled about on the stage, displaying so much of her person that the gentlemen in the pit stood on their seats to see the better, so displeasing those behind them that this gave rise to much dissension.

There was one in his box who watched the scene with an avid interest. This was Charles Sackville, Lord Buckhurst, a wit and poet, and he was filled with a great desire to make Nell his mistress.

Consequently after the play the first person to reach the tiring room to beg Mrs Nelly to dine with him was Charles Sackville.

*　　*　　*

They dined at the Rose Tavern in Russell Street, and the innkeeper, recognizing his patrons, was filled with the desire to please them.

Nell had refused to ask the gentleman to her lodgings, as she had refused to go to his. She knew him for a rake and, although he was an extremely handsome one as well as a wit, she had no intention of giving way to his desires. Some of these Court gentlemen stopped at little. My lord Rochester and some of his boon companions, it was said, were beginning to consider seduction tame and were developing a taste for rape. She was not going to make matters easy for this noble lord.

He leaned his elbows on the table and bade her drink more wine.

'There's not an actress in the town to touch you, Nelly,' he said.

'Nor shall any touch me – actress or noble lord – unless I wish it.'

'You are prickly, Nell! Wherefore?'

'I'm like a hedgehog, my lord. I know when to be on my guard.'

'Let us not talk of guards.'

'Then what should we talk of, the Dutch war?'

'I can think of happier subjects.'

'Such as what, my lord?'

'You . . . myself . . . alone somewhere together.'

'Would that be so happy? You would be demanding, I should be refusing. If you need my refusal to make you happier, sir, you can have it here and now.'

'Nelly, you're a mad thing, but a little beauty like you should have better lodgings than those in Old Drury!'

'Is it a gentleman's custom to sneer at the lodgings of his friends?'

'If he is prepared to provide a better.'

> '*My lodging is on cold boards,*
> *And wonderful hard is my fare.*
> *But that which troubles me most*
> *Is the impertinence of my host . . .*'

sang Nell, parodying the song in *The Rivals*.

'I pray thee, Nell, be serious. I offer you a beautiful apartment, a hundred pounds a year . . . all the jewels and good company you could wish for.'

'I do not wish for jewels,' she said, 'and I doubt you could provide me with better company than that which I now enjoy.'

'An actress's life! How long does that go on?'

'A little longer than that of a kept woman of a noble lord, I imagine.'

'I would love you for ever.'

'For ever, forsooth! For ever is until you decide to pay court to Moll Davies or Beck Marshall.'

'Do you imagine that I shall lightly abandon this . . .'

'Nay, I do not. It is after seduction that such as you, my lord, concern themselves with the abandonment of a poor female.'

'Nell, your tongue's too sharp for such a little person.'

'My lord, we all have our weapons. Some have jewels and a hundred a year with which to tempt the needy; others have a love of straight speaking with which to parry such thrusts.'

'One of these days,' said Charles Sackville, 'you will come to me, Nell.'

She shrugged her shoulders. 'Who knows, my lord? Who knows? Now, if you would prove to me that you are a good host, let me enjoy my food, I beg of you. And let me hear a piece of that wit for which I hear you are famous. For the man from whom I would accept jewels and an apartment and a hundred a year must needs be a witty man, a man who knows how to play the perfect host, and that – so my brief spell in high society tells me – is to talk, not of the host's own inclinations, but of those of his guest.'

'I am reproved,' said Sackville.

He was exasperated, as he and his friends always were by the refusal of those they wished to fall immediate victims to their desires, but after that meal he was even more determined to make Nell his mistress.

*   *   *

The King was furious with his players. It was unlike the King to lose his temper; he was, it was said by many, the sweetest tempered man at Court. But there was a great deal to make him melancholy at this time.

A terrible disaster had overtaken the country. The Dutch fleet had sailed up the Medway as far as Chatham. They had taken temporary possession of Sheerness; they had burned the *Great James*, the *Royal Oak*, and the *Loyal London* (that ship which London had so recently had built to ennoble the Navy). They had sent up in smoke a magazine of stores worth £40,000 and, afraid lest they should reach London Bridge and inflict further damage, the English had sunk four ships at Blackwall and thirteen at Woolwich.

The sight of the triumphant and arrogant Dutchmen sailing up the Medway, towing the *Royal Charles*, was, many sober Englishmen declared, the greatest humiliation the English had ever suffered.

So the King, who loved his ships and had done more than any to promote the power of his Navy, was melancholy indeed; this melancholy was aggravated by those who went about the country declaring that this was God's vengeance on England because of the vices of the Court. There came to him news that a Quaker, naked except for a loin-cloth, had run through Westminster Hall carrying burning coals in a dish on his head and calling on the people of the Court to repent of their lascivious ways which had clearly found disfavour in the eyes of the Lord.

Charles, the cynic and astute statesman, said to those about him that the disfavour of the Lord might have been averted by cash to repair his ships and make them ready to face the Dutchmen. But he was grieved. He could not see that the fire and the plague which had preceded it – and which in the crippling effects they had had on the country's trade were the reasons for this humiliating defeat – had any connection with the merry lives he and his followers led. In his opinion God would not wish to deny a gentleman his pleasure.

The plague came on average twice a year to London, and had done so for many years; he knew this was due to the crowded hovels and the filthy conditions of the streets, rather than to his licentiousness; the fire had been so disastrous because those same houses were built of wood and huddled so close together that there was no means – except by making gaps in the buildings – of stopping the fire once it had started on such a gusty night.

But he knew it was useless to tell a superstitious people

these things, for they counted it Divine vengeance when aught went wrong and Divine approval when things went right.

But even a man of the sweetest nature could feel exasperated at times and, when he heard that in the *Change of Crowns* which was being done at his own playhouse John Lacy was pouring further ridicule on the Court, Charles was really angry. At any other time he would have laughed and shrugged his shoulders; he had never been a man to turn from the truth; but now, with London prostrate from the effects of plague and fire, with the Dutch inflicting the most humiliating defeat in the country's history and rebellion hanging in the air as patently as that miasma of haze and stench which came from the breweries, soap-boilers and tanneries ranged about the city, this ridicule of Lacy's was more than indiscreet; it was criminal.

The King decided that Lacy should suffer a stern reprimand and the playhouse be closed down for a while. It was incongruous, to say the least, that the mummers should be acting at such a time; and the very existence of the playhouse gave those who were condemning the idle life of the Court more sticks with which to beat it.

So, during those hot months, Lacy went to prison and the King's Theatre was closed.

Once more Nell was an actress without a theatre to act in.

*   *   *

Afterwards she wondered how she could have behaved as she did.

Was it the desperation which was in the London air at that time? Was it the long faces of all she met which made her turn to the merry rake who was importuning her?

She who loved to laugh felt in those weeks of inactivity that she must escape from a London grown so gloomy that she was reminded of the weeks of plague, when she had lived that wretched life in a deserted city.

Charles Sackville was at her elbow. 'Come, Nelly. Come and make merry,' he said. 'I have a pleasant house in

Epsom Spa. Come with me and enjoy life. What can you do here? Cry "Fresh herrings, ten a groat"? Come with me and I'll give you not only a handsome lover but a hundred pounds a year.'

In her mood of recklessness, Nell threw aside her principles. 'I will come,' she said.

* * *

So they made merry, she and Charles Sackville, in the house at Epsom.

There they were in pleasant country, but not too quiet and not so far from London that their friends could not visit them.

Charles Sedley joined them. He was witty and amusing, this Little Sid; and highly amused to see that Nell had succumbed at last. He insisted on staying with them at Epsom. He hoped, he said, to have a share in pretty, witty Nell. He would disclaim at length on the greater virtues of Little Sid as compared with those of Charles Sackville, Lord Buckhurst, and he was so amusing that neither Nell nor Buckhurst wished him to go.

They were wildly merry; and all the good people at Epsom talked of these newcomers in their midst. Little groups hung about outside the house hoping to catch a glimpse of the Court wits and the famous actress; and it seemed that a spirit of devilment came to all three of them, so that they acted with more wildness than came naturally even to them; and the people of Epsom were enchanted and shocked by turns.

Other members of the Court came down to see Lord Buckhurst and his newest mistress. Buckhurst was proud of his triumph. So many had laid siege to Nell without success. There was Sir Carr Scrope, squint-eyed and conceited, who made them all laugh by assuring Nell that he was irresistible to all women and, if she wished to be considered a woman of taste, she must immediately desert Buckhurst for him.

Rochester came; he read his latest satires. He told Nell that he set his footmen to wait each night at the doors of those whom he suspected of conducting intrigues, that he might be the first to compile a poem on their activities and circulate it throughout the taverns and coffee houses. She believed him; there was no exploit which would be too fantastic for my lord Rochester.

Buckingham came; he was at this time full of plans. He swore that ere long they would see Clarendon out of office. He was working with all his mind and heart and he could tell them that his cousin, Barbara Castlemaine, was with him in this. Clarendon must go.

And so passed the weeks at Epsom – six of them – mad, feckless weeks, which Nell was often to remember with shame.

It was Sir George Etherege – Gentle George – who came riding to Epsom with news from London.

Lacy was released; the King had pardoned him; he could not remain long in anger against his players; moreover he knew the hardship this brought to those who worked in his theatre. The ban was lifted. The King's Servants were playing once more.

Nell looked at her player's livery then – a cloak of bastard scarlet cloth with a black velvet collar. In the magnificence of the apartment which Buckhurst had given her she put it on; and she felt that the girl she had now become was unworthy to wear that cloak.

She had done that which she had told herself she would never do. She had loved Charles Hart in her way, and if her feeling for him had not proved a lasting affection, at least she had thought it was at the time.

She accepted the morals of the age; but she had determined that her relationship with men must be based on love.

And then, because of a mood of recklessness, because she had been weak and careless and afraid of poverty, she had become involved in a sordid relationship with a man whom she did not love.

Buckhurst came to her and saw her in the cloak.

'God's Body!' he cried. 'What have we here?'

'My player's livery,' she said.

He laughed at it and, taking it from her, threw it about

his own shoulders. He began to mince about the apartment, waiting for her applause and laughter.

'You find me a bore?' he asked petulantly.

'Yes, Charles,' she said.

'Then the devil take you!'

'He did that when I came to you.'

'What means this?' he cried indignantly. 'Are you not satisfied with what I give you?'

'I am not satisfied with what there is between us.'

'What! Nelly grown virtuous, sighing to be a maid once more?'

'Nay. Sighing to be myself.'

'Now the wench grows cryptic. Who is this woman who has been my mistress these last weeks, if not Nelly?'

''Twas Nelly, sure enough, and for that I pity Nelly.'

'You feel I have neglected you of late?'

'Nay, I feel you have not neglected me enough.'

'Come, you want a present, eh?'

'Nay. I am going back to the playhouse.'

'What, for a miserable pittance?'

'Not so miserable. With it I get back my self-respect.'

He threw back his head and laughed. 'Ah, now we have become high and mighty. Nelly the whore would become Nelly the nun. 'Tis a sad complaint but no unusual one. There are many who would be virtuous after they have lost their virtue, forgetting that those who have it are for ever sighing to lose it.'

'I am leaving at once for London.'

'Leave me, and you'll never come back!'

'I see that you and I are of an opinion. Good day to you, sir.'

'You're a fool, Nelly,' he said.

'I am myself, and if that be a fool . . . then Nelly is a fool and must needs act like one.'

He caught her wrist and cried: 'Who is it? Rochester?' Her answer was to kick his shins.

He cried out with pain and released her. She picked up her player's cloak, wrapped it about her, and walked out of the house.

*   *   *

70

Charles Hart was cool when she returned to the theatre. He was not sure, he told her, whether she could have back any of her old parts.

Nell replied that she must then perforce play others.

The actresses were disdainful. They had been jealous of her quick rise to fame; and even more jealous of her liaison with Lord Buckhurst and the income which they had heard he had fixed upon her. They were delighted to see her back – humbled, as they thought.

This was humiliation for Nell, but she refused to be sub-dued. She went on the stage and played the smaller parts which were allotted to her, and very soon the pit was calling for more of Mrs Nelly.

'It seems,' said Beck Marshall, after a particularly noisy demonstration, 'that the people come here not to see the play but my lord Buckhurst's whore.'

Nell rose in her fury and, facing Beck Marshall, cried in ringing tones as though she were playing a dramatic part: 'I was but one man's whore, though I was brought up in a bawdy-house to fill strong waters to the guests; and you are a whore to three or four, though a Presbyter's praying daughter.'

This set the green room in fits of laughter, for it was true that Beck Marshall and her sister Ann did give themselves airs and were fond of reminding the rest that they did not come from the slums of London but from a respectable family.

Beck had no word to say to that; she had forgotten that it was folly to pit her wits against those of Nell.

The dainty little creature was more full of fire than any, and had the weapon of her wit with which to defend herself.

They all began to realize then that they were glad to have Nell back. Even Charles Hart – who, though in the toils of my lady Castlemaine, had regretted seeing Nell go to Buckhurst – found himself relenting. Moreover he had the business of the playhouse to consider, and audiences were poor, as they always were in times of disaster. Anything that could be done to bring people into the theatre must be done; and Nell was a draw.

So, very soon after her brief retirement with Lord Buck-hurst, she was back in all her old parts; and there were many who declared that, if there was one thing which could make them forget the unhappy state of the country's affairs, it was pretty witty Nell at the King's playhouse.

All through that autumn Nell played her parts.

Meanwhile the country sought a scapegoat for the disasters, and Clarendon was forced to take this part. Buckingham and Lady Castlemaine were working together for his defeat, and although the King was reluctant to forsake an old friend he decided that, for Clarendon's own safety, it would be wiser for him to leave the country.

So that November Clarendon escaped to France, and Buckingham and his cousin Castlemaine rejoiced to see him go, and congratulated themselves on bringing about his eclipse.

But it was not long before Buckingham and his cousin fell out. Lady Castlemaine with her mad rages, Buckingham with his mad schemes, could not remain in harmony for long. The Duke then began to make further wild plans, and this time they were directed against his fair cousin.

He conferred with his two friends, Edward Howard and his brother, Robert Howard, who wrote plays for the theatre.

Buckingham said: 'The Castlemaine's power over the King is too great and should be broken. What we need to replace her is another woman, younger, more enticing.'

'And how could this be?' said Robert. 'You know His most gracious Majesty never discards; he merely adds to his hand.'

'That is so; but let him add such a glorious creature, so beautiful, so enchanting, so amusing, that he has little time to spare for Castlemaine.'

'He would fain be rid of her and her tantrums now, but still he keeps her.'

'He was ever one to love a harem. Our gracious Sovereign says "Yes yes yes" with such charm that he has never learned to say "No".'

'He is too good-natured.'

'And his good-nature is our undoing. If Castlemaine remains mistress *en titre* she will ruin the country and the King.'

'Not to mention her good cousin, my lord Buckingham!'

'Aye, and all of us. Come, we are good friends – let us do something about it. Let us find the King a new mistress. I suggest one of the enchanting ladies of the theatre. What of the incomparable Nelly?'

'Ah, Nelly,' said Robert. 'She's an enchantress, but every time she opens her mouth Cole-yard comes out. The King needs a lady.'

'There is Moll Davies at the Duke's,' said Edward. Buckingham laughed, for he knew Moll to be a member of the Howard family – on the wrong side of the blanket. It was reasonable that the Howards should want to promote Moll, for she was a good choice, a docile girl. She would be sweet and gentle with the King and ready to take all the advice given her.

But Buckingham was the most perverse man in England. It would be such an easy matter to get Moll Davies into the King's bed. But he liked more complicated schemes; he wanted to do more than discountenance Castlemaine. Moreover how would Moll stand up to her ladyship? The poor girl would be defeated at every turn.

No, he wanted to provide the King with a mistress who had some spirit; someone who could deal with Lady Castlemaine in a manner to make the King laugh, if he should witness conflict between them, and there was one person he had in mind for the task.

Let the Howards do all in their power to promote the leading actress from the Duke's Theatre; he would go to the King's own playhouse for his protégée.

Mrs Nelly! She was the girl for him. She had at times the language of the streets. What of it? That was piquant. It made a more amusing situation: a King and a girl from the gutter.

He turned to the Howards. 'My friends,' he said, 'if there is one thing His Majesty would appreciate more than one pretty actress, it is two pretty actresses. You try him with Moll;

I'll try him with Nelly. 'Twill be a merry game to watch what happens, eh? Let the pretty creatures fight it out for themselves. Her ladyship will be most disturbed, I vow.'

He could scarcely wait to bid them farewell. Nor did they wish to delay. They were off to the Duke's to tell Moll to hold herself in readiness for what they proposed.

Buckingham was wondering whether he should first call Charles' attention to Nell or warn Nell of the good fortune which awaited her. Nell was unaccountable. She had left Buckhurst and gone back to the comparative poverty of the stage. Mayhap it would be better to speak to Charles first.

He began to frame his sentences. 'Has Your Majesty been to the playhouse of late? By God, what an incomparable creature is Mrs Nelly!'

Buckingham was in high spirits by the time he reached Whitehall.

THREE

THE King took several brisk turns round his privy gardens. It was early morning; it was his custom to rise early, however late he had retired, for his energy outstripped that of most of his courtiers, and when he was alone in the morning he walked at quite a different pace from that which he employed in his favourite pastime of sauntering, when he would fit his steps to those of the ladies who walked with him, pausing now and then to compliment them or throw some witty remark over his shoulder in answer to one of the wits who invariably accompanied him at sauntering time.

But in the early morning he liked to be up with the sun, to stride unattended through his domain – quickly round the privy garden, a brisk inspection of his physic garden, perhaps a turn round the bowling green. He might even walk as far as the canal in the park to feed the ducks.

During these walks he was a different man from the indolent, benevolent Charles whom his mistresses and courtiers knew. Those lines of melancholy would be more pronounced on his face as he took his morning perambulation. Sometimes he recalled the carousal of the previous day and regretted the promises he had made and which he knew he would not be able to keep; on other occasions he meditated on the virtuous and noble actions which he had left undone and all the subterfuges into which his easygoing nature and love of peace had led him.

It was more than seven years since he had ridden triumphantly into Whitehall, and this city had been gay with its flower-strewn streets, the banners and tapestries, the fountains flowing with wine, and most of all its cheering hopeful citizens.

And during that time how far had his people's hopes been realized? They had suffered plague in such degree as had rarely been known in all previous visitations; their capital city had been in great part destroyed; they had suffered ignoble defeat by the Dutch and had experienced the humiliation of seeing Dutchmen in their own waters. They had deplored the Puritan spoilsports but what had they in place of them? A pleasure-loving King who more frequently dallied with his mistresses and the debauched Court wits who surrounded him, than attended to affairs of state! The fact that he was in full possession of a lively mind, that he could, if he had been less indolent and more in love with politics than with women, have grown into one of the most astute statesmen of the times, made his conduct even the more to be deplored.

But even while he walked and considered himself and his position in his country, a sardonic smile curved his lips as he remembered that when he went into the streets the people still cheered him. He was their King and, because he was tall and commanding in appearance, because the women at the balconies who waved to him as he passed recognized that overwhelming charm in him, because the men, in their way, recognized it no less and were compensated for all the hardships they suffered when the King addressed them in the easy familiar way he had towards his subjects, rich or poor, they were satisfied and well content.

Such was human nature, thought Charles wryly; and why should I wish to change it when it is so beneficial to myself?

He had made peace with the French, Danes, and Dutch at Breda in the summer, and soon he hoped to conclude the triple alliance by which England, Sweden, and Holland bound themselves to assist Spain against the French. The French had recently proved themselves no friends of his and although it had been deplorable that there should be open strife between them, Charles knew that the one man he must watch more carefully than any other was Louis XIV of France.

There were times when he was excited by the game of politics, but he tired quickly. Then he would want the witty gentlemen of his Court about him – and most of all the beautiful women – for during his years of exile he had grown so cynical that he found it difficult to have much faith in anything, or any man. Pleasure never failed him. It always gave what he asked and expected. So many times he had seen plans come to nothing through no fault of the planners; he had seen men work diligently towards an ideal, only to be cheated of it by a trick of fate. He could not forget the years of bitterness and exile, the heartbreak of Worcester. Then he had given all his youthful idealism to regaining his kingdom; the result – dismal failure and humiliation. He had changed after Worcester. He had gone back to his life of wandering exile, the excitement of his days being not the plans he made for the regaining of his kingdom but those for the conquest of a new woman; and then suddenly Fortune had smiled on him. Through little effort of his own, without conflict and bloodshed, he was called back to his kingdom. He was welcomed with flowers and music and shouts of joy. England welcomed the debauchee, the careless cynic; almost ten years before, after disastrous Worcester, they had hounded the idealist from their shores. Such experiences made a deep impression on a pleasure-loving nature.

So now, as he walked through his garden, his cynical smile expanded. He must keep disaster at bay and enjoy life.

But even in this matter of enjoyment life had changed. He was heartily tired of Barbara Castlemaine. In the first years of their relationship he had found her tantrums amusing; he no longer did so. Why did he not banish her from the kingdom? Her *amours* were notorious. He could not bring himself to do it. She would storm and rage; and he had formed a habit, long ago, of avoiding Barbara's storms and rages. It was simpler to let her alone, to avoid her, to let her continue with her love affairs. They said of him, in the language of the card tables: 'His Majesty never discards; he adds to his hand.' It was true. Discarding was such an unpleasant affair; you could keep the uninteresting cards in your hands even though you rarely used them. It was much the more peaceable method.

Frances Stuart had bitterly disappointed him. Silly little Frances, with her child's mind and her incomparably beautiful face and figure. In spite of her simplicity, he would have married Frances if he had been free to do so, for her beauty had been such that it haunted him day and night. But Frances had run away and married that sot Richmond. Much good had this done her. Now poor Frances was a victim of the smallpox, and had lost her beauty and with it her power to torment the King.

Then there was Catherine, his wife – poor Catherine, with her dusky looks and her rabbits' teeth and her overwhelming desire to please him. Why had his own wife to fall in love with him? It was a situation which the wits of his Court regarded as extremely piquant. Piquant it might have been, but he was a man of some sensibility and if there was one thing he hated more than having to refuse something that was asked, it was to see a woman distressed. He must live continually with Catherine's distress. She had been brought up in the strict Court of Portugal. He hated hurting her, yet he could no more help doing so than he could help being himself. He must saunter with his mistresses; his mistresses were more important to him than his crown. He was a deeply sensual man and his sexual appetite was voracious so that the desire to appease it surmounted all other desires.

Therefore with his countless mistresses he must displease his queen who had had the childish folly to fall in love with him.

He was beset by women. By far the more satisfactory mistresses were those who could be called upon when desired and made few demands. It was small wonder that the Dutch had made cartoons of him, clinging to his crown as he ran, pursued by women.

He it was who had brought change to England. Less than ten years ago there had been strict puritanism everywhere; he liked to think that he had brought back laughter to England; but it was often laughter of a satirical kind.

The conversation of the people had changed; they now openly discussed subjects which, ten years ago, they would have blushed to speak of and would have pretended did not even exist. Throughout the country the King's example was followed, and men took mistresses as naturally as previously they had taken walks in the sunshine. The poets jeered at chastity. Maidens were warned of flying time, of the churlishness of holding out against their lovers; the plays were frankly bawdy and concerned mainly with one subject – sexual adventure.

The King had brought French manners to England, and in France a King's mistress – not the Queen whom he had married for expedience – ruled with him in his Court.

The men of letters who surrounded him – and his greatest friends, and those who received his favours, were the witty men of letters – were, almost every one of them, rakes and libertines. Buckingham had recently been involved in a brawl with Henry Killigrew in the Duke's Theatre, where they had bounded from their boxes to fight in the pit while the play was in progress; and the cause of this was Lady Shrewsbury, that lady whose reputation for taking a string of lovers matched that of the King's own mistress, Castlemaine. Killigrew, himself a rake and a notorious liar, had fled to France.

Henry Bulkeley had fought a duel with Lord Ossory and had been involved in a tavern brawl with George Etherege. Lord Buckhurst had recently been making merry at Epsom in the company of Sedley and an actress from the King's own theatre. Rochester, the best of the poets and the greatest wit and libertine, possessed of the most handsome face at Court, had abducted a young heiress, Elizabeth Malet. It had been deemed necessary to imprison him in the Tower for a spell – though not for long, as Charles liked to have the gay fellow at his side. There was not another who could write a lampoon to compare with his; and if they were most scurrilous and that scurrility was often directed against the King himself, they were the most pointed, the most witty to be found in the kingdom. Rochester, the most impudent and arrogant of men, had since married the very willing Elizabeth Malet, confounded her family, and taken charge of her great fortune.

All these happenings were characteristic of life at the Court.

As the King walked through his gardens he saw coming

towards him a young man; and as he gazed at the tall and handsome figure, the cynicism dropped from his face. For this young man, who was by no means possessed of the wit the King loved, had the King's love as no other had at Court.

'Why, Jemmy!' he called. 'You're early abroad.'

'Following Your Majesty's customs,' said the young man.

He came and stood before the King without ceremony, and Charles put his arm about the young man's shoulders.

'I had thought, after your revelry of last night, that you would have lain longer abed.'

'I doubt my revelry equalled that of Your Majesty.'

'I am accustomed to combining revelry and early rising – a habit few of my friends care to adopt.'

'I would follow you in all things, Father.'

'You would do better to follow a course of your own, my boy.'

'Nay, the people love you. Thus would I be loved.'

Charles was alert. James' words were more than flattery. James was looking ahead to a time when he might wear the crown; he was seeing himself riding through the Capital, smiling at the acclaim of the people, letting his eyes rest on the prettiest of the women in the balconies.

Charles drew his son towards him with an affectionate gesture.

He said: 'Fortunate James, you will never be in the public eye as I am. You can enjoy the pleasures of the Court without suffering its more irksome responsibilities.'

James did not answer; he was too young and not clever enough to hide the sullen pout of his lips.

'Come, Jemmy,' said Charles, 'be content with your lot. 'Tis a good one and might have been not good at all. You are more fortunate than you know. Do not seek what can never be yours, my son. That way can disaster lie – disaster and tragedy. Come, let us make our way back to the Palace. We'll go through my physic garden. I want to show you how my herbs are progressing.'

They walked arm-in-arm. James was conscious of the King's display of affection. Charles knew he was glancing towards the Palace, hoping that many would see him walking thus with the King. Alas, thought Charles, his desire to have my arm through his is not for love of me; it is for love of my royalty. He is not thinking of my fatherly affection but implying: See, how the King loves me! Am I not his son? Does he not lack a legitimate heir? Will that rabbit-toothed woman ever give him one? He is rarely with her. With what passion could such a woman inspire a man like my father? See how he scatters his seed among the women around him. He has many children, but not one by Rabbit-teeth to call his legitimate son and heir to the throne. I am his son. I am strong and healthy; and he loves me dearly. He has recognized me; he has made me Baron Tyndale, Earl of Doncaster, and Duke of Monmouth. I have precedence over all Dukes except those of the royal blood. I am empowered to assume the royal arms – with the bar sinister, alas – and all this shows how the King delights to honour me. Why should he not make me his legitimate heir, since it is clear that the Portuguese woman will never give him one?

Ah, Jemmy, thought Charles, I would it were possible.

But had he, in his affection, showered too much favour on this impetuous boy who was not twenty yet, and because of the love the King had for him was fawned upon and flattered by all?

How often did Charles see his mother in him! Lucy with the big brown eyes; Lucy who had seemed the perfect mistress to the young man Charles had been in those days of exile. Those were the days before he had suffered the defeat at Worcester. He had loved Lucy – for a little while, but she had deceived him. Poor Lucy! How could he blame her, when he understood so well how easy it was to deceive? Even in those days he had understood. And out of that relationship had come this handsome boy.

He was glad he had loved Lucy. He would long ago have forgotten her, for there had been so many mistresses, but how could he ever forget her when she lived in this handsome boy?

James had inherited his mother's beauty and, alas, her

81

brains. Poor Jemmy! He could never pit his wits against such as Rochester, Mulgrave, Buckingham, and the rest. He excelled in vaulting, leaping, dancing; and had already given a good account of himself with the ladies.

Now Charles thought it necessary to remind James of his lowly mother, that his hopes might not soar too high.

'It was on such a day as this that Ann Hill brought you to me, Jemmy,' he said. 'That was long before I regained my kingdom, as you know. There was I, a poor exile confronted with a son only a few years old. A bold little fellow you were, and I was proud of you. I wished that your mother was a woman I could have married, and that you could have been my legitimate son. Alas, it was not so. Your mother died in poverty in Paris, Jemmy, and you were with her. What would have happened to you, had good Ann Hill not brought you and your sister Mary to me, I know not.'

James tried not to scowl; he did not like to be reminded of his mother.

'It is so long ago,' he said. 'People never mention my mother, and Your Majesty has almost forgotten her.'

'I was thinking then that I never shall forget her while I have you to remind me of her.'

There was a brief silence and, suddenly lifting his eyes, the King saw his brother coming towards him. He smiled. He was fond of his brother, James, Duke of York, but he had never been able to rid himself of a faint contempt for him. James, it seemed to him, was clumsy in all he did – physically clumsy, mentally clumsy. He was no diplomatist, poor James, and was most shamefully under the thumb of his wife – that strongminded lady who had been Anne Hyde, the daughter of disgraced Clarendon.

'What!' cried Charles. 'Another early riser?'

'Your Majesty sets such good examples,' said the Duke, 'that we must needs all follow them. I saw you from the Palace.'

'Well, good morrow to you, James. We were just going to look at my herbs. Will you accompany us?'

'If it is your pleasure, Sir.'

Charles grimaced slightly as he looked from one to the

other of the two men who fell into step beside him: Young James, handsome, sullen, and aloof, unable to hide his irritation at the intrusion; older James, less handsome, but equally unable to hide his feelings, his face clearly showing his mistrust of young Monmouth, his speculation as to what the young man talked of with his father.

Poor James! Poor brother! mused Charles. Doomed to trouble, I fear.

James, Duke of York, was indeed a clumsy man. He had married Anne Hyde when she was to have his child, ignoring convention and the wishes of his family to do so – a noble gesture in which Charles had supported him. But then, being James, he had repudiated her just when he was winning the support of many by his strong action; and in repudiating her – after the marriage of course – he had deeply wounded Anne Hyde herself, and Charles had no doubt that Anne was a woman who would not easily forget. Anne was now in control of her husband.

Poor James indeed. Contemplating him, Charles was almost inclined to believe that it might have been a good idea to have legitimized young Monmouth.

Monmouth was at least a staunch Protestant while James was flirting – nay, more than flirting – with the Catholic Faith. James had a genius for drifting towards trouble. How did he think the people of England would behave towards a Catholic monarch? At the least sign of Catholic influence they were ready to cry 'No Popery!' in the streets. And James – who, unless the King produced a legitimate heir, would one day wear the crown – must needs consider becoming a Catholic!

If he ever becomes King, thought Charles, God help him and God help England.

Charles was struck by the significance of the three of them walking thus in the early morning before the Palace was astir. Himself in the centre – on one side of him James, Duke of York, heir presumptive to the crown of England; and on the other side, James, Duke of Monmouth, the young man who would have been King had his father married his mother, the young man who had received such affection and such honours that he had begun to hope that the greatest honour of all would not be denied to him.

Yes, thought Charles, here am I in the centre, keeping the balance . . . myself standing between them. Over my head flows mistrust and suspicion. This uncle and nephew are beginning to hate one another, and the reason is the crown, which is mine and for which they both long.

What an uneasy thing a crown can be!

How can I make these two, good friends? There is only one way: produce a legitimate son. It is the only answer. I must strike the death knell of their hopes and so disperse that suspicion and mistrust they have for one another; remove that state of affairs and, in place of growing hate, why should there not be growing affection?

The King shrugged. There is no help for it. I must share the bed of my wife more frequently. Alas, alas! It must not be that for want of trying I fail to provide England with a son.

*　　*　　*

Later that morning the Howards sought audience of the King.

Charles was not eager for their company; he found them dull compared with sharp-witted Rochester. It was typical of Charles that although he personally liked the Howards and disliked Rochester, he preferred the company of a man who could amuse him to that of those whom he admitted to be of better character.

Edward Howard had recently been subjected to the scorn of the wits who criticized his literary achievements unmercifully. Shadwell had pilloried him in the play, *The Sullen Lovers*, and all the wits had decided that Edward and Robert Howard should not be taken seriously as writers; only the mighty Buckingham who was, of all the wits, more interested in politics and diplomacy, remained their ally.

Now Robert said to Charles: 'Your Majesty should to the Duke's Theatre this day. Pretty little Moll Davies never danced better than she has of late. I am sure that the sight of her dancing would be a tonic to Your Majesty.'

'I have noted the lady,' said Charles. 'And mighty charming she is.'

The brothers smiled happily. 'And seeming to grow in beauty, Your Majesty, day by day. A good girl, too, and almost of the gentry.'

Charles looked at the brother slyly. 'I have heard that she has relations in high places. I am glad of this, for I feel sure they will do all in their power to elevate her, doubtless in compensation for her begetting on the wrong side of the blanket.'

'It may be so,' said Robert.

'And would it please Your Majesty to call at the Duke's this day to see the wench in her part?' asked Edward a little too eagerly.

Charles ruminated. 'Tis true, he thought; they are dunces indeed, these Howards. Why do they not say to me: Moll Davies is of our family – a bastard sprig; but we would do something for her. She is an actress and high in her profession; we should like to see her elevated to the position of your mistress? Such plain speaking would have amused him more.

'Mayhap. Mayhap,' he said.

Robert came nearer to the King. 'The wench believes she saw Your Majesty look with approval upon her. The foolish girl, she was almost swooning with delight at the thought!'

'I was never over-fond of the swooning kind,' mused Charles.

'I but spoke metaphorically, Your Majesty,' said Robert quickly

'I rejoice. I would prefer to keep my good opinion of little Moll Davies. A mighty pretty creature.'

'And gentle in her ways,' said Edward. 'A grateful wench, and gratitude is rarely come by in these days.'

'Rarely indeed! Now, my friends, I will bid you goodbye. Matters of state . . . matters of state . . .'

They bowed themselves from his presence, and he laughed inwardly. But he continued to think of Moll Davies. For, he said to himself, my indolent nature is such, I am amused that my friends should bring my pleasures to me rather than that I should go in search of them. There are so many beautiful women. I find it hard to choose, therefore deem it thoughtful of my courtiers to do the choosing for me. This avoids my turning with regret from a beautiful creature and having to murmur apologies: Not yet, sweet girl. I am mighty capable, but even I must take you all in turn.

*   *   *

Buckingham presented himself.

'Your Majesty, have you seen Mrs Nell Gwyn in the Beaumont and Fletcher revival of *Pilaster*?'

Charles' melancholy eyes were brooding. 'Nay,' he answered.

'Then, Sir, you have missed the best performance ever seen upon the stage. She plays Bellario. Your Majesty remembers Bellario is sick of love and follows her lover in the disguise of a page boy. This gives Nelly a chance to swagger about on the stage in her breeches. What legs, Sir! What a figure! And all so small that 'twould seem a child's form but for those delicious curves.'

''Twould seem to me,' said the King, 'that you are enamoured of this actress.'

'All London is enamoured of her, Sir. I wonder your fancy has not turned to her ere this. What spirit! What zest for living!'

'I am weary of spirit in ladies – for a while. I have had over-much of spirit.'

'My fair cousin, eh? What a woman! Though she be my kinswoman and a Villiers, I pity Your Majesty. I pity you with all my heart.'

'I conclude you and the lady have fallen out. How so? You were once good friends.'

'Who would not fall out in due time with Barbara, Sir? You know that better than any of us. Now Nelly is another matter. Lovely to look at, and a comedienne to bring the tears of laughter to the eyes. Nelly is incomparable, Sir. There is not another on the stage to compare with Nelly.'

'What of that pretty creature at the Duke's – Moll Davies?'

86

'Bah! Forgive me, Sir, but Bah! and Bah! again. Moll Davies? A simpering wench compared with Nelly. No fire, Your Majesty; no fire at all.'

'I am a little scorched, George. Mayhap I need the soothing balm that comes from simpering wenches.'

'You'd tire of Moll in a night.'

Charles laughed aloud. What game was this? he wondered. Buckingham is determined to put Barbara out of countenance; I know they have quarrelled. But why should the Howards and my noble Duke have turned procurers at precisely the same time?

Moll Davies? Nell Gwyn? He would have one of them to entertain him that night.

He was a little put out with Buckingham, who had for most of last year been under a cloud, and, not so long before that, banished from Court for returning there without the King's permission. Buckingham was a brilliant man, but his brilliance was marred continually by his hare-brained schemes. Moreover the noble Duke gave himself airs and had an exaggerated opinion of his own importance and the King's regard for him.

Charles laid his hand on the Duke's shoulder. 'My dear George,' he said, 'your solicitude for little Nelly touches me. It is clear to me that one who speaks so highly of a pretty actress desires her for himself. You go to my theatre this day and court Nelly. I'll go to the Duke's and see if Moll Davies is the enchanting creature I have been led to believe.'

* * *

Nell heard the news; it sped throughout the theatre.

The King had sent for Moll Davies. She had pleased him, and he had given her a ring estimated to be worth every bit of £700.

He was often at the Duke's Theatre. He liked to see her dance. He led the applause, and everyone in London was talking about the King's latest mistress, Moll Davies.

Lady Castlemaine was sullen; she stayed away from the theatres. There were wild rumours about the number of lovers who visited her daily.

Then one afternoon, instead of going to the Duke's, the King came to his own theatre.

In the green room there was a great deal of excitement.

'What means this?' cried Beck Marshall. 'Can it be that His Majesty is tired of Moll Davies?'

'Would that surprise you?' asked her sister Ann.

'Indeed it would not surprise *me*,' put in Mary Knepp. 'A more stupid simpering ninny I never set eyes on.'

'How can the King . . . after my lady Castlemaine?' demanded Peg Hughes.

'Mayhap,' said Nell, 'because Moll Davies is unlike my lady Castlemaine. After the sun the rain is sweet.'

'But he sends for her often, and he has given her a ring worth £700.'

'And this night,' said Beck, 'he is here. Why so? Can it be that he has a taste for actresses? Has Moll given him this taste?'

'We waste time,' said Nell. 'If he has come here for a purpose other than watching the show, that is a matter which we soon shall know.'

'Nell's turning to wisdom. Alas, Nell, this is a sign of old age. And, Nelly, you are growing old, you know. You're turned eighteen, I'll swear.'

'Almost as old as you are, Beck,' said Nell. 'Of a certainty I must soon begin to consider myself decrepit.'

'I'm a good year younger than you,' cried Beck.

'You have a remarkable gift,' retorted Nell. 'You can make time turn back. This year you are a year younger than last. I have remarked it.'

Ann interrupted: 'Calm yourselves. You'll not be ready in time; and will you keep the King waiting?'

While Nell played her part she was conscious of him. All were conscious of him, of course, but Nell was playing her part for him alone.

What did she want? Another affair such as that in which she had indulged with my lord Buckhurst, only on a more exalted plane? No. She did not want that. But Charles Stuart was no Charles Sackville. She was sure of that. The King was libertine-in-chief in a town of libertines, yet he was apart from all others. She sensed it. He had a quality which was possessed by none other. Was it kingship? How could Nelly, bred in Cole-yard, know what it was? She was aware of one thing only; she wanted that night, above all things, to hear those words: The King sends for Nelly.

She was a sprite that night, richly comic, swaggering about the stage in her page's garb. The pit was wildly applauding; the whole theatre was with her; but she was playing only for the dark-eyed man in the box, who leaned forward to watch her.

She made her bow at the end. There she stood, at the edge of the apron stage so close to the royal box. He was watching her – her only; she was aware of that. His dark eyes glistened; his full lips smiled.

She was in the green room when the message came.

Mohun brought it. 'Nelly, you are to go to Whitehall at once. The King wishes you to entertain him in his palace.'

So it was happening to her as it had happened to Elizabeth Weaver. She did not see the glances of the others; she was aware of a great exaltation.

Mohun put a rich cloak about her shoulders.

'May good fortune attend you, Nelly,' he said.

*   *   *

In the great apartment were assembled the ladies and gentlemen of the King's more intimate circle. Many of these were personally known to Nell. Rochester and his wife were there. She was glad, for, notwithstanding his often spiteful quips, she knew Rochester to be her friend. There was one thing he admired above all others – wit – and Nell, possessing this in full measure, had his regard. Buckingham and his Duchess were also present. The Duke's eyes were shining with approval. He had worked to bring this about, and he was enjoying the rivalry with the Howards who were putting forward Moll Davies. At last he had succeeded in getting Nell to the Palace, and he had no doubt that pretty witty Nelly would soon triumph over pretty, rather spiritless Moll Davies.

Bulkeley, Etherege, Mulgrave, Savile and Scrope were

also there. So were the Dukes of York and Monmouth, with several ladies.

Nell went to the King and knelt before him.

'Arise, sweet lady,' said the King. 'We wish for no ceremony.'

She rose, lifting her eyes to his, and for once Nell felt her bravado desert her. It was not that he was the King. She had suspected it was something else, and now she knew it was.

More than anything she wanted to please him; and this desire was greater even than that which she had once felt when her ambition was to become an orange-girl, and later to act on the stage.

Nell, shorn of her high spirits, was like a stranger to herself.

But Buckingham was beside her.

'I trust Your Majesty will prevail on Mrs Nelly to give us a song and dance.'

'If it should be her wish to do so,' said the King. 'Mrs Nelly, I would have you know that you come here as a guest, not as an entertainer.'

'I am right grateful to Your Majesty,' said Nell. 'And if it be your wish, I will sing and dance.'

So she sang and she danced; and her spirits returned. This was the Nell they had met so many times before – Nell of the quick wits; the Nell who could answer the remarks which were flung at her from my lords Rochester and Buckingham, neither of whom, she was sure, had any wish other than to make her shine in the eyes of the King.

There was supper at a small table during which the King kept her at his side. His glances showed his admiration, and he talked to her of the plays in which she had acted. She was astonished that he should know so much about them and be able to quote so much of their contents, and she noticed that it was the poetic parts which appealed to him.

'You are a poet yourself, Sire?' she asked.

He disclaimed it.

But Rochester insisted on quoting the King:

> '*I pass all my hours in a shady old grove,*
> *But I live not the day when I see not my love;*
> *I survey every walk now my Phyllis is gone,*
> *And sigh when I think we were there all alone;*
> *O then, 'tis O then that I think there's no hell*
> *Like loving, like loving too well.*'

'Those are beautiful words,' said Nell.

The King smiled wryly. 'Flattery abounds at Court, Nelly,' he said. 'I had hoped you would bring a breath of change.'

'But 'tis so, Your Majesty,' said Nell.

Rochester had leaned towards her. 'His Most Gracious Majesty wrote the words when he was deep in love.'

'With Phyllis?' said Nell. 'His Majesty most clearly says so.'

'Some beautiful lady cowers behind the name of Phyllis,' said Rochester. 'I begin to tire of the custom. What say you, Sir? Why should we call our Besses, our Molls, and our little Nells by these fanciful names? Phyllis, Chloris, Daphne, Lucinda! As our friend Shakespeare says: "That which we call a rose by any other name would smell as sweet."'

'Some ladies wish to love in secret,' said the King. 'If you poets must write songs to your mistresses, then respect their desire for secrecy, I beg of you.'

'His Royal Highness is the most discreet of men,' said Rochester with a bow. 'He's too good-natured. No matter whether it be politics, love, or religion.'

Rochester began to quote:

> '*Never was such a Faith's Defender,*
> *He like a politic prince and pious,*
> *Gives liberty to conscience tender*
> *And does to no religion tie us.*
> *Jews, Turks, Christians, Papists, he'll please us*
> *With Moses, Mahomet, or Jesus.*'

'You're an irreverent devil, Rochester,' said Charles.

'I see the royal lip curve in a smile, which I trust was inspired by my irreverence.'

'Nevertheless there are times when you try me sorely. I see, my lady Rochester, that you are a little tired. I think you are asking for leave to retire.'

'If it should please Your Most Gracious Majesty . . .' began Lady Rochester.

'Anything that pleases you, my dear lady, pleases me. You are tired, you wish to retire. So I will command your husband to take you to your apartments.'

This was the signal. They were all to go. The King wished to be alone with Nell.

Nell watched them all make their exit. This was performed with the utmost ceremony, and as she watched them she felt her heart beat fast.

When they had gone, the King turned to her, smiling.

He took her hands and kissed them.

'They amuse me . . . but such amusements are for those times when there are less exciting adventures afoot.'

Nell said tremulously: 'I trust I may please Your Majesty.'

He replied: 'My friends have put me in the mood to rhyme,' and he began to quote Flecknoe's verse:

> *But who have her in their arms,*
> *Say she has a hundred charms,*
> *And as many more attractions*
> *In her words and in her actions.'*

He paused, smiling at her, before he went on: 'It continues, I believe:

> *"But for that, suffice to tell ye,*
> *'Tis the pretty little Nelly."*

And 'tis written of you, I'll swear, by one who knew you well.'

'By one, Sire, who but saw me on the stage.'

Charles drew her to him and kissed her lips. ''Twas enough to see you, to know it were true. Why, Nell, you are afraid of me. You say, This is the King. But I would not be a King tonight.'

Nell said softly: 'I am but a girl from the Cole-yard, one of Your Majesty's most humble servants.'

'A King should love all his subjects, Nell, however humble. I never thought to see you humble. I have noted your subduing of the pit.'

'Sire, I do not now face the pit.'

'Come with me and, for the sake of your beauty, this night let us forget that I am Charles Stuart, and you Nell of old Drury. Tonight I am a man; you a woman.'

Then he put his arm about her and led her into a small adjoining chamber.

And here it was that Nell Gwyn became the mistress of the King.

*   *   *

Nell left the Palace in the early hours of the morning. She was bemused. Never had her emotions been so roused; never had she known such a lover.

She was carried to her lodgings in a Sedan chair; it would not have been meet for her to have walked through the streets in the fine gown she had been wearing. She was no longer merely Mrs Nelly, the play actress. Her life had changed last night. People would look at her slyly; they would marvel at her; they would whisper about her; many would envy her; many would censure her.

And I care not! she thought.

When she reached her lodgings she kicked off her shoes and danced a jig. She was happier than she had ever been in her life. Not because the King had sent for her; not because she had joined the King's seraglio; but because she was in love.

There was never one like him. It was not that he was the King. Or was it? Nay! All kings were not kind, gentle, passionate, charming, all that one looked for in a lover. He was no longer Your Majesty to her; he was Charles. She had called him Charles last night.

'Charles!' She said it now aloud. And: 'Charles, Charles, Charles. Charles is my lover,' she sang. 'The handsomest, kindest lover in the world. He happens to be the King of

93

England, but what matters that? To me he is Charles . . .
my Charles. He is the whole country's Charles . . . but mine
also . . . especially mine.'

Then she laughed and hugged herself and recalled every
detail of the night. She wished passionately then that she had
never known any other Charles, never known Charles Hart;
never known Charles Sackville.

There have been too many Charleses in my life, she
mused. I would there had been only one. Then she wept
a little, because happy as she was there was so much to
regret.

*　　　*　　　*

The King forgot Nell for some time after that night. She
was very pretty, but he had known many pretty women.
Perhaps he had been disappointed; he had heard her wit
commended by such as Buckingham; that did not count of
course, as Buckingham had his own reasons for promoting
Nell, which was the discomfiture of his cousin Barbara and
doubtless the Howards. Yet Rochester seemed to have had
some praise for her. Could it to be that Rochester had been
or still was her lover?

The King shrugged his shoulders. Nell was just a pretty
actress. She had been a very willing partner in an enjoyable
interlude, as had so many. He fancied she was very experienced; he had heard of an escapade with Buckhurst.
Doubtless the pretty creature was not averse to changing
from Duke to King.

Moll Davies suited his present mood more frequently.
Moll was so gentle; there had been no pretence of quick wits
there; she was just a lovely young woman who could learn
a part and speak it prettily; and she could dance as well as
anyone on the stage.

He found he was sending more frequently for Moll than
for any.

He had grown a little weary since the disasters. Was he
ageing somewhat? Beneath the periwig he had plenty of
silver showing among his dark hairs.

Now that Clarendon was gone he was missing him. He

would have to form a new Council. Buckingham was pressing for a place and of course would have it.

State affairs claimed his attention; when he turned from them, little Moll Davies, who smiled so sweetly while speaking little, provided that which he needed. She was the completest contrast to Barbara. Then of course Will Chaffinch and his wife – who held the post of seamstress to the Queen – would often usher ladies up the back stairs to his apartments during the night, and lead them down to the river in the early hours of morning when their barges would be waiting for them. Chaffinch was a discreet and wily fellow, and his apartments were situated near those of the King. He had for long looked after his master's more intimate and personal business.

But now and then Charles remembered the sprightly little actress from his theatre, and sent for her.

He enjoyed her company. She was mightily pretty; she was now becoming amusing, and often he would catch glimpses of that wit which had amused Buckingham.

Then he forgot her again; and it seemed that Moll Davies was going to replace Lady Castlemaine as the woman, among all his women, who could best please him.

*   *   *

Nell was sad and her chief task during those days was to hide her sadness. She was nothing to him but just another harlot. She realized that now. She had been mistaken. The courtly manners, the charm, the grace – they were generously offered to any light-o'-love who could amuse him for a night.

She was nothing more than one of dozens. Tonight it might be her turn – perhaps not.

For her there was no £700 ring. Moll Davies had won. The Howards were triumphant.

As for Buckingham, he had forgotten his intention to promote Nell. His object had been achieved by the Howards and Moll Davies, for his cousin Barbara flew into a flaring rage every time the girl was mentioned. Barbara's pride had been lowered; Barbara knew that she must take care

95

when she thought she might insult the great Duke of Buckingham – her cousin and one-time lover though he was. What part had Nell in Buckingham's schemes? None at all. He had forgotten he had ever exerted himself to bring her to the King's notice. Thus it was with all his schemes. He dallied with them for a while and then forgot. So Moll Davies was provided with beautiful clothes and jewels by the Howards, who brought her before the King whenever he seemed inclined to forget her, while Nell's benefactor ignored her.

So Nell was desolate.

In the green room the women laughed together, their eyes on Nell, Nell who had enjoyed the privilege of being sent for by the King.

'Cole-yard,' whispered Beck Marshall, 'could not go to Whitehall. 'Twas a mistake. His Majesty would be the first to realize it. Poor Nelly soon got her marching orders.'

'She has been called back once or twice,' said her sister Ann.

Peg Hughes, who was being courted by Prince Rupert, was inclined to be kind. 'And doubtless will be called again. The King was never a man to fix his love on one. Nell will remain one of his merry band, I doubt not.'

'She'll be in the twice-yearly class,' said Beck.

'Well, 'tis better to play twice yearly than not at all,' said Peg quietly.

When Nell came among them, Beck said: 'Have you heard the latest news, Nell? Moll Davies is to have a fine house and, some say, leave the stage.'

Nell for once was silent. She felt that she could not speak to them about the King and Moll Davies.

She had changed. She wondered: Shall I one day be like Elizabeth Weaver, waiting in vain for the King to send for me?

*   *   *

Early that year the Earl of Shrewsbury had challenged Buckingham to a duel on account of the Duke's liaison with Lady Shrewsbury; the result of this was that Shrewsbury

was killed. The King was furious. He had forbidden duel-
ling, and Buckingham awaited the outcome in trepidation.
He had now completely forgotten that he had decided to
launch Nell at Whitehall.

In the summer she had the part of Jacintha in Dryden's
An Evening's Love; or the Mock Astrologer. Charles Hart played
opposite her.

Dryden, such an admirer of Nell's, invariably had her in
his mind when he wrote his plays, and Jacintha *was* Nell,
so said all, 'Nelly to the last y.'

The King was in his usual box and, as she played her part,
Nell could not help gazing his way. Perhaps there was a
mute appeal in her eyes, in her voice, in her very actions.

To love a King – that was indeed a tragedy, she had come
to understand. She had no means of being with him unless
sent for, no way of learning where she had failed to please.

Charles Hart as Wildblood wooed her on the stage before
the King's eyes.

'"What has a gentleman to hope from you?"' he asked.

And Nell, as Jacintha, must answer: '"To be admitted
to pass my time with while a better comes; to be the lowest
step in my staircase, for a knight to mount upon him, and a
lord upon him, and a marquis upon him, and a duke upon
him, till I get as high as I can climb."'

The audience laughed loud and long.

Many covert glances were thrown at the King in his royal
box and pert Nell on the stage. She had had her lord; she
had reached her King; but she had not kept her King.

There was no sign on the King's face to show how he
received this piece of impudence. But Nell, intensely aware
of him, believed he was displeased.

She went straight to her lodgings that night and wept a
little, but not much. She had to show the world a bold
front, and the next day she was a merry madcap once more.

'Nelly . . . the old Nelly . . . is back,' it was said.

And after a while it was forgotten that she had ever
changed. There she was, the maddest and most indiscreet
creature who had ever played in the King's Theatre, and
the people crowded into the playhouse to see her.

Now and then the King came. Occasionally he sent for Nell. But Moll Davies had her fine house near Whitehall, and had left the stage.

All the actresses talked of Moll's good fortune, and many wondered why it was that pretty witty Nell had pleased the King so mildly and Moll had pleased him so much.

*　　*　　*

The company performed Ben Jonson's *Cataline*. Lady Castlemaine sent for Mrs Corey who was playing Sempronia – a most unattractive character – and gave her a sum of money on condition that she would, when playing the part, mimic Lady Castlemaine's great enemy of the moment, Lady Elizabeth Harvey, whose husband had recently left London for Constantinople as the King's ambassador.

During the very first performance, when the question was asked, 'But what will you do with Sempronia?' Lady Castlemaine leaped to her feet and shouted at the top of her voice: 'Send her to Constantinople.'

Lady Harvey was so incensed that she arranged that Mrs Corey should be sent to prison for the insult. Lady Castlemaine then used all her influence, which was still great, to have her released. And when Mrs Corey next played the part she was pelted with all manner of obnoxious objects, and men, hired by Lady Elizabeth, snatched oranges from the orange-girl's baskets to throw at the actors on the stage.

Each night the play was performed there was an uproar between men hired by Lady Elizabeth Harvey and those hired by Lady Castlemaine. It was bad for the play and the actors, but good for business; for the theatre was filled each time that play was performed.

Later, Dryden's *Tyrannic Love; or the Royal Martyr* was produced; and in this Nell played Valeria, daughter of the Emperor Maximin who persecuted St Catherine. It was a small part in which Nell stabbed herself at the end; then came the epilogue, which was to be her great triumph.

She felt exalted that day. She had escaped from the dismal creature she had become. She had been a fool to harbour such romantic thoughts about a King.

'Nelly, grow up,' she said to herself. 'Have done with dreaming. What are you to him – what could you ever be – but a passing fancy?'

She lay dead on the apron stage and when the stretcher-bearers approached with her bier, she leaped suddenly to her feet, crying:

> *'Hold! Are you mad? You damned confounded dog!*
> *I am to rise and speak the epilogue.'*

Then she came to the very front of the apron stage – mad Nelly, the most indiscreet of all the actresses, pretty witty Nell who had won their hearts.

The King, sitting in his box, leaned forward. She felt his approving eyes upon her. She knew that, try as he might, he could not withdraw them, and she believed then that neither Lady Castlemaine nor Moll Davies could have made him turn his eyes from her.

She cried in her high-pitched, mocking tones:

> *'I come, kind gentlemen, strange news to tell ye:*
> *I am the ghost of poor departed Nelly.*
> *Sweet ladies, be not frightened, I'll be civil;*
> *I'm what I was, a little harmless devil . . .'*

The audience was craning forward to listen as she went on with the lines which were setting some rocking with laughter, while others, fearful of missing Nelly's words, cried: 'Hush!'

> *'O poet, damned dull poet, who could prove*
> *So senseless to make Nelly die for love!*
> *Nay, what's yet worse, to kill me in the prime*
> *Of Easter term, in tart and cheese-cake time!'*

She had thrown back her head; her lovely face was animated. Many caught their breath at the exquisite beauty of the dainty little creature as she continued:

99

'*As for my epitaph when I am gone,*
I'll trust no poet, but will write my own:
"Here Nelly lies who, though she lived a slattern,
Yet died a princess, acting in Saint Cattern." '

The pit roared its approval. Nell permitted herself one look at the royal box. The King was leaning forward; he was clapping heartily; and he was smiling so intimately that Nell knew he would send for her that night.

She felt light-headed with gaiety. She had tried to act a part because she had loved a King. In future she would be herself. Who knew, had he known the real Nelly, Charles might have loved her too.

*　　　*　　　*

Charles did send for Nell that night, but secretly. Will Chaffinch came to her lodgings to tell her that His Majesty wished her to visit him by way of the back stairs.

In high good spirits Nell prepared herself for the journey and, very soon after Chaffinch had called at her lodgings, she was mounting the privy stairs to the King's chamber.

Charles was delighted to see her.

'It is long since we have met, Nell,' said he, 'in these intimate surroundings, but I have thought of you often – and with the utmost tenderness.'

Nell's face softened at the words, even while she thought: Does he mean it? Is this another of those occasions when his desire to be kind triumphs over truth?

But perhaps his greatest charm was that he could make people believe, while they were in his presence, all the kind things he said to them. It was only after they had left him that the doubts crept in.

'Matters of state,' he murmured lightly.

And indeed, he mused, that which had kept him from Nell was indeed a matter of greatest importance to the state. Of late he had been spending his nights with Catherine, his wife.

He had done his duty, he decided with a grimace. He fervently hoped that the exercise would bear fruit.

I must get a legitimate son, he told himself a hundred

times a day. Every time he saw his brother James, every time he saw that handsome sprig, young Monmouth, swaggering about the Court eager that none should forget for a moment that he was the King's son, Charles said to himself: I must get me a son.

Here was a perverse state of affairs. He had many healthy children, sons among them, growing up in beauty to manhood, many of them bearing the stamp of his features – and all bastards. There was scarcely one of his mistresses who had not borne a child which she swore was his. Od's fish, I am a worthy stallion, he thought. Yet, in my legitimate bed I am sterile – or Catherine is. Poor Catherine! She yearns for a child equally with me. Why in the name of all that's holy should our efforts meet with no success?

And it was a great burden to follow the call of duty, to spend long hours of the night with Catherine – cloying, clinging Catherine – when superb creatures such as Barbara, charmingly pretty dolls such as Moll Davies, and exquisitely lovely sprites, such as this little Nelly, had but to be brought at his command.

When he had seen Nell on the stage this day, rising from her bier, looking the very embodiment of charm and wit and all that was fascinating and amusing, he had determined to evade his duty that night.

'My dear wife,' he had said to Catherine, 'I shall retire early this evening. I feel unwell.'

She was startled, that good wife of his. He was never ill. There was not another at Court who enjoyed his rude health. In the game of tennis he excelled all others; and if he spent his afternoons in the theatre and his evenings in amusing the ladies, his mornings were often devoted to swimming, fishing, or sailing. His laziness was of the mind – never of the body. He slept little, declaring that the hours a man spent in unconsciousness were lost hours; he had not yet had such a feast of the good things life had to offer that he could afford to waste long periods of his life in sleep. He merely disliked what he called 'that foolish, idle, impertinent thing called business', and much preferred to take 'his usual physic at tennis' or on horseback.

Mayhap he had been unwise to make the excuse of ill-health. Catherine was all solicitude. She was a simple soul, who yet had much to learn of him; and he was his most foolish self in that he could not bring himself to say – as my lord Buckingham would have told his wife, or my lord Rochester his – that he needed an occasional escape from her company; he must tell his lies for, if he did not, he would hurt her, and to see her hurt would spoil his pleasure; and that was one thing he could not endure – the spoiling of his pleasure.

When they next met she would smother him with her concern and he would have to feign a headache or pain somewhere, and remember the exact position of the pain. He might even have to endure a posset of her making since the dear simple creature was ever eager to display her wifely devotion.

But enough of that – here was Nell, risen from her bier, prettier than ever, her eyes sparkling with wit and good humour.

This little Nelly grows on me, pondered the King; and lifting from the bed one of the many spaniels which were always in his bedchamber, he embraced her warmly; and Nell with delight gave herself up to that embrace.

They made love. They dozed, and they awakened to find Will Chaffinch's wife at their bedside.

'Your Majesty! Your Majesty! I pray you awake. The Queen comes this way. She brings a posset for you.'

'Out of sight, Nelly!' said the King.

Nell whisked out of bed and, naked as she was, hid herself behind the hangings.

Catherine entered the room just as Nell was hidden; she approached the bed, her long and beautiful hair hanging about her shoulders, her plain face anxious.

'I could not sleep,' she said. 'I could do naught but think of you in pain.'

The King took her hand as she sat on the bed and looked at him anxiously.

'Oh,' he said, 'the pain is to be deplored, only because it

disturbed your slumbers. It has gone. In fact I have forgotten where it was.'

'I very much rejoice. I have brought this dose. I am sure it will bring immediate relief should you need it.'

Nell, listening, thought: here are the King and Queen of England, and he treats her in the same charmingly courteous way in which he treats his harlots.

'And you,' he was saying, 'should be resting in your bed at this hour. I shall be the one who has to bring you doses if you wander thus in your night attire.'

'And you would,' she said. 'I know it. You have the kindest heart in the world.'

'I pray you do not have such high opinions of me. I deserve them not.'

'Charles . . . I will stay beside you this night . . .'

There was a sudden silence and, unable to stop herself, Nell moved the hangings and looked through the opening she had made.

She saw that one of the King's spaniels had leaped on to the bed and was bringing Nell's tiny slipper in his mouth and laying it there as though offering it to Queen Catherine.

Nell, in that quick glance, took in the scene – the King's discomfiture, the Queen's face scarlet with humiliation.

The Queen quickly recovered her dignity. She was no longer the same inexperienced woman who had swooned when she had come face to face with Barbara Castlemaine, and the odious woman had kissed her hand.

She said abruptly: 'I will not stay. The pretty fool who owns that little slipper might take cold.'

The King said nothing. Nell heard the door close.

Nell came slowly back to the bed. The King was gently stroking the ears of the little spaniel who had betrayed them. He stared moodily before him as Nell got in beside him.

He turned to her ruefully. 'There are many strange things happening in the world,' he said. 'Many women are kind to me; but I am a King, and it pays to be kind to kings, so that presents little mystery. But there is one mystery I have been unable to solve: Why does that good and virtuous woman who is my Queen love me?'

Nell said: 'I could tell you, Sire.'

And she told him; her explanation was lucid and witty. She restored him to his good humour, and shortly after that occasion Nell discovered that she was to bear the King's child.

*   *   *

Now that Nell was with child by the King, it was no longer possible for her to play all her old parts. She was helped by Will Chaffinch, who had charge of such items of the royal expenditure, and she moved into Newman's Row, which was next to Whetstone Park.

Nell was elated by the thought of bearing the King's child. Charles was only mildly interested. He had so many illegitimate children; it was a legitimate one which he so desperately needed. Even before he had been restored to his throne he had a large and growing family, of which the Duke of Monmouth was the eldest son. Some he kept about him; others passed out of his life. One of the latter was James de la Cloche who had been born to Margaret de Carteret while Charles was exiled in Jersey. He believed that James was now a Jesuit. Lady Shannon had given him a daughter; Catherine Pegge a son and a daughter. There were many others who claimed to be his. He accepted them all in his merry good humour. He was proud of his ability to create sons and daughters; and when some of his subjects called him 'Old Rowley', after the stallion in the royal stables who had sired more fine and healthy colts than any other, he did not object. Barbara Castlemaine had already borne him five children. He loved them all tenderly. He adored his children; there was nothing he liked better than to talk with them, and listen to their amusing comments. He enjoyed his visits to Barbara's nursery more than to their mother's chamber. They were growing more amusing – young Anne, Charles, Henry, Charlotte, and George – than their virago of a mother.

He had an acknowledged family of nine or ten; he did what he could for them, raising them to the peerage, settling money on them, keeping his eyes open for profitable marriages. Oh, yes, he was indeed fond of his children.

And now little Nell was to provide him with another.

It was interesting; he would be eager to see the child when it put in an appearance; but meanwhile there was much elsewhere with which to occupy himself.

He was faintly worried once more by the shadows cast over his throne by his son Monmouth, and his own brother, the Duke of York.

Monmouth was turning out to be a rake. In the sexual field, it was said, he would one day rival his father. Charles could only shrug his shoulders tolerantly at this. He would not have had young Jemmy otherwise – nor could he have expected it with such a father and such a mother.

He wished though that his son did not indulge in so much street-fighting. Charles had given him a troop of horse, and when he had inspected fortifications at Harwich recently it was reported that he and his friends had had a right merry time debauching the women of the countryside.

It would be churlish of me to deny him the pleasure in which I myself have taken such delight, the King told himself. Yet he would have preferred young Jemmy to have had a more serious side to his character. It was true that the King's friends indulged in like pleasures; but these were men of wit; they were rogues and libertines, but they were interested in the things of the mind as well as those of the body – even as Charles was himself. So far it seemed to him that his son Jemmy had taken on himself all the vices of the Restoration and none of its virtues.

Jemmy was growing more arrogant, more speculative every day. He was providing the biggest shadow over the crown. Brother James also caused anxieties. He was very different from young Jemmy. James had his mistresses – many of them – and he visited them and got them with child whenever he could escape from Anne Hyde. James was not a bad sort; James was merely a fool. James had a perfect genius for doing that which would bring trouble – mainly on himself. 'Ah,' Charles would murmur often, 'protect me from *la sottise de mon frère*. But most of all, protect my brother from it.'

Now James was having trouble with Buckingham. There

was another who was doomed to make trouble for others and chiefly for himself. Two trouble-makers; if they could but put their heads together and make one brewing of trouble 'twould be easier, mused Charles. But they must needs busy themselves with their separate brews and give me double trouble.

Buckingham – by far the cleverer of the two – had decided that James should be his friend. He made advances to the Duke, suggesting that they sink their differences and work together. Buckingham wished to rid himself of his greatest rival in the Cabal, my lord Arlington, and had solicited James' help to this end.

James, with sturdy self-righteousness, had set himself apart from their schemes. He intimated that he considered it beneath him to enter into such Cabals; he was resolved to serve the King in his own way.

More tact should have been used when dealing with the wild and reckless Buckingham.

Buckingham now saw James as an enemy; and how could such an ambitious man tolerate an enemy who was also heir presumptive to the crown?

Buckingham raged, and mad schemes filled his imaginative brain. The King must get legitimate children; the Duke of York must never be allowed to mount the throne.

So now it was that Buckingham brought out his wild plans for a divorce between the King – that mighty stallion, who had proved many times that he was capable of getting children with a variety of women – and sterile Catherine, whose inability to perform her duties as Queen could plunge the country into a desperate situation.

Charles had declined Buckingham's efforts on his behalf, which had ranged from the divorcing of Catherine to the kidnapping of her and carrying her off to some plantation where she would never be heard of again.

Moreover Charles had sought out James.

'My lord Buckingham's wild mind teems with wild plans,' he said. 'And the very essence of these plans is that you shall never follow me. Do not laugh at them, James. Buckingham is a dangerous fellow.'

Buckingham was looking to Monmouth. What wild seeds could he sow in that wild mind?

So the shadows deepened about the throne, and the King had little time to think of the child which Nell would soon be bringing into the world.

*   *   *

There was not a breath of air in the room. Hangings had been drawn across the windows to shut out the light; candles burned in the chamber. Nell lay on her bed and thought her last hour had come. So many women died in childbirth.

Rose was with her, and she was glad of Rose's company.

'Nelly,' whispered Rose, 'should you not be walking up and down the chamber? 'Twill make an easier birth, they say.'

'No more, Rosy. No more,' moaned Nell. 'I have walked enough, and these pains seem fit to kill me.'

Her mother sat by the bed; Nell saw through half-closed eyes that she had brought her gin bottle with her.

She was crying already. Nell heard her talking of her beautiful daughter who had captivated the King. Her mother's voice, high-pitched and shrill, seemed to fill the bedchamber.

'That little bastard my girl Nell is bearing is the King's son. Who'd have thought it . . . of my little Nell!'

It is a long way, thought Nell, from a bawdy-house in Cole-yard to child-bed of the King's bastard.

And where was the King this day? He was not in London. He was riding to Dover to greet visitors from overseas. 'Matters of state,' he would murmur. 'Matters of state. That is why I cannot be at hand at the birth of our child, sweet Nell.'

He would say such things to have her believe that the child she was bearing was as important to him as those borne by his lady mistresses. Actress or Duchess . . . it was the same to him. That's what he would imply. If he had been beside her and said it, she would have believed him.

'I always said,' Mrs Gwyn was croaking to Mary Knepp and Peg Hughes, who had come into the chamber to swell the crowds and see Mrs Nelly brought to bed of the King's bastard, 'I always said that my Nell was too little a one to bear children.'

Then Nell suddenly sat up in bed and cried aloud: 'Have done with your caterwauling, Ma. I'm not a corpse yet. Nor do I intend to be. I'll live, and so will the King's bastard.'

That was so typical of Nell that everyone fell to laughing; and Nell herself kept them in fits of laughter until the pain grew worse and she called to Rose and the midwife.

Not long after that Nell lay back exhausted, with the King's son in her arms.

There was a fluffy dark down on his head.

The women bending over him cried: 'He's a Stuart! Yes, you can see the royal stallion in Nelly's brat.'

And Nell, holding him close, believed she was discovering a new adventure in happiness. She had never felt so tired nor so contented with her lot.

This tiny creature in her arms should never sprawl on the cobbles of Cole-yard; he should never hold horses for fine gentlemen; indeed he should be a fine gentleman himself – a duke no less!

And why not? Were not Barbara's brats dukes? Why should not Nell's most beautiful babe become one also?

'What'll you call him, Nelly?' asked Rose.

'I shall call him Charles,' said Nell, and she spoke very firmly. 'Charles, of course, after his father.'

And as she lay there, for the first time in her life Nell knew the real meaning of ambition. It was born in her, strong and fierce; and all her hopes and desires for greatness were for this child who lay in her arms.

*   *   *

Charles, travelling to Dover, did not give Nell and their child a thought. He knew that he was approaching one of the most important moments of his reign.

This meeting at Dover would not only bring him a sight of his beloved sister, but it would mean establishing that alliance which was to be forged between himself and France, himself and France rather than England and France, for the treaty which he would sign would be a secret treaty, the contents of which would be known only to himself and four of his most able statesmen – Arlington, Arundel, Clifford, and Bellings.

Secrecy was necessary. If his people knew what he planned to sign, they would rise against him. They hated the French; and how was it possible to explain to them that their country tottered on the edge of bankruptcy? How was it possible to explain that the effects of plague, fire, and a Dutch war lingered on? England needed France's money and, if France demanded concessions, these concessions must be made. Whether they would be kept or not was a matter with which Charles must concern himself when the time came for keeping them. Meantime it was a matter of signing the secret treaty or facing bankruptcy, poverty, famine, and that sorry state which invariably followed on the heels of these disasters and was the greatest of them all – revolution.

Charles had seen one revolution in England; he had no intention of seeing another. Ten years ago he had come home; and he was determined – if it were in his power to prevent it – never to go wandering again.

So he rode to Dover.

There were so many compensations in life. Here he was to meet his sweet Minette, that favourite of all his brothers and sisters, the youngest of them all, whom he had always loved so dearly and who, in the letters she wrote so frequently to him, seemed like a constant companion. She was married – poor sweet Minette – to the most loathsome Monsieur of France, who treated her shamefully; and she was in love – she betrayed this in her letters, and he had his spies in the French Court who had confirmed this – with Louis XIV, the brilliant and handsome monarch of France. It was Minette's tragedy that the restoration of her brother had come too late for her to marry the King of France, and that she had been forced to take Monsieur his brother.

But it would be wonderful to see his sister, to talk with her, to listen to her news and tell his, and to assure each other how much those frequent letters meant in their lives;

to tell each other that brother and sister never loved as they did.

It was small wonder that Charles forgot that one of his minor mistresses was being delivered of a son. He fêted his sister and he signed the treaty which, if it had become universal knowledge, would have put his crown in as much danger as that which had surrounded his father more than twenty years before.

But he would not let the facts depress him. His dearest sister was his guest for two short weeks – that odious husband of hers would allow her to stay no longer – and Louis was to pay him two million livres within six months that he might, when the opportune moment arose, declare himself an adherent of the Catholic Faith. Charles shrugged his shoulders. There was no stipulation as to when Charles should make that declaration; had there been, he could never, however tempting the reward, have signed that treaty. He could declare himself a Catholic, at his own pleasure. That would be years ahead – mayhap never. And very badly England needed those French livres.

He was to declare war on Holland when Louis asked him to, and for his services in this respect he would receive three million livres a year as long as the war continued.

That gave him few qualms. The Dutch were England's enemies and, with the aid of pamphleteers, it was not difficult to rouse the country's hatred against an enemy who had recently sailed up one of England's rivers and burned the nation's ships under their very noses.

Nay, thought Charles, they'll go to war readily enough. 'Tis my turning papist they'd not stomach.

But he remembered the words of his maternal grandfather, the great Henri Quatre – when he had entered Paris and ended the wars of religion.

We are of a kind, thought Charles. A good bargain this. My country almost bankrupt, and myself to be paid two million livres to declare myself a Catholic at the right moment. Who knows, the right moment may never come, but my two million livres will, and prove most useful.

So he signed the treaty and delighted his dear sister, for

Louis, whom she loved, would be pleased with her when she came back to France to make a present to him of her brother's signature on that treaty.

Sweet Minette. Back to France she must go. Back to her odious husband.

She held out her jewel case to him and said: 'Choose what you will, dearest brother. Anything you may wish for I would have you take in memory of me.'

Then he lifted his eyes and saw the charming girl who stood beside his sister, and who had brought the jewel case when Henriette had bidden her do so.

'There is only one jewel I covet,' he said. 'This fair one who outshines all in your box, sweet sister.'

The girl dropped her eyes and blushed warmly.

Minette said to her: 'Louise, my dear, I pray you leave me with my brother.'

The child curtseyed and was gone, but not before she had thrown a quick look over her shoulder at the King of England.

'Nay, Charles,' scolded Minette, 'she is too young.'

'It is a fault easily remedied,' said Charles. 'Time passes, and those who are young are . . . not so young.'

'I could not leave her behind.'

Charles was somewhat regretful. He had rarely pursued women; it had never been necessary. Louise was a charming child, but he doubted not that here in Dover there were other charming children, his own subjects. The only time he had ever pursued a woman was during his infatuation for Frances Stuart.

'I shall regret her going,' said Charles. 'Had she stayed she could have provided some small consolation for your loss.'

'Mayhap, dear brother, one day soon I shall come again to England, and I pray that next time I come it will not be necessary for me to depart so soon.'

'My poor Minette, is life so difficult?'

She turned to him, smiling. 'Life is full of happiness for me now,' she said.

Then she embraced him and wept a little.

'When I return to France,' she said, 'write to me regularly, Charles.'

'Indeed I will. It is the only solace that is left to us.'

'Tell me all that happens at your Court, and I will tell you all that happens at Versailles. Louis is jealous of my love for you.'

'And I of yours for him.'

'It is different, Charles.'

'I am but the brother and he . . .'

She smiled sadly. 'Often there have been only your letters reminding me that I am entirely yours to make me feel my life is worth while.'

He smiled at her tenderly; he understood so well. She loved him – but second to the King of France – and she had had to choose between them when she came on this mission as the agent of the King of France. Yet he loved her no less because of that.

* * *

He saw his sister's young maid of honour before they left for France.

He came upon her suddenly in an antechamber as he was about to go to his sister's apartments. He wondered whether she had arranged that it should be so.

She curtsied prettily, and then as though wondering whether she complied with the English custom, fell on her knees.

'Nay,' he said, 'such obeisance is not necessary. Let not beauty kneel to any – not even royalty.'

She rose and stood blushing before him.

'You are a charming child,' he said. 'I asked my sister to leave you behind that we might become good friends, but she will not do so.'

'Sire,' said the girl. 'My English is not of the best, you see.'

'You should be taught it, my child; and the best way to learn a country's language is to take up residence in that land. When I was your age and after, I spent many years in your country, and thus I spoke your country's language.'

He began to speak in French, and the young girl listened eagerly.

'Would you like to come and stay awhile in England?'

'But yes, Your Majesty.'

'Stay at Court, shall we say, where I might show you how we live in England?'

She laughed childishly. 'It would give me the greatest pleasure.'

'Alas, my sister says she owes an obligation to your parents and must take you back with her.' He placed his hands on her shoulders and drew her towards him. 'And that,' he said, 'makes me desolate.'

'I thank Your Majesty.'

'Thank me not. Thank the Fates which gave you this beautiful curling hair.' He fondled it tenderly. 'This soft skin . . .' He touched her cheeks and throat.

She waited breathlessly. Then he bent gracefully and kissed her on the lips. There was a movement in the room beyond them.

He said: 'Mayhap we shall meet again.'

'I do not know, Your Majesty.'

'Tell me your name before we part.'

'It is Louise.'

'Louise. It is a charming name. What other names have you?'

'I am Louise Renée de Penancoët de Kéroualle.'

'Then adieu, sweet Mademoiselle de Kéroualle; I shall pray that ere long we meet again.'

FOUR

WHEN Louise de Kéroualle came to England with Charles'
sister, Henriette, Duchess d'Orléans, she was already
twenty years old. She looked much younger; this was due
not only to her round babyish face but to her manners.
These looks and manners were no indication of the real
Louise, who was shrewd and practical in the extreme.

As the daughter of Guillaume de Penancoët, the Sieur de
Kéroualle, a gentleman of noble lineage, she could not hope
for a brilliant marriage, since her family had fallen into
poverty and could not provide her with an adequate dowry.
Louise, ever conscious of her lineage, was never tired of
reminding those who seemed likely to forget it that, through
her mother, she was connected with the family of de Rieux.
Her position was an unfortunate one – so proud and yet so
poor. Louise was older than her sister Henriette by some
years, so her problem was the more immediate. She had one
brother, Sebastian, who was serving abroad with the King's
armies.

Men could distinguish themselves in the service of their
Kings, mused Louise; there was only one way open to
women: marriage. Or so she had thought.

She had remained at the convent, where she had received
her education, so long that she had thought she would never
leave it. She had had visions of herself growing old, past a
marriageable age, perhaps taking the veil. For what was
there left for noble women, who could not marry with their
equals, but the veil?

And then, suddenly had come the summons to return to
her parents' Breton home.

She would never forget the day she arrived at the great
mansion, where all the family lived since none of them could
afford to go to Court. She had wondered whether Sebastian
had distinguished himself, whether the King had honoured

him, and their fortunes were changed, whether some miracle had happened and a man of wealth and family had asked for the elder daughter's hand in marriage.

It was none of these things, but it concerned herself.

Her parents received her ceremoniously. Never did her father forget that he was Sieur de Kéroualle, and ceremony in his house was as closely observed as it was at Versailles.

She curtsied before them both and received their embrace. Her father had waved his hand to dismiss the servants, and then he had turned his face to her and, smiling, said: 'My daughter, a place has been found for you at Court.'

'At Court!' she had cried, in her excitement forgetting that she should not show her surprise but accept all that was suggested, with the utmost decorum.

'My dear child,' said her mother, 'the Duchess d'Orléans is to take you into her suite.'

'And . . .' Louise looked from one to the other, 'this can be done?'

'Indeed it can be done,' said her father. 'Wherefore did you think we had sent for you if it could not be so?'

'I . . . I merely thought it might prove too costly.'

'But it is a great opportunity, and one which we could not miss. I shall sell some land and make it possible for you to go to Court.'

'And we hope that you will be worthy of the sacrifice,' murmured her mother.

'I will,' said Louise. 'Indeed I will.'

'In the service of Madame you will meet the very highest in the land. His Majesty himself is often in Madame's house. They are great friends. I hope you will find favour in the King's sight, daughter. Much good could come to our family if he found one of its members worthy of his regard.'

'I see, Father.'

They dismissed her then, for they said she was tired from her journey. She went to her room, and her mother followed her there. She made her lie down, and had food brought for her.

While she ate, her mother looked at her earnestly. She stroked the fine curling chestnut hair.

'Such pretty hair,' she said. 'And you are pretty, my dear Louise. Very pretty. Different from the Court ladies, I know; but sometimes it is a good thing to be different.'

When her mother left her, Louise had lain staring at the canopy of her bed.

She was to go to Court; she was to do her utmost to please the King. There was something her parents were trying to tell her. What was it?

*   *   *

She quickly discovered.

They talked constantly of the King. The most handsome man in all France, they said; and what a pleasure it was to have a young King on the throne, a King who looked as a King should look. They recalled his magnificence at his coronation; what a fine sight it had been to see him in the ceremonial cloak of purple velvet embroidered with the golden lilies of France, and the great crown of Charlemagne on his noble head. All who had watched in the great Cathedral of Notre-Dame de Rheims had said that this was more than a King; it was a god come among them. He was pink and white and gold, this King of theirs; and he had a nature to match his face – benign and beautiful. It was a pleasure for all to serve him – man and woman alike.

They recalled his love for Marie Mancini, how idealistically he had wanted to marry her; and he would have done so too, had not his mother and Cardinal Mazarin set themselves against the marriage. Of course it would have been quite impossible for the King of France to marry a woman who was not of royal birth, but did it not show what a kindly, what a charming nature he had, to think of the marriage?

What did the King look like? Anyone who wanted to know that only had to read the romances of the day. It was said that, when she described her heroes, Mademoiselle de Scudéry used Louis XIV as her model.

'He is married now, our King,' said Louise regretfully;

for she had begun to picture herself in the place of Marie Mancini, and she believed that had she been that young woman she would have married the King in spite of his mother, the unpopular Anne of Austria, and Cardinal Mazarin who was equally unpopular. She and Louis would have conspired together to bring about that marriage.

Marriage with a King! It was foolish to dream such dreams.

'He is married now, yes,' said her mother. 'He is married to the dumpy little Spanish Princess, Marie Thérèse. She looked well enough in her wedding garments. But divested of them! Oh, I shudder for our beloved King, he who is such a connoisseur of beauty. There will be others.' Her mother lifted her shoulders and smiled tenderly. 'How could it be otherwise? I have heard that, when he was very young, he loved Madame de Beauvais.' She laughed aloud. 'Madame de Beauvais! Years older than he was – a fat woman – and I have heard that she has but one eye. Yet . . . he has never forgotten her. He has shown her great favour. *There* is an indication of the kind of King we have. A King who never forgets to reward those who have pleased him . . . even if it was only for a short time and long ago.'

Now Louise began to understand. She could not make a brilliant marriage because she had no suitable *dot*; but if she could become the good friend of the King, all sorts of honours might fall to her; and there were many men who then might wish to share her fortunes. How much more desirable was a royal mistress – even a discarded one – than a penniless virgin!

*   *   *

So to Court came Louise. She was pretty enough, but this prettiness was due to her youthful appearance. Her hair was lovely, so was her complexion, unpitted by the pox and unmarked by any blemish. Her round plump face gave her an innocent expression rare at this time, and this was appealing. Her eyes were rather closely set, and there was a suggestion at times of a cast in one of them. However, she was accounted a pretty young girl; and, because her appearance was not one of conventional beauty, this brought her some attention.

She had been thoroughly schooled in social etiquette, both in her home and in the convent, and as a result of her training was possessed of a natural grace. Her education had not been neglected and she was considered to be a cultured young woman, though lacking in the imagination which would have made her an outstandingly clever one. Louise then, when she came to the Court, was a well-bred, well-educated girl with some pretensions to good looks, certain graceful charm, and shrewd ideas, beneath that calm and babyish brow, of making a comfortable existence for Mademoiselle de Kéroualle.

Louise was a born spy. Her poverty and pressing need had nourished this quality in her. She told herself that it was a matter of great urgency that she must understand all that was going on about her; she had no time to spare. She was already twenty, no longer very young; a place at Court might not remain open to her. Therefore she quickly grasped the state of affairs at St Cloud.

Henriette d'Orléans, the wife of the King's brother, and sister to the King of England, was a charming woman – quick-witted, clever, and though no conventional beauty, one of the most attractive women in the Court of le Roi Soleil. Here, thought Louise, was a good model for herself. She studied Henriette and, watching her closely, being her intimate companion, she began to probe her secrets.

Not that Monsieur – Henriette's husband – made any secret of the life they led together. Monsieur had his *mignons*, his dear friends who meant more to him than any woman could. Monsieur was the most conceited man in France and Louise discovered that his wife pleased him very much in one respect. There were occasions when he felt proud of her.

Louise understood the meaning of this one day when Louis himself paid a visit to St Cloud.

This was the first time Louise had seen him. She was prepared. She was looking younger than ever; she kept close to her mistress. Here was her first chance to shine before His

Majesty. She wore the most youthful of her gowns and her magnificent hair was elaborately dressed but falling in curls over her shoulders, as a young girl would wear it. She was sure she did not look more than fifteen.

The King came into the apartment, tall and as handsome as he had been made out to be, dressed in cloth of gold trimmed with black lace, diamonds flashing in his hat; he strode to Henriette.

She would have knelt, but he would not allow her to do so. He was agitated, Louise guessed.

He said: 'No ceremony, dear sister.'

'Your Majesty has urgent business with me,' said Henriette. 'I had hoped to present my new maid of honour, Mademoiselle de Kéroualle.'

Louis' eyes flickered lightly over Louise.

She came forward and fell to her knees.

He said: 'Welcome to the Court, my dear. Welcome.'

She lifted her eyes to his face; this was the moment for which she had longed and hoped. But he was looking at the Duchesse.

'You wish to speak to me alone?' asked Henriette.

'I do wish that,' said the King.

It was the signal for attendants to retire.

One of her companions put her arms about Louise's shoulders. 'Don't be hurt, my child,' she said. 'It is always thus. When he comes, he has no eyes for anyone but Madame. Moreover if you would have pleased him you should not have seemed such a very little girl. His Majesty once liked matrons – now he likes no one but Madame.'

After that she began to understand a good deal.

Here was intrigue which interested Louise, not only because it was of vital importance to her, but because intrigue in any form fascinated her.

When her mistress danced in such a sprightly way, when she joked so readily, when she appeared to be gay, she was really full of sadness; and it was due to the fact that she had married the wrong man – Monsieur – when she loved the King himself.

Louise did not give up hope of attracting the King.

There was a great deal of gossip concerning Louis and his sister-in-law. Louise discovered that both the King's mother, Anne of Austria, and Henriette's mother, Queen Henrietta Maria, had pointed this out to the lovers.

It was at this time that the King began to show a little interest in that foolish and perfectly unworthy creature, Louise de la Vallière.

How could he look at the silly creature, Louise de Kéroualle wondered; then she began to understand. It was Madame who had decided that he should pay attention to La Vallière, Madame who had selected the girl. Louise de la Vallière was just the sort whom a woman who was in love would choose, if choose she must. Madame could feel confident that the King would never fall in love with the silly creature.

If only she had chosen me! thought Louise. How different it would have been then!

She thought of her family in their Breton home. They would hear the rumours from the Court. Such rumours always travelled fast. They would shake their heads and perhaps have to sell more of their possessions. Would they say: 'Is it worth the expense of keeping Louise at Court?'

*   *   *

One day Madame called Louise to her and said: 'Louise, would you like to accompany me to England?'

'To England, Madame?' answered Louise. 'Indeed I would!'

'It will be but a short visit.' Henriette had turned away. There was, had she known it, no need for her to curb her tongue; she could have said all that was in her mind, because Louise knew it already.

Louise knew that she longed to get away from her husband, that she longed to see her brother who wrote to her so often and so lovingly. Louise was fully aware of the great affection between her mistress and the King of England. She had heard Monsieur, in one of his wild quarrels with Madame, declare that the love between his wife and her brother was more than that which it was meet and proper for two of such a relationship to share. She knew that, white-faced and horrified, Henriette had cried out to him that he was a liar, and that at that moment her self-control had broken.

Louise knew these things. She had a good pair of ears, and saw no reason why they should not be pressed into service. Those shrewd little eyes too were sharp. Louise trained them to miss nothing.

So if Henriette had decided to break free from that iron control which she kept on her feelings, and blurt out the truth to little Louise de Kéroualle, it would not have mattered. She would have told Louise very little that she did not already know.

'We shall stay no longer than two weeks,' said Henriette. 'My brothers will meet me at Dover. I doubt I shall have time to visit the Capital.'

'Monsieur will not part with you for longer than that, Madame,' said Louise.

Henriette looked at her quickly, but there was no trace of malice in the babyish face. She is a child, thought Henriette, who was unaware that she was twenty years old – not so very much younger than herself. Louise, looking so un-concernedly youthful, conveyed such an appearance of innocence. I must try to make a match for her before she loses that innocence which is so charming, thought the kindly Madame. May it be a happier one than my own, and may she preserve that faith in life for as long as it shall exist.

'My brother is most eager for the visit,' said Henriette, and her face softened. 'It is years since I have seen him.'

'I have heard, Madame, that a great affection exists between you and the King of England.'

''Tis true, Louise. My childhood was lived in such un-certain times. I saw so little of him. I was with my mother, a beggar almost at the Court of France, and my brother, the King of England, but a wandering exile. We saw little of each other, but how we treasured those meetings! And we have kept our love for one another alive in our letters. Hardly a week passes without our hearing one from the

121

other. I think one of the most unhappy periods of my life was when France and England were not good friends.'

'All France, and I doubt not all England, knows of your love for your brother, Madame. And all is well between England and France at this present time.'

Henriette nodded. 'And I hope to make that bond of friendship stronger, Louise.'

Louise knew. She had been present on those occasions when King Louis had visited Henriette. Sometimes they forgot she was present. If they saw her they would think: Oh, it is but the little Louise de Kéroualle – a sweet child but a baby, a little simpleton. She will not understand what we talk of.

So it was that often they disclosed certain secret matters in her presence; often they betrayed themselves.

They loved, those two. Louis would have married Henriette had he not married dull Marie Thérèse before Charles Stuart regained his kingdom. Louise had heard it said that, before that time, Madame had been a shy girl who had not shown to advantage against the plump pink and white beauties so admired by the King of France. But when her brother regained his throne, Henriette's gaucheries had dropped from her and she emerged like a butterfly from a chrysalis, it was said – brilliant, exquisite, the most graceful, charming, amusing, and clever woman at the Court. Then Louis had realized too late what he had missed; now he contented himself with the shyness of La Vallière and the flamboyant beauty of Montespan, in an effort to make up for all he had lost in Madame.

This interested Louise and she rejoiced therefore when she was chosen to accompany her mistress into England.

*   *   *

So she travelled with Madame to Dover, and all the pomp of a royal visit accompanied them.

She realized that Henriette was uneasy; and she guessed that it was due to the treaty which she was to induce her brother to sign.

Louis had prevailed upon Henriette to do this, and Louise

surmised that the treaty, which would be signed at Dover, was one to which the King of France was very eager to have the King of England's signature. Henriette was uncertain. Louise knew by her abstracted air that she was torn between her love for her brother and the King of France; and Louise knew that the King of France had won. For all her professed love for Charles of England, Henriette was working for the King of France whom she regarded in the light of a lover.

There was one thing to learn from this: emotions should never become involved when it was a question of one's position in society. For all her cleverness, for all her wit, Henriette of Orléans was nothing but a weak woman, torn by her love for two men.

And so they came to Dover and were greeted, not only by the tall dark King of England, but by his brother, the Duke of York, and his natural son, the Duke of Monmouth.

There were banquets and dancing. The treaty was signed and dispatched to France. The days sped by. Henriette seemed to be indulging in frantic gaiety.

She loved her brother undoubtedly; yet, wondered Louise, how far had she sacrificed him to Louis?

She longed to know. The thought of such plots and counter-plots was highly fascinating.

There came the time when they were due to leave the shores of England. Louise would never forget that occasion. It was a moment full of significance in her life, for it was then that new avenues of adventure were opened to her.

The King of England was looking at her with the approval which she had sought in vain to arouse in the King of France. He was referring to her as a brighter jewel than any in the casket which his sister was offering him. Those dark eyes, passionate and slumbrous, were fixed upon her. Louise realized then that the King desired her.

This in itself was no unusual thing. The King of England desired many women, and it was rarely that his desires went unfulfilled. Yet Louise, the daughter of a poor Breton gentleman, had already deeply considered what the admiration of a King could mean.

She was blushing now, because the King was asking that

she might stay behind in England, and her mistress was telling him that she had her duty to the child's parents.

Child! They seemed unaware that she was twenty years old.

Louise, considering her age, was filled with sudden panic. What if she failed to fulfil her parents' hopes? Would she have to return to the convent; perhaps make a marriage which would not lift her from the poverty from which she had determined to escape?

The admiration of kings could do a great deal for a woman. Her thoughts went to Louise de la Vallière – but all were aware that La Vallière was a simpleton who knew not how to exploit her lover. If ever the time came for Louise de Kéroualle to exploit such a lover, she would know full well how to do this to the best advantage to herself.

There was little time left, but she determined to do all in her power to see that the King of England did not forget her. She kept near her mistress because she knew that where Henriette was, there would Charles be.

And then there was that last encounter when she had stood before him.

Louis might like matrons, but Charles was clearly attracted by more youthful charms.

There was no doubt that he was attracted by her. He took her hands, and he spoke to her in her native French. He kissed her with a mingled passion and tenderness, and he told her he would not forget her and that he hoped one day she would come again to England, and that he would teach her the customs of the English.

She railed against the ill-fortune which had brought her face to face with Charles such a short time before she was due to leave.

She longed to tell him that her parents would have no objection to her staying at the Court of England; that they had hoped she would become the mistress of the King of France, so they would not wish to refuse her to the King of England.

But how could she say these things? She could only stand on the ship, waving farewell and standing close to her mistress, so that the last Charles saw of the departing company was his dear sister and her maid of honour who had so charmed him.

* * *

Louis welcomed them back with great rejoicing. He was delighted with his dear Duchesse. At all the balls and masques he was at her side.

On one of these occasions, Henriette turned to the girl beside her and said to Louis: 'Louise greatly impressed my brother.'

'Was that so?' said Louis.

'Indeed yes. He begged me to leave her with him in England.'

Louis looked with amusement at Louise, who had cast down her eyes.

'And did you wish to stay, Mademoiselle de Kéroualle?' he asked.

'If Madame had stayed, I should have wished to, Sire,' said Louise. 'My wish is to serve Madame.'

'That is as it should be,' said Louis. 'Serve her well. She deserves good service.'

His gaze was kind and doting. His mother was dead now; so was Madame's mother, and he and Madame could not be reproved because they were so much together. None would dare reprove Louis now.

Louis laughed suddenly. 'The King of England is governed by women, they say. I could tell you tales of the King of England, Mademoiselle de Kéroualle, but I would not do so before Madame who loves him dearly, nor would I wish to bring the blushes to your cheeks.'

'Your Majesty is gracious,' murmured Louise.

* * *

Louise was in her own apartments. She was stunned by the news. There had been a most unexpected turn of events, which she knew must affect the course of her life. Madame was dead.

It had happened so suddenly, though Madame had been

frail for a long time. She had been dining with her women and, during the meal, they had thought how ill she looked; when it was over she had risen from the table and lain on some cushions; she felt exhausted, she had said. Then she had asked for a drink and, when Madame de Gourdon had brought her a glass of iced chicory water, she was in sudden and acute pain.

She had cried out that she was poisoned, and her eyes had turned accusingly to Monsieur who had come into the apartment. Everyone present had thought: Monsieur has poisoned Madame.

Louise, in extreme panic, had hurried out of the apartment to bring help. It was imperative that Madame be treated at once, for she looked close to death, and if she died what would become of Louise?

The doctors had come. The King had come. Louise witnessed the strange sight of the magnificent Louis kneeling by Madame, his handsome face distorted with grief; she had heard the sobs in his throat, and his muttered endearments.

But Louis could not save her; nor could the doctors. A few short weeks after her return from her brother's Court Henriette d'Orléans was dead.

And now, thought Louise, what will become of me?

She waited for the summons to return to her father's estate. She had failed. There was no place for her at Court; she realized that now.

Each day she expected the summons to come.

*   *   *

There was a summons; but not from her home.

Madame de Gourdon came to her one day. Poor Madame de Gourdon! She was a most unhappy woman. She was not allowed to forget that she it was who had brought the glass of iced chicory water to Madame. Rumour ran wild throughout the Court. Madame was poisoned, it was whispered. Monsieur had done this; and his partner in crime was the Chevalier de Lorraine, his latest friend. But who had administered the draught? One of Madame's women.

Why, it was Madame de Gourdon. In vain did Madame de Gourdon sob out her devotion to Madame. People looked at her with suspicion.

Now she spoke listlessly: 'Mademoiselle de Kéroualle, the King wishes you to attend him immediately.'

'His Majesty!' cried Louise, springing to her feet and smoothing down the folds of her dress.

'I will take you to him,' said Madame de Gourdon. 'He is ready to receive you now.'

The King had come to St Cloud to see her! It was incredible. She could think of only one thing it could mean. He *had* noticed her after all.

If he had come to see her all would soon know it. They would talk of her as they talked of La Vallière and Montespan. And why not? She was as good-looking as La Vallière surely. She touched her chestnut hair. The soft curls reassured her, gave her courage.

'I will go and prepare myself,' she said.

'You cannot do that. His Majesty is waiting.'

He was striding up and down the small apartment when Madame de Gourdon conducted her thither.

Madame de Gourdon curtsied and left Louise alone with the King.

Louise went hurriedly forward and knelt as though in confusion, but a confusion which was charming. She had practised this often enough.

'Rise, Mademoiselle de Kéroualle,' said the King. 'I have something to say to you.'

'Yes, Sire?' she said, and she could not keep the breathless note from her voice.

He did not look at her. He was staring at the tapestry which covered the walls of this small chamber, as though to find inspiration there. Louise took a quick glance at his face and saw that he was trying to compose it. What could this emotion of the King mean?

She was prepared to register the utmost surprise when he should tell her he had noticed her. She would be confused, overcome with astonishment and modesty. She would stammer out her gratitude and her fear. She believed that was what Louis would expect. She had the shining example of La Vallière to follow.

The King began to speak slowly: 'Mademoiselle de Kéroualle, I have just suffered one of the greatest griefs of my life.'

Louise did not speak; she merely bowed her head; the handsome eyes were turned upon her, and there were tears in them.

'And I know,' went on Louis, 'that you too have suffered. Any who had lived near her must feel her loss deeply.'

'Sire . . .' murmured Louise.

The King raised his hand. 'You have no need to tell me; I know. Madame's death is a great loss to our Court, and none in that Court suffers as I do. Madame was my own dear sister and my friend.' He paused. 'There is one other who suffers . . . almost as deeply as I. That is Madame's brother – the King of England.'

'Indeed yes, Your Majesty.'

'The King of England is prostrate with grief. I have heard from him. He writes harshly. He has heard evil rumours, and he is insisting that if it be true that Madame was hurried to her death those who are her murderers should be discovered and dealt with. But, as I am sure you will have heard, Mademoiselle de Kéroualle, at the autopsy which I insisted should be immediately performed no poison was found in Madame's body. She had been in bad health for some time, and the very chicory water of which she drank was drunk by others, and these suffered not at all. We know that it was Madame's own ill health which resulted in her death, and no one here was in the least to blame. But the King of England bitterly mourns his sister whom he loved so well, and I fear we shall find it difficult to convince him. Now, Mademoiselle de Kéroualle, you are a very charming young lady.'

Louise drew a deep breath. Her heart was beating so fast that she could scarcely follow what the King was saying.

'And,' went on Louis, 'I wish my brother of England to understand that my grief is as great as his own. I wish someone to convey my sympathy to him.'

'Sire,' said Louise, 'you . . . you would entrust me with this mission?'

Louis' large eyes were benign. He laid a white, heavily ringed hand on her shoulder. 'Even so, my dear,' he said. 'Madame herself has told me of a little incident which occurred while you were in England. King Charles was attracted by you; and, my dear Mademoiselle, it does not surprise me. It does not surprise me at all. You are most . . . most personable. I am going to send you to my brother in England to convey my sympathy and to assure him that Madame his sister has always been treated with the utmost tenderness in this land.'

'Oh . . . Sire!' Louise's eyes were shining.

She fell to her knees.

'Rise, my dear Mademoiselle,' said Louis. 'I see you are sensible of the honour I would do you. I want you to prepare for your journey to England. I will acquaint King Charles of your coming. Mademoiselle de Kéroualle, you are the daughter of one of our noblest houses.'

Louise drew herself up to her full height. There was pride in her eyes. So the King himself recognized the standing of her family. It was only money that it lacked.

'And,' continued the King, 'it is from our noblest families that we expect and receive the utmost loyalty. I believe, Mademoiselle, that you loved your mistress dearly. But as in all good subjects of our beloved country there is one love which is above all others. That is love of France.'

'Yes, Sire.'

'I knew it. That is why I am going to entrust you with a great mission. To the King of England you will take comfort; but you will always serve France.'

'Your Majesty means that during my stay in England I shall work for my country?'

'My ambassador across the water will be your very good friend. He will help you when you need help. Before you leave for England you will be further instructed. I have lost, in Madame, not only a very dear friend but one who, in view of her relationship to the King of England, was able to bring about great understanding between us two. Mademoiselle,

I believe that such a charming and intelligent young lady as you so evidently are – and as one who has already attracted the attention of His Majesty of England – can, in some measure, give me . . . and your country . . . something of that which we have lost in Madame.'

The King paused. Louise sought for words and could find none.

'I have taken you by surprise,' said the King. 'Go now and think about this.'

Louise again fell to her knees and said in clear tones: 'Your Majesty, I rejoice in this opportunity to serve my King and my country.'

When she stood up, Louis placed his hands on her shoulders; then inclining his head with the utmost graciousness he kissed her lightly on both cheeks.

'I have the utmost confidence in you, my dear,' he said. 'France will be proud of you.'

Louise left the apartment in a state of exaltation.

How often had she dreamed of being sent for by the King! At last it had happened.

The result was surprising, but no less promising for all that.

*   *   *

George Villiers, Duke of Buckingham, presented himself at the French Court.

He had come to sponsor a treaty between his master and the King of France.

As several members of the Cabal were ignorant of the real Treaty of Dover, it had been necessary for Charles to devise another with which he might dupe them. This he had done, and Buckingham was selected to take it to St Germain and at the same time to represent the King at the funeral of Madame. With Buckingham went Buckhurst and Sedley, and the Duke's chaplain, Thomas Sprat.

Buckingham had been chosen – as a prominent Protestant – because the King and those who were in the secret feared that the news of the King's promising to adopt the Catholic Faith might have leaked out. Since Buckingham was commissioned to sign the treaty in France, this would silence such rumours, as it would be generally believed that anything to which Buckingham would give his signature could not possibly concern the King's becoming a Catholic.

There was another matter with which he was entrusted. He was to escort to England the late Henriette's maid of honour who had attracted Charles when she had come to England in his sister's train.

This was a task after the Duke's own heart. It had been clear to him that his cousin Barbara was losing her hold over the King. Barbara's beauty, which had once been incomparable, was fading. None could live the life Barbara lived and keep fresh. Any but Charles would have turned her away long ago, tiresome virago that she was. It was true that in the heyday of her youth no one could compare with Barbara for beauty and for sensuality; the King had found her – tantrums and all – irresistible. But Barbara was ageing, and even with an easy-going man such as Charles she could not continue to hold the title of mistress-in-chief. Sooner or later Barbara must be replaced.

The King had his women – many of them. The chief mistress at the moment was Moll Davies, and Nell Gwyn was a close runner-up. But these were play-actresses, and Moll, aping the nobility, showed her origins as clearly as Nell who made no secret of her beginnings.

The mistress-in-chief should be a lady of high degree. She should feel at home at Court; and although Barbara's manners were atrocious, she was a noble Villiers and there could at times be no doubt of this.

But with Barbara fading from favour, someone else would soon be called upon to take her place. This Frenchwoman was surely the one to be selected for that task.

Louise de Kéroualle was a lady of noble birth. She had been educated and coached for a life at Court. She was not exactly beautiful. When Buckingham remembered what Barbara had been at her age he could call the new woman positively plain. But Louise had that which Barbara lacked – poise, gracious manners, and a quiet charm. At this time he believed that Louise was destined to become the most important of the King's mistresses.

It was great good fortune that he had been sent to bring her to England, for it gave him a great advantage over all those who would later seek to reach the King's ear through his mistress. Buckingham would ingratiate himself with the woman and so establish himself as her friend.

The King of France was delighted to receive Buckingham. He had Madame's own apartments made ready for him at St Germain. It seemed meet and fitting that Buckingham should be in France at that time for, ten years before when Henriette had visited her brother in England at the time of the Restoration, the Duke had professed to be deeply in love with her. He had, in fact, made something of an exhibition of these feelings which had been an embarrassment not only to Henriette herself but to others; Monsieur had declared himself jealous of the Duke, with the result that it had been necessary to recall Buckingham to London. Who, therefore, was better suited to attend the funeral of Madame as her brother's representative, than the Duke of Buckingham who had once loved her so madly?

Louis – anxious to show in what great esteem he had held Madame, and eager that the King of England should banish from his mind all thought that his sister had met her death by poison – greeted Buckingham warmly. He gave him one of the royal coaches and with it the service of eight royal footmen. All the expenses Buckingham incurred while in France were to be met from the King's exchequer.

Louis – being French – believed firmly in the power of a man's mistresses, and realizing Buckingham's infatuation for Anna, Lady Shrewsbury, offered to pay that lady a pension of four hundred pounds a year, because his ambassador in England had already warned him that the lady had said that she, for such recognition, would make sure that Buckingham complied with Louis' desires in all things. Louis also sent a bribe for Lady Castlemaine as, although the lady was no longer enjoying the favour she once had, it was clear that she would continue to wield certain influence as long as she lived.

Louis was fully aware of the power of these women. They were both deeply sensual; they had both enjoyed numerous lovers; therefore Louis believed that they were skilled in the arts of love-making. Each was a strong-minded woman. Barbara Castlemaine had proved this again and again. As for Anna Shrewsbury, she too had shown the world that she could be formidable – a good ally, a bad enemy.

Louis had heard of the duel which had been fought between Lord Shrewsbury and the Duke of Buckingham and which had resulted in Shrewsbury's death; he had heard rumours of how Anna Shrewsbury had been a witness of the duel; how, some said, she had acted as page to her lover so that she might be present; and how later, unable to forgo the immediate satisfaction of their lust, Buckingham and Anna had forthwith slept together, Buckingham still in the shirt spattered with her husband's blood.

There was another rumour concerning this woman. Harry Killigrew had been one of her numerous lovers, and there had been a notorious scene in the Duke of York's playhouse when Buckingham and Killigrew had fought together; as a result of that, Killigrew had been sent into exile, from which he had returned sullen and determined to be revenged on the Duke and his mistress. He had declared in many public places that Anna Shrewsbury would still be his mistress if he wished it, and that indeed she was any man's who cared to take her. She was like a bitch in season – only Anna Shrewsbury's season was every hour of the day or night.

Anna set out in her coach one dark night to see performed a certain deed which she had arranged. It happened near Turnham Green when Harry Killigrew was on his way to his house there. Harry Killigrew was set upon, his servant killed, and, only by a miracle it seemed, Killigrew escaped the same fate.

Yes, the King of France was certain that Anna Shrewsbury was worth a pension of four hundred pounds a year.

He was sure too that Buckingham was worth cultivating, even though the King had seen fit to keep him ignorant of the real Treaty of Dover.

So he arranged great treats for the Duke. Special banquets were prepared for him. He was presented not only with the coach, footmen, and living expenses, but with other costly gifts.

He was able to fit himself into the formal ceremony of Louis' magnificent Court. Handsome and witty, he was in his element. Mock sea-fights on the Seine were arranged for his benefit and he was introduced to the splendours of Versailles.

The Comte de Lauzun – a man of diminutive stature and a great friend of the King of France – asked him to a supper party. A splendid banquet was prepared, and next his host, in the place of honour, sat the Duke. Beside him was Louise de Kéroualle, formal and distant; but, the Duke assured himself, he would soon win her regard. She was a cold creature, he decided; not what he would have expected from the French, nor the sort he would have thought would find favour in his master's eyes. However, it was his task to ingratiate himself with her, and this he would do – all in good time. At the moment he was too busy being the guest of honour.

During that banquet three masked figures entered the banqueting hall. One was a man, tall and richly clad; the others were ladies. They came graciously to the table and bowed to Lauzun and Buckingham. The musicians, who had been playing in the gallery, changed their tune to a stately ballet, and the three began to dance with such grace and charm that all at the table held their breath – or pretended to – since all had guessed the identity of the masked cavalier.

There were murmurs of 'Perfection!' 'But who could dance with such exquisite grace?' 'I know of only one I have seen to equal that dancer – His Majesty himself.' 'We must have the fellow perform before Louis. Nothing will content him but to see such perfection.'

Now the ladies were miming charmingly. They had pointed to a sword which the masked man wore. All saw that its hilt was studded with brilliant diamonds. One of the masked ladies danced to Buckingham's side and implied, by her gestures, that the cavalier should bestow the sword upon their country's most honoured guest. The cavalier retreated, clung to his sword, his gestures indicating that the sword was his dearest possession. The ladies continued to persuade; the cavalier continued to hold back.

The music stopped.

'Unmask! Unmask!' cried Lauzun.

With seeming reluctance the ladies did so first, and there was loud applause when one of these proved to be Madame de Montespan herself, the King's flamboyant and beautiful mistress.

Now Madame de Montespan turned to the cavalier. She removed his mask, and there were exposed the handsome features so well known throughout the country.

All rose; men bowed and women curtsied; and the handsome young Louis stood there smiling happily and benignly on them all.

'Our secret is out,' said Louis. 'We are unmasked.'

'I could not believe that any but Your Majesty could dance with such grace,' said Lauzun.

Now Madame de Montespan had taken the sword from the King and carried it to the guest of honour.

Buckingham stared down at the flashing diamonds, calculating its cost; then rising, fell on his knees before the King of France and thanked him, almost in tears, for his magnificent gift and all the honour which had been done to his master through him.

The King and his mistress took their places at the table; and the King talked to Buckingham of his love for the King of England, of his grief in Madame's death; nor did he forget to pay some attention to little Louise. Louise understood. He would have my lord Buckingham know that Mademoiselle de Kéroualle was to be treated with the same respect in England as in France.

How different had been her position when Madame was alive! Then she had been Madame's maid of honour – an insignificant post. Now she was the spy of the King of France, and that was indeed important.

'We have prepared many entertainments for you, my lord Duke,' said the King. 'There shall be masques and the ballet – we in France are devoted to the ballet.'

'Your Majesty is the ballet's shining light,' said Louise.

The King smiled, well pleased. 'And we must show you our operas and comedies. They shall be acted in illuminated grottoes.'

'I am overwhelmed by all the honour Your Majesty does unto me,' said the Duke.

The King momentarily laid his hand over that of Louise. 'And when you take this little subject of mine into England, you will give her the benefit of your care?'

'With all my heart,' said Buckingham.

*　　　*　　　*

Later he made plans with Louise.

'I would have you know, Mademoiselle de Kéroualle,' he said, 'that from henceforth I serve you with all my heart.'

Louise accepted this outward profession of service with graceful thanks but she attached little importance to it. Since she was to act as French spy in England it had been necessary to acquaint her with certain political aspects of the state of affairs between the two countries. She knew that, although the Duke held a high position in his country's government and was a member of the famous Cabal, he was ignorant of his master's true plans.

He was quite unaware that the King of France was planning war with Holland in the spring of next year, and in this war the King of England would be his ally; and that as soon as it was satisfactorily concluded Charles was to declare his conversion to Catholicism.

Therefore she had little faith in Buckingham. Herself calm and rarely losing control of her emotions, she thought the Duke a tempestuous man who, clever though he might be, could be driven into great folly by his uncontrolled passions.

He was, he told her, although he had been so flatteringly received in France, looking forward to returning to his own country.

He talked of Anna Shrewsbury in glowing terms; he was indeed deeply infatuated with the woman. Louise listened and said little. He began to think her a little simpleton, one who would never hold his King's affection. He compared her with Anna, with Barbara, with Moll Davies and Nell Gwyn. Those four were possessed of beauty – outstanding beauty which would have marked them for notice anywhere. It seemed to Buckingham that Louise de Kéroualle lacked even that first essential. Why, there were indeed times when the woman positively squinted. And she was always so formal; he thought of Anna and Barbara in their rages, of Nell's wit and high spirits. It was true Moll Davies never raged, was never witty and rarely showed any spirits, but she was an extremely lovely woman. Nay, the more he pondered the matter, the more certain he became that Louise de Kéroualle would not hold the King's attention for long.

He was wondering whether he was not wasting his time in ingratiating himself with her. He was longing to be back with Anna.

He said to her: 'There are certain matters to which I have to attend in Paris. My master, the King of England, is growing impatient to receive you. I think much time would be saved if you travelled to Dieppe in company which I will arrange for you and set out at once. I will conduct with all speed my business in Paris, arrange for a yacht to carry you to England, and I'll swear I'll be at Dieppe before you arrive there. Then I can have the great honour of conducting you to England.'

'I consider that an excellent arrangement,' said Louise, who was longing to set out on her journey and fearful, with every passing day, that the King of England might change his mind and, realizing that a young woman who came from Louis' Court might have been schooled in the arts of espionage, decide that he would be wise to content himself with the ladies of his own Court.

'Then let it be so,' cried Buckingham. 'I will inform His Majesty of my plans.'

So it was arranged. Louise travelled to Dieppe; Buckingham lingered in Paris. He wanted to buy clothes, not only for himself, but for Anna.

Paris was always a step ahead of London with the fashions,

and Anna would be delighted with what he would bring her.

*   *   *

When Louise arrived in Dieppe – and the journey there from St Germain had taken two whole weeks – it was to find that Buckingham had not yet arrived.

No one there had heard anything of the yacht which Buckingham had promised to have ready for her. Louise was weary after the journey from St Germain and at first was not sorry to rest awhile – but not for long. She was fully aware of the importance of the task which lay before her. She had discovered all she could concerning the King of England, and she knew that, once she arrived in England, she would be well received. What terrified her was that, before she had an opportunity of being with the King, he might suggest that she did not cross the Channel.

She knew that Lady Castlemaine would do all in her power to prevent her arrival, and Lady Castlemaine still wielded some power.

So when the days began to pass she grew really alarmed.

Two days – three – a whole week, and there was still no sign of the Duke.

With the coming of the next week she grew frantic. She sent a messenger to Ralph Montague, the ambassador in Paris, and begged to know what she should do.

She waited most anxiously for news. Each time a messenger arrived at her lodgings she would start up in a sweat of trepidation. During those two anxious weeks in Dieppe the continual threat of failure was before her; she imagined herself being sent back to her parents' home in Finisterre, an ignoble failure, knowing that if she did not go to England there would now be no place for her at the French Court.

She watched the sea, which was rough and choppy, for a sight of the yacht which would come to take her away. Mayhap the weather was too rough for Buckingham to reach her. She clutched at any explanation.

And while she waited there, one of her maids came to tell her that a traveller had arrived from Calais and, hearing

138

that she was awaiting the arrival of the Duke of Buckingham, had news for her if she would care to hear it.

The man was brought in.

'Mademoiselle de Kéroualle,' he began, 'I have heard that you are awaiting the arrival of the English Duke. He left Calais more than a week ago.'

'Left Calais! For where?'

'For England.'

'But that is impossible.'

''Tis true, Mademoiselle.'

'But did he say nothing of calling at Dieppe?'

'He said he was sailing for England. He filled the yacht with presents, which had been given him, and goods which he had bought. He said he hoped to arrive in England very soon as the tide was favourable.'

Louise dismissed the man. She could bear no more. She shut herself into her room, lay on her bed, and pulled the curtains about it.

She knew that she had been deserted. She felt certain now that the King of England had changed his mind, that he had not been serious when he had asked for her to be sent to his Court, that he recognized her coming as the coming of a spy, and had commanded Buckingham to return to England without her.

It was all over – her wonderful dream which was to have saved her from an ignoble future. She should have known; it had been too wonderful, too easy. It was like something that happens only in a dream: To have gone to the Court in the hope that she would be chosen as the mistress of Louis Quatorze, and to have qualified for the same post at the Court of the King of England!

How long could she stay here in this desolate little seaport? Only until her parents sent for her or came to take her home.

*   *   *

There was someone to see her.

She allowed her maid to comb back her hair from her hot face. She did not ask who the visitor was. She did not want to know. She guessed it was her father or someone from him, come to take her to her home, for they would know that the Duke of Buckingham had left without her.

Waiting for her was Ralph Montague, Charles' ambassador, whom she had often seen in Paris.

He came towards her, took her hand, and kissed it with great ceremony.

'I came with all speed on receiving your message,' he said.

'It was good of you, my lord.'

'Nay,' he said, ''twas my duty. My master would never have forgiven me had I not come in person to offer my assistance.'

'My lord Buckingham did not arrive,' she said. 'I have been waiting here for two weeks. I hear now that he left Calais some time ago.'

'Buckingham!' Ralph Montague's lips curled with disgust. 'I offer humble apologies for my countryman, Mademoiselle. I trust you will not judge us all by this one. The Duke is feckless and unreliable. My master will be incensed when he returns without you.'

Louise did not say that his master would doubtless know of his return by now and had done nothing about arranging for her journey.

'I wondered whether he was acting on the King's instructions.'

'The King is eagerly awaiting your arrival, Mademoiselle.'

'I was led to believe that was so,' said Louise. 'But I doubt it now.'

'And still is. Mademoiselle, I have already arranged for a yacht to call here in a few hours' time. It shall be my pleasure to make these arrangements. My friend, Henry Bennet, Earl of Arlington, will be waiting to receive you when you arrive in England. He and his family will look after you until you are presented to His Majesty. I trust you will give me this great pleasure in arranging your safe conduct.'

The relief was so great that Louise, calm as she habitually was, was almost ready to break into hysterical tears.

She managed to say: 'You are very good.'

Montague said: 'I will remain here in Dieppe and see you aboard if I have your permission to do so.'

'I shall not forget this kindness,' she replied. And she thought: Nor the churlish behaviour of Buckingham. 'My lord, have they offered you refreshment?'

'I came straight to you,' said Montague. 'I thought my first need was to impress upon you that all Englishmen are not so ungallant.'

'Then will you take some refreshment with me, my lord?'

'It would give me the greatest pleasure,' said Montague.

*   *   *

Montague, as he took refreshment with Louise, was congratulating himself on the folly of Buckingham. What could have possessed the Duke to sail away from France, leaving the King's potential mistress in the lurch?

Surely Buckingham realized that, if ever Louise came to power, she would never forgive the insult.

He thought he understood, on consideration. His friend Arlington, with Clifford, was inclined towards Catholicism. Buckingham was staunchly Protestant. Buckingham would assess the influence the Catholic Frenchwoman would have on Charles, and mayhap had decided to do all in his power to prevent her arrival in England; so he had left her at Dieppe, hoping that careless Charles would forget her, as indeed it seemed he had. But Arlington, whose protégé Montague was, would hope to benefit from a Catholic mistress's influence over the King. Therefore it was Montague's duty to see that Charles had no chance to forget his interest in Catholic Louise.

He watched her as he took refreshment.

He admired her, this Frenchwoman, for her poise and calm. She looked almost a child with her plump, babyish face, and yet, in spite of the days of anxiety through which she had passed, she was completely controlled.

She was no beauty. At times it seemed as though she squinted slightly. Yet her figure was shapely, her hair and complexion lovely. Her charm was in her graceful manners;

that complete air of the *grande dame* which the King would appreciate and would have missed in other mistresses.

Montague felt that if Louise de Kéroualle conducted herself with care she might find great favour with the King.

So while they waited for his yacht to arrive at Dieppe, he frequently talked to her. He told her of the King's character, that most easy-going nature, that love of peace.

'He has had little of that from those he loves,' said Montague. 'Even his Queen, a gentle, docile lady, was far from calm when His Majesty wished her to receive Lady Castlemaine into her bedchamber. It is my belief – and that of others – that, had the Queen been tolerant of the King's desire on this occasion, she would have won great love from him and kept it.'

Louise nodded. This was friendly advice, and she took it to heart. It meant, Never be out of temper with the King. Give him peace, and he will be grateful.

'His Majesty greatly loved Mrs Stuart before her marriage to the Duke of Richmond. He would have married her if he had been free to do so. But he was not free, and she held out until he was well-nigh maddened in his desire for her and would have offered anything, I verily believe, for her surrender.'

'So many,' said Louise, 'must be ready to give the King all he asks, that it is small wonder that, when he finds one who holds back, he is astonished.'

'And enamoured . . . deeply enamoured. If the Queen had died, many people believe, he would have married Mrs Frances Stuart. And indeed that was the bait which was held out to him when . . .' He paused.

'When?' prompted Louise gently.

'It was my lord Buckingham with his wild schemes. He wished the King to divorce his wife and marry again.'

'My lord Buckingham, it seems, would wish to run the affairs of his King's country,' said Louise smoothly.

'A foolish man!' said Montague. 'But he had his reasons. He did not like the Catholic marriage; he is a Protestant. Moreover, he was eager for the King to have an heir. One of his greatest enemies is the Duke of York.'

Louise thought: From this moment he has a greater.

'And,' went on Montague, 'if the King does not get an heir, James, Duke of York, will one day be King of England. My lord Buckingham sought to replace the Queen with a fruitful woman who would provide the King with an heir and so ruin the Duke's chance of ascending the throne.'

'It does not then seem that he is so foolish.'

'He has moments of lucidity, superseded by moments of great folly. That is my lord Duke.'

Louise was silent, looking into the future.

It was not long after that when the yacht which had been chartered by Ralph Montague arrived at Dieppe. As the tide was favourable, Louise left France for England, and when she arrived there, was greeted so warmly by Arlington and his friends that she no longer had need to complain of neglect.

Now she had two projects in view. The first and most important was to enslave the King; the second was revenge on the careless Duke who had given her so many hours of anxiety.

But, born spy that she was, cold by nature, calculating and in complete control, her eyes were now fixed on that distant goal which, she had suddenly made up her mind, should be marriage with the King of England. For if he had been prepared to marry Frances Stuart, why should he not marry Louise de Kéroualle?

*   *   *

In the Palace of Whitehall Louise came face to face with the King.

When she would have knelt before him he raised her in his arms and there were tears in his eyes.

'Welcome,' he said, 'doubly welcome, my dear Mademoiselle de Kéroualle. It does my heart good to see you at Whitehall. But I cannot forget the last time we met, and I am deeply affected because I remember one who was with us then.'

Louise turned away as though to hide her own tears.

There was none; of course there was none; how could she regret the death of Henriette when it had given her a chance to reach such heights of glory as even her parents had not hoped for her?

The King was smiling at her now, his eyes alight with admiration. She was exquisitely gowned and wore fewer jewels than Castlemaine would have affected on such an occasion. Louise had the air of a queen, and Charles was reminded of Frances Stuart who had been brought up in France.

He was excited by the French girl, and he determined to make her his mistress with as little delay as possible.

He said: 'The Queen will receive you into her bedchamber.'

Louise murmured her thanks graciously; but she knew, of course, that Barbara Castlemaine had been a lady of his wife's bedchamber. Louise had no intention of going the way Barbara had gone.

She met the Queen; she met the courtiers; she met the Duke of Buckingham, and she betrayed not even by a gesture that she was in the least angered by his treatment of her; none watching her would believe that her anger rose so high that she feared that, if in that moment she attempted to speak, the effort might choke her.

She could content herself with waiting. The first task was the capture of the King; then she could proceed to annihilate the Duke.

The King had her sit beside him at the banquet which was held in her honour; he talked of his dear brother Louis and the French Court. All about them were saying, This will be the King's newest mistress.

The King himself believed it. But Louise, smiling so charmingly, looking so young and innocent, had other plans. Before her there was the shining example of Frances Stuart, the girl who had so plagued the King with refusals to surrender that, had he been able, he would have married her. She had seen the Queen – and it occurred to Louise that the Queen did not look over-healthy.

The King deceived himself if he thought he could make

Louise de Kéroualle his mistress as easily as a play-actress from his theatre.

He said to her: 'So eagerly have I awaited your coming that I gave myself the pleasure of preparing your apartments for you.'

She smiled into that charming face, knowing full well that his eagerness for her arrival was feigned. He had doubtless been so sportive with his play-actresses – and perhaps Madame Castlemaine too was by no means the discarded mistress she had been led to believe – that he had omitted to ask my lord Buckingham, when he arrived in England, what he had done with the lady whom he was supposed to be escorting.

'Your Majesty is good to me,' she said with a smile.

He came closer; his eyes were on her plump bosom; his hands caressed her arm.

'I am prepared to be very kind,' he murmured. 'I have given you apartments near my own.'

'That is indeed good of Your Majesty.'

'They overlook the privy garden. I am proud of my privy garden. I trust you will like it. You can look down on the sixteen plots of grass and the statues. It is a mighty pretty view, I do believe. I long to show you these apartments. I have had them furnished with French tapestries, because I wished you to feel at home. No homesickness, you understand.'

'I can see Your Majesty is determined to be kind to me.'

'Would you wish me to dismiss these people, that you might be alone and . . . rest?'

'Your Majesty is so good to me that I crave a favour.'

'My dear Mademoiselle de Kéroualle, you have given me the great gift of your presence here. Anything you might ask of me would be but small in comparison with what you have given me. And were it not, I have no doubt that I should grant it.'

'I have had a long journey,' said Louise.

'And you are weary. It was thoughtless of me to have given such a banquet so soon. But I wished to make you sure of your welcome.'

'I am indeed grateful for the honour you have shown me, but my lord Arlington and Lady Arlington, who have been so good to me, have placed apartments in their house at my disposal.'

'I am glad my lord Arlington and his lady have been so hospitable,' said Charles a little wryly.

'I am very weary, and I fear that the etiquette of the Court, in my present state, would overtax my strength,' said Louise.

Charles' glance was ironic. He understood. Louise was jealous of her dignity. She was not to be sent for like any play-actress. She had to be wooed.

Inwardly he grimaced. But he said with the utmost charm: 'I understand full well. Go to the Arlingtons. His lady will make you very comfortable. And I trust that ere long you will be ready to exchange Lord Arlington's house for my palace of Whitehall.'

Louise thanked him charmingly.

She believed she had won the first round. The King was eager for her; but he was realizing that a grand lady such as Louise de Kéroualle must be courted before she was won.

*   *   *

Louise stayed with the Arlingtons. The King visited her frequently, but she did not become his mistress. Charles was often exasperated, but Louise attracted him with her perfect manners and babyish looks. There was in her attitude a certain promise which indicated that, once the formalities had been observed, he would find the waiting well worth while. Louise remembered other ladies from the past who, by careful tactics, had won high places for themselves. Elizabeth Woodville in her dealings with Edward IV. Anne Boleyn with Henry VIII. The latter was not a very happy example, but Louise would not be guilty of that Queen's follies; nor did Charles resemble in any way the Tudor King. The poverty of Louise's youth, the knowledge, which was always before her, that she must make her own way for herself had fired her with great ambition, so that no sooner did one goal appear in sight than she must immediately aim at another. King's mistress had been the first goal. She could achieve that at any moment. Now she was trying for another: King's wife. It might seem fantastic and wild. But there was the example of Frances Stuart. Moreover the Queen was ailing, and she could not produce an heir. These were the exact circumstances which had helped to put Anne Boleyn on the throne. Anne had had the good sense to withhold herself for a long time from an enamoured monarch, but after marriage she had lost that good sense. Louise would never lose hers.

So she held back. She reminded the King by a hundred gestures that she was a great lady; she hinted that she found him very attractive but, because she was not only a great lady but a virtuous one, the fact that he was married prevented her from yielding to his desires.

Charles hid his growing exasperation under great charm of manner. He was ready to play her game, for he knew she would eventually surrender. Why else should she have come to England? And while he waited, he amused himself with others. Occasionally he visited Barbara, Moll, and Nell; Chaffinch continued to bring certain ladies up to his apartments by way of the privy stairs. Thus he could enjoy the game of waiting which he must play with Louise.

Apartments were furnished for her at Whitehall; beautiful French tapestries adorned the walls; there was furniture decorated with the new marqueterie; there were exquisite carpets, cabinets from Japan, vases of china and silver, tables of marble, the newest kind of clocks with pendulums, silver candelabra and everything that was exquisite.

Louise moved into these apartments, but she made it clear to the King that such a great and virtuous lady as herself could only receive him at one time of the day. This was nine o'clock in the morning.

Colbert de Croissy, the French ambassador, watched uneasily. He even remonstrated with her. He greatly feared that she would try the King's patience too far.

Louise was determined.

She would serve, not only the cause of France, but her own ambition.

*   *   *

Those three women who had been the King's leading mistresses watched the newcomer with apprehension. They knew that they owed the King's occasional company to the continued reserve of the Frenchwoman. They knew that, once she decided to surrender, the King's interest in them would wane. And what would be the effect of that waning? Barbara knew that she was fast losing her hold on the King. Her beauty was no longer fresh and appealing; her rages did not diminish with her beauty; she had taken so many lovers that she had become notorious on that account. Her adventures with Charles Hart and a rope-dancer named Jacob Hall had created the greatest scandal, because, it was said, she had chosen these men as lovers in retaliation for the King's preoccupation with Moll Davies and Nell Gwyn. Barbara still clung to her waning influence with the King, knowing that he would still be prepared to give way in some respect, if not for love of her, for love of peace.

Moll Davies was rarely visited now. She had her fine house and her pension, but the King was growing tired of her gentle qualities. It was due to his habit of 'not discarding' that she remained his mistress.

As for Nell, her baby took up a great deal of her time, but her preoccupation with the little boy made her thoughts turn often to his father. The King must not tire of her; she must cease to be as frivolous-minded as she had previously been. There was the boy to think of.

'I'll get a fine title for you, my little man,' she would whisper to the child. 'You shall be a Duke, no less.' She would laugh into the big wondering eyes which watched her so intently. 'You . . . a Duke . . . that slut Nelly's brat – a royal Duke. Who would have believed it?'

But dukedoms were not easily come by.

The King was delighted with the child. Those were pleasant days when he came to visit Nell and took the boy in his arms.

'There is no doubt,' cried Nell, leaning over him like any proud wife and mother, 'that this boy is a Stuart. See that nose! Those eyes!'

'Then God have mercy on him!' said the King.

'Come, my little one,' said Nell. 'Smile for Papa.'

The child surveyed the King with solemn eyes.

'Not yet, eh, sir!' murmured Charles. 'First wait and see what manner of man this is who has fathered you.'

'The best in the world,' said Nell lightly.

The King turned and looked at her.

'Od's Fish!' he cried. 'I believe you mean that, Nelly.'

'Nay!' cried Nell, ashamed of her own emotion. 'I am sowing the first seeds which will flower into a dukedom for our boy.'

'And strawberry leaves for yourself! Oh, Nell, you go the way of all the others.'

Nell snatched the child from his father's arms and began dancing round the apartment with him.

'What do I want for you, my son? A coronet, a great title, all that belongs by right to a King's bastard. Already, my son, you have the King's nose, the King's eyes, and the King's name. Od's Fish! I trust His Majesty will not think you adequately endowed with these, for they will make little story in the world, I suspect.'

Then she laid him in his cradle and bent and kissed him.

The King came to her and put his arms about her shoulders.

He thought in that moment that, although Louise de Kéroualle was becoming an obsession with him, he would be loath to part with little Nell.

* * *

Rose came to see Nell in her new house.

It was a small one at the east end of Pall Mall, not far from the grand mansion in Suffolk Street where another of the King's mistresses – Moll Davies – had her residence.

Nell's house was a poor place compared with that of Moll. Moll liked to ride past Nell's in her carriage and lean forward to look at it as she passed, smiling complacently, flashing her £700 ring on her finger.

'Keep your house, keep your ring, Moll!' called Nell from her house. 'The King has given me something better still.'

Then Nell would snatch up her child from one of the servants and hold him aloft.

'You've never got the King's bastard yet, Moll!' screeched Nell.

Moll bade her coachman drive on. She thought Nell a fool. She had had every chance to escape from her environment, and yet she seemed to cling to it as though she were reluctant to let it go.

'What a low wench!' murmured Moll in her newly acquired refined voice. 'Why His Majesty should spend an hour in her company is past my comprehension.'

Moll smiled complacently. Her house was so grand; Nell's was such a poor place. Did it not show that the King appreciated the difference between them? Nell went into the house where Rose was waiting for her.

Rose took the baby from Nell and crooned over him.

'To think that he is the King's son,' said Rose. ''Tis past understanding.'

'Indeed it is not,' cried Nell. 'He made his appearance through all the usual channels.'

'Oh, Nell, why did you move from your good apartments in Lincoln's Inn Fields to this little house? The other was far grander.'

'It is nearer Whitehall, Rose. I have one good friend in the world, and I want to be as near him as possible.'

'He acknowledges little Charlie as his own?'

'Indeed he does. And could you mistake it? Look! The way he sucks his finger is royal, bless him.'

'It makes me wonder whether I ought to drop a curtsy to him when I pick him up.'

'Mayhap you will have to one day,' said Nell, dreaming.

Rose kissed the child.

'To think I've kissed where the King has kissed!' said Rose.

'If that delights you,' Nell retorted, 'you may kiss me any time – and anywhere – you wish.'

That made them both laugh.

'You're just the same, Nell. You haven't changed one little bit. You have fine clothes, and a house of your own, and the King's bastard . . . and yet you're still the same Nell. That's why I've come to talk to you. It's about a man I met.'

'Why, Rosy, you're in love!'

Rose admitted this was so. 'It's a man named John Cassels. I met him in one of the taverns. I want to marry him and settle down.'

'Then why not? Ma would like to have one respectable daughter in the family.'

'Respectable! Ma cares not for that. She's prouder of you than she could ever have been of any respectably married daughter. She talks of you continually. "My Nelly, the King's whore . . . and my grandson Charlie . . . the King's little bastard. . . ." She talks of nothing else. . . .'

Nell laughed. 'Ma's one dream was to make good whores of us both, Rosy. I fulfilled her dreams, but you – you're a disgrace to the family. You're thinking about respectable marriage.'

'The trouble with John is the way he gets his living.'

'What is that?'

'He's a highwayman.'

'A perilous way of making a living.'

'So say I. He longs to be a soldier.'

'Like Will. How is cousin Will?'

'Speaking of you often and with pride, Nelly.'

'It seems that many are proud of the King's whore.'

'We are all proud of you, Nell.'

Nell laughed and threw her curls off her face. 'Marry your John, if you wish it and he wishes it, Rose. Mayhap he will be caught. But if he should end his days by falling from a platform while in conversation with a clergyman . . . at least you will have had your life together, and a widow is a mighty respectable thing to be. And Rose . . . if it should be possible to drop a word in the right quarter . . . who knows, I may get my chance to do it. I do not forget poor Will and his talk of being a soldier. I often think of it. One day Will shall be a soldier, and I will do what I can for your John Cassels. That's if you love the man truly.'

'Nell, Nell, my sweet sister.'

'Nay,' said Nell, 'who would not do all possible for a sister?'

And when Rose had gone she thought that it would be a comparatively easy thing to find places in the army for Will and John Cassels.

'But, my little lord,' she whispered, 'it is going to be rather more difficult to fit a coronet on to that little head.'

*   *   *

Nell stayed on in her small house and the months passed. Louise had not surrendered to the King. Moll Davies still flaunted past Nell's house in her carriage.

My lord Rochester visited Nell in her new house, and shook his head over what he called 'Nell's squalor'.

He sprawled on a couch, inspecting his immaculate boots, and glancing up at Nell with affection.

He gave advice. 'The King does not treat you with the decencies he owes to a royal mistress, Nell,' he said. 'That is clear.'

'While Madam Davies rides by in her coach to her fine house, flashing her diamond ring!' cried Nell.

''Tis true. And poor Nelly is now a mother, and the infant's face would proclaim him as the King's son even if His Majesty had reason to suspect this might be otherwise.'

'His Majesty has no reason to suspect that.'

'Suspicion does not always need reason to support it, little Nell. But let us not discourse on such matters. Let us rather devote ourselves to this more urgent business: How to get Mrs Nelly treated with the courtesy due to the King's mistress. Barbara got what she wanted by screams, threats and violence. Moll by sweet, coy smiles. What have you, sweet Nell, to put in place of these things – your Cole-yard wit? Alas, alas, Cole-yard is at the root of all your troubles. His Majesty is in a quandary. He is fond of his little Nell; he dotes on his latest son; but little Charles is half royal, half Cole-yard. Remember that, Nell. There have been other little Charleses, to say nothing of Jemmies and Annes and Charlottes. Now all these have had mothers of gentle birth. Even our noble Jemmy Monmouth had a gentlewoman for his mother. But you, dear Nell – let's face it – are from the gutter. His Majesty fears trouble if he bestows great titles on this Charles. The people accept the King's lack of morals. They like to see him merry. They care not where he takes his pleasure. What they do care about, Nell, is to see one of themselves rise to greatness through the King's bed. "Why," they say, "that might have happened to me . . . or my little Nell. But it did not. It happened to *that* little Nell." And they cannot forgive you that. Therefore, though you bear the King's bastard, they do not wish that titles should be bestowed on him. They wish it to be remembered that his mother is but a Cole-yard wench.'

''Tis so, I fear, my lord,' said Nell. 'But it shall not stay so. This child is going to share in some of that which has been enjoyed by Barbara's brats.'

'Noble Villiers on their mother's side – those little bastards of Barbara's, Nelly!'

'I care not. I care not. Who is to say they *are* the King's children? Only Barbara.'

'Nay, not even Barbara. For how could even their mother be sure? Now listen to my advice, Nell. Be diplomatic in your attitude towards the King. When the Frenchwoman surrenders, as undoubtedly she will, there may be changes in His Majesty's seraglio. The lady may say, "Remove that object. I ask it as the price of my surrender." And believe me, little Nell, that object – be she noble Villiers or orange-girl – may well be removed. Unless, of course, the object makes herself so important to His Majesty that he cannot dispense with her.'

'This Frenchwoman, it seems, would have great powers.'

'She uses great diplomacy, my dear. She holds out hopes to our most gracious King, and then withdraws. It is a game such women play – a dangerous game unless the woman has the skill. She is skilled, this French Louise. It is her manners and this game she plays which make her so desirable. For the love of God I cannot see what else. The woman sometimes seems to squint.'

'And so Squintabella will throw us all out of favour!' cried Nell wrathfully.

'Squintabella will, if she wishes to. Mayhap she will not consider a little one-time orange-girl from Cole-yard a worthy adversary. But listen to me, Nelly. For this time make no demands upon the King. Administer to his peace. Laugh for him. See that he laughs. He will come to you for refuge, as a ship comes into harbour. Squintabella will not rage and storm as Barbara raged and stormed, but yet I fancy he will have need of refuge.'

Nell was silent for a while. Then she looked at the handsome dissolute face of my lord Rochester and said: 'I cannot understand, my lord, why you should be so good to me.'

Rochester yawned. He said: 'Put it down, if you will, to my dislike of Squintabella, my desire for His Majesty's peace and enjoyment of the most charming lady in London, and my pleasure in helping a fellow-wit.'

'Whichever it should be,' said Nell, 'I'll follow your advice, my lord, as far as I'm able. But since the days when I sat on the cobbles in Cole-yard, I have never been in control of my tongue. And, as I know myself, I am certain I shall continue to ask favours for my young Charles until he is a noble duke.'

'Aye!' cried Rochester. 'Go your own way, Nelly. There is one thing that's certain. 'Twill be a way no other went before.'

*   *   *

So Nell continued at the eastern end of Pall Mall. The King came less frequently. Will Chaffinch regretted that his purse was not as deep as he would have liked, and Nell had developed extravagant tastes.

She would not dress young Charles in garments unsuited to his state. She had never been thrifty; debts began to mount.

One day she said to Rochester: 'I cannot keep my little Charles, in the state to which I intend he shall become accustomed, on what I get from Chaffinch.'

'You could remind the King of his responsibilities,' suggested Rochester. 'Remind him gently. Be not like Barbara with her demands.'

'I'll not be like Barbara,' said Nell. 'And my son shall not be dressed in worsted. Nothing but silk shall touch his skin. It's going to be a duke's skin before he dies, and I want to make it duke's skin from the start. He was born high, and he'll stay high.'

'Nell, I see plans in your eyes. What mad pranks do you plan?'

'Since what Chaffinch gives me is not enough, I must work for more.'

'You would take a lover?'

'Take a lover! Nay, one man at a time was ever my way. I have my friend the King, and we have our child. We are too poor, it seems, to keep him in the state due to him. Therefore I must work.'

'You . . . work!'

'Why not? I was once an actress, and it was said that many people crowded into the theatre just to see me. Why should they not again?'

'But now you are known as the King's mistress and the mother of his son. King's mistresses do not work. They never have.'

'This one will set a fashion,' said Nell. 'If his father is too poor to give young Charles his due, his mother shall not be.'

'Nay, Nell. It is unheard of.'

'From tomorrow it shall not be. For then I go back to the stage.'

FIVE

James, Duke of Monmouth, was whipping himself to a rage. He strutted about his apartments before those young men whose pleasure it was to keep close to the King's son and applaud him in all that he did.

Monmouth was handsome in the extreme. He had inherited his father's physique and his mother's beauty; and there was just enough of the Stuart in his features to convince everyone that he was the King's son. All knew of the King's devotion to this young man, the liberties allowed him, the King's unending patience; for it had to be admitted that Monmouth was an arrogant fellow, proudly conscious of that stream of royal blood which flowed in his veins. At the same time he bore a great grudge against that fate which had made him an illegitimate son of such an indulgent father.

There was a hope, which never left him, that one day the King would legitimize him. There were many to surround him and tell him that this would be so, for the Queen's pregnancies continued to end in miscarriages, and the dislike of the country for the King's brother's religion was growing.

James, Duke of York, was suspect. He had not proclaimed himself a Catholic, but it was clear by his absence from the church that he was uneasy in his mind concerning his religion, and rumour ran riot. It was for Monmouth and his friends to foster those rumours.

In the meantime Monmouth gave himself up to pleasure. He was a glutton for it. He had his father's interest in women, but he lacked his father's good-natured tolerance. Charles had the gift of seeing himself exactly as he was; Monmouth saw himself larger than life. Charles had had no need to bolster up the picture of himself, since his forbears were Kings of Scotland, England, and France. He was entirely royal. Monmouth had to link his royal ancestors with those of his mother; and, although he was the King's son, there were many who declared he would never wear the crown. There was a burning desire within him to override those who would stand in the way of his ambitions. This coloured his life.

His education had not been of the best; he had left the environment of a simple country gentleman to become a petted member of his father's Court. His head was not strong enough for him to imbibe such a strong draught and remain sober.

So he strutted, raged, posed, and made many enemies; and those who were his friends were in truth either enemies of the Duke of York or those who thought to curry favour with the King because of the love he bore his son.

Monmouth's time was devoted to fortune-tellers, looking after his appearance, collecting recipes for the care of his skin, and keeping his teeth white and his hair that lustrous black which was such a contrast to his smooth fair skin; soldiering attracted him; he wished to be a famous soldier and to make great conquests; he pictured himself riding through the streets of London with his military glory like a halo about his handsome head; for thus, he believed, the people would realize his worth and, when they cried 'Down with the Catholic Duke of York,' they would add, 'Up with the Protestant Duke of Monmouth!'

It was seven years since he had married the little Countess of Buccleuch, a very wealthy Scottish heiress whom his father had been pleased to bestow upon his beloved Jemmy. Monmouth had been fourteen then; Anne, his little bride, twelve. He remembered often how his loving father had merrily attended the ceremony of putting them to bed together, yet insisting on the ceremony's stopping there, since the pair were so young.

It had proved a far from happy marriage. But Anne Scott was proud. Monmouth thought her callous. She gave no sign of any distress which her husband's wildness caused her, and some said she was as hard as the granite hills of her native land.

Monmouth was pursuing a lady of the Queen's bed-chamber, Mary Kirke. It was not that Mary appealed to him more than any other; but he had heard that his uncle, the Duke of York, was enamoured of the lady and, in his slow and ponderous way, was attempting to court her.

That was enough to inspire young Monmouth's passion, for it was necessary for him continually to flaunt what he felt to be his superiority over his uncle. He must do it in every possible way, so that all – including James, Duke of York – should realize that, should King Charles die without legitimate heirs, James II would not be James, Duke of York, but James, Duke of Monmouth.

Now, as he walked about his apartment, he was ranting to his companions on what he called an insult to royalty.

Sir Thomas Sandys was with him; also a Captain O'Brien. He had called these men in because he wished them to help in a wild plan which was forming in his mind. His great friends, the young Dukes of Albemarle and Somerset, sprawled on the window-seat listening to Jemmy's ranting.

'My father is too easy-going by far!' cried Monmouth. 'He allows low fellows to insult him – and what does he? He shrugs his shoulders and laughs. It is all very well to take that attitude, but insolence should be punished.'

'His Majesty's easy temper is one of the reasons for the love his people bear him,' suggested Albemarle.

'A King should be a King,' said Monmouth boldly.

None spoke. Monmouth, as beloved son, had a right to criticize his father which was denied to them.

'Have you fellows heard what this insolent Coventry said in the Parliament?'

All were silent.

'And who is this John Coventry?' demanded the young Duke. 'Member for Weymouth! And what is Weymouth, I pray you tell me? This obscure gentleman from the country would criticize my father and go free. And all because my father is too lazy to punish him. 'Tis an insult to royalty, I tell you; and if my father will not avenge it, then should his son do so.'

The Duke of Albemarle said uneasily: 'What was said was said in the Parliament. There, it is said, a man has a right to speak his mind.'

Monmouth swung round, black eyes flashing, haughty lips curled. 'A right . . . to speak against his King!'

'It has been done before, my lord,' ventured Somerset. 'What this man Coventry did was to ask that an entertainment tax should be levied on the theatres.'

''Twas a suggestion worthy of a country bumpkin.'

'He proposed it as a means of raising money, which all agree the country needs,' said Somerset.

'My good fellow, the King must be amused. He loves his theatres. Why should he not have his pleasures? The theatres give much pleasure to His Majesty.'

'That was said in Parliament,' said Albemarle grimly.

'Aye,' cried Monmouth. 'And 'twas then that this John Coventry – *Sir* John Coventry – rose in his seat to ask whether the King's pleasure lay among the men or the women who acted therein.'

''Twas an insult to His Majesty, 'tis true,' admitted Albemarle.

'An insult! It was arrogance, *lèse majesté*. It shall not be permitted. All the country knows that the King finds pleasure in his actresses. There are Moll Davies from the Duke's and Nell Gwyn from the King's to prove it. Coventry meant to insult the King, and he did so.'

'His Majesty has decided to allow the insult to pass,' said Albemarle.

'But *I* shall not allow it to pass,' cried Monmouth. '*I* shall make these country bumpkins realize that my father is their King, and any who dare insult him shall live to regret that day.'

'What does Your Grace plan?' asked Sir Thomas Sandys.

'That, my good friends, is what I have assembled you here to discuss,' said the Duke.

*   *   *

The King was very uneasy. He sought out his brother James in his private apartments.

James was sitting alone, a book before him.

James, thought Charles, so tall and handsome – far handsomer than I – and clever enough in his way; why is it that James is a fool?

'Reading, James?' said Charles lightly. 'And the book?' He looked over his brother's shoulder. 'Dr Heylin's *History of the Reformation*. Ah, my Protestant subjects would be pleased to see you reading such a book, James.'

James' big dark eyes were puzzled.

He said: 'I find much food for thought 'twixt these pages.'

'Give over thinking so much, James,' said Charles. 'It is a task ill-suited to your nature.'

'You mock me, Charles. You always did.'

'I was born a mocker.'

'Have you read this book?'

'I have skimmed its pages.'

''Tis worth more than a skimming.'

'I am glad to hear you say so. I trust this means your feet are set in what my Protestant subjects would call the path of the just.'

'It fills me with doubts, Charles.'

'Brother, when I die you will inherit a crown. The managing of a kingdom will take every bit of that skill with which nature has provided you. You will be at your wits' end to keep the crown upon your head, and your head upon your shoulders. Remember our father. Do you ever forget him? I never do. You are over-concerned with your soul, brother, when your head may be in danger.'

'What matters a head where a soul is in the balance?'

'Your head is there for all to see – a handsome one, James, and that of a man who may well one day be King. Your soul – where is that? We cannot see it, so how can we be sure that it has any existence?'

'You blaspheme, Charles.'

'I'm an irreligious fellow; I know it. 'Tis my nature. My mind is a perverse one, and to such as I am faith is hard to come by. But put away the book, brother. I would talk to you. 'Tis this affair of Coventry.'

James nodded gloomily. 'A bad affair.'

'Young Jemmy grows too wild.'

'The fellow will live?'

'I thank God that he will. But those wild young men have slit his nose and the Parliament is filled with anger.'

''Tis to be understood,' said James.

'I am in agreement with you and the Parliament, James. But my Parliament is displeased with me and it is a bad thing when parliaments and kings are not of one accord. We have a terrible example before us. When I came home I determined to live in peace with my subjects and my Parliament. And now young Jemmy has done this. He was defending my royalty, he proclaims.'

'That boy has such a deep sense of Your Majesty's royalty, largely because he believes himself to have a share in it.'

''Tis true, James. There are times when young Jemmy gives me great cause for anxiety. The Parliament has passed an act whereby any who shall put out an eye, cut a lip, nose, or tongue of His Majesty's liege people or in any other manner wound or maim any Parliament man, shall be sent to prison for a year, besides incurring other heavy penalties.'

''Tis just,' said James.

'Aye, 'tis just. Therefore I like not to see young Jemmy conduct himself thus.'

'A little punishment, inflicted by Your Majesty, might be useful.'

'Indeed it might. But I was never a punishing man, James, and I find it hard to punish those I care for as I do for that boy.'

'Nevertheless he will bring trouble on himself, and on you one day.'

'That is why I wish you to help me, James. Could not you two be friends? I like not to see this strife between you.'

''Tis your natural son who causes the strife between us. He fears I shall wear the crown to which, in his heart, he believes himself to have prior claim.'

'There is only one thing which can make you two become friends, I fear; and that is a family of healthy sons for me, so that there is no hope for either of you to wear the crown.'

'Charles, there are some who say you love that boy so much that you would make him your heir in all things.'

''Tis true I love the boy. He is my own flesh and blood. There are a thousand things to remind me of that each day. He is my son – my eldest son. He is handsome, he delights me. I'll deny it not. But you too, brother, are our father's son and you are my heir. Never would I make Jemmy legitimate, while there is one who, it is right and proper, should take my place. If I die childless, James, you are the heir to the throne. I never forget that. Lightminded though I may be, on this point I am firm and strong. But there is one other matter I must settle with you. It is this dabbling with the Catholic Faith.'

'We cannot control our thoughts, brother.'

'Nay, but we can keep them to ourselves.'

'I could not be false to what I believed to be the true religion.'

'But you could keep your thoughts to yourself, brother. Remember our grandfather, Henri Quatre. You're his grandson no less than I. Think of the control he kept on his religion, and because of this a country, which had known disastrous war, at last knew peace. England is a Protestant country – as firmly Protestant as France in the days of our grandfather was firmly Catholic. England will never again accept a Catholic King. If you would have peace in England when I am gone, you must come to the throne a Protestant.'

'And if my heart and mind tell me the Catholic Faith is the true one?'

'Subdue the heart, dear brother. If you let the mind take control, it will say this: Worship in secret. Remain outwardly what the country wishes you to be. Remember our grandfather . . . the greatest King the French ever had. He put an end to civil war, because he, who had been Huguenot, professed to be a Catholic. Stop this flirting with the Catholic Faith, James. Show yourself with me in the church when the occasion demands it. Let the country see you as a good Protestant. Then, brother, we shall more quickly put an end to this unhealthy fostering of young Jemmy's ambitions. Do this – not for my sake – but for your own and that of an England you may one day rule.'

James shook his head gravely. 'You know not what you ask, brother. If a man follows the Catholic Faith, how can he go to a Protestant church and worship there?'

Charles sighed wearily.

Then he shrugged his shoulders. James was a fool . . . always had been a fool and, he feared, always would be. Charles could console himself with the thought that whatever trouble James brought on himself he, Charles, would be in his grave and not concerned with it.

He turned to a happier subject. 'How fares your family?'

James' face lightened. 'Mary is solemn as ever. Anne grows plump.'

'Come, take me to them. I would have them know their uncle forgets them not.'

In the Duke's apartment Charles met Anne Hyde. Anne's welcome was fond, and not entirely so because her brother-in-law was King. Anne was a clever woman, and she and Charles had ever been good friends. Anne did not forget that, when all had deserted her soon after her marriage and Henrietta Maria was demanding that she be ignored, it was Charles the King who had been her best friend.

'Your Majesty looks in good spirits,' she said.

''Tis the prospect of talk with you,' said Charles, ever gallant even to the over-fat and ageing. 'Od's Fish! James is a gloomy fellow with his holy problems. Where are these children of yours?'

'I'll send for them,' said Anne. 'They'll be eager to come, now they know Your Majesty is here.'

Charles, looking at Anne, thought she was more sallow than usual; her very fat seemed unhealthy.

He asked if she had news of her father, Edward Hyde, Earl of Clarendon, who was living in exile in France.

Anne had heard. He passed his days pleasantly enough, she told the King. He was finding compensation for his exile in writing his memoirs.

'They should make interesting reading,' said the King.

Now the little girls were coming into the room: Mary and

Anne, the only two who had survived, thought the King, among the seven – was it seven? – which Anne Hyde had borne the Duke of York.

Yet James, with his two girls, had been more fortunate than his brother. Why was it that royal folk, for whom it was so necessary to produce heirs, were usually so unfortunate? Lack of heirs was the curse of royalty.

Mary, the elder, took his hand and solemnly kissed it. Charles lifted her in his arms. He loved children and he was particularly fond of solemn little Mary.

He kissed her affectionately, and she put her arms about his neck and rubbed her cheek against his. Next to her father she loved her Uncle Charles.

Anne was tugging at his coat.

'Anne's turn,' said Anne stolidly.

'Now, Mary, my dear,' said the King, 'you must give place to plump Anne.'

He set Mary down and made as though to lift Anne from the ground. He wheezed and puffed, and both children shrieked with delight.

'Anne is too fat to be lifted,' said Mary.

'I confess,' said the King, 'that this great bulk of my niece defeats me.'

'Then give me sweetmeats instead,' said Anne.

'It is because she eats that she is so fat, Uncle Charles,' said Mary. 'If she eats more she will become fatter and fatter, and *nobody* will be able to lift her.'

Anne gave them a slow, friendly smile. 'I'd rather have sweetmeats than be lifted,' she said.

'Ah, my dear Anne, you present a weighty problem,' said the King. 'And knowing your fancies, and that I should be admitted to your ponderous presence, I came well armed.'

Both little girls looked at his face; for he had knelt to put his on a level with theirs.

'Armed,' said Mary. 'That means carrying swords and such things, Anne.'

'Swords made of sweetmeats?' said Anne, interested.

'Feel in my pocket, nieces, and you may find something of interest,' said their uncle.

Anne was there first, squealing with delight, and cramming the contents of the King's pocket into her mouth.

Mary put her hand in that of the King. 'I will show you Papa's greyhounds. I love them.'

'I love them too,' mumbled Anne as best she could, while the sweet juices ran down her plump chin.

'They are so thin,' said the King, giving her his melancholy smile.

'I like others to be thin,' said Anne. 'It is only Anne who must be fat.'

'You fear that if they grow as fat as you they will acquire similar tastes. If we all loved sweetmeats as does Mistress Anne, there would not be enough in the world to satisfy us all.'

Anne was solemn for a while, then she smiled that affectionate and charming smile. 'Nay, Uncle Charles,' she said, 'the confectioners will make more sweetmeats.'

They went to look at the Duke's greyhounds. Their father forgot his preoccupation with religious problems and played games with his little girls. Charles showed them how to throw in *pelmel*.

And, as he guided Mary's hand when she would throw the ball and as little Anne toddled beside him, Charles thought: If these two were but mine I should end this dangerous rivalry between Jemmy and James; I should not need to feel concerned because I see my brother deep in doubt when he reads Dr Heylin's *History of the Reformation*.

*　　　*　　　*

Charles came to see Nell after she had been playing on the stage of the King's Theatre for a few weeks.

He was amused by her return to the stage; but, as he pointed out, everyone knew that the child who was sleeping in the cradle was his son, and it was hardly fitting for that child's mother to remain an actress.

'It is necessary for that child's mother to provide food for the King's bastard,' said Nell characteristically. 'And if play-acting is the only way she can do it, then play-act she must. Should an innocent child starve because his mother is too lazy and his father too poor to feed him?'

'Have done,' said the King. 'Leave the stage and you shall not want – nor shall he.'

'If I leave the stage I shall be obliged to see that this is a promise Your Majesty shall keep,' said Nell. 'For myself I ask no pension; but for my child – who is known by the name of Charles, and none other – I would ask a good deal.'

'All that can be done for you and him shall be done,' promised the King.

He was visiting her more frequently now. Louise de Kéroualle was still holding him at bay. He thought a great deal of Louise; she seemed to him infinitely desirable, indeed the most desirable woman in his kingdom, but he was too lighthearted to sigh on that account. Louise would succumb eventually, he felt sure; in the meantime there was Moll – still charming enough to be worth a visit now and then; Barbara on whom he still called occasionally, if only that he might congratulate himself on having almost broken with her; and Nell, who could always be relied upon to amuse and come up with the unexpected. The others – the ladies who provided amusement for a night or so – there would always be. He was well supplied with women.

Charles realized Nell's problems, and he had decided that it would be convenient if she lived even nearer to him at Whitehall.

He reminded her that he had given her the house in which she now lived.

'And that,' retorted Nell, 'I do not accept, since I discover it to be leasehold. My services have always been free under the Crown. For that reason, nothing but freehold will satisfy me.'

'Nell,' said the King with a laugh, 'you grow acquisitive.'

'I have a son to think for.'

'It has changed you – becoming a mother.'

'It changes all women.'

The King was sober temporarily. 'You do well,' he said, 'to consider the boy. You do well to remind me of your needs. Why, look you, Nell, it is a long step here from Whitehall.'

'But Your Majesty's chief pleasure – save one – is sauntering, so I've heard.'

'There are occasions when I would wish to have you near me. And now that you have left the stage, I am going to make you a present of a fine house – freehold. The only freehold in the district on which I can lay my hands.'

'It is near Whitehall?'

'Nearer than this one, Nell. Indeed, it is nearer by a quarter of a mile. I do not think you will have reason to find this house unworthy of our son, Nell.'

'And it is freehold?' insisted Nell.

'I swear it shall be.'

*　　*　　*

Nell was climbing in the world now.

She had her residence in the beautiful wide street at that end which was the home of many of the aristocrats of the Court. Nell's new house was three storeys high, and its gardens extended to St James' Park, from which it was separated by a stone wall. At the end of Nell's garden was a mound, and when she stood on this she could see over the wall and into the Park; she could call to the King as he sauntered there with his friends.

Now Nell was indeed treated with the 'decencies of a royal mistress'. Her near neighbours were Barbara Castlemaine, the Countess of Shrewsbury, and Mary Knight who had once been one of the King's favoured mistresses. Lady Greene and Moll Davies were not far off.

There was a difference in the attitude of many people towards her now. She was Madam Gwyn more often than Mrs Nelly; tradesmen were eager for her custom; she was treated with the utmost servility.

Nell of the old days would have ridiculed these sycophants; Nell the mother enjoyed their homage. She never forgot that the more honour paid to her the easier it would be for honours to find their way to that little boy, and she was determined to see him a Duke before she died.

There were some who often tried to remind her that she had been an orange-girl and an actress, bred in Cole-yard. Mary Villiers, the Duke of Buckingham's sister, had refused to receive her and this, Nell was delighted to learn, had aroused the King's deep displeasure. He had reminded the noble lady: 'Those I lie with are fit company for the greatest ladies in the land.' And Mary Villiers had had to change her attitude.

The Arlingtons were cool. They were all for the promotion of Mademoiselle de Kéroualle; but she, it seemed, was chained to celibacy by her virtue. Let her remain thus, thought Nell, while the rest of us enjoy life and grow rich.

There was some rivalry with Moll Davies.

Nell could not endure Moll's affected airs of refinement. She wondered that the King – a man of such wit – did not laugh them to scorn. He still visited Moll, and there were occasions when Nell, expecting him to call at the house or even vault the wall as he sometimes did, would see him passing on his way to visit Moll Davies.

Moll sometimes called on Nell after the King's visit. She would sit in Nell's apartment, displaying her £700 ring, and talking of the latest present the King had brought her.

'He even brings me sweetmeats such as I like. He says I am almost as great a glutton for them as the Princess Anne.'

One day, early that spring, Moll called at Nell's house in a twitter of excitement expressly to tell her that the King had sent a message that he would be calling on her that night.

'It surprises me, Nelly,' she said, 'that he should come so far. *You* are nearer now, are you not, and yet he comes to me! Can you understand it?'

'All men, even Kings, at times act crazily,' said Nell quickly.

She was anxious. He son was without a name. She was not going to have him called Charlie Gwyn. He was growing. He needed a name. Many times she had suggested that some honour be given to the boy, but the King was always vague and evasive. He promised to do all that he could, but Charles' promises were more readily given than fulfilled. He

168

was fond of the boy; yet to have ennobled him would have caused much comment. Rochester was right about that. The affair of Sir John Coventry was still remembered, and there were times when the King was eager not to arouse too much criticism in his subjects.

'Let be, Nell,' he had said. 'Let the matter rest awhile. I promise you the boy shall lack nothing.'

And tonight he would go to that scheming Moll Davies. It was not to be borne.

'I am a good hand at making sweetmeats,' Nell said to Moll.

'I was never taught to perform such menial tasks,' said Moll.

'I used to make them to sell in the market,' Nell told her. 'Sweetmeats!' she cried in a raucous cockney voice. 'Good ladies, buy my sweetmeats!'

Moll shuddered. She looked about her at the beautifully furnished apartment and wondered how such a creature as Nell had ever managed to obtain it.

Nell pretended not to see Moll's disgust. 'I shall bring you some sweetmeats,' said Nell. 'My next batch shall be made especially for you.'

Moll rose to go; she had preparations to make, she reiterated, for the reception of the King that night.

When she had gone, Nell picked up the baby.

A fine healthy boy; she kissed him fondly.

She was ready to fight all the duchesses in the land for his sake.

Now she went to her kitchen and, rolling up the fine sleeves of her gown, made sweetmeats; and as soon as they were ready she set out with them for Moll Davies' house.

Moll was surprised to see her so soon.

'I made these for you,' said Nell; 'and I thought I would bring them to you while they were fresh.'

'They look good indeed,' said Moll.

'Try one,' suggested Nell.

Moll did so, flourishing her diamond under Nell's eye. Nell's gaze dwelt on it enviously, so it seemed to Moll.

'It's beautiful,' said Nell simply.

'It is indeed! Every time it catches my eye it reminds me of His Majesty's devotion.'

'You are indeed fortunate to have that outward symbol of the King's devotion. Do try another of these fondants.'

Moll tried another.

'How clever to be able to make such delicious things! I was never brought up to be so useful.'

'Nay,' said Nell with a high laugh. 'You were brought up to wear a diamond ring and play high-class whore to a merry King.'

Nell went into peals of laughter which made Moll frown. Moll had never been sure of Nell since the impudent girl from Cole-yard had imitated her on the stage of the King's Theatre.

'I laugh too readily,' said Nell, subdued. 'It was a habit I learned in the Cole-yard. I would I were a lady like yourself. Pray have another.'

'You are not eating any.'

'I ate my fill in my own house. These are a present for you. Ah, you are thinking, why should I bring you presents and what do I want in exchange? I see the thoughts in your eyes, Moll. 'Tis true. I do want something. I want to learn to be a lady such as you are.' Nell held out the box in which she had put the sweets, and Moll took yet another.

'You know well what flavours appeal to my palate,' said Moll.

'I'll confess it,' said Nell. 'I study you. I would ape you, you see. I would discover why it is His Majesty visits you when he might visit little Nell from the Cole-yard.'

'Nell, you are too low in your tastes. You laugh too much. You speak with the tongue of the streets. You do not try to be a lady.'

''Tis true,' said Nell. 'Pray have another.'

'I declare I grow greedy.'

''Tis a pleasure to please you with my sweetmeats.'

Moll said: 'You are good at heart, Nell. Listen to me. I will tell you how to speak more like a lady. I will show you how to walk as a lady walks, how to treat those who are your inferiors.'

'I pray you do,' said Nell.

And Moll showed her, eating the sweetmeats Nell had brought as she did so. When she had finished she had cleared the whole dish.

Nell rose to go. 'You have preparations to make for His Majesty,' she said. 'I must detain you no longer. Pray keep the dish. When you look at it you will think of me.'

Nell went out to her chair which was waiting for her.

'Hurry back,' she said to her professional carriers whom she hired by the week. 'I have certain preparations to make.'

And when she reached her own house she went into the room where the baby was sleeping.

She picked him up and, kissing him fiercely, cried: 'We must prepare for Papa. He will be coming here this night, I doubt not. And, who knows, when he is here I may be able to wheedle a nice little title from him for my Charley boy.'

Then she laid him gently in his cradle.

There was no time to lose. She called her cook and bade him prepare pies of meat and fowl, to set beef and mutton roasting.

'I have a fancy,' she said, 'that His Majesty will be supping here this day.'

Then she put on a gown of green and gold lace with slippers of cloth of silver.

She was ready; she knew that the King would come. Moll Davies would be unable to entertain him that night, for the sweets with which she had supplied her unsuspecting rival had been filled with jalap made from the root of a Mexican plant.

Moll had taken a good dose. Nell had little doubt that ere this day was out the King and she would be laughing heartily over Moll's predicament.

'It may be,' said Nell aloud, 'that Mrs Moll will realize this night that there is something to be learned from my Cole-yard ways.'

She was not disappointed. The King joined her for supper. He had discovered what had happened to Moll, and he had had a shrewd notion who had played the trick on her.

He could not contain his mirth as he and Nell sat over supper.

'You are the wildest creature I ever knew,' he told her.

And she saw that he liked well that wildness, and was beginning to feel that, whoever came into his life, he must keep Nelly there to make him laugh and forget his troubles.

* * *

It seemed to the King that, during that difficult year, Nell was his main refuge from his burdens. He was still pursuing Louise de Kéroualle who, although she was maid of honour to the Queen and had her apartments in Whitehall, still expressed her horror at the thought of becoming his mistress.

'How could that be?' she asked. 'There is only one way in which Your Majesty could become my lover, and that way is closed. Your Majesty has a Queen.'

In vain did Charles point out the irksomeness of royal lives. Queens were not to be envied. Look at his own Queen Catherine. Did she seem to be a happy woman? Yet look at merry little Nell. Was there a happier soul in London?

Louise appeared to be puzzled. It was a trick of hers when she wished to appear vague.

'I must work harder at learning to understand the English,' she would say in her lisping voice which matched her baby face.

The King gave her more beautiful tapestries to hang in her apartments; he gave her jewels and some of his most treasured clocks. Still she could only shake her head, open her little eyes as wide as possible, and say: 'If I were not the daughter of such a noble house, why then it would be easier for me to be as these others. Your Majesty, it would seem there is only one way open to me. I should go to a convent and there pass my days.'

Charles was torn between exasperation and desire. He could not endure his lack of success. It was Frances Stuart's inaccessibility which had made her doubly attractive. Louise realized this, and played her waiting game.

It was many months since she had come to England. The

King of France sent impatient messages. Daily the French ambassador warned her.

The Seigneur de Saint Evremond – who was a political exile from France and residing in England where, on account of his wit and literary qualities, Charles had granted him a pension – was eager to see his countrywoman an influence in the land of their adoption. He wrote to Louise. He had heard the rumour that she had declared her intention of entering a convent, so he wrote of the wretched life of nuns, shut off from the world's pleasures, with nothing to sustain them but their religious devotions.

'A melancholy life this, dear sister, to be obliged for custom's sake to mourn a sin one has not committed, at the very time one begins to have a desire to commit it.

'How happy is the woman who knows how to behave herself discreetly without checking her inclination! For, as 'tis scandalous to love beyond moderation, so 'tis a mortification for a woman to pass her life without one *amour*. Do not too severely reject temptations, which in this country offer themselves with more modesty than is required, even in a virgin, to hearken to them. Yield, therefore, to the sweets of temptation, instead of consulting your pride.'

Louise read the advice with her childish smile, and her shrewd brain worked fast. She would surrender at the right moment, and that moment would be one which would bring great profit to herself and to France.

*   *   *

The Duke of Monmouth, having been reprimanded by the King for the part he had played in the Coventry affair, was inclined to sulk.

'But, Father,' he said, 'I sought but to defend your honour. Should a subject stand aside and see slights thrown at his King's honour?'

'Mine has had so many aimed at it that it has developed an impenetrable shell, my son. In future, I pray you, leave its defence to me.'

'I like not to see your royalty besmirched.'

'Oh, Jemmy, 'tis so tarnished that a little more is scarce noticeable.'

'But that these oafs should dare condemn you . . .'

'Coventry's no oaf. He's a country gentleman.'

Monmouth laughed. 'He'll carry a mark on his face all the days of his life to remind him to mend his manners.'

'Nay, to remind us that we should mend ours,' said the King seriously. 'But have done with these wild adventures, Jemmy. I frown on them. Now let us talk of other matters. How would you like to come with me to Newmarket? You and I will race together and see who shall win.'

Monmouth's sullen smile was replaced by one of pleasure. He was quite charming when he smiled. He brought such a vivid reminder of his mother's beauty that Charles could believe he was young again.

Jemmy was eager to go to Newmarket. Not that he cared so much for the racing, or for his father's company. What meant so much to Jemmy was that he should be seen at his father's side. He liked to observe the significant looks of courtiers, to hear the cries of the people. 'See, there is the Duke of Monmouth, the King's natural son! They say His Majesty is so fond of the boy – and can you doubt it, seeing them thus together? – that he will make him his heir.' Jemmy fancied that many people would be pleased to see this done. And why not? Did he not look every inch a prince? And was he not a Protestant, and were not the rumours growing daily concerning the King's brother's conversion to the Catholic Faith? Monmouth and his friends would see to it that there was no lack of such rumours.

Contemplating the trip to Newmarket, he was in high spirits. The King doted on him. There was nothing he could not do and still keep Charles' favour. And everyone would know it. More and more people would rally to his support. They would say he was the natural heir to the throne. All would know that, in spite of the affair of Sir John Coventry, he had lost none of his favour with the King.

He called to Albemarle and Somerset: 'Come,' he said, 'let us go out into the town. I have a desire to make good sport.'

Albemarle was eager to accompany his friend. He, with

others, marvelled at the King's softness towards Monmouth. The affair of Sir John Coventry was a serious one, yet the King had made as light of it as possible – because of who was involved. Albemarle was certain that his friendship with such an influential young man could bring him much good. Somerset shared Albemarle's ideas.

It was fun to roam through the city at dusk, to see what they could find and make good sport with. What excitement to come upon some pompous worthy being carried in his chair, turning it over, and rolling the occupant in the filth of the street! There might be a young girl out late at night, and if a young girl wandered late at night what more could she be expecting than the attentions of such as Monmouth and his friends?

They made their way to one of the taverns, where they dined. They sat about drinking, keeping their eyes open for any personable young woman who came their way. The innkeeper had taken the precaution of locking his wife and daughters away out of sight, and was hoping with all his heart that the dissolute Duke had not heard that these had a reputation for beauty.

Monmouth had not, so he contented himself with the innkeeper's wine and, when they staggered into the street, he and his friends were so befuddled that they lurched and leaned against the wall for support.

It was when they were in this condition that they saw an elderly man and a girl approaching them.

'Come,' cried Monmouth drunkenly, 'here's sport.'

The girl was little more than a child and, as the three drunken men barred the way, she clutched at her grandfather in terror.

'Come along, my pretty,' hiccupped Monmouth. 'You are but a child, but 'tis time, I'll swear, you left your childhood behind you. Unless you already have . . .'

The old man, recognizing the men as courtiers by their fine clothes and manner of speaking, cried out in terror: 'Kind sirs, let me and my granddaughter go our way. We are poor and humble folk . . . my granddaughter is but ten years old.'

''Tis old enough!' cried Monmouth, and laid his hands on the child.

Her screams filled the street; and a voice called: 'What goes on there? Who calls?'

'Help!' screamed the child. 'Robbers! Murderers!'

'Hold there! Hold there, I say!' called the voice.

The three Dukes turned and looked; coming towards them was an old ward beadle, his lanthorn held high. He was so old that he could scarcely hobble.

'Here comes the gallant knight!' laughed Monmouth. 'I declare, I tremble in my shoes.'

The little girl had seized her grandfather's hand, and they hurried away.

The drunken Dukes did not notice they had gone, for their attention was now centred on the ward beadle.

'My lord,' said the man, 'I must prevail upon you to keep the peace.'

'On what authority?' demanded Monmouth.

'In the name of the King.'

That amused Monmouth. 'Do you know, fellow, to whom you speak?'

'A noble lord. A gallant gentleman. I implore you, sir, to go quietly to your lodging and there rest until you have recovered from the effects of your liquor.'

'Know you,' said Monmouth, 'that I am the King's son?'

'Nevertheless, sir, I must implore you . . .'

Monmouth was suddenly angry. He struck the man across the face.

'Down on your knees, sir, when you address the King's son.'

'My lord,' began the old man, 'I am a watchman, whose duty it is to keep the peace . . .'

'Down on your knees when you speak to the King's son!' cried Albemarle.

'Kneel . . .' cried Somerset. 'Kneel there on the cobbles, you dog, and ask pardon most humbly because you have dared insult the noble Duke.'

The old man, remembering the recent outrage on Sir John Coventry, was seized with trembling. He held out a

176

hand appealingly, and laid it on Monmouth's coat. The Duke struck it off, and Albemarle and Somerset forced the man down to his knees.

'Now,' cried Monmouth, 'what say you, old fellow?'

'I say, sir, that I but do my duty . . .'

Somerset kicked the old man, who let out a shriek of agony. Albemarle kicked him again.

'He is not contrite,' said Monmouth. 'He would treat us as dogs.'

He administered a kick to the old man's face.

Monmouth's drunken rage was increasing; he had forgotten the girl and her grandfather, his first quarries. His one thought now was to teach the old man that he must pay proper respect to the King's son. Monmouth suspected all, who did not immediately pay him abject homage, to be sneering at him because of his illegitimacy. He needed twice as much homage as the King himself, because he needed to remind people of that in him which, in the King, they took for granted.

The watchman, sensing the murderous indifference to his plight in Monmouth's attitude, forced himself to get to his knees.

'My lord,' he said, 'I beseech you do nothing that would ill reflect upon your character and good nature . . .'

But Monmouth was very drunk; and he was obsessed with the idea that his royalty had been slighted.

He kicked the man with such ferocity that the poor watchman lay prone on the cobbles.

'Come!' screeched Monmouth. 'Let us show this fellow what happens to those who would insult the King's son.'

Albemarle and Somerset followed his lead. They fell upon the old man, kicking and beating him. The blood was now running from the watchman's mouth; he had put up his hands to protect his face. He cried piteously for mercy. But still they continued to inflict their murderous rage upon him.

Then suddenly the man lay still, and there was that in his attitude which somewhat sobered the three Dukes.

'Come,' said Albemarle, 'let us go from here.'

'And be quick about it,' added Somerset.

The three of them staggered away; but not before many, watching from behind shutters, had recognized them.

Before daybreak the news spread through the town.

Old watchman, Peter Virmill, had been murdered by the Dukes of Monmouth, Albemarle, and Somerset.

*   *   *

Charles was worried indeed. People were saying that there was no safety in the streets. A poor old ward beadle murdered, and for keeping the peace!

All were watchful. What would happen now? My lord Albemarle who had recently inherited a great title, my lord Somerset who was a member of a noble house, and my lord Monmouth, son of the King himself, were all guilty of murder. For, said the citizens of London, the murder of a poor watchman was as much murder as that of the highest in the land.

The King sent for his son. He was cooler towards him than he had ever been before.

'Why do you these things?' he asked.

'The man interfered with our pleasure.'

'And your pleasure was . . . breaking the peace?'

''Twas a young slut and her grandfather. Had they come quietly all would have been well.'

'You are a handsome young man, James,' said the King. 'Can you not find willing ladies?'

'She would have been willing enough once we had settled the old grandfather.'

'So rape was your business?' said Charles.

''Twas but for the sport,' growled Monmouth.

'I am not a man who is easily shocked,' said the King, 'but rape has always seemed to me a most disgusting crime. Moreover it exposes a man as a mightily unattractive person.'

'How so?'

'Since it was necessary to make a victim of the girl instead of a partner.'

'These people were insolent to me.'

178

'James, you too readily see insult. Take care. Men will say, since he looks for insults, does he know that he deserves them?'

Monmouth was silent. His father had never been so cold to him.

'You know the penalty for murder,' said Charles.

'I am your son.'

'There are some who call me a fool for accepting you as that,' said Charles brutally.

Monmouth winced. Charles knew where to touch him in his most vulnerable spot. 'But . . . there is no doubt.'

Charles laughed. 'There is the greatest doubt. Knowing what I now know of your mother, I myself have doubts.'

'But . . . Father, you have made me believe that you never had these doubts.'

Charles stroked the lace on his cuff. 'I had expected you to have your mistresses. That is how I would expect a son of mine to act. But to behave thus towards helpless people, to show such criminal arrogance to those who are not in a position to retaliate . . . these things I understand not at all. I am a man of much frailty, I know. But that which I see in you is so alien to my nature that I have come to believe that you cannot be my son after all.'

The beautiful dark eyes were wide with horror.

'Father!' cried the Duke. 'It is not true. I am your son. Look at me. Can you not see yourself in me?'

'You, such a handsome fellow – I, such an ugly one!' said the King lightly. 'Yet never did I have to resort to rape. A little wooing was enough on my part. I think you cannot be a Stuart after all. I shall have you taken away now. I have no more to say to you.'

'Father, you mean . . . You cannot mean . . .'

'You have committed a crime, James. A great crime.'

'But . . . as your son . . .'

'You remember I have my doubts of that.'

The Duke's face was twisted with his misery. Charles did not look. He was soft and foolish where this young man was concerned. He had made too much of him, spoiled him, petted him.

For Jemmy's own sake, he must try to instil some discipline into that turbulent proud nature which lacked the balanced good sense to understand the temper of the people he so fervently hoped to rule.

'Go to your apartments now,' he said.

'Father, I will stay with you. I will make you say you know I am your son.'

'It is an order, my lord Duke,' said Charles sternly.

Monmouth stood uncertainly for a moment, a pretty petulant boy; then he strode towards Charles and took his hand. Charles' was limp, and the melancholy eyes were staring out of the window.

'Papa,' said Monmouth, 'Jemmy is here . . .'

It was the old cry of childhood which had amused Charles in the days long ago when he had come to see Lucy, this boy's mother, and the boy, fearing he was not receiving his due of the King's attention, had sought to draw it to himself.

Charles stood still as a statue.

'To your apartments,' he said crisply. 'There you will stay until you hear what is to be done.'

Charles withdrew his hand and walked away.

Monmouth could do nothing but leave the apartment.

When he had gone, Charles continued to stare out of the window. He looked down at the river, beyond the low wall with its semicircular bastions. He did not see the shipping which sailed past. What to be done? How to extricate the foolish boy from the results of this mad prank? Did he not know that it was acts such as this which set thrones tottering?

There would be murmuring among the people. The Coventry scandal had not died down.

If he were strong, those three would suffer the just punishment of murderers. But how could he be strong where his warmest feelings were concerned?

He had to take a bold step. But he would do it to save that boy. There was very little he would not do for the boy. He must at all costs resist the temptation to give him what he so earnestly desired – the crown. That he would not do – love him as he did, he would see him hanged first. Jemmy had to learn his lesson; he had to learn to be humble. Poor Jemmy, was it because he feared he was too humble that he strutted as he did? Had he been a legitimate son . . . then what a different boy he might have been. Had he been brought up with the express purpose of wearing the crown, as he, Charles, had been, there would have been no need for him to make sure that everyone recognized him as the King's son.

I make excuses for him – not because he deserves them; but because I love him, thought Charles. A bad habit.

Then he did what he knew he must do. It was weakness, but how could he, a loving father, do aught else?

He issued a pardon 'Unto our dear son James, Duke of Monmouth, of all murders, homicides, and felonies whatsoever at any time before the 28th day of February last past, committed either by himself alone or together with any other person or persons . . .'

There! It was done.

But in future Jemmy must mend his ways.

* * *

While the King was brooding on the wildness of Monmouth, news came to him that his brother's wife, Anne Hyde, had been taken ill. She was so sick, came the message, and in such agony that none of the physicians could do aught for her.

Charles went with all haste to his brother's apartments. He found James distracted with grief; he was sitting, his face buried in his hands; Anne and Mary were standing bewildered on either side of him.

'James, what terrible news is this?' asked the King.

James dropped his hands, lifted his face to his brother's, and shook his head with the utmost sadness.

'I fear,' he began, 'I greatly fear . . .'

He choked on his sobs and, seeing their beloved father thus, the two little girls burst into loud wailing.

Charles went through to the bedchamber where Anne Hyde was lying, her face so distorted with pain that she was scarcely recognizable.

Charles knelt by her bed and took her hand.

Her lips twisted in a smile. 'Your Majesty . . .' she began.

'Do not speak,' said Charles tenderly. 'I see that it is an effort.'

She gripped his hand firmly. 'My . . . my good friend,' she muttered. 'Good friend first . . . King second.'

'Anne, my dear Anne,' said Charles. 'It grieves me to see you thus.' He turned to the physicians who stood by the bed. 'Has all been done?'

'All, Your Majesty. The pains came so suddenly that we fear it is an internal inflammation. We have tried all remedies. We have bled Her Grace . . . We have purged her. We have applied plasters to the afflicted part, and hot irons to her head. We have tried every drug. The pain persists.'

James had come to stand by the bedside. The little girls were with him, Mary holding his hand, Anne clinging to his coat. Tears flowed from James' eyes, for Anne was half-fainting in her agony, and it was clear to all in that chamber that her life was ebbing away.

James was thinking of all his infidelities which had occurred during their married life. Anne herself had not always been a faithful wife. James thought bitterly of his repudiation of her in the early days of their marriage, and he wondered if his weakness at that time was responsible for the rift between them.

He could have wished theirs had been a more satisfactory marriage. Mayhap, he thought, had I been different, stronger when my mother was against us, if I had stood out, if I had been more courageous, Anne would not have lost her respect for me and mayhap we should have been happier together.

One could not go back. Anne was dying, and their married life was over. He wondered what he would do without her, for always during their life together he had respected her intelligence and relied on her advice.

There were his two little girls who needed a mother's care. If the King did not get a legitimate child, the elder of those little girls could inherit the throne.

'Anne . . .' he murmured brokenly.

But Anne was looking at Charles; it was from the King's presence that she seemed to gain comfort. She was remembering, of course, that he had always been her friend.

'Charles . . .' she murmured, 'the children.'

Then Charles bade the little girls come to him and, kneeling, he placed an arm about each of them.

'Have no fear, Anne,' he said. 'I shall care for these two as though they were my own.'

That satisfied her. She nodded and closed her eyes.

James, weeping bitterly, flung himself on his knees. 'Anne,' he said. 'Anne . . . I am praying for you. You must get well . . . you must . . .'

She did not seem to hear him.

Poor James! thought Charles. Now he loves his wife. She has but an hour to live and he finds he loves her, though for so long he has been indifferent towards her. Poor ineffectual James! It was ever thus.

Charles said: 'Let her chaplain be brought to her bedside.'

He could tell by her stertorous breathing that the end was near.

The chaplain came and knelt by the bed, but the Duchess looked at him and shook her head.

'My lady . . .' began the man.

James said: 'The Duchess does not wish you to pray for her.'

There were significant glances between all those who had come in to witness the death of the Duchess of York.

Anne half raised herself and said on a note of anxiety: 'I want him not. I die . . . in the true religion . . .'

James hesitated. Charles met his eyes. The words which James was about to utter died on his lips. There was a warning in Charles' eyes. Not here . . . not before so many witnesses. He turned to the bed. Anne was lying back on her pillows, her eyes tightly shut.

'It is too late,' said the King. 'She will not regain consciousness.'

He was right. Within a few minutes the Duchess was dead.

But there were many in that room of death to note her

last words and to tell each other that when she died the Duchess was on the point of changing her religion. It seemed clear that, if the Duke was not openly a Catholic, he was secretly so.

Monmouth must lie low for a while. He must curb his wild roistering in the streets; but that did not prevent him from spreading the rumour that the Duke – heir presumptive to the throne – was indeed a Catholic. Had not the English, since the reign of Bloody Mary, sworn they would not have a Catholic monarch on the throne?

* * *

Nell was now enjoying every minute of her existence. She had indeed become a fine lady.

She had eight servants in the house in Pall Mall, and from 'maid's help', at one shilling a week, to her lordly steward, they all adored her. The relationship between them was not the usual one of mistress and servants. Nell showed them quite clearly that she was ever ready to crack a joke with them; never for one instant did she attempt to hide the fact that she had come from a lowlier station than most of them.

She liked to ride out in her Sedan chair, calling to her friends; and to courtiers and humble townsfolk alike her greeting was the same. She would call to the beggar on the corner of the street who could depend on generous alms from Mrs Nelly, and chat as roguishly with the King from the wall of her garden. Nor would she care who his companions were. They might be members of his government or his church, and she would cry: 'A merry good day to you, Charles. I trust I shall have the pleasure of your company this night!' If those who accompanied the King were shocked by her levity, he seemed all the more amused; and it was as though he and Nell had a secret joke against his pompous companions.

Nell entertained often. She kept a goodly table. And there was nothing she liked better than to see her long table loaded with good things to eat – mutton, beef, pies of all description, every fruit that was in season, cheese cakes and tarts, and plenty to drink. And about that table, she liked to see many faces; she liked every one of the chairs to be occupied.

Nell had only one worry during that year, and that was the King's failure to give her son the title she craved for him. But she did not despair. Charles was visiting her more frequently than ever. Moll Davies rarely saw him now, and it was not necessary to administer jalap in sweetmeats to turn the King from her company to that of Nell. He came willingly. Her house was the first he wished to visit.

Louise was still tormenting him and refusing to give way. Many shook their heads over Louise. She will hold out too long, it was whispered. Mayhap when she decides to bestow herself the King will be no longer eager.

Barbara Castlemaine, now Duchess of Cleveland, was growing of less and less importance to the King. Her *amours* were still the talk of the town, partly because they were conducted in Barbara's inimitable way. When Barbara had a new lover she made no attempt to hide the fact from the world.

That year her lustful eyes were turned on William Wycherley, whose first play, *Love in a Wood*, had just been produced.

Barbara had selected him for her lover in her usual way.

Encountering him when he was walking in the park and she was driving past in her coach, she had put her head out of the window and shouted:

'You, William Wycherley, are the son of a whore.'

Then she drove on.

Wycherley was immensely flattered because he knew, as did all who heard it, that she was reminding him of the song in his play which declared that all wits were the children of whores.

It was not long before all London knew that Wycherley had become her lover.

So with Barbara behaving so scandalously, and Louise behaving so primly, and Moll ceasing to attract, Nell for a few months reigned supreme.

Rose was a frequent visitor. She was now married to John Cassels, and when this man found himself in trouble Nell managed to extricate him, and not only do this but obtain for him a commission in the Duke of Monmouth's Guards, so that instead of having a highwayman for a husband Rose had a soldier of rank. Nell had also found it possible to bring her cousin, Will Cholmley, his heart's desire. Will Cholmley was now a soldier, and she hoped that ere long there would be a commission for him.

Rose came to her one day, and they talked of the old days.

Rose said: 'We owe our good fortune to you, Nell. It is like you, Madam Gwyn of Pall Mall, the King's playmate and the friend of Dukes, not to forget those you loved in the old days. We have all done well through you. I'll warrant Ma wishes she had used the stick less on you, Nell. Little did she think to what you would come.'

'How fares she?' asked Nell.

'She will not fare for long.'

'The gin?'

'It is as bad as ever. She is more often drunk than sober. I found her lying in the cellar – that old cellar; how long ago it seems! – dead drunk. John says she'll not live long.'

'Who cares for her?' asked Nell.

'There are plenty to care for her. She can pay them with the money you send her. But 'tis a foul place, that cellar in Cole-yard. The rats are tame down there. 'Tis not as it was when Ma used it as her bawdy-house.'

'She will die there,' said Nell. ''Tis her home. I give her money. That is enough.'

''Tis all you can do, Nell.'

'She needs care,' said Nell. 'We needed it once. But we did not get it. We were neglected for the gin bottle.'

''Tis true, Nell.'

'Had she been different . . . had she loved the gin less and us more . . .' Nell paused angrily. ''Tis no concern of ours . . . if she be ill and dying of gin. What is that to us? What did she do to you, Rose? What would she have done for me? I'll never forget the day the flesh-merchant said you stole his purse. There she stood before you, and there was terror on your face . . . and she pushed you to him. Rose, she cared not for us. She cared for nothing but that you should sell yourself to pay for her gin. What do we owe to such a mother?'

'Nothing,' said Rose.

'Then she will die in her cellar, her gin bottle beside her . . . die as she lived. 'Tis a fate worthy of her.'

Nell was angry; her cheeks were flushed; she began to recount all the unhappiness and neglect she and Rose had suffered at their mother's hands.

Rose sat listening. She knew Nell.

And as soon as Rose had left, Nell called for her Sedan chair.

'Whither, Madam?' asked the carriers.

'To Cole-yard,' said Nell.

That night Nell's mother slept in a handsome bed in her daughter's house in Pall Mall.

'Old bawd that she is,' said Nell, 'yet she is my mother.'

Many were disgusted to discover the bawdy-house keeper installed in her daughter's house; many applauded the courageous action of the daughter, which had brought her there.

Nell snapped her fingers at them all. She cared not, and life was good. She was again pregnant with the King's child.

*　　　*　　　*

That was a happy summer for Nell. She was with the King at Windsor, and it was a pleasure to see his affection for her little son.

Never, declared Nell, had she known such happiness as she had with her Charles the Third. Charles the First (Charles Hart) had been good to her and taught her to become an actress. Charles the Second (Charles Sackville, Lord Buckhurst) was a regrettable incident in her life, but with Charles the Third (the King) she found contentment. She did not ask for his fidelity. Nell was too much of a realist to ask for the impossible, but she had his affection as few people had; she knew that. She had discovered that she could keep that affection by means of her merry wit and her constant good humour. Charles had been accustomed to women who asked a great deal; Nell asked for little for herself, but the needs of her son were ever in her mind.

The little boy was now called Charles Beauclerk – a name given him by his father as a consolation while he waited for a title. He was called Beauclerk after Henry I, who had received it because he could write while his brothers were illiterate. This Henry I had been the father of a greater number of illegitimate children than any English King before Charles – Charles, of course, had beaten him. It was characteristic of the King to remind the world of this fact in naming Nell's son.

So temporarily Nell had to be content with the name Beauclerk which, while it brought no earldom nor dukedom for which she craved, at least was a royal name and a reminder to the world that Charles accepted Nell's son as his own.

Louise was growing a little anxious. Nell Gwyn was becoming too formidable a rival. It was rather disconcerting that, as in the case of his other mistresses, the King seemed to grow more rather than less affectionate towards Nell. It was incredible that the girl from Cole-yard should have such power to hold the elegant and witty King's attention where fine ladies failed.

Louise began to listen to the warnings of her friends.

Louis Quatorze had work for her to do. He was very impatient with her on account of her delay. Lord Arlington, who had Catholic inclinations and who had made himself her protector, was decidedly worried.

Louise had declared so frequently that she was too virtuous to become the King's mistress that, unless she made a complete *volte face*, she did not see how she could be. Yet she, too, had come to realize that to delay any longer would be dangerous.

'The King is an absolute monarch,' she said to Arlington. 'Why should he not, if he wishes, have two wives?'

Arlington saw the implication. He approached the King. Mademoiselle de Kéroualle loved His Majesty, said Arlington, and there was only one thing which kept her aloof – her virtue.

The King looked melancholy. 'Virtue,' he said, 'is indeed a formidable barrier to pleasure.'

'Mademoiselle de Kéroualle,' mourned Arlington, 'as a lady of breeding, finds it difficult to fill a part which has been filled by others who lack her social standing. If in her case an exception were made . . .'

'Exception? What means that?' asked the King, alert.

'If her conscience could be soothed . . .'

'I have been led to believe that only marriage could do that.'

'A mock marriage, Your Majesty.'

'But how is this possible?'

'With Kings all things are possible. What if Your Majesty went through a ceremony with the lady . . .?'

'But how could such a ceremony be binding?'

'It would serve one useful purpose. It would show a certain respect to the lady. With none of those who pleased you has Your Majesty gone through such a ceremony. It would set Mademoiselle de Kéroualle apart from all others. And, although she cannot be Your Majesty's wife, if she were treated as such her pride would be soothed.'

'Come, my lord, I see plans in your mind.'

'What if, when Your Majesty is at Newmarket, you called at my place of Euston. What if we had a ceremony there . . . a ceremony which seemed in the outward sense a marriage . . . then, Your Majesty . . .'

The King laughed. 'Let it be!' he cried. 'Let it be! My dear Arlington, this is a capital idea of yours.'

Arlington bowed. It was his greatest pleasure to serve his King, he murmured.

So, when the King set out for Newmarket, he did so with more than his usual pleasure. Racing delighted him. Monmouth, now fully restored to favour, was at his father's side most of the time. They went hawking together, and matched their greyhounds. They rode together against each other, and the King won the Plate although his young son was among the competitors. Charles, at forty-one, had lost little of the attractiveness of his youth. His grey hair was admirably concealed under the luxuriant curls of his periwig; there were more lines on his face, but that was all; he was as agile and graceful as he had ever been.

Every day he was at Euston; often he spent the night there; and all the time he was courting Louise who was growing more and more yielding.

And on one October day Arlington called in a priest who murmured some sort of marriage service over the pair, and after that Louise allowed herself to be put to bed with all the ribald ceremonies in which it was the custom to indulge.

Now Louise was the King's mistress and, in view of her rank and the high value she set upon herself, was being regarded as *maîtresse en titre* – that one, of all the King's ladies, to take first place.

Nell realized that her brief reign was over. There was another who now claimed the King's attention more frequently than she did; and because she was what Louise would call a vulgar play-actress, she knew that the Frenchwoman would do all in her power to turn the King's favour from her.

That December Nell's second son was born. She called him James, after the Duke of York.

As she lay recovering from the exhaustion of childbirth, which, because of her rude health, was slight, Nell determined to hold her place with the King and to fight this new favourite with all the wit, charm, and cockney shrewdness at her disposal.

She did not believe she would fail. Her own love for her Charles the Third strengthened her resolve; moreover she had the future of little Charles and James Beauclerk to think of.

SIX

NELL saw little of the King during the months which followed. He was completely obsessed by Louise, who gave
herself the airs of a queen; she had only to imply that the
apartments at Whitehall which had been hers before the
mock ceremony were now no longer grand enough to house
her, to have them remade and redecorated at great expense.
With Louise it was possible not only to make love but to talk
of literature, art, and science; and this the King found
delightful. He realized that for the first time he had a
mistress who appealed to him physically and intellectually.
Barbara had been outrageously egoistical and her own
greed and desires had shadowed her mind to such an extent
that it had been impossible to discuss anything with her in
an objective manner. Nell had sharp wits and a ready
tongue, and there would always be a place for Nell in his
life, but what did Nell know of the niceties of living? And
Frances Stuart had been a foolish little creature for all her
beauty. No! In Louise he had a cultured woman, moreover
one who was well versed in the politics of her country, which
happened to be at this time of the utmost importance to
Charles.

It seemed that Louise had succumbed at exactly the right
moment, for Louis Quatorze was about to undertake that
war in which, under the terms of the Treaty of Dover,
Charles had promised to help him.

Louise had received the French ambassador; she had
been informed of the wishes of the King of France; it was
for her to ensure that the King of England kept to his
bargain. Louise was happy. She was pleased with her progress. She had held out against the King until it would have
been dangerous to remain longer aloof. It had taken her
some time to realize that her greatest rival could have been
the common little play-actress, Nell Gwyn, simply because

her aristocratic mind refused to accept the fact that one brought up in Cole-yard could possibly be a rival to herself. But at length she had realized that this play-actress – low as she was – had certain qualities which could be formidable. Her pretty, saucy face was not the most formidable of her weapons. Had Nell Gwyn received even the rudiments of education it might have been hopeless to do battle with her. As it was she must be treated with respect.

French soldiers were now crossing the Rhine and marching into Holland. The gallant Dutch, taken off their guard, were for a short time stunned – but only for a short time. They rose with great courage against the aggressors. In fury those men, the brothers De Witt who had advocated a policy of appeasement, were torn to pieces by the mob in the streets of The Hague. Dutchmen were calling on William of Orange to lead them against their enemies, declaring they would die in the last ditch. They were ready to open the dykes, an action which had the desired effect on the invaders by showing the French that no easy victory would be theirs when they came against Dutchmen.

Louise, in the King's confidence, assured him of the advisability of carrying out his obligations under the treaty. Charles had no intention of not carrying out this particular clause. He too badly needed the French gold which had been coming into his exchequer to offend Louis so flagrantly. Therefore Charles decided to send an expeditionary force of 6,000 men to aid the French.

Monmouth came to the King and asked if he might speak to him alone. Louise was with Charles, and Duke and King's mistress eyed each other with some suspicion. Each of them, favoured by the King, was jealous of Charles' regard for the other. As yet they were unsure of the other's power. There was one great cause for dissension between them. Louise was Catholic, Monmouth Protestant. Monmouth knew – not that he had realized this himself, but those such as Buckingham whose interest it was to persuade the King to legitimize him had told him this – that Louise was an ambitious woman whose hopes went beyond becoming the King's mistress. Therefore she was dangerous.

Monmouth did not believe for a moment that Charles would divorce Queen Catherine; but if the Queen died and Louise was able to fascinate the King enough, who knew what might happen? Louise was already pregnant, and she was delighted that this should be so. If she proved that she could give the King sons, as she was a lady of nobility there was a possibility that Charles might marry her. The thought that that child she now carried might one day take all that Monmouth so passionately longed for was unbearable to him.

Louise saw the King's natural son as an upstart. Monmouth's mother had been of little more consequence than the play-actress of whom the King was so fond. Little Charles Beauclerk had as much right to hope for the crown as this other bastard.

'You may speak as though to me alone,' said the King.

Monmouth glared at Louise who, proud of her breeding, was clever enough to know that the King was so enchanted with her because he could be sure of decorous handling of any situation. Louise was determined to impress upon Charles that her manners were impeccable.

Now she inclined her head graciously and said with quiet dignity: 'I see that my lord Duke would have speech with Your Majesty alone.'

Charles gave her a grateful look and she was rewarded. She was smiling as she left father and son together. She would in any case very quickly discover what Monmouth had to say.

Monmouth scowled after her.

'Well,' said Charles, 'having succeeded in dismissing the lady, I pray you tell me what is this secret matter.'

'I wish to go to Holland with the Army.'

'My son, I doubt not it can be arranged.'

'But as the King's son I wish to have a rank worthy of me.'

'Oh, Jemmy, your dignity rides ahead of your achievements.'

Monmouth's handsome face was flushed with anger. 'I am treated as a boy,' he protested.

Charles laid his hand on his son's shoulder. 'Would you remedy it, Jemmy? Then grow up.'

'There is only one post worthy of your son, Sir,' he said. 'Commander of the Army.'

'You may command it, Jemmy. In time . . . in time . . .'

'Now is the time, Father. Wartime is the time to command an army.'

''Tis true that at such times honours can be won. But disgrace can also be the lot of the commander who fails.'

'I should not fail, Father. Always I have longed to lead an army. I beg of you, give me this chance.'

He had thrown himself at Charles' feet, had taken his father's hand and was kissing it. The dark eyes with their curling black lashes were appealing. Lucy lived again in those eyes. Charles thought: Why is he not my legitimate son? What a happy state of affairs we should have if he were! Then he would have been trained with a difference; then he would not have been so eager always to maintain his dignity. We would have made a bonny King of Jemmy. Brother James could have continued to worship his graven images in peace, and none would have cared; there would not have been this enmity between them. What an unfortunate father I am! But how much more unfortunate is this pretty boy of mine!

'Get up, Jemmy,' he said.

'Your Majesty will grant me this one small request?'

'You underestimate it, Jemmy. 'Tis no small one.'

'Father, I swear you will be proud of me. I will lead your armies to victory.'

'You know the temper of our enemies. You have seen what fighters these Dutchmen are.'

'I know them, Father. They are an enemy worthy of the conquering.'

'Jemmy, a commander of a great army must have more care for his men than for himself.'

'I know it, and so would I have.'

'He must be ready to face all that he asks his men to face.'

'So would I face death to win my country's battles . . .'

'And glory for yourself.'

Monmouth hesitated for a while and then said grudgingly: 'Yes, Sir, and glory for myself.'

Charles laughed. 'I see new honesty in you, Jemmy, and it pleases me.'

'And this I ask you . . . ?'

'I'll think of it, Jemmy. I'll think of it . . .'

'Father, do not put me off with promises such as those you give to others. I am your son.'

'There are times when I think it had been better if you had been the son of another of your mother's lovers.'

'Nay!' cried Monmouth. 'I would rather be dead than own another father.'

'You love my crown too much, Jemmy.'

''Tis yourself, Sir.'

'And I had just complimented you on your honesty! Nay, do not look hurt. 'Tis natural to be dazzled by a crown. Do I not know it? I was dazzled all through the years of exile.'

'Father, you are turning me from my point. My uncle of York has the Navy. It is only right that I, your son, should have the Army.'

'Your uncle is the legitimate son of a King, Jemmy. There is a difference. Moreover he is many years older than you; he is possessed of great experience. He has proved himself to be a great sailor.'

'I will prove myself to be a great soldier.'

Charles was silent for a while. He had never seen Jemmy so fervently eager. It was a good sign; he at least was asking for some means of proving himself to be worthy of a crown. Previously he had thought mainly of possessing it.

'There is nothing I would like better,' said Charles, 'than to see you at the head of the Army.'

'Then you will . . . ?'

'I will do all that is possible.'

Monmouth had to accept that but he was not satisfied. He was fully aware of his father's easy promises.

But Charles had decided that he would do something. He discussed the matter with Louise and she agreed with him that the young Duke should be given some duties. Moreover if he were sent with the Army there was the possibility of his disgracing himself or even being killed. It seemed to Louise an excellent way of getting the troublesome young man out of the kingdom for a while.

Charles sent for Arlington.

'Let the Duke of Monmouth have the *care* of the Army,' he said, 'though not the command of it. Make him a Commander – in name only. Then we shall see how he shapes as a soldier.'

Arlington was very willing. He was eager not to be on bad terms with one so close to the King as the Duke was; he could see that Monmouth could save him a great deal of trouble without taking any of his power and profit from him.

So when the expeditionary force left England, Monmouth was with it.

And Charles, with fatherly devotion, waited to see how the young man would acquit himself.

* * *

The war continued. It was popular in spite of the fact that press-gangs roamed the streets and, invading the taverns and any place where men might be gathered together, carried off protesting recruits. There came news of the successes achieved by Louis with the aid of Monmouth. Charles was proud to hear that Jemmy was proving himself to be both brave and daring in battle, harrying the enemy with the same abandon with which he had attacked innocent citizens of London.

Several of the Court gallants, considering the victories of Monmouth, planned to take a band of volunteers abroad to join the Duke. Buckingham, restless, always eager to be at that spot where he could enjoy most limelight, begged the King to be allowed to go as Commander-in-Chief.

Charles talked of this with Louise, as he talked of most things.

Louise smiled; she had visions of the Duke, returning to London a conqueror. It seemed as if that other Duke, Monmouth, might do this. Two Protestant Dukes to ride through the streets as conquering heroes! It would not do.

Moreover she had a score of long standing to settle with Buckingham.

'Nay,' she said. 'Send not my lord Buckingham. He is as a weather-vane. He turns this way and that, according to the winds that blow. Has it occurred to you, Charles, that the noble Duke is the most unreliable man in your kingdom?'

'Oh, George is a good fellow at heart. Wild he may be at times, and there has been trouble between us, but I have never doubted that George is my friend. We grew up together, shared the same nursery. I have a fondness for George, as I have for brother James.'

'He has not Your Majesty's good heart. And forget not, he is a Protestant.'

Charles laughed. 'As are most of my subjects, and as I am . . . as yet.'

'As yet,' agreed Louise. 'But you will not remain so.'

The King was alert. He knew Louise spent occasional hours in the company of the French ambassador and he did not doubt that instructions for Louise would be continually arriving from Louis.

'I shall declare my conversion in my own time,' said Charles. 'That time is not yet.'

'Nay, but mayhap after the war has been satisfactorily concluded. . . .'

'Who shall say when that will be! These Dutch are stubborn fellows. And we were talking of George's desires to lead the volunteers . . .'

'I long for Your Majesty to be a true Catholic in thought and deed.'

'You share the desires of my dear brother Louis, which is mayhap not surprising since you are a subject of his.'

Louise lowered her eyes and said quickly: 'When one loves there is a wish for the loved one to share all things. This applies in particular to something so precious as Faith.'

'Faith is one of the most difficult possessions for an honest man to acquire,' said the King lightly. 'Shall I give George his wish? Shall we turn him into a gallant soldier?'

This was characteristic. Stop this talk of my promise to

declare myself a Catholic and you shall have your wish regarding Buckingham. Louise smiled gently.

'If my lord Buckingham left England, Lady Shrewsbury would miss him sorely,' she said. 'Is it kind to her ladyship to inflict such hardship upon her?'

The King laughed. She had given a witty turn to the discussion and that appealed to him.

He sent for Buckingham.

'You are not to lead the volunteers, George,' said Charles, 'for we could not bear to break Anna's heart. Therefore we will not deprive her of your company.'

Buckingham's face was purple with suppressed anger. Louise was delighted to see him thwarted. It mattered not to her that he did not realize she was the one who had prevented his attaining his desires. Louise enjoyed working in the dark. Her aim was to destroy the man who had slighted her, not merely to enjoy the transient pleasure of snapping her fingers in his face.

*   *   *

There came news of the battle of Southwold Bay which, while it proved indecisive, cost much in men's lives. Now the press-gangs were more rapacious, and mothers and wives were terrified when any able-bodied young man ventured into the streets. What was this war? it was asked. The English, sternly Protestant, were fighting Protestant Holland at the side of Catholic France. They were suffering great losses. For what reason? To spread the Catholic Faith across Europe. The King's brother, commanding the Navy, was almost certainly a Catholic. The King's favourite mistress was a Catholic. The King himself was so easygoing that he would adopt any faith if he were asked to do so prettily enough.

There were increasing scandals concerning the Court. That July, Barbara Castlemaine gave birth to a daughter whom she tried to foist on the King, but who everyone was sure was John Churchill's child. In spite of Barbara's importuning him, the King refused to acknowledge the girl.

Louise's son was born the same month. He was called

Charles. Louise insisted on the name, although the King mildly protested that this would be his fourth son named Charles, and he feared he might at times be wondering which was which.

'My Charles,' said Louise, 'will be different from all the others.'

She was certain of this, and she was furious when she saw the youngest of the King's Charleses – little Charles Beauclerk – amusing his father with his quaint manners which seemed to belong half to the Court and half to the slums of London.

Louise sighed over her Charles. He would be more handsome, more courtly than any. Only the greatest titles in the land would suit him.

'For I am different,' she told Charles. 'I am not your mistress. I am your wife, and Queen of England. That is how I see myself.'

'As long as no others see it so, that is a happy enough state of affairs,' said the King.

'I see no reason why you should not have two wives, Charles. Are you not Defender of the Faith?'

'Defender of the faithless sometimes,' said Charles lightly. He was thinking of Barbara, who, since he had refused to acknowledge John Churchill's child, was making demands on behalf of those whom he had already accepted. She wanted her Henry, who was nine years old, raised to the peerage without delay. Earl of Euston, she thought, should be the title for him; then he would be fit to marry my lord Arlington's daughter, a charming little heiress. Charles had reminded her that her eldest was already Earl of Southampton, and young George was Lord George Fitzroy.

'I was never a woman to favour one child more than another,' said Barbara virtuously. 'And what of poor dear Anne and Charlotte? I must ask you to allow them to bear the royal arms.'

Charles was beset on all sides.

Louise was less blatant in her demands than Barbara. But Charles knew that they would be no less insistent. Indeed, Louise's schemes went deeper than those of Barbara ever had. The Queen was ill, and Louise's small squinty eyes were alert.

It was not easy for her to hide her satisfaction as the Queen grew more languid. If the Queen died, Louise would get her little Charles legitimized at once through her marriage with the King. The little Breton girl, for whom it had been so difficult to find a place at the Court of France, would be the Queen of England.

Charles pointed out to Louise that he could not give her honours equal to those of Barbara's, for she was still a subject of the King of France, and therefore not in a position to accept English titles, so Louise lost no time in appealing to Louis. She must become a subject of the King of England, for England was now her home. Louis hesitated for a while. He wondered whether the granting of her request might mean the relinquishing of his spy. Louise assured him through the ambassador that, no matter what nationality she took, her allegiance would always be to her native land.

Louise's hopes were high. She believed she knew how to manage the King. She had shown him that she could bear his sons. She had all the graces which a queen should possess. And the Queen was sick. Once Louis had agreed to her naturalization she would be the possessor of noble titles, and with great titles went wealth. And she would never swerve from the main goal, which was to share the throne with Charles.

One of her minor irritations was the presence at Court of the orange-girl.

She suspected that the King often slipped away from her company to enjoy that of Nell Gwyn. He would declare he was tired, and retire to his apartments; but she knew that he slipped out of the Palace and climbed the garden wall to the house in Pall Mall.

Louise knew that she was often referred to as Squintabella because of the slight cast in her eye, and Weeping Willow because, when she wanted to make some request, she would do so sadly and with tears in her eyes. Both of these names had been given her by the saucy comedienne, who made no secret of the fact that she looked upon herself as Louise's rival. To Nell Squintabella was no different from Moll Davies or Moll Knight or any low wench to be outwitted for the attentions of the King.

She would call to Louise if their carriages passed:

'His Majesty is well, I rejoice to say. I never knew him in better form than he was last night.'

Louise would pretend not to hear.

All the same, Nell had her anxieties. Barbara's children flaunted their honours; it was said that the King was only waiting for Louise's naturalization to make her a Duchess; and meanwhile Nell remained plain Madam Gwyn with two little boys called Charles and James Beauclerk.

When the King called on her she indignantly asked him why others should find such favour in his sight while two of the most handsome boys in the kingdom were ignored.

Young Charles, now just about two years old, studied his father solemnly, and the older Charles felt uncomfortable under that steady stare.

He lifted the boy in his arms. Little Charles smiled cautiously. He was aware that his mother was angry, and he was not quite sure how he felt towards this man who was the cause of that anger. Little Charles looked forward to his father's visits, but his merry mother, who laughed and jigged and sang for him, was the most wonderful person in his world, and he was not going to love even his fascinating father if he made his mother unhappy.

'Are you not glad to see me, Charles Beauclerk?' asked Charles Stuart. 'Have you not a kiss for me?'

Little Charles looked at his mother.

'Tell him,' said Nell, 'that you are as niggardly with your kisses for him as he is lavish with the honours he showers on others.'

'Oh, Nelly, I have to be cautious, you know.'

'Your Majesty was ever cautious with Madam Castle-maine, I understand. Those whom you fondly imagine to be your children – though none else does – are greatly honoured. Yet for those who are undoubtedly your sons you have nothing but pleas of poverty.'

'All in good time,' said the harassed King. 'I tell you this boy shall have as fine a title as any.'

'Such a fine title that it is too fine for the human eye to perceive, I doubt not!'

'This is indeed Nelly in a rage. Fighting for her cub, eh?'

'Aye,' said Nelly. 'For yours too, my lord King.'

'I would have you understand that this is something I cannot do as yet. If you had been of gentle birth . . .'

'Like Prince Perkin's mother?'

Charles could not help smiling at her nickname for Jemmy. He said: 'Lucy died long ago, and Jemmy is a young man. There is plenty of time for this little Charles to grow up. Then I think he shall have as grand a title as any of his brothers.'

'Should his mother be so obliging as to die then,' cried Nell dramatically. 'Shall I jump in the river? Shall I run a sword through my body?'

Young Charles, vaguely understanding, set up a wail of misery.

'Hush, hush,' soothed the King. 'Your mother will not die. She but acts, my son.'

But young Charles would not be comforted. Nell snatched him from the King.

'Nay, nay, Charlie,' she said, ''twas but a game. Papa was right. There's naught to fret us but this: You are a Prince by your father's elevation, but you have a whore to your mother for your humiliation.'

Then she laughed and jigged about the room with him until he was laughing and the King was laughing too.

He was so delighted that he could not resist promising Nell that he would think what he could do for the boy. And he remembered too that her sister Rose suffered from her poverty, and he would grant her the pension of one hundred pounds a year for which Nell had asked him on her behalf.

As for Nell herself, she did him so much good even when she scolded for her son's sake that he would make her a countess, indeed he would.

'A countess,' said Nell, her eyes shining. 'That would please me mightily. Young Charlie and Jamie, having a

King for a father, should indeed have no less than a countess for a mother.'

The King wished he had been more discreet, but Nell went on: 'I could be Countess of Plymouth. It is a title which someone will have ere long. Why should it not be Nelly? Barbara has done as well.'

'All in good time,' said the King useasily.

But Nell was happy. Countess of Plymouth – and that meant honours for her boys. And why not? Indeed why not?

*   *   *

Nell did not become Countess of Plymouth. Boldly she had applied for the documents which would have staked her claim to this title, only to be told that these could not be supplied. The King told her that he had but been jesting when he had made the suggestion; he asked her to understand the state of the country. They were engaged in a war which was proving to be more costly than they had expected; the Dutch were determined not to lose their country; not content with opening the dykes and causing the utmost confusion to the invaders, young William of Orange, Stadholder and Captain-General, was a determined young man who seemed to be possessed of military genius.

'Who would have guessed this of that gauche young nephew of mine!' cried Charles. 'Never will I forget his visit to my Court. A little fellow, pale of visage, afraid to dance lest it should make him breathless on account of his weak lungs. He was glum and I had to do something to rouse him, so I had Buckingham ply him with wine, and what do you think he did? Fall into a torpor? Not he! His true character came to the surface then. Before he could be prevented he had smashed the windows of those apartments which housed the maids of honour, so eager was he to get at them. "Dear nephew," I said, "it is customary at my Court to *ask* the ladies' permission first. A dull English custom, you may doubtless think, but nevertheless one which I fear must be respected." Ah! I might have looked for greater depth in a young man who appeared so prim and whom his cups betrayed as a lecher. Then he was drunk with wine. Now he is drunk with ambition and the desire to save his country. Again we see that this nephew of mine can be a formidable young fellow indeed.'

'We talked of Plymouth, not of Orange,' Nell reminded him.

'Ah, we talked of Plymouth,' agreed the King. 'Then let me explain that the war is costly. The people dislike the press-gang and the taxes, both of which are necessary to maintain our Navy. When the people are angry they look for someone on whom to vent their anger. They are asked for taxes, so they say, "Let the King pay taxes, let him spend less money on his women, and mayhap that will serve to supply the Navy." Nelly, I can do nothing yet. I swear to you that I shall not forget these sons of ours. I swear I shall not forget you.'

'Swearing comes easy to a gentleman,' said Nell, 'and the King is the first gentleman in his country.'

'Nevertheless here is one promise I shall keep. You know my feelings for the boys. 'Twould be impossible not to love them. Nay, Nell, have patience. Come, make me laugh. For with the Dutch on one side and the French on the other and the Parliament at my heels I have need of light relief.'

Then Nell softened; for indeed she loved him, and she loved him for what he was, the kindest of men, though a maker of promises he could never keep; and she remembered too the words of my lord Rochester. She must soothe the King.

If she plagued him with her tongue, as Barbara had, she would drive him away. She, the little orange-girl and play-actress, had to be every bit as clever as the *grande dame* from France, who was her most formidable rival.

*   *   *

Charles was now very anxious. He did not believe that his subjects would continue to support the war. He knew that he must act. Louis had taken possession of large tracts of Holland and had even set up a Court at Utrecht; but

Charles saw very clearly that, once he had beaten the Dutch, Louis would look for fresh conquests and that he would try to make his pensioner Charles, his slave.

He therefore planned to make a separate peace with Holland, doing all in his power to make them accept terms which would not displease Louis.

William of Orange was, after all, his nephew, and it was wrong, he declared, that there should be strife between them.

He decided to send two emissaries to Holland to sound young William; and he chose Arlington, one of the most able members of the Cabal, and the ebullient Buckingham of whom he still had great hopes. Moreover he wished to compensate poor George for his churlish refusal to allow him to take the troop abroad as its commander-in-chief.

He felt sure that twenty-year-old William would be ready enough to make peace on his terms. He did not ask a great deal; he wanted recognition of England's claim to be saluted by all ships of any other nation; he wanted a subsidy of £200,000 for the cost of the war, he would ask for the control of the ports Sluys, Flushing, and Brill; a subsidy for herring fishing; new arrangements regarding English and Dutch trade in the East Indies; time enough for the English planters in Surinam to sell their effects and retire; and as William was his nephew he would help him to enjoy favourable conditions in his own country.

Buckingham, ever ready to undertake some new venture, was delighted to convey these terms to Orange.

He landed in Holland, the benign peacemaker, and he and Arlington were greeted with expressions of joy by the people, for these two were the Protestant members of the Cabal, and the Dutch had hopes that they were in truth on their side. Monmouth joined them, and all knew that the King's natural son was a staunch Protestant even if only because his uncle, the heir presumptive to the throne, was suspected of Catholicism.

But the Princess-Dowager, Amalia, who was William's grandmother and had always been a power in the land, did not trust the English emissaries, and she made this clear.

Arlington's exuberance was quelled; Monmouth was silent; but Buckingham sought to assure her of their good-will.

'We are good Hollanders, Your Highness,' he told the Princess.

She answered: 'We would not ask so much of you, my lord Duke. We would only expect you to be good Englishmen.'

'Ah!' cried the irrepressible Buckingham. 'We are not only good Englishmen but good Dutchmen. We do not use Holland like a mistress but like a wife.'

'Truly,' said the Princess, 'I think you use Holland just as you do your wife.'

Buckingham could say nothing to that; he knew that she had heard that when he brought his mistress, Anna Shrewsbury, to his wife, and that poor wronged lady had protested that there was not room for her and Anna under the same roof, he had replied: '*I* had thought that, Madam. Therefore I have ordered your carriage.'

He felt therefore that he could not hope for a quick capitulation by the Princess, so he sought out young William over whom he imagined he would have an easy victory.

He remembered that it was in his apartments that William had become drunk during his stay in London. He remembered how difficult it had been to make the young man drink, for his opinions of wine seemed to be the same as those he had of gambling and the play; but he had managed it, and what fun it had been to see the solemn young Hollander smash the windows to get at the maids of honour! No! He did not foresee any great difficulty with young William.

'I rejoice to see Your Highness is in such good health,' cried Buckingham, and went on to tell William that the King of France had seen the terms set out by the King of England and agreed that, as Holland was a conquered country, they were fair indeed. 'It is because of your uncle's fondness for his sister who was your mother. His Majesty remembers that he promised his sister to keep an eye upon you. It is for this reason that, even though your country is a conquered one, His Majesty of England will insist that you shall be acclaimed King of Holland.'

This young man was quite different from the youth who had tried to storm the dormitory of the maids of honour. His cold face was alight with determination to drive the conquerors from his ravaged country.

He said coolly: 'I prefer to remain Stadtholder, a condition which the States have bestowed upon me; and I – and all Dutchmen – do not consider we are a conquered people.'

'Your Highness would suffer not at all. You would be proclaimed King and accepted as such by France and England.'

'I believe myself bound in conscience and honour not to prefer my interests to my obligations.' The two Dutch statesmen who had accompanied him, Beverling and Van Beuning, nodded gravely, and William went on: 'The English should be our allies against the French. Our countries are of one religion. What good would England reap were Holland to be made merely a province of France, myself a puppet – as I should certainly be – the French King's puppet? Picture it, my friends. Holland ruled by Louis through me. What is Louis looking for? Conquest. Why, having secured my country he might conceivably turn to yours.'

'By God,' murmured Buckingham, 'there is truth in what His Highness says.' The volatile Duke was immediately swayed to the side of the Dutchman. He saw a Catholic menace over England. He wanted to make new terms there and then which would make England and Holland allies against the French.

'But His Highness forgets,' said Arlington, 'that his country is already conquered.'

'We in Holland do not accept that,' said William hastily.

'You have called a halt to Louis,' said Buckingham, 'by flooding your land. But with the winter frosts it may well be laid open.'

William said firmly: 'You do not know us Dutchmen. We are in great danger, but there is one way never to see our country lost and that is to die in the last dyke.'

There was no more to be said to such a fanatical idealist as this young Prince. It was vain to tell him that his ideals were part of his youth. William of Orange believed he had been selected to save his country.

Arlington, Buckingham, and Monmouth joined Louis' encampment at Heeswick. New terms were submitted to Dutch William; again they were rejected.

Then news came that the states of Brandenburg, Lüneburg, and Münster, determined to stem the conquests of Catholic Louis, were about to join William of Orange in his fight against the invaders. Louis, having found the war had brought him little gain at great expense, decided to withdraw, and marched his armies back to Paris, and there was nothing for the English diplomats to do but return to England.

Louise was contented.

Buckingham had failed miserably. He had wasted a great deal of money – the account he put in for his expenses amounted to four thousand seven hundred and fifty-four pounds and a penny – and he had brought nothing but ridicule to his country.

With Arlington he was accused by the people of England of making this disastrous war with the Dutch.

Louise was not the only one in England who had decided to bring about the downfall of the Duke.

*   *   *

Charles could at last be proud of Monmouth. Whatever he had done at home, he had acquitted himself well abroad.

Charles liked to hear the account of how his son had fought at Brussels Gate. Beside him had marched Captain John Churchill, and it had been hard to say which of the two young men – Churchill or Monmouth – had been the braver.

'Only one man could pass at a time,' Charles was told by one who had witnessed the action. 'We marched, swords in hand, to a barricade of the enemy's. There was Monsieur d'Artagnan with his musketeers, and very bravely these men carried themselves. Monsieur d'Artagnan did his best to persuade the Duke not to risk his life by attempting to lead his men through that passage, but my lord Duke would have none of his advice. Monsieur d'Artagnan was killed, but the Duke led his men with such bravery and such contempt for death as had rarely been seen. Many will tell Your Majesty that they never saw a braver or more brisk action.'

Jemmy came home, marching through the streets of London to Whitehall, and the people came out in their hundreds to see him pass.

He had grown older but no less handsome. There was a flush under his skin which made his eyes seem brighter and more lustrous. The women at the windows threw flowers to Monmouth, and the cry in the streets was: 'Brave Jemmy's come marching home.'

This was what he wanted. This acclaim. This glory.

And Charles saw with some anxiety that they were very ready to give it to this handsome boy – partly because he was handsome, partly because he was brave, but largely because the Duke of York was a Catholic and they had sworn that never again should a Catholic sit on the throne of England. Jemmy seemed more serious now, and Charles hoped his son might have realized it was better to jettison those dangerous ideas of his.

Jemmy had a new mistress – Eleanor Needham – who obsessed him. He was eager to found two packs of foxhounds at Charlton. His son – named Charles – was born, and the King himself with the Duke of York were godparents.

This was a happier way for a young man to conduct himself, thought the King. And the looks he bestowed on young Monmouth were very affectionate.

*   *   *

There were rumours throughout England that the Duke of York was about to remarry, and that the Princess chosen for him was Mary Beatrice, sister of the reigning Duke of Modena. The girl was young – she was fourteen – beautiful, and seemed capable of bearing children. There was one thing against her: She was a Catholic.

This marriage had caused Louise a great deal of anxiety. Since she had left for England, Louis had given her three main tasks. She was to work for an alliance with France against Holland, make Charles give a public profession of the Catholic Faith, and bring about a match between the Duke of York and a Princess of Louis' choice.

Louis' choice was the widow of the Duc de Guise, who was worthy, being Elizabeth d'Orléans before her marriage, second daughter of Gaston, brother of Louis XIII. Louise had stressed to Charles and James the advantage of this match, but she was clever enough to know that she must not work too openly for France.

The Duke of York, in remorse on the death of his wife, had given up his mistress, Arabella Churchill, but he had almost immediately formed an attachment with Catharine Sedley, Sir Charles Sedley's daughter. Catharine was no beauty but, as his brother had said, it was as though James' mistresses were chosen for him by his priest as a penance. But James had perversely decided that although he would forgo beauty in a mistress, he would not in a wife, and that Madame de Guise, no longer young and beautiful, would not suit him. So failing a French wife, Louise was ready to support the choice of Mary Beatrice since she was a Catholic, and a Catholic Duchess of York would certainly be no hindrance to one of her main duties – the bringing about of that open profession of the King's acceptance of the Catholic Faith.

Louise felt therefore that, although she had failed to persuade the King and his brother to take Madame de Guise, she had not altogether displeased the King of France by throwing in her support for the marriage with Mary Beatrice, particularly as there was a great deal of opposition throughout the country to a Catholic alliance for the Duke.

A new wave of anti-Catholic feeling was spreading over England. It was long since fires had burned at Smithfield, but there were people still living who remembered echoes of those days.

'No popery!' shouted the people in the streets.

Louise had as yet failed to obtain any promise from

Charles as to when he would declare himself a Catholic. He had, however, abolished certain laws against the Catholics. He wanted toleration in religious matters, he declared. But many of his subjects were demanding to know whether he had forgotten what happened to English sailors who fell into the hands of the Inquisition. Had he forgotten the diabolical plot to blow up the Houses of Parliament in his grandfather's reign? The King, it was said, was too easygoing; and that with his brother a Catholic, and the French mistress at his ear, he was ready to pay any price for peace.

'If the Pope gets his big toe into England,' declared Sir John Knight to the Commons, 'all his body will follow.'

The House of Commons then asked Charles to revoke his Declaration of Indulgence. To this Charles replied that he did not pretend to suspend any laws wherein the properties, rights, or liberties of his subjects were involved, or to alter anything in the doctrine or discipline of the Church of England, but only to take off the penalties inflicted on dissenters.

The Commons' reply was to resolve not to pass the money bill until there was a revocation of the Liberty of Consciences Act.

Then Charles, finding both Houses against him, had no alternative but to give his assent to the Test Act, which required all officers, civil or military, to receive the sacrament according to the rites of the Church of England, and to make a declaration against transubstantiation.

Having done this, he immediately sought out James.

'James,' he said, 'I fear now you must make a decision. I trust it will be the right one.'

''Tis this matter of the Test Act?' asked James. 'Is that what puts the furrow in your brow, brother?'

'Aye; and if you were possessed of good sense it need be neither in mine nor yours. James, you must take the sacrament according to the rites of the Church of England. You must take the Oath of Supremacy and declare against transubstantiation.'

'I could not do that,' said James.

'You will have to change your views,' said Charles grimly.

211

'A point of view is something we must have whether we want it or not.'

'Wise men keep such matters to themselves.'

'Men wise in spiritual matters would never enter a holy place and commit sacrilege.'

'James, you take yourself too seriously in some ways – not seriously enough in others. Listen to me, brother. I am past forty. I have not one legitimate child. You are my brother. Your daughters are heiresses to the throne. You are to marry a young girl ere long, and I doubt not she will give you sons. If you want to run your own foolish head into danger, what of their future?'

'No good ever grew out of evil,' said James firmly.

'James, have done with good and evil. Ponder on sound sense. You will come to Church with me tomorrow and by my side you will do all that is expected of you.'

James shook his head.

'They'll not accept you, James,' insisted Charles, 'they'll not have a Catholic heir.'

'If it is God's will that I lose the throne, then lose it I must. I choose between the approval of the people and that of God.'

'The approval of the people is a good thing for a King to have – and even more important for one who hopes to be King. But that is for the future. You have forgotten, my lord High Admiral, that all officers, under the Test Act which I have been forced to bring back, must receive the sacrament according to Church of England rites, make a declaration against transubstantiation, and take the Oath of Supremacy. Come, brother, can you not take me as head of your Church? Or must it be the Pope?'

'I can only do what my conscience bids me.'

'James, think of your future.'

'I do . . . my future in the life to come.'

'The life here on Earth could be a good one for you, James, were you to bring a little good sense to the living of it.'

'I would not perjure my soul for a hundred kingdoms.'

'And your soul is more important to you than your

daughters' future, than the future of the sons you may have with this new wife?'

'Mary and Anne have been brought up as Protestants. You asked for that concession and I gave it.'

'My solicitude was for your daughters, James. Has it ever occurred to you that if I die childless, and if you have no sons, one or both of those girls could be Queens of England?'

'It has, of course.'

'And you jeopardize their future for a whim!'

'A whim! You call a man's religion a whim?'

Charles sighed wearily. 'You could never give up your post as Commander of the Navy. You love the Navy. You have done much to make it what it is this day. You'd never give up that, James.'

'So they are demanding that?' said James bitterly.

'It has not been mentioned, but it is implied. Indeed how could it be otherwise? Indeed, James, I fear your enemies are at the bottom of the desire to have this revocation of the Declaration for the Liberty of Consciences.'

'Who would take my place?'

'Rupert.'

'Rupert! He is no great sailor.'

'The people would rather a Protestant leader who knew not how to lead their Navy, than a Catholic one who did. People are as fierce in their religion – one against the other – as they were in our grandfather's day.'

'You constantly remind me of our grandfather.'

'A great King, James. Remember his word, "Paris is worth a Mass."'

James opened his candid eyes very wide. 'But that was different, brother. He . . . a Huguenot . . . became a Catholic. He came out of error into truth.'

Charles gave his brother his melancholy smile. He knew that he had lost his Lord High Admiral.

*   *   *

It was a misty November day when the royal barges sailed down the Thames to meet James and his new bride recently come from Dover. The people crowded the banks of the river to see the meeting between the royal barges and those which were bringing the bridal party to London. There was still a great deal of murmuring about this marriage. A strong body of opinion – set up by Anthony Ashley Cooper, Earl of Shaftesbury – had declared firmly against it. Charles had been petitioned by this party in the Commons to send to Paris at once and stop the Princess from coming to England to consummate her marriage.

'I could not in honour dissolve a marriage which has been solemnly executed,' said Charles.

In a fury of indignation the Commons asked the King to appoint a day of fasting, that God might be asked to avert the dangers with which the nation was threatened.

'I could not withhold my permission for you gentlemen to fast as long as you wish,' was the King's reply.

It was unfortunate that the anniversary of the Gunpowder Plot should have fallen at this time. When the feeling against Catholicism ran high, the ceremony of burning Guy Fawkes was carried out with greater zest than usual, and that year Guy Fawkes' Day was watched with great anxiety by the King and his brother. They feared that the burning of the effigies of Guy Fawkes, the Pope, and the devil would develop into rioting.

Arlington suggested then, since the King would not prevent the departure of the Princess of Modena from Paris, he might insist that, after his marriage, James and his new bride should retire from the Court and settle some distance from London, where he might enjoy the life of a country gentleman.

'Your suggestions interest me,' said the King. 'But the first is incompatible with my honour, and the second would be an indignity to my brother.'

So Mary Beatrice of Modena had with regret left the shores of France where she had been treated with great kindness by many people in high places.

The young girl was terrified of her new husband. He was forty, and that seemed a great age. She had implored her aunt to marry the Duke of York, instead of her; she would be quite happy, she had declared, to go into a convent; any life would seem better to her than that which included marriage to a man, old enough to be her father, who had a reputation for keeping as many mistresses as his brother.

She was a lovely child; she resembled her mother who had been Laura Martinozzi, a niece of Cardinal Mazarin, and, like all the ladies of that family, noted for her beauty. But to be fourteen and torn from her home to start life in a new country with a man who seemed so old, was a terrifying experience, and she was too young not to show her repugnance.

James was fully aware of what his young bride's feelings might be and was determined to do all in his power to put her at ease.

He was on the shore at Dover to greet her in person, and he was touched when he saw her, for her youth reminded him of his own daughter Mary, who was not much younger than this child who had left her home and all she loved to come to a new country to be his wife. He took her into his arms and embraced her warmly. But Mary Beatrice had taken one horrified look at her husband and burst into tears.

James was not angry; he could only find it in his kindly nature to be sorry for her. He assured her that although he was old and feared he must seem mighty ugly to one so young and fresh and beautiful, she had nought to fear, as it would be his delight to love and honour her all the days of their lives.

He was fervently wishing that he had Charles' easy manner, which he was sure would quickly have put the child at ease.

But James' gaucheries were balanced by his gentle kindness, and he decided that until the child had grown accustomed to his company he would not force himself upon her.

'I would not add to your fears,' he soothed her. 'I think of my little Mary and Anne.'

They set out from Dover, and the bride was glad that her mother and the Prince Rinaldo d'Esté travelled with them. They journeyed by slow stages to Canterbury, Rochester, and Gravesend, and the people came out of their houses to watch. The little girl charmed them so much that they were astonished to think that she might bring evil into their country.

At Gravesend they embarked and sailed to meet the royal barges. When they met these James took his bride to meet the King.

Charles was surrounded by the ladies and gentlemen of the Court. The Queen was there, ready to be tender and kind, remembering her own coming into this land to marry the most fascinating of kings only to discover that he was far from faultless, and to learn that it was impossible to fall out of love with him. Louise was beside the King, less flamboyantly dressed than most, yet seeming to be more richly clad; less heavily jewelled so that each jewel which adorned her person seemed to glow with a special lustre. It was this lady whom Mary Beatrice took to be the Queen. Louise held herself like a queen, thought of herself as a queen. She had recently become naturalized and this meant that she had been able to accept the titles and estates with which the King had been pleased to endow her. She had now several resounding titles – Baroness Petersfield, Countess of Fareham and Duchess of Portsmouth. She was a lady of the Queen's bedchamber. She was, in all but name, the Queen of England. Nor did she despair of being entirely so. Her small eyes rested often on the pallid face of the Queen. She hoped the lady would not live long, for indeed what joy could there be in life for one such as Catherine of Braganza who could not adapt herself to her husband's Court? She could surely have no great wish to live. The Queen's death was what Louise ardently desired, for she knew the King would never divorce his wife. Louise had discovered something about Charles. Easygoing as he was, ready to make promises to all, once he made up his mind that he would take a firm stand on some point, he was the most obstinate man in the world. She must be continually grateful for his indulgence, but infatuated as she had managed to keep him, she did not forget that all others had a share in that indulgence – Catherine, the Queen, no less than any other. And if the King's desire was fixed on Louise, his pity went to Catherine his wife.

Mary Beatrice was aware of other ladies and gentlemen. She noticed beautiful Anna Shrewsbury with the Duke of Buckingham, and Lord Rochester, that handsomest of all courtiers, although debauchery was beginning to mar his good looks; and close to him a lively and pretty creature with chestnut curls and bright tawny, mischievous eyes, most flamboyantly dressed, and attracting the attention of everyone. Even the King's eyes strayed often towards her. Her name, it seemed, was Madam Gwyn. There were gentlemen whose names she had heard mentioned with that of the King: Earl of Carbery, Earl of Dorset, Sir George Etherege, Earl of Sheffield, Sir Charles Sedley, Sir Carr Scrope.

Then Mary Beatrice was aware of a pair of dark eyes watching her intently. She fell to her knees and she was raised by the King's elegant hands, and he, looking into her face, saw the too-brilliant eyes which suggested tears, noted the trembling lips.

'Why,' he said in that gentlest and most musical of voices, 'my little sister. I am mighty glad to see you here. You and I shall be friends.'

Mary Beatrice put her hands in his. She did not care that he was the King; she only knew that his words, his smile, his infinite charm made her feel happy and no longer afraid.

The King kept a hold on her hand, and she felt that while he held it thus she could be almost pleased that she had come.

He kept her beside him during the festivities. He implied that he would be her special friend until she felt quite at home in her new country. He told her that she reminded him of her kinswoman, Hortense Mancini – one of the most beautiful women he had ever seen in the whole of his life. He had wanted to marry Hortense, but her uncle had put his foot down. 'In those days I was a wandering exile. No good match at all. But I never forgot beautiful Hortense, and you remind me of her . . . with pleasure . . . with the utmost pleasure.'

She was beside him as they sailed to Whitehall. She heard the people acclaim him from the banks, and she knew that they all loved him, that they felt that irresistible charm even as she did.

He pointed out his Palace of Whitehall whither they were bound.

She was relieved to stand beside him. Her mother was delighted to see the King's easy affability towards her daughter, delighted to see the lightening of her daughter's spirits.

The courtiers watched them.

'Am I mistaken?' drawled Rochester. 'Is it Charles who is bridegroom or is it James?'

'His Majesty but puts the child at ease,' said Nell.

'James has tried to do so,' said Buckingham, 'without success. Alas, poor James! It strikes me that in all things our gracious sovereign could, if he would; and his brother would, if he could.'

Louise had strolled towards them. She glanced with some amusement at Nell's brilliantly coloured gown.

Nell's eyes smouldered. It was galling to be reminded, every time she saw the woman, that she was now the Duchess of Portsmouth while her young Charles and James were merely surnamed Beauclerk and she was plain Madam Gwyn. The Duchess thought Nell scarcely worthy of notice. Yet she was kindly condescending.

'You are grown rich, it would seem by your dress,' she said lightly. 'You look fine enough to be a queen.'

Nell cried: 'You are entirely right, Madam. And I am whore enough to be a duchess.'

The Duchess passed on; the laughter of Nell, Buckingham, and Rochester followed her.

Louise's face betrayed nothing. She was thinking that Rochester was a fool, continually banished from Court on account of his scurrilous attacks on all, including the King; his debauchery would soon carry him to the grave; there was no need to think of him. As for the orange-girl, let her remain – buffoon that she was. Moreover, the King delighted in her and would be stubborn if it were suggested she be removed; Nell Gwyn's attack was with words, an art in which Louise could not compete with her. Those quips never rose easily to Louise's lips even in her own language. But there was one who should soon feel the full weight of her displeasure. My lord Buckingham should not have long to flaunt his power if she could help it.

*　　*　　*

The Duke of Monmouth was delighted with the marriage of the Duke of York.

'There is nothing he could have done,' he told his cronies, 'which could have pleased me more. The people are incensed. And do you blame them? My uncle is a fool if he thinks he can bring popery into England.'

He was told that Ross, his old governor, wished to see him; and when Ross was admitted to him it was clear that the fellow had something to say which was for his ear alone.

Monmouth lost no time in taking the man to a place where they could speak privately. Ross was looking at him with that admiration which Monmouth was accustomed to see in many eyes.

'For this moment,' said Ross, 'I would but ask to look at Your Grace. I remember when you were a little fellow – the brightest, handsomest little fellow that ever came under my charge. It does me good to see Your Grace enjoying such fine health.'

Monmouth was indulgent. He loved praise. 'Pray continue,' he said.

'There is but one thing which irks me concerning Your Grace.'

'The bend sinister?' Monmouth prompted.

''Tis so. What a King you would make! How those people down there would line the streets and cheer, if only you were James, Prince of Wales, instead of James, Duke of Monmouth.'

'Just a ceremony . . . just a signature on a document . . .' muttered Monmouth.

'And for that a country loses the best King it could ever have.'

'You did not come merely to tell me this, Ross.'

'Nay, my lord. When I watched you on your horse or learning how to use your sword, I used to let myself imagine that one day the King would acknowledge you as his legitimate son. I used to see it all so clearly . . . His Majesty sending for you when you were a year or so older . . . and that came true. His Majesty bearing great love for you . . . and that came true also. His Majesty declaring that in truth he had married your mother and that you would inherit the crown.'

'And that did not come true,' said Monmouth bitterly.

'It might yet . . . my lord.'

'How so?'

'I feel in my heart that there *was* a ceremony between your father and Lucy Walter.'

'My father says there was not, and I verily believe that since the Portuguese woman is barren he would most happily acknowledge me as his son if his conscience would let him.'

'The consciences of kings often serve expediency . . . saving your royal presence.'

'You mean my father would deny a marriage which had taken place. But why so?'

'Why so, my lord? Your mother was . . . again I crave pardon . . . a woman who took many lovers. She was not of state to marry with a king. Your father was young at the time – but eighteen – and young men of eighteen commit their indiscretions. She who was worthy to be a wife to an exiled prince, might not be owned by a reigning king.'

'You know something, Ross. You are suggesting that my father was married to my mother.'

'I asked Cosin, Bishop of Durham, to give me the marriage lines.' Ross smiled slyly. 'He could have had them. He was chaplain at the Louvre for those who belonged to the Church of England at the time of the association.'

'Ross, you are a good fellow. What says he?'

'He insisted that there were no marriage lines. He asked me indignantly if I were suggesting that he should forge them.'

'And . . . now he has promised to produce them?'

'He is dead.'

'Then what good is he?'

Ross smiled slowly. 'Friends of mine – and yours – are ready to swear that, as he died, he murmured of a black box which contained marriage lines proving that Lucy Walter was the wife of your father.'

'Ross, you are the best friend a man ever had . . .'

'I looked on you as my son when I became your governor in the house of my lord Croft. There is nothing I would not do to give you your heart's desire.'

'I thank you, Ross; I thank you. But my father lives . . . What will he say of this . . . black box?'

Ross was silent for a while; then he said: 'The King, your father, loves you. The country does not want a Catholic King. The Duke of York, in giving up his post as Lord High Admiral, has exposed himself as a Papist. Now there is this marriage. The King loves peace . . . He loves peace more than truth. He loves you. He loves all his children, but everyone knows that his favourite is his eldest son. It may be that he – and I, feeling as a father towards you, understand his feelings – would accept this tale of the black box for love of you and for love of peace.'

Monmouth embraced his old governor.

'Man,' he said, 'you are my good friend. Never shall I forget it.'

Ross fell on his knees and kissed the Duke's hands.

'Long live the Prince of Wales!' he said.

Monmouth did not speak; his dark eyes glittered; he could hear the shouts of the people, feel the crown on his head.

*   *   *

Rumour was raging through London as fiercely as, a few years before, the fire had raged – and, said some, as dangerously.

The King was married to Lucy Walter. The Bishop of Durham died speaking of a black box . . . a black box which contained the fateful papers, the papers which would one day place the crown on the head of the Protestant Duke of Monmouth.

'But where is the black box?' asked some. 'Will it not be necessary to produce it?'

'It is in the interest of many to keep it hidden. The Duke of York's men will swear that it has no existence.'

The country was Protestant and so hated the idea of a Catholic King. As for the wildness of young Monmouth, they would be ready to forget that. It was remembered only that he was young, handsome, and had acquitted himself with valour in the wars, that he was a Protestant and son of King Charles.

Monmouth awaited his father's reactions. He could not be sure what went on behind those brooding, cynical, and often melancholy eyes.

He had asked to be formally acknowledged as the head of the Army.

Meeting his uncle, he told him so. James, unable to hide his feelings concerning this nephew of his, knowing of the rumours which were abroad, gruffly told him that he thought he lacked the experience for the post.

'It could not go to you, my lord,' said Monmouth with a smile. 'You are disqualified under the Test Act. You know that all officers of the military services or civil ones must conform to the rites of the Church of England.'

'I know this well,' said James. 'But your present position gives you as much power as you need.'

'I am sorry I have not your friendship and support,' Monmouth retorted sullenly.

James flushed hotly. 'Indeed you are not sorry.'

Then he left his nephew.

Monmouth sent for his servant, Vernon.

'Vernon,' he said, 'go to the clerks who are drawing up the documents which will proclaim me head of the Army. I have seen how these will be worded. The title of head of the armed forces is to go to The King's *natural* son. Vernon, I want you to tell the clerks that you have had orders to scratch out the word "natural" if it has been already put in; and if the papers are not completed let it be that the phrase reads: "The King's son, James, Duke of Monmouth."'

Monmouth fancied that Vernon's bow was a little more respectful than usual. Vernon believed he was in the presence of the heir to the throne.

* * *

James, Duke of York, was with his brother when the papers were put before the King. James took them from the messenger and looked sadly at them.

Charles was carelessly fond where his emotions were involved. Many believed, though, that Monmouth would do well in the Army. He had the presence, the confidence for it. Moreover his handsome looks and likeness to the King made people fond of him.

He spread the papers out on a table.

'Your signature is wanted here, Charles,' he said.

Charles sat down and, as his eyes ran over the papers, the blood rushed into James' head.

He pointed to an erasure. The word 'natural' had been removed.

'Brother!' said James, his face stricken. 'What means this?'

Charles stared at the paper in astonishment.

'It is so then,' said James. 'This talk of the black box is no rumour. You admit that a marriage took place between you and Lucy Walter?'

'There is no truth in that rumour,' said Charles. He called the man who had brought it to the chamber.

'Who commanded that that word should be erased?' he asked.

'It was Vernon, the Duke of Monmouth's man, Your Majesty.'

'I pray you bring me a knife,' said Charles, and when it was brought he cut the paper into several pieces.

'It will have to be rewritten,' he said. 'When that is done, I shall sign the paper giving my *natural* son the command of the Army.'

Later that day, when he was surrounded by courtiers,

ladies, and men from the Parliament, he said in a loud voice: 'There have been rumours afoot of late which displease me. There are some who talk of a mysterious black box. I have never seen such a black box and I do not believe it exists outside the imagination of some people. What is more important, I have never seen what that box is reputed to contain, and I know – who could know better? – that these documents never were in existence. The Duke of Monmouth is my very dear son, but he is my natural son. I say here and now that I never married his mother. I would rather see my dear son – my bastard son, Monmouth – hanged at Tyburn than I would give support to the lie which says he is my legitimate son.'

There was silence throughout the hall.

Monmouth's face was black with rage. But the King was smiling as he signed for the musicians to begin to play.

* * *

Louise, walking in the gardens of Whitehall Palace, came upon the newly created Earl of Danby and graciously detained him. She had decided that the two men who could be of most use to her were Danby and Arlington. She had been eager to bring about the disgrace of Buckingham ever since he had humiliated her at Dieppe, but her nature was a cold one and she cared more for consolidating her position at Court and amassing wealth than for revenge.

Danby, it seemed to her, must be her ally if she were to enrich herself as she intended to, for Danby was a wizard with finance and it was into his hands that the King would place the exchequer.

Much as Louise delighted in her title of Duchess, there was one thing that was more important than any English title. It was at the French Court that she had suffered her deep humiliation, and one of her most cherished dreams was that one day she would return there to receive all that respect which had been denied her in the past. She would rather have a *tabouret* at the Court of Versailles, on which she would be permitted to sit in the presence of the Queen, than any English honours. The ducal fief of Aubigny had reverted to the crown on the death of the Duke of Richmond, on whose family it had been bestowed by a King of France as far back as the early part of the fifteenth century. Louise's acquisitive mind had already decided that she must be granted the title of Duchesse d'Aubigny – for with it went the *tabouret* – and she would need Charles' help to plead with Louis for the title; and if the pleas of a man who was rising, as Danby surely would, were added to that of the King, it would be helpful, for Louis would be pleased to grant favours to those who held influential positions at the English Court.

Arlington was ready to turn against Buckingham. Together they had supported the Dutch war, and together they had sought to make peace. The country was saying that both these activities had been conducted with incompetence and inefficiency. Therefore a man such as Arlington, to save himself, would be ready to throw the larger share of blame on his companion in misfortune. Buckingham had already done his best to weaken Arlington's position by trying to persuade the King not to proceed with the proposed marriage between Arlington's girl, Isabella, and Barbara's son, the Duke of Grafton. He had held out a better match as bait – the Percy heiress – and Arlington was furious at Buckingham's attempt to spoil the linking of his family with the royal one.

But Louise felt that Danby was the man who could help her most. He was quiet, a man who would be happy to work in secret, and he had come to his present place by quiet determination, working by devious ways towards his goal. If he lacked altogether the brilliance of Buckingham, he also lacked the Duke's folly which was ready to trip him at every step. As Sir Thomas Osborne, Danby had come to London when he was made member for York. He had first come to notice when he was appointed commissioner for examining public accounts some seven years before. Since then his rise had been rapid. He had been Treasurer of the Navy, Privy Councillor, and, with the reinstatement of the Test Act and the banishment of Clifford, he had become Lord High Treasurer.

Louise believed that he would rise to even greater power. She feared him. He founded his policy, she had heard, on the Protestant interest and thus he was opposed to the French. This meant that she and he must necessarily be in opposite camps. Yet at this point their interests were similar. Buckingham was to blame for the alliance with France and the Dutch war. Buckingham was even suspected of having Catholic interests, for he had received many costly presents from Louis Quatorze, and all knew that Louis did not give his presents for nothing.

Therefore she and Danby, who it would seem must follow diametrically different courses, could meet in one desire: to see the downfall of Buckingham. And Louise, ever fearful that she would fail to mould the King of England in the manner desired by the King of France, was ready to go to great lengths to secure the friendship of men whose animosity could ruin her. Her great dread was that she should be sent back to France without her *tabouret* – back to humiliation and obscurity.

'I trust I see you well, my lord Treasurer,' said Louise.

'As I trust I see Your Grace.'

Louise took a step nearer to him and lifted her eyes to his face. 'You have heard the sad news of your predecessor?'

'My lord Clifford?'

Louise nodded. 'He has grieved greatly since he resigned his post in accordance with the Test Act. He died – some say by his own hand.'

Danby caught his breath. It was into Clifford's shoes that he had stepped. Was she warning him that a man held a high position one day and was brought low the next? He was bewildered. He could not believe that he could ally himself with the King's Catholic mistress. Was she suggesting this?

She smiled charmingly, and said in her quaint English: 'There are disagreements between us, my lord Treasurer, but as we are both near the King, should we allow these to make us the enemies?'

'I should be sad if I thought I were Your Grace's enemy,' said Danby.

Louise laid her hand very briefly on his sleeve. It was almost a coquettish gesture. 'Then from now on I shall hope that we are friends? Please to call on me when you have the wish.'

Danby bowed and Louise passed on.

* * *

Shaftesbury had been dismissed. Clifford was dead. The Commons declared that the remaining members of the Cabal – Lauderdale, Arlington, and Buckingham – were a triumvirate of iniquity.

The result of the Cabal's administration was an unchristian war with Holland and an imprudent league with France. Protestant England had put herself on the side of Catholic France against a country which, entirely Protestant, should have been an ally. The King had been traitor-ously ensnared by pernicious practices.

Charles remained aloof. He could not disclose the clauses of the secret Treaty of Dover; he could not come to the rescue of his politicians by explaining that it had been necessary at one time to accept bribes from France in order to save England from bankruptcy. That clause in the treaty, referring to his conversion to Catholicism to be proclaimed at an appropriate moment, meant that it must never be disclosed while he lived.

If he attempted to defend his ministers, he could plunge his country into disaster.

He could only look on with the melancholy smile which came to his lips at times such as these, and await results. He could not regret the replacement of Clifford by Danby; Danby, juggling with figures, was beginning to balance accounts as they never had been balanced before.

So Lauderdale was indicted; Arlington followed; and Buckingham's turn came.

He was called to defend himself, which he did in person and, as ever being unable to control his tongue, answered questions put to him in his jaunty, witty, and fearless way. He spoke long of the misfortunes which had occurred during his administration of the Cabal, but declared that he felt it his duty to remind the assembly that this was not so much due to the administration as to those in authority over it.

He could not resist adding: 'I can hunt the hare with a pack of hounds, gentlemen, but not with a brace of lobsters.'

As this last epithet was flung at the King and the Duke of York, it was hardly likely that the reckless Buckingham would receive much sympathy in the only quarter from which at this time he could have hoped for it. Yet it was typical of the Duke that he would fling away years of ambition and all his bright hopes for the future for the sake of giving his tongue full play.

The result of this investigation was that Buckingham was dismissed, and the people clamoured for peace with Holland. The clever young Prince of Holland asked for the hand of Mary, eldest daughter of the Duke of York, who, should the King and his brother fail to produce further offspring, would one day inherit the crown.

Louise was flung into a panic by this suggestion. She knew that she must exert all her influence with Charles to have it quashed. Louis would consider she had indeed failed in her duty if there was a marriage between Holland and England.

She talked to Charles. He was non-committal. Easygoing as he always was, he was quick to sense the temper of the people. And the dissatisfaction with the Cabal had given rise to much murmuring among the people who knew that the King was involved, even as were his ministers. Charles wished to please those he favoured, but not to the extent of angering his people against him.

Terrified that she would cease to find favour with Charles, picturing Louis' indifference if she returned humiliated to France, Louise turned in panic to Danby. She was ready to do anything – just anything – for a strong man who would help her hold her position at this difficult time.

*   *   *

Buckingham's health collapsed rapidly. He suffered, said his doctors, more from fever of the mind than of the body.

Louise, watching, knew that the Duke had too many enemies for her to worry greatly about bringing about his downfall. Moreover she had more immediate troubles of her own.

A few days after he had suffered his ordeal and while he was a very sick man, the guardians of the fifteen-year-old son of Anna Shrewsbury arranged that the boy should bring a charge against Buckingham of the murder of his father and the public debauchery of his mother.

As the death of Shrewsbury had occurred six years before, and almost every man at Court was living in open adultery, this was clearly yet another of his enemies' moves to destroy the Duke.

He was aware that temporarily he was a defeated man, and he obtained absolution from the House of Lords only on paying a heavy fine, and promising never to cohabit with Lady Shrewsbury again.

The greatest of his troubles then was the knowledge that, now he was a defeated man, Anna Shrewsbury was finished with him. She had been faithful to him for many years, and had even been known as the Duchess of Buckingham, while Buckingham's wife had been called the Dowager-Duchess. Their relationship had seemed as though it would go on for ever.

Now he knew that she too had deserted him – for had she not done so, nothing would have kept her away from him nor him from her – he was as low as he had ever been. Charles, no doubt finding it impossible to forgive the reckless Duke for referring to him and his brother publicly as lobsters, deprived him of the Mastership of the Horse. There was one waiting to receive it whose handsome looks would well become it: the Duke of Monmouth.

So Buckingham retired from Court. But his exuberant spirits would not let him stay long in exile. Little Lord Shaftesbury (who as Ashley had been a member of the Cabal and was now the leading light of the Opposition and secretly intriguing to legitimize Monmouth) made friendly advances; and Buckingham was already planning his return.

Louise had not betrayed by one glance how delighted she was in the Duke's misfortune.

But Nell knew it – although she knew nothing of politics – and decided that, since Louise was the enemy of the fallen Buckingham, she would be his friend.

SEVEN

Nell was a little sad at the beginning of that year. She had seen the disgrace of my lord Buckingham who had seemed such a brilliant ornament at the Court, and although she never really gave her mind to politics, she knew that even if Louise had not brought this about, she had had a hand in it. She was aware too of the growing friendship between the Lord Treasurer, the Earl of Danby, and Louise. Nell firmly believed that, while these two held their present positions, she would remain Madam Gwyn and never become a countess; and, what was more important, her two little boys would never be anything but Charles and James Beauclerk.

It was true that recently Charles had given her five hundred pounds for new hangings in her house, but even in this there was some cause for sadness. Charles was graciously apologizing for spending so little time with her.

She was not poor, but she realized that, compared with the establishments of Barbara in her heyday and Louise at present, her home was a comparatively humble one. Nell had never learned thrift, and money slipped through her hands. She was over-generous and never refused loans or alms. She had eight servants to feed, as well as her mother, herself, and her two sons. Rose's husband, Captain Cassels, had been killed while fighting with his regiment in Holland, and there was Rose to help along.

She had her own Sedan chair, and of course she must have her French coach; six horses were needed to draw it, and bills came in for oats and hay. She liked to have people around her and was a lavish hostess.

Nell's mother needed medicines from the apothecaries for her constant complaints, and Nell was continually paying for ointments and cordials, plague-water and clysters. The children were in need of sugar candy, pectoral syrup, and plasters. Charles was a healthy little boy; James was almost as healthy; but they suffered from the usual childish ailments and Nell was determined that they were both going to live to hold as great titles as any held by Louise's or Barbara's brats.

Nell had always loved the theatre; she attended frequently, and the King's mistress must have one of the best seats. She was a gambler at heart and she enjoyed a flutter either on horses or gamecocks. Mr Groundes, her steward, remonstrated with her but, as Nell said: 'If I cannot pay for my fancies, then must the bills be passed on to Mr Chaffinch.'

She enjoyed riding forth in her coach, stopping at the Exchange to examine the goods for sale, her footman following her ready to carry her purchases. She would only buy the best for Charles and James. 'Dukes' skins they were going to be from the start,' she would declare.

But as she entertained her friends and was jolted forth in her coach, she was a little sad. It was a long time since the King had visited her, and although when they met he was friendly and always had a smile and joke for Nelly, his nights were spent with the Frenchwoman. It was almost as though he, like Louise, looked on that mock marriage as a true one and felt the need to treat it as such.

Lord Rochester, returned to Court after one of his many exiles from it, shook his head sadly.

''Tis a pity,' he said, 'that His Majesty is so enamoured of the Frenchwoman.'

'There are times when I think Charles bewitched,' said Nell crossly. 'When the woman isn't squinting she is weeping, and when she's doing both she's spying for France. What can he find so alluring in a weeping, squinting spy?'

'Novelty in the squint, mayhap, for though he has witnessed tears and spies in plenty, I have never before seen His Majesty enamoured of a squint.'

When he wandered through the Palace of Whitehall he thought of Nell who so sadly missed the King, and paused outside the door of that chamber occupied by Louise to stick on it one of those couplets for which he was renowned.

'*Within this place a bed's appointed*
For a French bitch and God's anointed.'

Louise was furious, as she always was at any affront to her
dignity, and as there was no doubt of the author of the
couplet she demanded that Rochester be once more banished from Court.

The King agreed that the noble Lord took liberties, and
that he should be dismissed. So Rochester's efforts to attack
Nell's enemy gained her nothing and lost her the presence
of one who – although in his scurrilous verses he did not
spare her – she regarded as her friend.

Moll Davies now had a daughter, but the King's visits
to her were rarer than those he paid Nell.

Louise continued to hold the King's attention. Louise was
clever and she was cautious. She had made several attempts
to turn the King from the suggested Dutch marriage, but
she was quick to realize that it would have been unwise to
be too insistent. Her strength lay in dignity; she must never
rant as Barbara had; she must never be vulgar as Nell was.
Moreover she had studied Queen Catherine, and from the
appearance of the Queen she judged that she would not live
long. If she could take the Queen's place Louise need never
fear Louis again. The crown of England was preferable
even to a *tabouret* at the Court of Versailles.

Nell Gwyn irritated her, but she would not lower her
dignity by showing jealousy of a girl who had sold oranges
at the King's Theatre.

In spite of the shadow cast by the proposed Dutch
marriage, Louise had never been feeling more sure of herself. Then, suddenly, a terrible misfortune befell her.

* * *

Nell first heard of it through Rochester. Back from exile
in the country, where the King never allowed him to stay
for long, he called on Nell and, settling himself in one of
the elaborate chairs, stretched his legs and smiling at his
toes, said: 'Nell, His Majesty is sick.'

Nell stood up in alarm, but Rochester waved a white

hand. 'I pray you calm yourself. 'Tis naught but the pox.
And he hath taken it lightly. 'Twas some slut brought to
him by Chaffinch. The royal body will be submitted to the
usual treatment. Rejoice in this, Nell. Out of evil cometh
good. Charles has not visited you of late. Rejoice, I say. For
although His Majesty hath taken the sickness but slightly,
the French bitch hath it far worse. 'Twill be many months
before she will share a bed with God's anointed.'

Nell laughed aloud, suddenly remembering the jalap she
had served to Moll Davies.

'You are sure of this?' she asked.

'I swear it. Our lady Duchess is in a fury. She strides up
and down her apartment, wailing in her own language.
Now is the time for the lucky Mrs Nelly to leap into her
shoes.'

'And Charles?'

'A week or two, the usual course of pills, and all will be
well. He was born healthy and, no matter to what he subjects the royal person, it remains healthy. Nelly, the enemy
is *hors de combat*. Forget it not! Prepare to reign supreme. I
hear that Louis Quatorze has sent her a diamond and pearl
necklace – just to keep her spirits up. I heard too that she is
to travel to Bath and Tunbridge Wells in the hope of a
speedy return to health. Be ready to welcome His Majesty
back to good health, sweet Nell. And remember what I tell
you. Administer to His Majesty's comfort. Let him see that
his merry Nell contributes more to his peace and enjoyment
than Madame Squintabella. And then . . . only then . . .
remind him of your brats.'

'I will remember to remind him,' said Nell grimly.

'Do not, dear Nelly, attempt to win the last battle first.
'Tis not the way to victory.'

Then began a joyous spring and summer for Nell. She
plunged right into the gaiety of the Court. The King was
well again – not so Louise; and her frequent visits to Bath
and Tunbridge Wells did little to relieve her. Her only
consolation was to put on the magnificent necklace sent her
by Louis – a reminder that she must get well quickly for
there was work for her to do. But Louise knew that, if she

failed to hold Charles, Louis would have little use for her. And there was nothing she could do but follow her doctor's advice and long to return to her place at Court.

The Court went to Windsor; and there was merry sport in the green fields. A mock battle was staged to represent the siege of Maestricht. Charles was particularly interested because that was the battle at which Monmouth had excelled.

He doted on that boy, thought Nell. 'Twas a pity he had not equal pleasure in little Charles and James Beauclerk. Not that he did not show the utmost affection towards them; not that it did not delight him to take the little fellows in his arms and lavish caresses on them.

Caresses! thought Nell bitterly. *They* won't make their fortunes.

Her anger against Charles' eldest son spurted out one day.

'Ha,' she cried, 'here comes Prince Perkin, to show us all how to win battles.'

The colour flamed in Monmouth's face. 'Who are you to speak thus to me?' he asked. 'You forget I am the King's son, whereas you . . . you belong to the gutter.'

''Tis true,' said Nell cheerfully. 'I and your mother are much of a piece – both whores and both come up from the gutter.'

Monmouth passed, cursing the low orange-girl whom his father was besotted enough to honour.

But Nell was not really angry with Monmouth. She found she could not be. She saw in him a resemblance to her own little Charles. They're half-brothers, she thought. She could understand Monmouth's ambitions. Had she not felt the same about her own boys?

Now she began to regard the handsome young man with a maternal eye. Strangely enough he found his arrogance quelled a little. Nell was low – none would deny that; but she was a born charmer; and to see those saucy eyes, momentarily sentimental and maternal as they rested upon him, could not but give the young Duke a feeling of pleasure.

He decided that, although she made the most outrageous comments and had no sense of the fitness of things, the little orange-girl was not without her attractions, and for the life of him he could not dislike her as he felt a young man in his position should.

Meanwhile Nell was back in high favour. Now Charles was wondering why he had neglected her so long. It was pleasant to escape from Louise's culture and enjoy a romp with Nell. Nell was so natural; moreover she learned quickly. She was already developing a taste for the kind of music which pleased the King.

It never failed to amuse him to see her in her apartments, the grand lady Madam Eleanor Gwyn. It grieved him that he could as yet do nothing for the boys, but he promised himself he would as soon as he felt it was safe to do so.

The King, recovered from his illness, was in good spirits. He recalled Rochester, for, although he could not entirely like the fellow, he knew of none who could write such witty verses and make him laugh so heartily – even though it was often at the King's expense.

The Court was merry. Charles refused to be worried by affairs of state. Louise was in retirement and, as there was no need to stand on dignity, there was much merrymaking during these months with Nell reigning supreme as the Queen of the Court, determined to enjoy every moment before that time when Louise must inevitably come forward and send her back a pace or two.

One day, when the King rose, it was to find one of Rochester's verses stuck on his door.

The courtiers gathered about him to read it.

Charles read aloud:

> *'Here lies our Sovereign Lord the King*
> *Whose word no man relies on.*
> *He never said a foolish thing*
> *And never did a wise one.'*

There was an expectant hush when the King finished reading. A man must indeed have a lively sense of humour to be able to laugh at what he knew to be so true of himself.

There was Rochester in the background, debonair and reckless, not caring if the verses earned him another banishment from the Court he loved to grace. How could he, his expression demanded, refrain from writing such neat and witty verses when they occurred to him and happened to be so true?

The King laughed suddenly and loudly.

'Why, my friends,' he said to the company, "'tis true, what he says, but the matter is easily accounted for – my discourse is my own, my actions are my Ministry's.'

Indeed it was a very merry Court during those months.

Nell gave a musical party in her finely furnished house; it was looking particularly grand, for if the King could not give her the titles she craved for her sons, he tried hard to make up for that with his gifts.

Nell, looking round the room, could hardly believe that this was now her home. It was not easy to conjure up the memory of that hovel in the Cole-yard now. Yet when she went up to that room where her mother would now be sleeping, the gin bottle not far out of reach, it was not so difficult.

But what a sight this was, with the candlelight gleaming on the rich dress of ladies and Court gallants! Nell glanced at her own skirts covered in silver and gold lace, at the jewels glittering on her fingers.

She, little Nell Gwyn of the Cole-yard, was giving a party at which the principal guests were the King and his brother, the Duke of York.

This was a particularly happy evening for Nell, because during it she would have a chance to do a good turn to a poor player from the theatre. He had a beautiful voice, this young Bowman, and she wanted the King to hear it and compliment him, for the King's compliments would mean that London playgoers would crowd into the theatre to hear the man; and it was a mighty pleasant thing, thought Nell, having had one's feet set on the road to good fortune to do all in one's power to lead others that way.

She watched the King's expression as he listened to the singing. She sidled up to him.

'A good performer, Nell,' he said.

'I am delighted so to please Your Majesty,' she told him. 'I wish to bring the singer to you that you may thank him personally. It will mean much to the boy.'

'Do so, Nell, if it be your wish,' said Charles and, as he watched her small figure whisk away, he thought affectionately that it was like Nell, in the midst of her extravagant splendour, to think of those less fortunate. He was happy with Nell. If she did not continuously plague him about those boys of hers he would know complete peace with her. But she was right, of course, to do what she could for their sons. He would not have her neglectful of their welfare. And one day she should be rewarded. As soon as it was possible he would give young Charles all that he had given Barbara's and Louise's.

Nell was approaching with young Bowman, who nervously stood before the King.

'I thank you heartily for your music,' said Charles warmly. He would not deny Nell the appreciation which she wanted. That cost nothing, and he wanted her to know that, were he in a position to do so, he would grant all her requests. 'I thank you heartily again and again.'

Nell was at his side. 'Sir,' she said, 'to show you do not speak like a courtier, could you not make the performers a worthy present?'

'Assuredly yes,' said the King, and felt in his pockets. He grimaced. He was without money. He called to his brother.

'James, I beg of you reward these good musicians in my name.'

James discovered that he, too, had left his purse in his apartments.

'I have nothing here, Sir,' he said, 'naught but a guinea or two.'

Nell stood, arms akimbo, looking from the King to the Duke.

'Od's Fish!' she cried. 'What company have I got into?'

There was laughter all round; and none laughed more heartily than the King.

Nell was happy, delighting in her fine apartments, the favour she enjoyed with the King, and the love she bore him.

All the same she did not forget to make sure that the musicians were adequately rewarded.

It was a successful evening among many.

Thus it was while Louise nursed herself back to health.

*   *   *

Louise was recovered, and now the King was dividing his time between her and Nell. Barbara, Duchess of Cleveland, although no longer in favour with the King, continued to fight for the rights of those children whom she declared were as much his as her own. Louise felt that by some divine right her own son should have the precedence over Barbara's. The King was pestered first by one, then by the other. Barbara's sons were to be the Dukes of Grafton and South-ampton; Louise's was to have the title of Duke of Richmond, which was vacant on the death of Frances Stuart's husband. But Charles must arrange that the patents be passed all at the same time, to avoid jealousy.

Still there were no titles for Charles and James Beauclerk. Nell was unable to conceal her chagrin. She could not refrain from insulting Louise on every possible occasion. 'If she is a person of such rank, related to all the nobility of France,' she demanded, 'why does she play the whore? I'm a doxy by profession, and I do not pretend to be anything else. I am constant to the King, and I know that he will not continue to pass over my boys.'

But Louise had now managed to win Danby to her side, and Danby's position was high in the country. Charles could not ignore him because his wizardry in matters of finance had made such marked improvements in Charles' affairs. Nell knew that she owed her own and her sons' lack of honours to the Danby–Portsmouth league, and she was also wise enough to know that while Danby remained in power she would find it very difficult to get the recognition she so eagerly desired.

Danby was fast building up the Court party of which he was the head. He wanted to revive the Divine Right of Kings and the absolutism of the monarchy as in the days of Charles I. In opposition, the Country party, led by Shaftesbury with Buckingham as his lieutenant, aimed to support the Parliament. Danby's party called Shaftesbury's party Whigs, which was a term hitherto only applied to Scottish robbers who raided the border and stole their neighbours' goods under a cloak of hypocrisy. Shaftesbury retaliated by dubbing Danby's party Tories, a term used in Ireland for those who were superstitious, bloodthirsty, ignorant, and not to be trusted.

The King watched the rivalry with seeming indifference, but he was alert. He recognized the skill of Shaftesbury – the cleverest and most formidable member of the Opposition party. Charles and his brother James had nicknamed him 'Little Sincerity'. He was a small man who suffered much from ill-health at this time; he had changed sides many times during the course of the last few years. When the civil war had started he had been cautious and retiring, waiting to see which side could serve him best. When it seemed the Royalists were winning he hastily joined them, and then was forced to desert to the other side with the greatest speed. He became a Field Marshal in Cromwell's armies; but while he kept close to Cromwell he took the precaution to marry a woman who was of a Royalist family. She died early, which was to the good, for Cromwell then became Lord Protector and the lady's background might have been an encumbrance to an ambitious man. Afterwards he married an heiress. He was clever enough to join none of the Royalist risings, but he was one of the first to present himself at Charles' exiled Court to welcome him back to England. He took a great part in the downfall of Clarendon, who held a post which he coveted. When the Great Seal was his, he was quick to see that the Opposition was likely to be very powerful; he had no wish to commit himself too hurriedly to support that which might prove to be a lost cause. But he was forced at this time to waver no longer. His way was clear. He must make Parliament supreme, for he clearly saw that his destiny lay therein. If Parliament were supreme, then Shaftesbury should be its head.

He did not underrate the King. Charles was lazy. As Buckingham had once said, 'he could if he would', and never had Buckingham said a truer word. It was only poor James of York who 'would if he could'. Between lazy Charles and aspiring James, one must walk with caution.

Charles had once said to him: 'I believe you are the wickedest dog in England.'

Shaftesbury, whose tongue was as quick as his mind, retorted: 'May it please Your Majesty, of a subject, I believe I am.'

Charles could never resist a witty rejoinder; he knew 'Little Sincerity' for a man without scruples, but he had to respect that quick and clever brain; in his continual tussles with his Parliament it was men such as Shaftesbury whom he must needs watch.

Nell, looking on, understanding little of politics, accepted Danby as her enemy because he and Louise were friends; Buckingham, friend of Shaftesbury, had been the means of bringing her to the attention of the King; so she looked upon Buckingham as her friend. The reckless Rochester was Buckingham's friend and therefore inclined to support the Shaftesbury party. So to her house these men came, and it was at her table they sat and discussed their plans. One of these, which was formulating in the agile brain of Shaftesbury, was to have Monmouth proclaimed legitimate and, on the King's death, set upon the throne as a puppet who would do his bidding; Shaftesbury and Buckingham were formidable enemies of the Duke of York.

Monmouth, too, came to Nell's parties, and an affection sprang up between them. Nell continued to refer to the proud young man as Prince Perkin and the Pretender, but Monmouth had to accept such inroads on his dignity as 'Nelly's talk'.

Charles knew of Nell's Whig friends, but he knew Nell. She was completely loyal to him as a man. She saw him, not only as the King, but in that inimitable way of hers which made him feel half husband, half son. She was lustily ready for passion, but the maternal instinct was always there; and Charles knew that Nell was the one person in his kingdom who could be relied upon for disinterested love. It was true she pestered at times: titles for her sons, a grand title for herself. But he always remembered that she had not done this until her sons were born, and it was that maternal instinct which prompted her to do so now. Honours for her sons she must have. And she wanted the boys not to be ashamed of their mother.

He made no effort to stop those entertainments she gave to these men whom he knew were trying to shatter the doctrine of the Divine Right of Kings. Nell was careless; she did not realize that she was dabbling in high politics. Often unconsciously she gave away little bits of information which were useful. His affection for her, as hers for him, burned steadily, no matter what he felt now and then for others.

As for Louise, he had not felt the same for her since their enforced separation. She had forgotten her gentle manners when she realized that she had caught the sickness. She had railed against him in her fury; it had been necessary to give her a handsome present to pacify her. Not, she had declared, that anything could pacify her for the loss of her health, and for the terrible indignity of being forced to suffer from such a disease, and he believed that her manner of fretting, her anger and railings had impeded her recovery.

He would not have been altogether displeased if Louise had told him she intended to return to France. He could not, of course, suggest that she should go. That would offend Louis, and he dared not do that at this stage. Moreover it was well for Louis to believe he had a spy close to the King of England.

Charles would employ tactics not new to him in his relationship with Louise. He would placate and promise; but it did not mean that he would keep his promises.

He brooded on these matters as he attended race meetings at Newmarket or sat fishing at Windsor, or strolled in St James' Park, feeding the ducks, his dogs at his heels, sauntering with the wits and ladies who delighted him.

He heard that Clarendon had died in Rouen, and that

saddened him a little, for he had never forgotten the old man who had served him so well in the days of his exile. John Milton, who had written *Paradise Lost*, died also. No one greatly cared. The witty and scurrilous verses of Rochester were more widely read than Milton's epic poetry. These reminders of death turned the King's thoughts into melancholy channels. He recalled Jemmy's unhealthy thoughts. If it were true that Shaftesbury planned to make Monmouth heir, what of James, Duke of York? James was at heart a good man, but he was by no means a clever one. James would deem it his duty to fight for what he believed to be right, and he was a Stuart who believed that kings ruled by Divine Right and that they were God's anointed.

Trouble lies ahead, thought the King uneasily. Then characteristically: But it is my death that sets light to the train of powder. When I am dead what concern shall it be of mine?

So he fished and sauntered, divided his time between Louise and Nell, vaguely wished that Louise would go back to France, vaguely hoped that he could give Nell her heart's desire and make her sons the little lords she would have them be.

*   *   *

With the coming of the new year there was a change at Court.

A small party on horseback came clattering through the streets. The leader of this party, wearing jacket, plumed hat, and a periwig, was Hortense Mancini, Duchess Mazarin. Her great eyes seemed black but on closer inspection were seen to be a shade of blue so dark as to resemble the colour of violets; her hair was bluish-black, her features classic, her figure voluptuously beautiful. She was known throughout Europe as the most beautiful woman in the world, and all those who saw her believed that she was justly described.

She had brought with her a few of her personal servants – five men and two women – and at her side rode her little black page who prepared her coffee.

She drew up at the house of Lady Elizabeth Harvey, who

243

came out to greet her and let her know that she was delighted to welcome her.

The citizens of London saw her no more that day. They stood about in the keen frosty air telling themselves that, the woman being so beautiful, and the King's reputation being what it was, she could have come to England for one purpose only.

They waited now to witness the discomfiture of Madam Carwell, as they had called Louise since her arrival in England. They refused to try to pronounce Kéroualle. Louise was Carwell to them, and no fine English title was going to alter that. It would please the Londoners to see her neglected whom they called The Catholic Whore.

Here was another foreigner, but this woman was at least a beauty, and they would be glad to see their King lured from the side of the squint-eyed French spy.

*   *   *

Louise was worried. She believed that she had lost her hold on the King. She knew that that hold had largely been due to the fact that she had not been easy to seduce. She could not, of course, have held out any longer; to have done so might have made the King realize that he did not greatly desire her.

The sickness which she had contracted had not only taken its toll of her looks; it had left her nervous, and she wondered whether she could ever regain the health she had once enjoyed. She had grown fat and, although the King had nicknamed her Fubbs with the utmost affection, she felt the name carried with it a certain lack of dignity. She was beginning to fear that had Charles been less indulgent, less careless, she would have been passed over long ago.

She did not believe that he did half those things which he promised he would do and which she was commanded by the French King through Courtin, the French ambassador, to persuade him to.

He would look at her with that shrewd yet lazy smile and say: 'So you would advise that, Fubbs? Ah, yes, of course, I understand.'

244

She often heard him laugh uproariously at some of Nell Gwyn's comments and frequently these were uttered to discountenance herself. And now this most disturbing news had reached her. Hortense Mancini was in London.

There was no one in England whom she could really trust. Buckingham, her enemy, was in decline, but for how long would he remain so? Shaftesbury hated her and would want to destroy her influence with the King, since he was anti-Catholic and she had heard through Courtin that he was planning to expunge all popery from the country. It might have been that Shaftesbury knew of that secret clause in the Treaty of Dover concerning the King's religion; if so, he would know that she had her instructions from Louis to make the King's conversion complete and public as soon as she could.

She was trembling, for she had lost some of her calmness during her illness.

She decided that there was only one person in England who would help her now, and that the time had come for her to redeem those vague promises which she had held out to him. She dressed herself with care. In spite of her increased bulk she knew well how to dress to advantage and she had taste and poise which few ladies at Court possessed.

She sent one of her women to Lord Danby's apartments with a message which was to be discreetly delivered and which explained that she would shortly be coming to see him, and she hoped he would be able to give her a private interview.

The woman quickly returned with the news that Lord Danby eagerly awaited her coming.

He received her with a show of respect.

'I am honoured to receive Your Grace.'

'I trust that in coming thus for a friendly talk I do not encroach on your time.'

'Time is well spent in your company,' said Danby. He had guessed the cause of her alarm. 'I hear that we have a foreign Duchess newly arrived among us.'

'It is Madame Mazarin . . . notorious in all the Courts of Europe.'

'And doubtless come to win notoriety in this one,' said Danby slyly.

Louise flinched. 'I doubt it not. If you know aught . . .' she began.

Danby looked at his fingernails. 'I gather,' he said, 'that she does not wish to live in the Palace, as Your Grace does.'

'She comes because she is poor,' said Louise. 'I have heard that that mad husband of hers quickly dissipated the fortune she inherited from her uncle.'

''Tis true. She has let His Majesty know that she must have an adequate income before taking up her apartments in Whitehall.'

Louise came closer to him. She said nothing, but her meaning was clear to him: You will advise the King against providing this income. You, whose financial genius enables you to enrich yourself while you suppress waste in others, you, under whom the King's budget has been balanced, will do all in your power to prevent his giving this woman what she asks. You will range yourself on the side of the Duchess of Portsmouth, which means that you will be the enemy of the Duchess Mazarin.

Why not? thought Danby excitedly. Intrigue was stimulating. Discovery? Charles never blamed others for falling into temptation which he himself made no attempt to resist.

He took her hand and kissed it. When she allowed it to remain in his, he was sure.

'Your Grace is more beautiful than before your illness,' he said; and he laughed inwardly, realizing that she, the coldest woman at Court, was offering herself in exchange for his protection.

He kissed her without respect, without affection. He was accustomed to taking bribes.

*   *   *

Hortense received the King at the house of Lady Elizabeth Harvey.

She had guessed that as soon as he heard of her arrival in his capital he would wish to visit her. It was exactly what Hortense wanted.

246

She lay back on a sofa awaiting him. She was voluptuously beautiful and, although she was thirty and had led a wild and adventurous life, her beauty was in no way impaired. Her perfect classical features would remain perfect and classical as long as she lived. Her abundant bluish-black hair fell curling about her bare shoulders; but her most beautiful assets were her wonderful violet eyes.

Hortense was imperturbably good-humoured, lazy, of a temperament to match the King's; completely sensual, she was widely experienced in amatory adventures. She had often been advised that she would do well to visit England, and had again and again decided to renew her acquaintance with Charles; but each time something had happened to prevent her, some new lover had beguiled her and made her forget the man who had wished to be her lover in her youth. It was sheer poverty which had driven her to England now – sheer poverty and the fact that she had created such a scandal in Savoy that she had been asked to leave. The last three scandalous years had been spent in the company of César Vicard, a dashing, handsome young man who had posed as the Abbé of St Réal. When the letters which had passed between the Duchess and the *soi-disant* Abbé had been discovered, they, completely lacking in reticence, had so shocked those into whose hands they fell, that the Duchess had been asked to leave Savoy.

So, finding herself poor and in need of refuge, Hortense had come to England. She knew no fear. She had faced the perilous crossing in the depth of winter, and with a few servants had come to a completely strange country, never doubting that her spectacular beauty would ensure for her a position at Court.

Charles strode in, took her hand, and kissed it while his eyes did not leave her face.

'Hortense!' he cried. 'But you are the same Hortense whom I loved all those years ago. No, not the same. Od's Fish, I should not have believed then that it was possible for any to be more beautiful than the youngest of les Mazarinettes. But I see that there is one more fair: the Duchess Mazarin – Hortense grown up.'

She laughed at him and waved him to be seated with a fascinating easy gesture as though she were the Queen, he the subject. Charles did not mind. He felt that he should indeed forget his royalty in the presence of such beauty.

The long lashes lay against her olive skin. Charles stared at the beautiful blue-black hair lying so negligently on the bare shoulders. This languid beauty aroused in him such desire as he rarely felt nowadays. He knew that his bout of sickness had changed him; he was not the man he had been. But he was determined that Hortense should become his mistress.

'You should not be here,' he said. 'You should come to Whitehall at once.'

'Nay,' she said, smiling her indolent smile. 'Mayhap later. If it could be arranged.'

'But it shall be arranged.'

She laughed. There was no pretence about her. She had been brought up at the French Court. She had all the graces of that Court and she had learned to be practical.

'I am very poor,' she said.

'I heard that you had inherited the whole of your uncle's fortune.'

''Twas so,' said Hortense. 'Armand, my husband, quickly took possession of it.'

'What! All of it?'

'All of it. But what mattered that? I escaped.'

'We have heard of your adventures, Hortense. I wonder you did not visit me before.'

'Suffice it that I have come now.'

Charles was thinking quickly. She would ask for a pension, and if it were large enough she would move into Whitehall. He must see Danby quickly and something must be arranged. But he would not discuss that with her now. She was Italian, brought up in France, and therefore, indolent as she seemed, she would know how to drive her bargain. It was not that he was averse to discussing money with a woman; but he feared she would ask too much and he be unable to refuse her.

He satisfied himself with contemplating that incomparable beauty and telling himself that she would be his mistress all in good time.

'We should have married,' he said.

'Ah! How it reminds me. And what an enchanting husband you would have made! Far better than Armand who forced me to fly from him.'

'Your uncle would have none of me. He did not wish to give his niece to a wandering prince without a kingdom.'

''Twas a sad thing that you did not regain your kingdom earlier.'

'I have often thought it . . . Now, having seen you, I regret it more than ever, since, had I been a King with a country when I asked for your hand, it would not have been refused me.'

'Marie, too, might have been a Queen,' said Hortense. 'But our uncle would not let her be. Think of it! Marie might have been Queen of France and I Queen of England – but for Uncle Mazarin.'

Charles looked into her face, marvelling at its perfections, but Hortense's dreamy thoughts were far away. She was thinking of the French Court where she had been brought up with her four sisters, Laura, Olympia, Marie, Mariana. They had all joined in the ballets devised for the little King and his brother Philippe; and her uncle, Cardinal Mazarin, and Louis' mother, Anne of Austria, had ruled France between them. All the Cardinal's nieces had been noted for their beauty, but many said that little Hortense was the loveliest of them all. What graces they had learned in that most graceful Court!

She remembered that Louis – impressionable and idealistic – had fallen in love first with Olympia and then more passionately, more seriously with Marie. She remembered Marie's unhappiness, the tears, the heartbreak. She remembered Louis, so young, so determined to have his own way and marry Marie. Poor Louis! And poor Marie!

It was the Cardinal who had ruined their hopes. Some men would have rejoiced to see a niece the Queen of France. Not Mazarin. He feared the French. They hated him and blamed him for all their misfortunes; he believed that if he allowed their King to marry his niece they would have risen against him, and there would have been revolution in France. He remembered the civil war of the Fronde. Perhaps he had been wise. But what misery the young people had suffered. Louis had married the plain little Infanta of Spain, Marie Thérèse, whom he would never love, and now his love affairs were the talk of the world. And poor Marie! She had been hastily married to Lorenzo Colonna who was the Grand Constable of Naples; and he had succeeded in making her as unhappy as she had made him and as, doubtless, Marie Thérèse, the meek and prim little Spaniard, had made Louis.

And Charles, seeing the young Hortense, and connoisseur of beauty that he was even in those days, had declared that he would be happy to make her his wife. He had urgent need of the money which would have helped him to regain his throne, and it was known that the Cardinal's wealth would go to his nieces. To the penurious exile the exquisite and wealthy child had seemed an ideal match.

But the Cardinal had frowned on Charles' offer. He saw the young man as a reckless profligate who would never regain his throne, and he did not wish his niece to link her fortunes with such a man.

So the Cardinal had prevented his two nieces from becoming queens. He had torn them from two charming people that they might make marriages with unhappy results to all concerned.

'Those days are long ago,' said Charles. ''Tis a sad habit to brood on what might have been. 'Tis a happier one to let the present make up for the disappointments of the past.'

'Which we should do?'

'Which we *shall* do,' said Charles vehemently.

'It is good of you to offer me refuge here,' said Hortense.

'Good! Nay, 'tis what all the world would expect of me.'

Hortense laughed that low and musical laugh of hers. 'And of me,' she said.

'Od's Fish! I wonder you did not come before.'

Hortense's dreamy eyes looked back once more into the

past. César Vicard had been an exciting lover. It had not been her wish to leave him. There had been others equally exciting, equally enthralling, and she would have been too indolent to leave any of them had circumstances not made it necessary for her to do so.

Yet she had left her husband and four children. So in a dire emergency she could rouse herself.

'It is an adventure,' she said, 'to come to a new country.'

'And to an old friend?' he asked passionately.

'It was so long ago. So much has happened. You may have heard of the life I led with Armand.'

'Vague rumours reached me.'

'You wonder why my uncle arranged that marriage,' she said. 'I might have had Charles Emmanuel, Duke of Savoy. He would have made a better husband. At least he was called Charles. Then there was Pedro of Portugal, and the Maréchal Turenne.'

'The last would have been a little aged for you, I imagine.'

'Thirty-five years older. But life with him could not have been worse than it was with Armand. Even the Prince de Cortenay who, I knew, concerned himself with my uncle's money rather than with myself . . .'

'The graceless fool!' said Charles softly.

'He could not have made my life more intolerable than did Armand.'

'Your uncle delayed marrying you so often that when he was on his deathbed he acted without due thought in that important matter.'

'To my cost.'

'It was so unsatisfactory?'

'I was fifteen, he was thirty. Some I could have understood. Some I could have excused. A libertine . . . yes; I have never pretended to be a saint. He had a fine title: Armand de la Porte Marquis de Meilleraye and Grand Master of the Artillery of France. Would you have expected such a one to be a bigot . . . a madman? But he was. We had not been married many months when he became obsessed with the idea that everyone about him was impure, and that it

251

was his duty to purify them. He sought to purify statues, pictures . . .'

'Sacrilege!' said Charles.

'And myself.'

'Greater sacrilege!' murmured Charles.

Hortense laughed lightly. 'Do you blame me for leaving him? How could I stay? I endured that life for seven wretched years. I saw my fortune being dissipated – and not in the way one would expect a husband to dissipate his wife's fortune. He agreed to take my uncle's name. Uncle thought he would be amenable. We became the Duc and Duchesse Mazarin. Uncle would not allow him to use the "de". He said: "Not Hortense, my fortune, and *de* Mazarin. That is too much. Hortense, yes. A fortune, yes. But you call yourself plain Duc Mazarin." '

Charles laughed. 'That is characteristic of the old man.'

'And so to me came the Palais Mazarin. You remember it – in the Rue de Richelieu – and with it came the Hôtel Tuboeuf and the picture and sculpture galleries, those which had been built by Mazard, as well as the property in the Rue des Petits Champs.'

'Such treasures! They must have been as good as anything Louis had in the Louvre.'

'Indeed yes. Pictures by the greatest artists. Statues, priceless books, furniture . . . It all came to me.'

'And he – your husband – sold it and so frittered away your inheritance?'

'He sold some. He thought it was wrong for a woman to adorn herself with jewels. He was verging on madness from the very beginning. I remember how I first came upon him before a great masterpiece, a brush in his hand. I said to him: "Armand, what are you doing? Are you imagining that you are a great painter?" And he stood up, pointing the brush at the painting, his eyes blazing with what I can only believe was madness. He said: "These pictures are indecent. No one should look on such nakedness. All the servants here will be corrupted." And I looked closer and saw that he had been painting over the nudes. There were his crude additions, ruining masterpieces. That was not all.

He took a hammer and smashed many of the statues. I dare not think how much he has wantonly destroyed.'

'And you lived with that man for seven years!'

'Seven years! I thought it my duty to do so. Oh, he was a madman. He forbade the maidservants to milk the cows, for he said this might put indecent thoughts into their heads. He wanted to extract our daughter's front teeth because they were well-formed and he feared they might give rise to vanity. He wrote to Louis, telling him that he had had instructions from the Angel Gabriel to warn the King that disaster would overtake him if he did not immediately give up Louise de la Vallière. You see he was mad – quite mad. But I was glad later that he had written to Louis thus, for when I ran away from him he asked Louis to insist on my returning to him, and Louis' answer was that he was sure Armand's good friend the Angel Gabriel, with whom he seemed to be on such excellent terms, could help him more in this matter than could the King of France.'

Charles laughed, 'Ah, you did well to leave such a madman. The only complaint I would make is that you waited so long before coming to England.'

'Oh, I was in and out of convents. And believe me, Charles, in some of these convents the life is rigorous indeed. I would as lief be a prisoner in the Bastille as in some of them. I was in the Convent of the Daughters of Mary, in Paris, and I was right glad to leave it.'

'You were meant to grace a Court, never a convent,' said Charles.

She sighed. 'I feel as though I may have come home. This is a country strange to me, but I have good friends here. My little cousin, Mary Beatrice, the wife of your own brother, is here. How I long to see her! And there is you, my dear Charles, the friend of my childhood. How fares Mary Beatrice?'

'She grows reconciled to her aged husband. I have become her friend. That was inevitable because, from the first, she reminded me of you.'

She smiled lazily. 'Then of course there is my old friend,

St Evremond. He has long been urging me to come to England.'

'Good St Evremond! I always liked the fellow. He has settled happily here; I like his wit.'

'So you have made him Master of your ducks, I hear.'

'A task well suited to his talents,' said Charles, 'for there is nothing he need do but watch the creatures and now and then throw them something to eat; but to perform this task he must saunter in the Park and converse while he stands beside the lake. It is a pleasure to saunter and converse with him.'

'I wonder does he grow homesick for France? Does he wish he had not been so indiscreet as to criticize my uncle at the time of the Treaty of the Pyrenees?'

'Does he tell you?'

'He tells me that he would never wish to leave England if I were there.'

'So he has helped to bring you. I must reward my keeper of the ducks.'

'He but spoke like a courtier, I doubt not.'

'All men would speak like courtiers to you, Hortense.'

'As they do to all women.'

'With you they would mean the fulsome things they say.'

She laughed. 'I will call my blackamoor to make coffee for Your Majesty. You will never have tasted coffee such as he can brew.'

'And while we talk, we will arrange for you to move to Whitehall.'

'Nay, I would not do so. I would prefer a house . . . nearby. I do not think Her Grace of Portsmouth would wish me to have my quarters in Whitehall Palace.'

'It is spacious. I have made improvements, and it is not the rambling mass of buildings it was when I came back to England.'

'Nevertheless, I would prefer to be nearby, you understand, but not too near.'

Charles was thinking quickly. He was determined to lose no time in making this exciting addition to his seraglio.

With amusement he accepted coffee from Hortense's little

slave, and as he sipped it he said: 'Lord Windsor, who is Master of Horse to the Duchess of York, would most gladly vacate his house for you. It faces St James' Park and would suit you very happily, I doubt not.'

'It seems as though Your Majesty is ready to make me very happy in England.'

'I shall set about that task with all my heart and soul,' said Charles, taking her hand and kissing it.

*   *   *

It was some months before Hortense moved to Whitehall. The question of money was a delicate one. Charles had placed himself in Danby's hands, for Danby had proved his worth in matters of finance.

Danby had summed up the character of the beautiful Hortense: Sensual, but by no means vicious; cultured, but by no means shrewd. She would let great opportunities elude her, not because she did not see them, but because she was too indolent to seize them.

He did not believe that she would long hold the King's undivided attention. She was more beautiful than any of the King's ladies, it was true, but Charles nowadays wanted more than beauty. Hortense desired a large pension because she needed it to live in the state to which she was accustomed. She had no wish to store up for herself great wealth as Louise did. She would not ask for honours, titles; she did not wish to reign as a queen in the Court. She wanted to be lazily content with good food, good wine, a lover capable of satisfying her. She would never intrigue.

Danby had decided that he would be well advised to support Louise. Therefore he held the King back from supplying the large income which Hortense demanded.

Hortense was, he knew, hoping that her husband would give her a bigger allowance than the four hundred pounds a year which was all he would allow her out of the vast fortune she had brought him. Danby believed that if Hortense received what she wanted she would accept Charles as a lover whether he supplied the income or not. That was Hortense's nature. She now asked £4,000 a year from

Charles. But, as Danby pointed out, that would not be all she would ask.

Hortense was extravagant by nature. She had told Charles of how, one day shortly before her uncle's death, she had thrown three hundred pistoles out of the window of the Palais Mazarin because she liked to see the servants scramble for them and fight each other.

'Uncle was such a careful man,' Hortense had said. 'Some say my action shortened his life. But it did not prevent his leaving me his fortune.'

Oh yes, Danby pointed out, if the King wished to keep his exchequer in order, they must be careful of such a woman.

But the whole country was talking of the King's latest mistress. Sir Carr Scrope wrote in the prologue to Etherege's *Man of Mode* which was produced in the King's Theatre that year:

> '*Of foreign women why should we fetch the scum*
> *When we can be so richly served at home?*'

And the audience roared its approval of the lines, although most people declared that anything was worth while if it put Madam Carwell's nose out of joint.

But Charles was impatient. He insisted on the pension's being paid, and as there was no hope of Hortense's being able to persuade Louis to force her husband to increase her allowance, she accepted Charles' offer and became his mistress.

*   *   *

Louise was distraught. Nell shrugged her shoulders. She was beginning to understand her position at Court. She was there when she was wanted, ready to make sport and be gay. She never reproached Charles for his infidelities. She knew she was safe and that no reigning beauty would be able to displace her. For one thing, Charles would never let her go. She was the buffoon, the female court-jester, apart from all others. This was a battle between Louise and

Hortense, and Hortense held all the cards which should bring victory. She was so beautiful that people waited in the streets to see her pass. She was deeply sensual. Louise was cold by nature, and had to pretend to share Charles' pleasure in their relations. Hortense had no need to pretend. Louise must constantly be considering instructions from France, and the King knew it. Hortense need consider nothing but her own immediate satisfaction. Hortense never showed jealousy of Louise; Louise continually showed jealousy of Hortense. Hortense offered not only sexual delight but peace. In this she was like Nell. But she lacked Nell's maternal devotion and she lacked Nell's constancy – although this was not apparent at this stage.

Edmund Waller wrote a set of verses called *The Triple Combat*, in which he portrayed the three chief mistresses struggling for supremacy. The country was amused; so was the Court. Charles acquired a new nickname – Chanticleer; and everyone was aware of how the affair progressed. Barbara had left for France, and Charles had at last made it clear that he wished to sever their relationship. 'All that I ask of you,' he had said, 'is to make as little noise as you can and I care not whom you love.'

Louise, who had been with child, suffered a miscarriage, and appeared at Court looking thin and ill. She had a slight affliction of one eye, and the skin round the affected eye became discoloured.

'It would seem,' said Rochester, 'that Her Grace, aware of the superior attractions of Madame Mazarin's dark eyes, would seek to transform herself into a brunette.'

The Court took up the story. Everyone was only too glad to jeer at Madam Carwell.

Louise was indeed melancholy. She feared that that nightmare, which had haunted her whenever she felt she was losing her hold on Charles, would become a reality. She was terrified that Hortense would persuade the King to send her, Louise, back to France and he, unable to deny his latest mistress what she asked, would agree. Louise need not have worried on that score, for Hortense would never bestir herself to make such demands.

Nell, as merry as ever, appeared at Court dressed in mourning.

'For whom do you mourn?' she was asked.

'For the discarded Duchess and her dead hopes,' explained Nell maliciously.

The King heard of this and was amused. He wished now and then that Louise would go back to France, but he was determined that whatever happened he would keep Nell at hand. It was pleasant to remember that she was always there, ready, without recriminations, to make good sport.

*   *   *

Louise lifted tearful eyes to the King. She had wept so much that those eyes, never big, seemed almost to have shrunk into her head. Her recent miscarriage and her illness of the previous year had undermined her health considerably. Charles would have been sorry for her had she been less sorry for herself. Although he was kind as always, Louise sensed that his thoughts were far away – she believed with Hortense – and she fancied she saw distaste in his eyes.

None of Charles' mistresses – not even Barbara – had been so acquisitive as Louise, and her great consolation now was that she and her sister Henriette, whom she had brought to England and married to the dissolute Earl of Pembroke, were very rich. But was that to be the only gratification of one who had sought to be a queen?

'I have served Your Majesty with all my heart,' began Louise.

She did not understand him. Recriminations dulled his pity.

'You are the friend of Kings,' he said.

She noticed that he used the plural, and her hopes sank. A less kindly man would have called her Louis' spy.

She said: 'I come to ask Your Majesty's leave to retire to Bath. There I think I might take the waters and regain my health.'

Her eyes were pleading with him: Forbid me to go. Tell me that you wish to keep me beside you.

But Charles had brightened. 'My dear Fubbs,' he said,

'by all means go to Bath. One of my favourite cities. There you will recover your health, I doubt not. Lose no time in going there.'

It was a sorrowing Louise who made arrangements for the journey.

She did not know that the King was no longer as completely enamoured of Hortense as he had been. She was beautiful – the most beautiful woman in his kingdom – he was ready to admit that. But beauty was not all. She had brought into her house a French croupier, Morin, and had introduced the game of basset to England. The King deplored gambling. He had always sought to lure his mistresses from the gaming table. It had always proved less costly in the long run to provide them with masques and banquets. He was therefore annoyed with Hortense for introducing a new form of gambling.

The little Countess of Sussex, Barbara's daughter, who was reputed to be Charles' also, was completely charmed by Hortense. She would not leave her side and Hortense, attracted by the little girl, gave herself up to playing games with her. This was very charming, but often when the King wished for Hortense's company Hortense could not tear herself away from his daughter.

There was another matter which was changing the King's attitude. She had a lover. This was the young and handsome Prince of Monaco who was visiting England. He had come, it was said, all the way from Monte Carlo with the express purpose of making Hortense his mistress.

Hortense was unable to resist his good looks and his youth. The young man became a constant visitor at her house, for Hortense was too reckless, too careless of the future, to hide her infatuation for him.

Barbara had taken lovers while she was the King's mistress, and he had gone back again and again to Barbara; but those were different days. He was almost forty-seven – no longer so young, and even his amazing virility was beginning to fade. Since he had recovered from his illness he appeared to be sterile, for he had fathered no child since the birth of Moll Davies' daughter.

He was growing old; therefore that immense infatuation he had felt for Hortense, and which had flared up so suddenly, as suddenly died down. He wanted to be amused. Louise was no good at amusing him. She would only weep and recount her ills. So he made his way to Nell's house in Pall Mall.

Nell was delighted to receive him. There she was, ready to act court-jester, ready to laugh at him, the disconsolate lover who had been disappointed in his mistress, but ready to comfort, ready to show beneath all that banter and high spirits that she felt motherly towards him and was really very angry with the foolish Hortense for preferring the Prince of Monaco.

Buckingham was often at Nell's house. So was Monmouth. Shaftesbury was there. Nell was getting herself embroiled with the Whigs, thought Charles with amusement.

But it was pleasant to have Nell dance and sing for them and, when Charles saw her imitation of Lady Danby, and Buckingham's of Lady Danby's husband, the King found himself laughing as he had not laughed for some weeks. He realized that he had been foolish to neglect the tonic only Nell could give.

Then, with Louise recuperating at Bath, and Hortense relegated to being just one of Charles' more casual mistresses, Nell stepped into chief place once more.

Rochester warned her: ''Twill only be for a while, Nell. Louise will be back to the fray – doubt it not. And she's a fine lady, while the dust of the Cole-yard still clings to little Nell. Not that I should try to wipe it off. That was where Moll failed. But do not be surprised if you are not number one all the time. Just fall back when required, but make hay, Nelly. Make hay while the sun shines.'

So Nell made the King visit her not only for parties but during the day, that he might come to better acquaintance with his two sons.

One day she called little Charles to tell him that his father had come.

'Come hither, little bastard,' she called.

'Nelly,' protested the King, 'do not say that.'

'And why should I not?'

'It does not sound well.'

'Sound well or not, 'tis truth. For what else should I call the boy since his father, by giving him no other title, proclaims him such to the world?'

The King was thoughtful, and very shortly after that one of Nell's dearest ambitions was realized.

Her son was no longer merely Charles Beauclerk; he was Baron Headington and Earl of Burford.

Nell danced through the house in Pall Mall, waving the patent which proclaimed little Charles' title.

'Come hither, my lord Burford,' she shouted. 'You have a seat in the House of Lords, my love. Think of that! You have a King for a father, and all the world knows it.'

The new Earl laughed aloud to see his mother so gay, and little James – my lord Beauclerk – joined with him.

She seized them and hugged them. She called to the servants, that she might introduce them to my lord Burford and my lord Beauclerk.

She could be heard, shouting all day: 'Bring my lord Burford's pectoral syrup. I swear he has a cough coming. And I doubt not that it would be good for my lord Beauclerk to take some too. Oh, my lord Burford needs a new scarf. I will go to the Exchange for white sarcenet this very day.'

She fingered delicate fabrics in the shops. She bought shoes, laced with gold, for the children. 'My lord Burford has such tender feet . . . and his brother, my lord Beauclerk, not less so.'

The house echoed with Nell's laughter and delighted satisfaction.

The servants imitated their mistress, and it seemed that every sentence uttered to any in that house must contain a reference to my lord Earl or my lord Beauclerk.

EIGHT

NELL was busy during the months which followed. These were the happiest of her life, she believed. Charles was a frequent visitor; his delight in my lord Burford and my lord Beauclerk was unbounded; the little boys were well; and Nell's parties were gayer than ever.

It was true that there was no title for her, but Charles had promised her that as soon as he could arrange it, he would make her a Countess.

Nell allowed herself to shelve this ambition. Little Charles was an Earl, and nothing could alter that. She was ready to be contented.

Hortense was friendly and wrote to Nell, congratulating her on the elevation of her sons.

Nothing could have delighted Nell more.

'I have a letter here,' she called to her steward, Mr Groundes. 'The Duchess Mazarin congratulates the Earl of Burford on his elevation.'

'That is good of her, Madam.'

'It is indeed good, and more than Madam Squintabella has had the good manners to do. Why, since the Duchess is so gracious concerning the Earl of Burford, I think I will call upon her and give her my thanks.'

So Nell called for her Sedan and was carried to the apartments of the Duchess Mazarin, calling out, as she went through the streets, to her friends. 'I trust I see you well?' 'And you too,' would come the answer. 'And your family?' 'Oh, my lord Burford is well indeed. My lord Beauclerk has a little cough.' Then she would call at the apothecary's. 'We are running short of pectoral syrup, and my lord Beauclerk's cough has not gone. I like to have it ready, for when my lord Beauclerk has a cough it very often happens that his brother, the Earl, catches it.'

It was disconcerting, on arriving at the Duchess' apartments in St James' Palace, to find the Duchess of Portsmouth already there.

Louise, who was chatting with the French ambassador, Courtin, gave Nell a haughty look. Lady Harvey, who was also present, smiled uncertainly. Only Hortense was gracious. But Nell did not need anyone to help her out of an awkward situation. She went to Louise and slapped her on the back.

'I always have thought that those who ply the same trade should be good friends,' she cried.

Louise was horrified; Nell was unperturbed. While Hortense smiled her sleepy friendly smile.

'It was kind of you to come,' she said.

'Indeed I came!' declared Nell. 'I was touched by your good wishes, Duchess. My lord Burford would have come to thank you in person, but he keeps my lord Beauclerk company.'

'You must be very happy,' said Hortense.

'And gratified,' said Louise, 'having worked so hard and so consistently to bring it about. Your son is fortunate indeed to have such a mother.'

'And such a father,' said Nell. 'There has never been any doubt as to who my lord Burford's father is – although 'tis more than can be said for some.'

Louise was taken aback although she could not believe the affront was meant for her. She had led an exemplary life – apart from that strange and somewhat tepid relationship she shared with Danby.

'And the same goes for my lord Beauclerk,' said Nell.

Louise recovered her equanimity quickly. 'I rejoice to say my own little Duke is well.'

Nell at that moment was determined that before she died my lord Burford should be a Duke.

Hortense said to Nell quickly: 'I have heard that you have petticoats which are the wonder of all that behold them.'

'I have a good seamstress,' said Nell. She stood up and, lifting her skirts, began to dance, twirling her lace petticoats as she did so.

Hortense laughed. 'You twirl so we can scarcely see them. I pray you let us examine them more closely.'

'You'll not find better work in London,' said Nell. 'And this woman will be making silk hoods with scarves to them for my lord Burford and my lord Beauclerk.' She became alert; she could never resist the pleasure of doing a good turn. 'Why, I doubt not this good woman would be ready to make for Your Graces if you should so wish it.'

Hortense said that she did wish it; Louise said she feared she must go, and left while the rest of the company were examining Nell's petticoats.

Nell's eyes fell on the French ambassador. 'Come, sir,' she said, 'like you not my petticoats? Portsmouth hath not finer, for all the presents that are sent to her by the King of France. Why, you should tell your King, sir, that he would do better to send presents to the mother of my lord Burford than to that weeping willow. I can tell you, sir, the King liketh me better than Fubbs. Why, almost every night he sleeps with me, you know.'

Courtin hardly knew what to answer. He bowed awkwardly, fixing his eyes on the petticoats. Then he said: 'Great matters need great consideration.'

And after a while Nell took her leave and went back to her chair, stopping to buy shoestrings merely for the pleasure of telling the keeper of the shop in the New Exchange that they would grace the little shoes of my lord Burford.

*   *   *

In Nell's house the Whigs gathered. Shaftesbury and Buckingham were excited. They believed that the country was behind them and that if they could bring about a general election they would have no difficulty in getting a majority.

Danby was nervous. He knew that, once Shaftesbury's party was in power, it would be the end of his career. He was determined to avoid the dissolution of the present parliament at all cost.

Shaftesbury and Buckingham planned to bring this about. And Nell, believing that Danby was the one who was preventing the King from giving her the patent which would make her a Countess, and knowing that he was the friend of Louise, assured them that she supported them wholeheartedly. Nell believed that once Shaftesbury was in power he would make her a Countess.

She did not realize that, in demanding a new election, Shaftesbury and Buckingham were going against the King's wishes, and that Charles' great desire was to rule without a Parliament, as he believed the Divine Right intended a King to rule. It was ever Charles' desire to put Parliament into recess, from which he only wished to call it when it was necessary for money to be voted into the exchequer.

Nell was awaiting the result of the meeting of Parliament and preparing for the banquet she would give that night. She believed that the diabolically clever Shaftesbury and the brilliant Buckingham would come back to her house to tell her how they had defeated Danby's administration, and how there was to be a new election which would certainly give them a majority over the Court Party in both Houses.

Then, she thought, I shall be made a Countess. Charles wishes to do it. It is only Danby who, to please Fubbs, prevents him.

While she waited a visitor called. This was Elizabeth Barry, a young actress in whom my lord Rochester was interested. He had found a place for her on the stage and was helping her to make a great career. He had begged Nell to do all she could for Elizabeth, and Nell, who would have been ready to give a helping hand to any struggling actress, even if she had not been a friend of Rochester's, had done so wholeheartedly.

Now Elizabeth was frightened.

'To tell the truth, Nell,' she said, 'I am with child, and I know not what my lord will say.'

'Say! He will find great pleasure in the fact. All men think they are so fine that the hope of seeing a copy of themselves fills them with pleasure.'

'My lord hates ties, as you know. He might look upon this child as such.'

'Nay, acquaint him with the facts, Bess. They'll delight him.'

'I understand him well,' said Elizabeth uneasily. 'He likes to laugh. He says that a weeping woman is like a wet day in the country. He hates the country as much as he hates responsibility. I once heard him say to a dog who bit him: "I wish you were married and living in the country!"'

''Tis the way he has with words. He must ever say what he thinks to be clever, no matter whether he means it or not. Nay, Elizabeth, you should have no fear. He will love this child, and you the more for bearing it.'

'I would I could believe it.'

'I'll see that he does,' said Nell fiercely. And Elizabeth believed she would, and was greatly comforted.

They talked of children then, and as Nell was discussing in detail her feelings and ailments while she was carrying my lord Burford and my lord Beauclerk, another visitor arrived. This was William Fanshawe, thin and poor, who held a small post at Court. He had married Lucy Walter's daughter, Mary, over whom the King had exercised some care, although he had refused to acknowledge the child as his own, since everyone was fully aware that she could not be.

''Tis William Fanshawe,' said Nell. 'He is proud because his wife is with child. He will boast and try to convince you that Mary was in fact the King's daughter, I doubt not. It is the main subject of his discourse.'

William Fanshawe was ushered in.

'Why, Will,' cried Nell, 'right glad I am to see you. And how fares your wife? Well, I trust, and happy with her belly.'

Fanshawe said that his wife was hoping the child would bear a resemblance to her royal father.

''Tis to be hoped,' said Nell, 'that the baby will not take so long to get born as her mother did.' This was a reference to the fact that Lucy Walter's daughter was born far more than nine months after Charles had left her mother. But Nell softened at once and offered a piece of friendly advice. 'And Will, spend not too much on the christening but reserve yourself a little to buy new shoes that will not dirty my rooms, and mayhap a new periwig that I may not smell your stink two storeys high.'

William took this in good part. He was delighted to be near one who was in such close touch with royalty.

But it was clear to Nell that he had not come merely to talk of his wife's pregnancy, and that he had something to say to her which was not for Elizabeth's ears.

So, finding some pretext for dismissing Elizabeth, she settled down to hear Fanshawe's news.

'Your friends are committed to the Tower,' he said.

'What friends mean you?' asked Nell, aghast.

'Shaftesbury, Buckingham, Salisbury, and Wharton . . . the leaders of the Country Party.'

'Why so?'

'By the King's orders.'

'Then he has been forced to this by Danby!'

'They argued that a year's recess automatically dissolved a Parliament. They should have known that His Majesty would never agree that this was so, since it is His Majesty's great desire that Parliament be in perpetual recess. The King was angry with them all. He fears, it seems, that the fact that they make such a statement may put it into the members' heads to pass a law making a year's recess a lawful reason for dissolution.'

'So . . . he has sent them to the Tower!'

'Nell, take care. You dabble in dangerous waters and you are being carried out of your depth.'

Nell shook her head. 'My lord Buckingham is my good friend,' she said. 'He was my good friend when I was an orange-girl. Should I fail to be his when he is a prisoner in the Tower?'

* * *

The King took time off from his troubles to enjoy a little domesticity with Nell. These were happy times, for Nell's contentment was a pleasure to witness.

Charles took great delight in discussing their sons' future. Ironically he copied Nell's habit of referring to them by their full titles every time he addressed them or spoke of them to Nell.

'Nell, my lord Burford and my lord Beauclerk must receive an education due to their rank.'

Nell's eyes sparkled with pleasure.

'Indeed yes. They must be educated. I would not like to see my lord Burford nor my lord Beauclerk suffer the tortures I do when called upon to handle a pen.'

'I promise you they shall not. You know, there is one place where they could receive the best education in the world – the Court of France.'

Nell's expression changed. 'Take them away from me, you mean?'

'They would merely go to France for a year or so. Then they would come back to you. They would come back proficient in all the graces of the noblemen you wish them to be.'

'But they wouldn't be my boys any more.'

'I thought you wished that they should be lords and dukes.'

'I do indeed; and forget not that you have promised they shall be. But why should they not be with their mother?'

'Because it is the custom for children of high rank to be brought up in the households of noblemen, Nell. Had I left Jemmy with his mother, he would never have been the young nobleman he is today.'

'Which might have been better for him and others. Mayhap then he would not have been strutting about as Prince Perkin.'

'You speak truth. I would not press this. It is a decision you must come to for yourself. Keep them with you if you wish it. But if you would have them take their place in the world beside others of their rank, then must they follow a similar course of education.'

'Why should I not have tutors for them?'

'It is for you to say.'

When the King left Nell, she was disturbed.

She found the boys playing with Mrs Turner, their

governess, in charge of them. They ran to her as she entered.

'Mama,' they cried. 'Here is Mama, come to sing and dance for us.'

Nell had rarely felt less like singing and dancing.

She dismissed Mrs Turner and hugged the boys. They were so beautiful, she thought. They had an air of royalty which, no matter what education they received, must surely carry them to greatness. Charles was the image of his father. My darling, darling Earl of Burford, thought Nell; and little James? Nay, he had not the same air as his brother. There were times when Nell thought she saw her mother in him. This was not a new idea. She had settled her mother in a house in Pimlico, where she was very contented to be. Nell did not want her mother to influence those two precious lives.

'Mama,' said Lord Burford, 'are you sad?'

'Nay . . . nay, my little lord. I'm not sad. How could I be when I have two such precious lambs?' She kissed them tenderly. 'Would you like to go to France?' she asked abruptly.

'Where's France?' asked Lord Beauclerk.

'Across the water,' said his brother. ''Tis a grand, a beautiful place. Papa lived there a long time.'

'I want to live there,' said little James.

'Is Papa coming with us?' asked Charles.

'No,' said Nell. 'If you went, you'd have to go alone.'

'Without you?' said Charles.

She nodded.

'Then I won't go,' he answered haughtily – royally, thought Nell. The Divine Right of the adored child shining in his eyes.

She thought, Mr Otway shall be his tutor. Poor Tom Otway, he'll be glad of a roof to his head and his food each day.

Little James had taken her hand and was staring into space. He was picturing himself in France.

Nell thought: Lord Beauclerk would not feel the break so much. Perhaps he should go to France. It is more important for a young son to have that air of nobility. Honours may not come so easily to him as to his brother. Nell snatched him up suddenly and held him tightly in her arms. I can't let him go, she told herself. He may be my lord Beauclerk, but he's my baby.

*   *   *

Charles was relieved to have the trouble-makers in the Tower. Their lodgings there were comfortable enough; they were allowed to have their own servants to wait upon them; they received visitors; in fact they lived like the noble lords they were; there was only one thing they lacked, and that was freedom.

Charles trusted none. To Danby, to Louise, he listened with sympathy; he visited Nell's house and talked with the utmost friendship to her Whig friends. But all the time he was playing the secret game. He had one great desire – to rule his country without the help of Parliament. Parliament, with its opposing parties, made continual trouble. The Whigs slandered the Tories and the Tories the Whigs. They were more concerned with their petty hatred for each other than their love of their country. Charles loved his country (as he would have been the first to admit, loving his country was tantamount to loving himself) and he was determined to use all his skill – which was considerable when he brought it into play – to prevent himself ever going on his wanderings again.

He supported Danby because Danby was a wizard who had managed his financial affairs as they had never been managed before. He did not believe he could afford to do without Danby. For the first time since he had come to England he felt his affairs to be in good order. He placated Louise because she was Louis' spy, and it was of the utmost importance that he should keep Louis' friendship. The bribes he was taking from France now, in exchange for which he kept aloof from the Continental war, were the very reason for his country's prosperity. Charles had always known that the country which stood aloof from war and concentrated on trade was the prosperous one. It was pleasant therefore to receive Louis' bribes for keeping a peace which in any case he had intended to keep. He pretended to take Louise's advice. Poor Louise! She must please Louis. He had to satisfy her in some way, and for the life of him he could not bring himself to visit her as often as he once had.

As for Nell, her dabbling in politics amused him so much that he could not keep away from her *salon*. She had as much understanding of politics as Old Rowley the stallion and Old Rowley the goat – who shared his nickname. Politics to Nell meant one thing: Who gives a dukedom to my lord Burford and makes the noble Earl's mother a Countess, shall have my support. Danby had been against elevating Nell – doubtless on account of Louise – therefore Nell was Danby's enemy.

So while Charles sympathized with Louise and Danby's Tories and turned a sympathetic ear to Nell's Whigs, he went his own way. And while he was accepting Louis' bribes he was trying to go ahead with the arrangements for the marriage between his niece, Mary, and William of Orange.

*   *   *

James sought his brother. James' face was dark with passion.

'Charles, you cannot mean this. My daughter Mary to marry that man!'

'Forget that he is the Protestant leader of the Dutch, and you'll see what an excellent match he is.'

'The man's a monster!' said James indignantly.

'The Prince is a brave soldier, Stadtholder of Holland, and our nephew.'

'My little girl is too young.'

'Your little girl is a Princess and therefore prepared for early marriage.'

'Have you forgotten his conduct when he was here?'

'That is a long time ago, and we made him drink too much. When a man drinks too much he does wild things. That is why I like only to drink when I am thirsty.'

'Brother, for the love of God do not give my little Mary to this man.'

271

'But this marriage is a necessary part of the peace between our two countries.'

'A man who smashed windows to get at the maids of honour. He is a lecher. He is debauched.'

'Oh, come . . . no more than the rest of us.'

James went away. He went to his little daughter and took her solemnly into his arms.

'Papa,' said Mary, 'what ails you?'

'My little one . . . My little one,' sighed James.

Charles had followed him. He said: 'Mary, a great future awaits you. You are to have a fine husband, and that is what every young lady – if she is wise – looks for.'

But Mary's frightened gaze was fixed on her father's face. She stared at him and slowly the tears began to fall down her cheeks. She understood. She would marry, and when a Princess married she was forced to leave her home.

*　　　*　　　*

The King liked to please Nell. Most of her requests – apart from the demand for that title which she felt should belong to the mother of her boys – were for others. She pleaded fiercely for Buckingham. His Majesty had so enjoyed the noble Duke's company. Could he ever be really angry with Lord Buckingham? Not for long, surely. They missed him at her parties; and had Charles forgotten how they had been friends together in their childhood?

Charles prevaricated. He was afraid of offending Louise and Danby, whom he wished to keep in the dark concerning the policy he was pursuing regarding the French. The fact that he wished to bring about the marriage of Mary and William of Orange would displease Louis and therefore Louise, though Louise, still unsure of her position, was giving little trouble concerning this marriage. He did not wish to sway too much to the side of the Whigs by releasing Buckingham.

But he hinted to Nell that if she visited Buckingham in his prison she might intimate that the King no longer wished his old friend and companion of his boyhood to remain in the Tower.

This Nell quickly did, with the result that Buckingham was granted leave for a month's freedom to help him throw off several indispositions which he had developed during his imprisonment. He did not return to prison, coolly taking up his quarters with his friend Rochester instead. They kept merry company with Nell Gwyn, and the King could not exclude himself from such entertainment as they gave.

Louise wept bitterly and told Charles that she feared he no longer had any regard for her. If he had, how could he show such friendship to those who sought to harm her?

The King softened towards Louise. He was more tender than he had ever been, because his love for her was gone. Poor Fubbs! She had never been the same since she had caught his sickness and she did not cease to remind him, with reproachful looks and hints, that she had suffered through him. He promised her that Buckingham should be dismissed from Whitehall; and he was as good as his word, knowing that Buckingham would not go far away. The Duke did indeed move to Nell's house in Pall Mall, and there the merry supper parties continued.

And the French ambassador was almost as concerned about the King's attendance at Nell's parties, those hotbeds of Whiggery, as he was about this proposed marriage between Mary and William of Orange.

*   *   *

Meanwhile Charles was playing his lonely political game. The proposed marriage had thrown Louis into a fluster of anxiety. Louis, engaged in Flanders, was finding that the Dutch were a race of brave men, and stubborn fighters. William of Orange had proved himself to be a leader of genius, and Louis' hopes of quick victory were not fulfilled. There was one thing Louis dared not face – an alliance between England and Holland.

Charles went with apparent heedlessness to Newmarket. He went to Windsor to fish. He laughed and made merry at the parties his mistresses arranged for him. Danby reproved him for his friendship with the Opposition, but he merely laughed at Danby. 'I declare,' he cried, 'I will not deny myself an hour's pleasure for the sake of any man.'

Danby, bewildered and unable to understand on whose side the King was, wrote to Louis making fresh demands and promises. Charles read his Treasurer's letters. To all of these Charles gave his royal sanction. 'This letter is writ by my order. C.R.'

Louis continued to pay to keep England aloof to enjoy that peace which her King was determined to have. Louis was assured that the talk of a marriage between England and Holland was necessary to keep the people quiet and to prevent their demanding intervention in the war on the side of Holland.

But in October of that eventful year Charles announced the engagement of William and Mary. England and Scotland went wild with joy because they saw in this marriage an end to the menace of popery.

Not all rejoiced. In her bedchamber a fifteen-year-old girl sobbed bitterly while her father knelt by her bed and sought to comfort her.

*   *   *

It was a misty November day, and in the Palace of St James' were assembled those who would attend the marriage ceremony of the little fifteen-year-old Princess Mary. In Mary's bedchamber an altar had been set up, for it was here in this room that the ceremony was to take place.

The bride's eyes were swollen; she had wept incessantly since her father had told her the news. She was terrified of the small pale young man with the grim face who seemed to her so cold and so different from her father and her Uncle Charles. They told her that she should be proud of her husband. He was a great soldier. He was called the 'hero of Nassau'. He had waged war on the invaders of his country; he had declared with such fervour his willingness to die rather than give in that his countrymen had rallied about him and followed his example. Nor had those been idle words. Mary was to marry a man whose name would be spoken of with awe every time military operations were mentioned. He was her cousin, her uncle had pointed out, his own sister's boy; and when that sister – Mary's own namesake – had died, Charles had promised his care of little Dutch William.

'And how could I relinquish that care to better hands than yours, my dearest niece?' asked Charles.

But Mary merely threw herself into the royal arms and sobbed bitterly. 'Let me stay, Uncle. Please, please, dearest Uncle, Your Majesty, let me stay with you and Papa.'

'Nay, nay, you'll be laughing at yourself in a short while, Mary. You are but a child, and we must all, alas, leave childhood behind us. You will rule Holland with your husband and, if this new child your new mother is to have should be a girl . . . well, then, one day you may rule England. If that became necessary, you'd have need of Dutch William.'

But Mary could only sob and refuse to be comforted.

Now in her familiar room the King and the bridegroom were present, and the King was saying: 'My little niece is the softest-hearted creature in the world. She and her sister Anne have been dear friends since their childhood. Poor Anne is suffering now from sickness, and her sister suffers with her. It is a pity that her dearest Anne cannot be present to witness the greatest moment her sister has yet experienced.'

Mary wanted to cry out: 'I do miss Anne. I would that she were here. But Anne will get well and, when she is well, I shall be far away. I shall lose all those I love, and in their place there will be this cold man who frightens me.'

Her father had entered now. She suppressed the desire to run to him, to fling herself into his arms. There were tears in James' eyes. Dearest Papa, she thought, he suffers as I do. With James was Mary's stepmother, Mary Beatrice; she was large with child, and her beautiful dark eyes were fixed with compassion on her stepdaughter. Mary Beatrice had offered as great comfort as any could during the preceding days. She herself had not been long in England, and when she had first come she had been every bit as frightened as poor Mary was now. 'That was different,' said Mary. 'You married Papa . . . my Papa . . . There is no one quite as kind as Papa.' 'I did not think so. I burst into tears when I first saw him. It is only now that I begin to know him that I realize there was no need for those tears. So you will find it with William.'

Mary had allowed herself to be comforted, but now, in the presence of Dutch William, her courage was failing her again.

Charles, looking anxiously at his niece, was eager to have the ceremony done with. He called impatiently to Compton, the Bishop of London, who was to perform the ceremony.

'Come, Bishop,' he cried. 'Make all the haste you can, lest my sister here, the Duchess of York, should bring us a boy, and then the marriage will be disappointed.'

William looked grim. His uncle's jovial cynicism astonished him. He was aware that Charles knew that, in marrying Mary, he was hoping that one day he would come to the throne of England, but he thought it astonishing that Charles should refer to it at the ceremony.

He looked with distaste at the poor blubbering child, in whom his hopes were centred. She did not attract him, but there would be others who did.

'Who gives this woman?' the Bishop was asking.

'I do,' said Charles, firmly.

The Prince said the words required of him. He put a handful of gold coins on the book, as he endowed Mary with all his worldly goods.

'Put it in your pocket, Mary,' said the King with a smile. 'For that is all clear gain.'

After that the ceremonies began. The bridegroom was aloof and indifferent to his bride, who continued to weep throughout the banquet in a quiet helpless way as though she had given up all hope of ever being happy again.

Charles was glad he had brought Rochester out of retirement. He found Dutch William and his friends a dull crowd, and was glad when the time came for him to officiate at the ceremony of putting the couple to bed.

Poor little Mary looked with dull eyes at those who

crowded into the bedchamber to break bread and drink the posset, and cut her and her husband's garters.

At last Mary and William were in the great bed together, and the King himself drew the curtains.

He did not look at Mary. He could not trust himself to meet the appeal in the tear-drenched eyes of his little niece.

He glanced at grim William, who looked like a man at a funeral rather than at his own nuptials.

'Now, nephew, to your work!' cried Charles. 'St George for England!'

*　　　*　　　*

Charles could no longer deceive Louis. The marriage with Holland was a fact, and the Parliament – Shaftesbury had now been released from the Tower and was back in the House – were demanding that an army be raised to assist Holland. Louis, through Danby and Louise, increased Charles' pension. Charles, in accepting this, continued to assure Louis that the raising of the army was being effected only to pacify his people and keep secret his friendship with France.

Louis was realizing that, in hoping to work through Charles, he had given himself a more difficult task than he might have had. There were others in England who could be of the utmost use to him. He considered the career of Shaftesbury, he whom Charles had named 'Little Sincerity', and he felt that the leader of the Opposition might be as useful to him as the King. Louis was rich; he offered more bribes, and it was not long before the members of the Opposition – those stern Protestants – were on his pension list.

Thereupon Parliament refused to advance the money necessary for the troops, and there was nothing to be done but disband the army. Charles was forced to pay them out of his own pocket, which again put him in the power of the Parliament, for it was necessary to ask for a further grant of money.

The old struggle between King and Parliament was revived. The Commons made it clear that they wished to control the country's affairs. Shaftesbury demanded the expulsion of the Duke of York. And Louis, furious at the way in which Danby had made him his dupe, passed over to the Commons Danby's letters in which he had arranged for Louis' bribes to be paid to the King.

Now Danby's enemies were at his throat.

Charles assured the Parliament that all Danby had done had been at his command; and indeed at the bottom of each letter was written in Charles' hand, 'This letter is writ by my order. C.R.' The Commons decided to ignore the King's part in these communications with Louis. They were out for Danby's destruction; and his impeachment was imminent.

Nell tore herself from the domestic flurries concerning my lord Burford's shoelaces and my lord Beauclerk's cough, and gave way to rejoicing. Danby and Louise had worked together, and she was sure that but for them she would have been a Countess by now, and my lord Burford a Duke.

Louise was afraid for, as Danby and she had worked together, she knew that many of his enemies strove to strike at her through him.

Then throughout the city there were rumours. They penetrated Whitehall.

Plots were afoot to murder the King and set the Duke of York on the throne.

People began to talk of a man named Titus Oates.

NINE

Terror swept over England. No one was safe from the accusations of Titus Oates. The Queen herself was in danger. As for Louise, the lampoons which the Whigs had been accustomed to pass round the coffee-houses were replaced by demands that she be brought to trial or sent back to France.

The King, hating trouble and realizing as few others did that Titus Oates was a rogue and a liar, did all in his power to keep himself aloof from the troubles. He dared not expose Titus; he dared not attempt to prevent the cruel executions which were taking place, for he knew that revolution was in the air and that he was in as dangerous a position as his father had been before he had laid his head on the block.

Louise was now known as the 'Catholic whore'. No sin was too black to be imputed to her. She trembled in her apartments and played with the idea of abandoning all she had worked for and slipping back to France.

Nell, on the other hand, was unaware of danger. The King seemed fonder of her than ever before. She wept now and then because Lord Beauclerk was in France, and thus her happiness could not be complete. Since the birth of her children her thoughts had been occupied with them almost to the exclusion of all else. Nell wanted to have the King and her sons with her, like any cosy family; then she could be happy. Plots whirled about her, but she was scarcely aware of them. Her so-called friend, Lady Harvey, had recently tried to bring to the notice of the King a lovely girl named Jenny Middleton. Lady Harvey – urged by her brother Montague – had sought Nell's help in bringing this girl to the King's notice, and Nell, her mind being taken up with her grief in the absence of my lord Beauclerk and the promotion of my lord Burford to a dukedom, had been quite unaware of Lady Harvey's intention of bringing to the King's notice one who would turn him from Nell herself.

The Middleton affair had collapsed unexpectedly when Montague, its instigator, who was suspected of being Jenny Middleton's father, was recalled to England. He was in deep disgrace because he had seduced Anne, Countess of Sussex (the young daughter of the King and Barbara) while they were both in France. As Montague had previously been Barbara's lover, Barbara was furious with the pair and had lost no time in acquainting the King with Montague's defection. The resulting disgrace of Montague meant that all connected with him were out of favour; thus the Middletons found it necessary to leave Court in a hurry; and Nell was safe. Only she herself was sublimely ignorant of the danger through which she had passed.

She was a Whig because her friends were Whigs. Buckingham and Rochester had been good to her, and Nell was the sort never to forget a friend. She was fond of Monmouth because he reminded her of her own little Charles, and he was her children's half-brother. She always felt that she wanted to ruffle that black hair and tell Prince Perkin to enjoy himself and not worry so much about whether he would inherit a crown. He seemed to forget that, if he ever received it, it could only be at the death of that one who, Nell believed, must be as beloved by his son as he was by her – King Charles, the fount of all their bounties.

She enjoyed life as best she could taking into account the absence of little James. She had a bonfire on November 5th, just outside her door in Pall Mall, and there she had a Pope to burn with the longest red nose that had ever been seen. The people rejoiced, calling her the 'Protestant whore'. And she was one of the few people at Court who was not in danger from Titus Oates.

Little Charles ran excitedly from the bonfire to his mother. He was throwing fireworks of such beauty that few had seen before.

'Now watch, good people,' cried Nell. 'My lord Burford will throw a few crackers.'

So Lord Burford let off his fireworks and threw squibs

at the long red nose of the burning Pope, and all the people about Nell's door that night rejoiced in her position at Court. They remembered that those who were poor had no need to ask help twice from Nell Gwyn. 'Long life to Nelly!' they cried.

Nell went into her house that night when the celebrations were over, and as she herself washed the grime from the little Earl's face, he noticed that she was crying; and to see Nell cry was a rare thing.

He put his arms about her and said: 'Mama, why do you cry?'

Then she hugged him. She said: 'It has been a good day, has it not, my lord Earl? I was wondering what my lord Beauclerk was doing in the great French capital. And I was crying because he was not here with us.'

Little Lord Burford wiped away his mother's tears. 'I'll never go,' he said. 'Never . . . never. I'll never go to France.'

*　　　*　　　*

The fury continued, and Charles temporized. He gave way to demands. He did all he could to save Danby, but was forced to submit to his imprisonment in the Tower. He found it necessary to dismiss the Duke of York and send him into temporary exile in Brussels. Louise, sick both mentally and physically, could not make up her mind whether or not to leave for France. Hortense continued to play basset and amuse herself with a lover. The people realized that Hortense should not give them cause for concern. It was Louise, the spy of Catholic France, who was the real enemy of the country.

There was talk of the Queen's attempt to poison the King. Charles characteristically intervened and, although he would have welcomed a new wife and a chance to get a son which he felt would have solved most of his immediate troubles, gallantly stood by the Queen and saved her life.

Nell continued to receive the Whigs at her house. She was cheered wherever she went. People crowded into a goldsmith's shop, where the goldsmith was making a very rich service of plate, admired this greatly and were pleased because they believed it was to be presented to Nell. When they discovered it was for Portsmouth, they cursed the Duchess and spat on the plate.

Nell was immersed in family affairs. Rose had married again on the death of John Cassels. This time her husband was Guy Forster, and Nell was working hard to get a bigger pension for Rose and her husband.

While Nell was at Windsor news came to her of her mother's accident.

Madam Gwyn had moved to Sandford Manor where, at the bottom of her garden, was a stream which divided Fulham from Chelsea. One day she had wandered out to her garden and, well fortified with her favourite beverage, had slipped and fallen into the stream. It was a shallow brook but, being too drunk to lift herself out of it, she had lain face down and drowned.

Nell hurried to London where Rose was waiting for her. They embraced and wept a little.

''Tis not,' said Nell, 'that she was a good mother to us, but she was the only mother we had.'

So Nell gave the old lady a fine funeral and many gathered in the streets to see it pass. Madam Gwyn was buried in St Martin's Church, and Nell ordered a monument to be erected over her grave

Whigs and Tories gathered in the streets. The Whigs called attention to the virtues of Nell; the Tories jeered. There was a new spate of Tory lampoons on Nell's upbringing in her mother's bawdy-house.

Nell snapped her fingers and went back to Windsor to join the King.

*   *   *

Charles knew that he was passing through the most dangerous time of his life. As an exile he had longed to regain his kingdom, but then he had been young. Now he was ageing; he had enjoyed almost twenty years of that kingdom, but he knew that if he did not walk with the utmost care he would lose it again; and he wondered whether, if he lost it, he would ever have the strength to recover it.

He tried to lead the life he loved – sauntering in his parks, his dogs at his heels, feeding his ducks, exchanging witty comments as he went. He sat for long hours fishing on the banks of the river at Windsor. He wished that he could prorogue Parliament and prevent its ever sitting again. If he had enough money with which to manage the affairs of the country, he believed he could rule in peace; he could put an end to this terror which hung over his country. He would demand freedom of thought in religious matters for all men. He saw no peace for any country when there was religious conflict. He wished to say: Think as you wish on these things, and let others go their way. He himself would never feel bound to any religion; he merely wished for freedom for all his subjects.

He wanted peace, and while Whig was at Tory's throat, and vice versa, there would never be peace. Let a pleasure-loving man such as himself rule; let the people take their pleasures as he did; give him enough money to fit out a navy which would hold all enemies from his shores, and there would be peace and plenty throughout the land.

But this terror had come upon the country, and there was nothing he could do to prevent it. He was powerless in the hands of his Parliament; he was caught between the Whigs and Tories, the Protestants and the Catholics.

James had reproved him for wandering too freely in his parks alone. 'Would his little spaniels protect him from an assassin's bullet?' James demanded. 'Do not worry on that score,' Charles had said. 'They will never kill me to make you King.'

He had said it with a laugh, but there was a great sadness in his heart. He feared for James; he greatly feared for James.

Oh, James, he mused again and again, if you would but turn from your holy saints, if you would but declare yourself a Protestant, England would accept you as my successor, and young Jemmy's nose would be out of joint. All this unrest would die down, for it flows out of the curse of this age – religious conflicts, and the curse of Kings: the inability to get sons.

He went to Nell for comfort.

Young Charles – my lord Burford, thought the King with a chuckle – came running to greet him.

'It is long since you have been to see me, Papa,' said Charles.

'"Tis but a few days.'

'It seems longer,' said the boy.

Charles ruffled the hair so like his own had been when he was a small boy roaming in the grounds of Hampton Court or lying on the banks at Greenwich watching the ships sail by.

'It was wrong of me.'

'You should pay a penalty for your sins, Father.'

'What would you suggest for me?'

'Stay all the time.'

'Ah, my son, that would be my pleasure, and penances are not for the pleasure of the sinner, you know. You and I will go to Portsmouth to watch the launching of one of my ships, shall we?'

Charles leaped into the air. 'Yes, Papa. When? . . . When? . . .'

'Very soon . . . very soon . . . I'll tell you something else. Ships have names, you know, just as boys have. What shall we call this one?'

Little Charles looked shyly at his father, waiting. 'Charles?' he suggested.

'There are so many Charleses. Who shall say which is which? Nay, we'll call her Burford.'

'Then she will be my ship?'

'Oh, no, my son. All those which bear our names do not necessarily belong to us. But the honour is yours. It will show the world how much I honour my son Burford. 'Twill make your mother dance a merry jig, I doubt not.'

'Shall we tell her?' asked small Charles with a laugh.

'Come! We'll do so now.'

And hand in hand they went to find Nell.

* * *

Charles, determined to follow the old life as far as possible, gave up few of his pleasures. He could not stop the execution of the accused, though he had managed to save the Queen. The mob had allowed him that, for such was his charm that he had only to appear before them to subdue their anger, and he had gone in person to Somerset House to bring Catherine to Whitehall at the very time when the mob was howling for her blood. But he could not save others, for Titus Oates, it seemed, was King of London during those days of terror.

So he sauntered and fished and played games, as he had always done. He had forgotten that he was fifty, he had enjoyed such robust health that he seemed to have a notion that he always would.

He had played a hard game of tennis and, walking along by the river, he had taken off his wig and jacket to cool down.

This he had done effectively enough at the time, but when he went to bed that night he became delirious and his attendants hurried to his bedside, to find him in a high fever.

Shaftesbury, Buckingham, and the whole of the Parliament were filled with consternation. If Charles should die now, there could be no averting civil war. James would never stand aside, and, although Monmouth had his supporters, there were many who would die rather than see a bastard on the throne.

James' friends sent word to Brussels, telling him that the King was on the point of death and that he should return immediately. James left Brussels at once, leaving Mary Beatrice there and taking with him only a few of his most trusted friends – Lord Peterborough, John Churchill, Colonel Legge, and his barber.

He dressed himself in simple dark clothes and wore a black periwig, so that on his arrival in England none would recognize him. This was very necessary, for with his brother, as he believed, dying, his life would be worth very little if he fell into the hands of his enemies.

James believed that a great ordeal lay before him and, as

John Churchill advised him, it was imperative that he should be at hand when his brother died, that he might be proclaimed King before Monmouth could be helped to the throne. James was very sad. He was a sentimental man and very fond of every member of his family. It seemed a terrible thing that a Stuart should be forced to fly the country while his brother was reigning King. Time and time again Charles had said to him: 'Give up your popery, James, and all will be well.' But, thought James, my spiritual well-being is of greater importance than what happens to me here on Earth.

He prayed and meditated on the future as he made the crossing in a French shallop, and when he arrived at Dover none knew that the Duke of York had come home.

Reaching London, he spent a night in the house of Sir Allen Apsley in St James' Square, and Sir Allen immediately brought his brother-in-law, Hyde, to him with Sidney Godolphin.

'It is necessary, Your Grace,' they told him, 'to make all haste to Windsor where the King lies. He is a little better, we hear. But for the love of God ride there, and ride fast. As yet Monmouth and his followers know nothing of His Majesty's indisposition.'

James set out for Windsor.

*   *   *

Charles' barber was shaving him when James burst in.

He rushed to his brother and knelt at his feet.

'James!' cried Charles. 'What do you here?'

'But you are yourself, brother. I had heard you were dying.'

'Nay, 'twas but a chill and touch of fever. The river breezes cooled me too quickly after tennis. And kneel not thus. Let me look at you. Why, James, did you think to find me a corpse and yourself a King?'

'Brother, I rejoice that it is not so.'

'I believe you, James. You have not the art of lying. And indeed you are wise to wish it at this time. I dare not think what would happen if I were so inconsiderate as to die now.

I should leave the affairs of this country in a sorry state. Think of it, brother: The English persecute the Jesuits and they owe my life, and what is more their concern the peace of their country – if this present rule of Titus can be called peace – to the Jesuits' powder, quinine. I swear this drug has cured me.'

He asked after Mary Beatrice and life in Brussels.

''Tis a sorry thing that you must be an exile, James,' he said. 'It would seem our family is cursed to be exiles. But, James, if you persist in acting as you have, and you should come to the throne, I'd not give you four years to hold it.'

'I would hold it,' said James, 'were it mine.'

'You must leave the country ere it is discovered that you returned.'

'Brother, is it justice, I ask you, that I should be exiled? Monmouth remains here. You know that were it not for Monmouth there would not be this trouble. This illness of yours has brought home to me how dangerous it is for me to be so far away when Monmouth is so near.'

Charles smiled wryly. James was right. It was unhealthy to have Monmouth in England during the Popish terror. Monmouth should go to Holland where he had so distinguished himself against the Dutch; and Catholic James should go to Protestant Scotland. It might be that both these men – both dearly beloved, but both recognized as sadly foolish – should learn something they both needed to learn, against a background which should be alien to them.

*   *   *

Shaftesbury and his Whigs were determined on the downfall of the Duke of York. They did not wish Monmouth to remain abroad and, believing that the King's love for his eldest son was as strong as ever, they brought him secretly back from Holland.

Monmouth was nothing loth. He was now certain that he was to wear the crown. It was true he had been sent to Holland, but that was only that the King might have an excuse to be rid of the Duke of York. The foolish and criminal exploits of his youth had been forgiven him. He knew how to placate the King, and Charles was never annoyed with him for long at a time.

It was the anniversary of Queen Elizabeth's coronation, and the Whigs had chosen this occasion as an opportunity for staging a demonstration which they believed would induce the King to legitimize Monmouth and make him his heir. It was easy to whip up the people of London to a state of excitement. They had already been shown the villainy of the papists by Titus Oates, according to whom new plots were continually springing up. It was therefore not difficult to rouse them to fury, and they were soon parading the streets holding aloft effigies of the Pope and the Devil which it was their intention to burn.

For several days these scenes took place; then they gave way to rejoicing. Charles, watching from a window of Whitehall, having heard the bells ring out, saw his son riding triumphantly at the head of a procession, holding himself as though he already wore the crown.

He stopped at Whitehall, and a message came to Charles that his dearly beloved son craved audience.

Charles sent back a message.

'Bid him go back whence he came. I have no wish to see him. I will deprive him of all his offices since he has disobeyed my wishes in returning to England when I commanded him to stay abroad. Tell him, for his own safety, to leave the country at once.'

Monmouth went disconsolately away.

Charles heard the crowds cheering him as he went. He shook his head sadly. 'Jemmy, Jemmy,' he murmured, 'whither are you going? The path you are taking leads to the scaffold.'

Then he recalled long-ago days in The Hague, when he had lightly taken Lucy Walter as his mistress. From that association had sprung this young man, and in him had been born such ambition as could set a bloody trail across this fair land and plunge it into civil war as hideous and cruel as that which had cost Charles' father his head. And all for the sake of a brief passion with a light-o'-love.

I must save Jemmy at all costs, Charles decided.

* * *

288

Nell was giving my lord Burford his goodnight kiss when she was told a visitor wished to see her.

She hoped it was my lord Rochester. She had need of his cheering company. Charles was melancholy. It was due to all these riots in the streets, all this burning of the Pope and the Devil. Poor Charles! She wished everyone would go about his business and let the King enjoy himself.

The visitor was shown in. He was wearing a long cloak which he threw off when they were alone.

'It's Perkin,' cried Nell. 'Prince Perkin.'

He did not frown as he usually did when she used that name. Instead he took her hand and kissed it. 'Nell, for the love of God, help me. The King has refused to see me.'

'Oh, Perkin, it was wrong of you to come. You know His Majesty forbids it.'

'I had to come, Nell. How can I stay away? This is my home. This is where I belong.'

'But if you are sent abroad on a mission . . .'

'Abroad on a mission! I am sent abroad because my uncle must go.'

'Well, 'tis only fair that if one goes so should the other.'

'My uncle goes because the people force him to. You have seen they want me here. Did you not hear them shouting for me in the street?'

Nell shook her head. 'All these troubles! Why cannot you all be good friends? Why are you always seeking the crown, when you know your mother was no better than I am. I might as well make a Perkin of little Burford.'

'Nell, my mother was married to the King.'

'The black box!' said Nell scornfully.

'Well, why should there not have been a black box?'

'Because the King says there's not.'

'What if the King tells not the truth?'

'He says it all the same, and if he says "no black box", then there should be none.'

'Nelly, you're a strange woman.'

'Strange because I don't bring my little Earl up to prate about a black box which carries my marriage lines?'

'Don't joke, Nell. Will you keep me here? Will you let me

stay? 'Twill only be for a short while, and mayhap you can persuade the King to see me. I've nowhere to go, Nell. There's no one I can trust.'

Nell looked at him. Dark hair, so like my lord Burford's. Dark eyes . . . big lustrous Stuart eyes. Well, after all, they were half-brothers.

'You must be well-nigh starving,' said Nell. 'And there'll be a bed for you here as long as you want it.'

*　　　*　　　*

Monmouth stayed in her house, and the whole of London knew. It was typical that the King, knowing, should have said nothing. He was glad Nell was looking after the boy. He needed a mother; he needed Nell's sharp common sense.

Nell pleaded with Charles to see his son.

'He grows pale and long-visaged, fearing Your Majesty no longer loves him.'

'It is well that he should have such fears,' said Charles. 'I will not see him. Bid him be gone, Nelly, for his own sake.'

Nell was universally known now as the 'Protestant whore'. In the turmoil that existed it was necessary to take sides. She was cheered in the streets; for the London mob, fed on stories of Popish plots, looked upon her as their champion.

They loved the King, for his easy affability was remembered by all, and in this time of stress they sought to lay blame for everything that happened in his name on the people who surrounded him. The Duchess of Portsmouth was the enemy; Nell was the friend of the people.

One day, as she was riding home in her carriage, the mob surrounded it, and, believing that it was Louise inside, they threw mud, cursed the passenger, and would have wrecked the vehicle.

Nell put her head out of the window and begged them to stop. 'Pray, good people, be civil,' she cried. 'I am the Protestant whore.'

''Tis Nelly, not Carwell,' shouted one and they all took up the cry: 'God bless Nelly! Long life to little Nell.'

They surrounded the coach, and they walked with her as she was carried on her way.

She was stimulated. It was pleasant to know that Squintabella, from whom it had been impossible to turn the King's favour, was so disliked and herself so popular. Nell enjoyed dabbling in their politics, even though she understood so little. Still she had understood enough to keep her place; she knew that she was no politician; she knew that the King could not discuss politics with her as he could with Louise. As she had said on one occasion: 'I do not seek to lead the King in politics. I am just his sleeping partner.'

So she was carried home.

* * *

The troublous winter had passed into spring and now it was June. Nell never forgot that June day, because some joy went out of her life then, and she knew that no matter what happened to her she would never be completely happy again.

A messenger arrived at her house. Her servants looked subdued and she knew at once that something had gone wrong and that they were afraid to tell her.

'What is this?' she asked.

'A messenger,' said her steward, Groundes. 'He comes from France.'

'From France. Jamie!'

'My lord Beauclerk was suffering from a sore leg.'

'A sore leg! Why was I not told?'

'Madam, it happened so quickly. The little boy was running about happily one day, and the next . . .'

'Dead,' said Nell blankly.

'Madam, all was done that could be done.'

Nell threw herself on to a couch and covered her face with her hands. 'It is not true,' she sobbed. 'There was nothing wrong with Jamie. He had a cough at times, that was all. Why was I not told? . . . My little boy, to die of a sore leg!'

'Madam, he did not suffer long. He died peacefully in his sleep.'

'I should not have let him go,' said Nell. 'I should have kept him with me. He was only a baby. My little boy . . .'

They tried to comfort her, but she would not be comforted. She drove them all away. For once Nell wanted to be alone.

Her little James, Lord Beauclerk, for whom she had planned such a glorious future, was now dead and she would never see those wondering dark eyes looking at her again, never hear the baby lips begging her to dance a jig.

'I let him go,' she said. 'I should never have let him go. He was only a baby. But I wanted to make him a Duke, so I let him go, and now I have lost him. I'll never see my little lord again.'

They sent Lord Burford in to comfort her. He wiped her eyes and put his arms about her.

'I'm here, Mama,' he said. 'I'm still here.'

Then she held him fiercely in her arms. She did not care if he was never a Duke. The only important thing was that she held him in her arms.

She would keep him with her for ever.

*   *   *

Nell shut herself in with her grief. Life seemed to have little meaning for her. She blamed herself. She had so wanted the child to be educated like a lord. How thankful she was that she had kept one of her sons at home.

She was still mourning the death of James when the news of another death was brought to her. It was that of the Earl of Rochester. Rochester had been a good friend to her; his advice had always been sound; and because he was merry and wicked and, although three years older than she was, had seemed but a boy to her, she grieved for him. It seemed a sad thing that he, after only thirty-three years of life, should have died, worn out by his excesses. Poor Rochester, so witty, so brilliant – and now there was nothing of him but the few verses he had left behind.

Death was horrible. Her mother was gone, but she was old and Nell had never loved her. It was a marvel that the gin had not carried her off long before. But these deaths of such as Rochester and little Jamie moved her deeply. She might laugh; she might dance and sing; but she was aware of change.

She was glad she had known nothing of that fever which had attacked Charles so recently. There had been no need to feel anxiety then, because he was well again before she heard of it. But it could happen suddenly and mayhap next time it would not end so happily.

Rochester . . . Jamie . . . She could not forget.

Charles, sharing her grief in the loss of their son though not by any means feeling it as deeply as she did, was sad to see the change in her.

He wanted his merry Nell back again.

He took her to Windsor and showed her a beautiful house not far from the Castle.

This was to be Burford House, and it was the King's gift to Nell. It was a delightful place. 'And so convenient to the Castle,' said the King with a smile.

It was impossible not be charmed with the house. It seemed a fitting residence for my lord Burford. And Nell showed her gratitude by trying to dismiss all thoughts of her lost child from her mind. She had the interior of Burford House decorated by Verrio, the Court painter, who was also working on the Castle at this time. And Potevine, her upholsterer in Pall Mall, furnished the place to her satisfaction. The gardens, facing south, were a delight, and she and the King planned them together, with my lord Burford running from one to the other, happy to see his mother more like herself, and his father with her in the new home.

*   *   *

With the terror at its height, the Whigs made an effort to force Charles to legitimize Monmouth. Thus only, they argued, could the King protect his own life and save his people from the Catholic plotters.

Charles, in the House of Lords, patiently pointed out that what they asked of him was illegal. He assured them that he intended to take great care of himself and his people.

It was pointed out to him that laws could always be changed in emergency.

'If that is your conscience,' said Charles, 'it is far from mine. I assure you that I love my life so well that I will take all the care in the world to keep it with honour. But I do not think it is of such great value after fifty to be preserved with the forfeiture of my honour, my conscience, and the law of the land.'

Monmouth was present and Charles watched the young man as he spoke. He saw the bitter look in Monmouth's face; and he thought: I was a fool to think he loved me. What did he ever love but my crown?

The King won the day. But Shaftesbury would not give in. He had gone so far he could not draw back and he knew he had proved himself to be such an enemy to the Duke of York that he must at all cost prevent his coming to the throne. He now tried to bring a new bill to force Charles to divorce the Queen. Charles retaliated with his old gambit: the dissolution of Parliament.

Louise meanwhile had been in constant touch with the new French ambassador, Barrillon, who had replaced Courtin. She believed she saw a chance to reinstate herself with Charles.

She had made herself aware, during the recent years of terror, of every twist and turn in the complicated policy of the King and Parliament. Now that Danby was a prisoner in the Tower she had turned her attention to Lord Sunderland, one of the most important men in the country. She had used all her wits to save herself and had found it convenient to turn to anyone who she thought could be of the slightest use to her. She even helped Shaftesbury to reinstate himself; she made friendly overtures to Monmouth, though she secretly hoped that her son, the Duke of Richmond, might be legitimized and named heir to the throne; but she said nothing of this to Monmouth.

Louise was desperate and, being full of cunning as well, she began to sidle back to the King, and her ability to discuss with intelligence any new political move made him seek her company. He was visiting her every day, although he was spending his nights with Nell. Louise did not greatly care that this should be so, because she was beginning to realize that if she were clever enough both Louis and Charles could come to look upon her as a person important to the policies they wished to pursue. For Charles she was that one to whom he could confide what he wished for from the King of France; to Louis she was the person who wielded an influence over the King of England which she could use as he bade her.

She sought out the King very soon after the dissolution of Parliament and, seeing that she wished to speak with him alone, he allowed her to dismiss all those about them.

One of his little dogs leaped into his lap, and he fondled its ears as they talked.

'What great good fortune,' said Louise, 'if it were never necessary to reassemble Parliament!'

'I agree with all my heart,' said Charles. 'But alas, it will be necessary ere long to do so.'

She had moved nearer to him. 'For what reason, Charles?'

'Money,' he said. 'I must have money. The country needs it. I need it. The Parliament must assemble and grant it me.'

'Charles, what if there were other means of filling your exchequer . . . would you then think it necessary to call the Parliament?'

He raised his eyebrows and smiled at her, but he was alert.

'If I could make certain promises to Louis . . .' she began.

'There have been promises.'

'Yes, and the Dutch marriage and your failure to confess yourself a Catholic angered Louis.'

Charles shrugged lightly. 'I was forced into the first,' he said. 'The people wished it. As for the second – that is something my people would not tolerate.'

'And you yourself, Charles?'

'I am an irreligious fellow. I cannot conform, you know. I think that the Catholic Faith is more befitting to a gentle-man than gloomy Presbyterianism certainly. But I am my grandfather again. England is worth a principle, as Paris was with him.'

'In the Treaty of Dover you promised to proclaim yourself a Catholic.'

'At the appropriate time,' said Charles quickly.

'And that will be . . .?'

'When my people will accept a Catholic King.'

'You mean . . . never as long as you live.'

'Who can say? Who can say?'

Louise was silent for a while. Religion, as with his grandfather who had saved France from the disaster into which religious conflict was plunging the nation, would always be for Charles a matter of expediency. She must shelve the great desire to fulfil that part of her duty to France. But she must seek to bind Charles closer to the country of her birth, not only to please the French King, but to make her own position secure.

'If you had money,' she said, 'if you had, say, four millions of livres over three years you would be able to manage your affairs without calling Parliament.'

'You think Louis would pay . . .'

'On conditions which me might arrange . . .'

Charles put down the lapdog and held out his hand. 'Louise, my ministering angel,' he said, 'let us talk of those conditions.'

*   *   *

Before the next Parliament was called Charles was to receive £200,000 a year for a promise of neutrality towards Louis' Continental adventures. Charles saw his chance to rule without a Parliament, which in the past he had needed merely to vote him the money he required for governing the country.

When the new Parliament met, the King's expression was inscrutable.

He called to the Lord Chancellor to do his bidding, and the Lord Chancellor declared that the Parliament was dissolved.

Charles left the chamber, where everyone was too astonished to protest. When he called to his valet to help him change, Charles was laughing. 'You are a better man than you were a quarter of an hour since,' he said. 'It is better to have one King than five hundred.'

He continued in high good humour. 'For,' he said, 'I will have no more Parliaments, unless it be for some necessary acts that are temporary only, or to make new ones for the general good of the nation; for, God be praised, my affairs are now in so good a position that I have no occasion to ask my Parliament to vote me supplies.'

Thus Charles, true ruler of his country through the French King's bribes, determined not to call a Parliament for as long as he lived. Nor did he.

Now he began to deal with the terror. Shaftesbury was sent to the Tower. Oates was arrested for slander. Monmouth was arrested and, although he was soon released, and Shaftesbury escaped to Holland, gradually there was a return to peaceful living.

TEN

IN a house not far from Whitehall a little group of men sat huddled about a table. They spoke in whispers and every now and then one of their number would creep to the door and open it silently and sharply, to make sure there was no one listening outside. At the head of the table sat a tall handsome young man whose brilliant eyes were now alight with ambition. Monmouth believed that before the year was out he would be King of England.

He listened to the talk of 'Slavery' and 'Popery', from which these men were swearing England should be freed for ever. Popery and Slavery had special meanings; one referred to the Duke of York, the other to the King.

Monmouth was uneasy. He hated Popery. But Slavery? He could not stop thinking of eyes which shone with a special affection for him, and he pretended to misunderstand when they talked about the annihilation of Slavery.

Rumbold, one of the chief conspirators, was saying: 'There could not be a spot more suited to our purpose. My farm – the Rye House – is as strong as a castle. It is close to the road where it narrows so that only one carriage can pass at a time. When Slavery and Popery ride past on their way to London from the Newmarket races we will block the way.'

Colonel John Rumsey said: 'We might overturn a cart. Would that suffice?'

'Amply.' Rumbold looked round the table at the men gathered there: Richard Nelthorpe, Richard Goodenough, James Burton, Edward Wade, and many more – all good countrymen; and the nobility was represented by the Earl of Essex, Lord William Russell, and Algernon Sydney.

Essex said: 'We would have in readiness forty armed men. They will quickly do their work.'

'And should there be trouble?' asked Captain Walcot,

another of the conspirators. 'What if the guards come to the aid of Popery and Slavery?'

'Then,' said Rumbold, 'we can retire to the Rye House. As I said, it is as strong as a castle and can withstand a siege until the new Government is set up. My lord Monmouth will be in London.'

'And,' said Sydney, 'he will but have to go into the streets and proclaim himself King.'

They were all looking at the young Duke, but Monmouth did not see them. He was remembering a room in a foreign house, a blowsy and beautiful woman upon whose bed he had climbed. He remembered playing soldiers with her sweetmeats; he remembered the arrival of a tall man who had tossed him to the ceiling and caught him as he fell. He remembered his own choking laughter of excitement; he remembered that wonderful feeling – the thrill of being thrown, and the certain knowledge that those hands which caught him would never fail.

Now they were asking him to aid in the murder of that kind father.

'You cannot,' said a voice within him.

But he could not shut out the thought of the glittering crown and the power that went with it.

*   *   *

Charles had settled into a life of ease.

Less vigorous than he had been, he had three favourites, and they were adequate. There was Louise – and he never forgot that it was Louise's advice and her negotiations with the French which had brought him the pension enabling him to rule without a Parliament – and he looked upon Louise as his wife. It was Louise who received foreign visitors, for she understood politics as poor Catherine never could. Louise looked upon herself as Queen of England, and acted the part with such poise and confidence that many had come to consider her as such. She felt herself to be so secure that she did not hesitate to leave England and take a trip to her own country. There she had been received as a Queen, for the French King, even more so than the King of England, was sensible of her services. She had demanded the right to sit on a *tabouret* in the presence of the Queen of France, and this had been granted her. Louis had done great honour to her and everywhere she had been received with the utmost respect. Louise, practical as ever, had set about wisely investing the great fortune she had amassed while in England. This was her real reason for coming to France. And, strangely enough, on her return to England she had been received with more honour than ever before. The people of England, hearing of the homage paid to her by the King of France for acting so ably as his spy, were ready to accord her that respect which hitherto they had always denied her.

Then there was Hortense – serenely beautiful, cultured, easygoing, very like the King in character – who was still the most beautiful woman in the kingdom, for her beauty was such that nothing seemed to mar it; and, although she took lovers and sat late at the basset table, she did all these things with such serenity, never departing from a mood of contentment, that there were no lines of dissipation to mark the beautiful contours of her perfect face. So lovely she was that men of all ages fell in love with her. Even her own nephew, Prince Eugène de Savoy-Carignan, when he visited London, did so, and had fought a duel for her sake with Baron de Bainer who was the son of one of the generals of Gustavus Adolphus; in this duel Bainer was killed, and at the Court of Versailles there was amazement that a woman who was a grandmother could arouse such passion in the heart of a young man who was moreover her nephew. But Hortense went on calmly playing basset, taking lovers, receiving the King now and then; not seeking power as Louise did; content with her position as casual mistress, that she might not be denied the right to take another lover if so she wished.

Then there was Nell. Nell's role, Charles came to realize, was the more maternal one. It was to Nell he went for amusement and for comfort. Nell's love was more disinterested than the others'. Nell loved him, not always as a lover, not as a King; but understanding that in him which –

cynic though he was – had never quite grown up, she was his playmate; she was his mistress when he desired her to be; she was his solace and his comfort.

Recently he had laid the foundation stone of Chelsea Hospital, which was to be a refuge for disabled old soldiers, and it was Nell who, with Sir Stephen Fox – for so many years Paymaster to the Forces – had urged him to this benevolent act. He smiled often remembering her enthusiasm and how, when she had seen Wren's plans of the hospital, she had protested angrily that it was too small. Then with a roguish laugh she had turned to the King. 'I beg Your Majesty to make it at least as big as my pocket handkerchief,' she had pleaded. He had answered: 'Such a modest request could not be denied you.' Whereupon she confounded him – and Wren – by tearing her handkerchief into strips and making a hollow square into which she fitted the plans. Charles was so amused that he agreed to increase the size of the proposed hospital.

He had come to know, in these years when he was aware of the slight ailments which must attack a man even as healthy as himself, that Nell was more important to him than any of his mistresses. Louise he admired as a clever woman who had risen from obscurity to be the power behind the throne; Hortense must be admired for her beauty; but it was Nell whom he could least bear to lose.

But he was a fortunate man. There was no need to lose any one of them. His pension from Louis enabled him to meet his and his country's commitments. He could dabble in scientific experiments in his laboratory; he could sit by the river and fish; he could go to the play with Louise on one arm and Nell on the other. He could spend his time between Whitehall and Windsor, Winchester and New-market.

Many of his friends were no longer with him. Buckingham, after the defeat of the Country Party, had left public life and retired to Helmsly in Yorkshire. He regretted George's gay company, but wherever George had been there also had been trouble. Rochester was dead. There would be no more witty verses stuck on bedroom doors; but those verses of his had been scurrilous indeed and had doubtless done much to dissatisfy the people. James, his brother, was back in England and, though he prophesied trouble for James when he came to the throne, and feared that James would not last long as King, he advised him now and then on ruling as he was ruling, keeping Parliament in recess and thus preventing that deadly rivalry between Whig and Tory which had almost brought the country to revolution. In any case he could tell himself that the ruling of the country would be James' affair, and any trouble that ensued could not reach him in the grave. His dear son, Monmouth, realized now that he had been foolish. He knew that he could never have the crown. 'Why you, Jemmy?' Charles had said. 'Think of all the sons I have who might as easily lay claim to the throne.' And Jemmy had looked sheepish, while Charles put his arm about his shoulders. ''Tis my wish,' he had said, 'that you thrust such thoughts from your mind since they can bring nought but suffering to you and to me.'

Then Jemmy had looked at him as the young Jemmy had when he had plunged his little hands into his father's pockets for sweetmeats. Charles remembered saying then: 'Why, Jemmy, is it the sweetmeats you are glad to find, or your father?' And the young Jemmy had considered this and suddenly thrown his arms about his father's neck. Jemmy, the young man, had not altered, thought Charles. He longs for a crown. But he knows it is dangerous longing.

Thus was his state when he travelled down to Newmarket for the season's races. The Duke of York was with him and they were seen together, the best of friends, the most loving of brothers. Charles wanted the whole country to know that, now that he had given up all hope of getting a son, his brother James was the only man who could follow him to the throne.

They planned to leave Newmarket on a certain day, and the journey home would be, as usual, through Hoddesdon in Hertfordshire and past the Rye House.

At the Rye House a group of men eagerly awaited the coming of the coach in which the royal brothers would be riding. All plans were completed. There was the cart which would be set across the road. There were the conspirators waiting in the Rye House. In London the Duke of Monmouth waited. He could scarcely contain his impatience.

But the conspirators waited in vain for the coach to ride into the trap, for the day before Charles was to leave Newmarket there was a great fire in that town and many houses were burned down. That in which Charles and James were staying did not escape, and the King decided that they might as well set out for London a day before they had intended to.

Thus, when they came to that narrow stretch of road through which it was only possible for one coach to pass at a time, they went straight through, having no idea that, in the house close by, their enemies were preparing to murder them on the following day.

*   *   *

It was some weeks later when important documents were brought to Charles. It appeared that a letter from a certain Joseph Keeling to Lord Dartmouth had been discovered, and in this letter was set out an account of the conspiracy which had been planned to bear fruit near the Rye House. Some of the minor conspirators, then feeling that it might be gainful to expose the plotters now that the plot had failed, were ready to come forward, explain all that had been planned, and incriminate those who had taken part in the plot.

There had been much talk of such plots. Only a short while ago the country had been roused to fury by the Meal-Tub plot, which had been concocted by the Papists as a retaliation for all the Popish plots which had grown out of the fevered imagination of Titus Oates. In that case papers relating to the plot, which was to raise an army and set up a Presbyterian republic, were supposed to have been discovered in a meal-tub. Therefore it was felt that the King would laugh to scorn this discovery of a new plot unless there was really tangible evidence to support it. Fortunately some letters of Algernon Sydney, as well as that of Keeling, were discovered, and when these were brought to Charles he could not doubt the existence of the Rye House plot.

Essex, Russell, and Sydney, with others, were arrested. But there was one name concerned in this which filled Charles with horror. There was no doubt that murder had been intended, and Jemmy was involved; Jemmy was one of the conspirators who had plotted the murder of his father.

The country was roused to fury. The death of all the traitors was demanded. The King was as popular now as he had been on the day of his restoration. Easygoing and affable, his people delighted in him, for he was never too proud to speak to the humblest of them, man to man; that was what they loved best in him. They laughed at the gay life he led. Why should he not? they demanded. Who would not support a seraglio if it were possible? All feared his death, for it was realized that he had but driven the threat of civil war underground. It was Charles with his disregard of Parliaments, his determination to keep England at peace, and living on the bribes of Louis, who was responsible for the peaceful state now enjoyed.

Russell and Sydney were executed. Essex took his own life in prison, and a new Lord Chief Justice was appointed to mete out justice to these men. His name was George Jeffreys and he had a reputation for severity.

The Rye House plot sealed Charles' triumph, for the Whig party was now completely out of favour. Nothing could have been more opportune than the discovery and frustration of such a plot.

Charles was safer than he had been since the early days of his Restoration; but his triumph was a bitter one.

He could not keep his eyes from that name which occurred again and again in the documents: James, Duke of Monmouth. James . . . Little Jemmy . . . who had plotted to murder his own father.

On the failure of the Rye House plot, Jemmy had hastily gone into hiding, but he was writing appealing letters to his father. 'I was in this plot, Father,' he wrote, 'but I did not understand they meant to kill you.'

Then how else, my son, said Charles to himself, could they have put you on the throne?

He knew that, had he cared, he could have drawn Jemmy out of his hiding-place. He could have put Jemmy in the Tower with those other would-be murderers. But he could not bring himself to do it. He could not shut out of his mind the memory of little Jemmy, bouncing on his mother's bed, holding up imperious arms to his father.

He did not want to know where Jemmy was. If he did he must take him from his hiding-place and put him in the Tower.

It was to Nell he turned for comfort. Nell was ashamed and angry because at one time she had helped 'Prince Perkin'; she had kept him in her house and asked the King to see him. Now she realized she had preserved him that he might live to attempt to take his father's life.

'I want no more of him,' said Nell; yet she could understand the King's grief. He loved the boy. He was his son. He was as dear to him as little Lord Burford.

Louise expressed anger against Monmouth, but the King sensed her pleasure. There were secrets in Louise's eyes, and Charles knew that at one time she had entertained hopes that her son, the Duke of Richmond, might be a possible heir to the throne. Louise was afraid because he had come near death, but that fear was really for the security of her own position.

Hortense expressed horror in her serene way. But Hortense was too careless of the future even to ponder what would become of her should her benefactor die.

And there in Charles' hands was the letter from Jemmy.

'What good can it do you, Sir, to take away your own child's life that only erred and ventured his life to save yours?'

That made the King smile. It was Jemmy's assurance that he had entered into the plot only to save the conspirators from violence. He would never have agreed to murder the father who had done everything for him.

'And now I do swear to you that as from this time I will never displease you in anything, but the whole study of my life

305

shall be to show you how truly penitent I am for having done it. I suffer torments greater now than your forgiving nature would know how to inflict.'

The Duke of York came to him as he sat with the letter in his hand.

'James,' said Charles, 'I have here a letter from Jemmy.' James' face hardened.

'Oh, I know you find it hard to forgive him,' said Charles. 'He is but a boy. He was carried away by evil companions.'

'Evil, indeed, since 'twas murder they plotted.'

'He had no intention to murder. He was there to restrain the others from violence.'

'Then,' said James grimly, 'he knew not the nature of the plot.'

'I like not to see this enmity between you two, James. I think of when I am gone. Why, brother, if you persist in your religion, I give you but four years as King – and mayhap then I am being over-generous. Peace between you and Jemmy would be a beginning of better things.'

'You would call him back?' said James incredulously. 'You could find it in your heart to forgive him when he has stood beside those who plotted to take your life!'

'He is my son,' said Charles. 'I cannot believe he is all bad. He was led away. And I do not think he intended to murder his father.'

'I think he intended to murder his uncle!'

'Nay, James. Let us have peace . . . peace . . . peace. Meet the boy half way. If he begs humbly for your pardon, if he can assure us that he had no intent to murder . . .'

James smiled wanly. Charles would have his way. And James understood. He was a father himself.

*　　*　　*

Charles embraced his son. The young Duke had been brought secretly into the Palace, and Charles had prepared a letter which he would require Monmouth to sign.

'Father,' said the young man with tears in his eyes.

'Come, Jemmy,' said Charles. 'Let bygones be bygones.'

'I would never have let them kill you,' sobbed Jemmy.

'I know it. I believe it. There! Sign this, and I will see that a pardon is issued to you.'

Monmouth fell to his knees and kissed his father's hand.

'Jemmy,' said Charles, 'you do not remember, but when you were a small boy you tried to catch hold of a burning log. I stopped you in time and I did my best to make you understand that if you attempted to touch the fire you would be badly hurt. You did understand. I am telling you just that now.'

'Yes, Father, and I thank you from the bottom of my heart.'

'Now you must leave me,' said Charles. 'It would not be well for you to be discovered here now. The people do not forgive you as readily as your father does.'

So Monmouth left his father, but, even as he moved quickly away from the Palace, he was met by some of his old friends. They knew where he had been and what he had done, and they pointed out to him that he had deserted those who had supported him and sought to put him on the throne, and once the confession he had signed was made public none of his supporters would ever plan for him again. He would be deemed but a fair-weather friend. Indeed, by signing the letter his father had prepared for him he had gone over to the enemy.

Monmouth, hot-blooded and impetuous, went back to Whitehall.

He faced his father. 'I must have that confession,' he said.

'Why so?' asked Charles coldly.

'Because it would do me great harm if it is known I signed it.'

'Harm you to have it known that you did not plot against your father's life?'

'I must have it,' persisted Monmouth.

Charles handed him the paper. Monmouth grasped it, but as he lifted his eyes to his father's face he was looking at a new man. He knew that Charles had thrown aside his illusions, had forced himself to accept his Jemmy for what he was – the son who would have murdered the father who had raised him up to where he was, and had done nought but what was for his own good; and this son would have murdered that father for his crown.

'Get out of here,' said Charles.

'Father . . .' stammered Monmouth. 'Where should I go?'

'From here to hell,' said Charles.

He turned away, and the Duke crept out into the streets. He was holding the confession in his hand.

There were crowds in the streets. They were talking of Rye House. He listened to them. He took a look at his father's Palace, and he knew that at this time there was no place for him in England.

That night he took ship for Holland.

*   *   *

Charles no longer thought of Monmouth. The Rye House plot had lost him his son, but it had brought an even greater power to him and with that power was peace. He was ruling as he believed a King, endowed with the Divine Right, should rule. His brother, the Duke of York, was reinstated as Lord High Admiral and, as James would not take the Test, Charles merely signed an order that, as brother to the King, he should be exempted from this.

Then began the happy months. His private life was as peaceful as his public life. All his children – with the exception of the one whom he had loved best – brought great pleasure to him.

He looked after their welfare, delighted in their triumphs, advised them in their troubles. He took charge of his brother's children's future, and married Anne to the Protestant George of Denmark – a not very attractive young man, no gallant, no wit, no scholar; but as his chief interest in life seemed to be food, Charles doubted not that Anne would be satisfied with him. He was over-fat, but Charles merrily advised him, 'If you walk with me, hunt with me, and do justice to my niece, you will not long be distressed by fat.'

It was Louise, strangely enough, who gave him cause for a slight attack of jealousy – but this was assumed more than deeply felt. A grandson of Henri Quatre and la Belle

Gabrielle, one of the most notorious of his mistresses, came to England. This was Philippe de Vendôme, the Grand Prior of France. Louise appeared to be experiencing real passion for the first time in her life, for she seemed blind to the danger in which she was placing herself. Charles, indifferent, happy with Hortense and Nell, had really no objection to Louise's amusing herself elsewhere; he who had given his affection to Louise more for her political significance than for her physical attractions, would have stood aside. But Louise's enemies, who had gone under cover, now came forward to do all they could to make trouble between her and the King. In the end Charles arranged that the Grand Prior should be expelled from England.

It was Louise who suffered most from the affair. She was terrified that the Grand Prior, on returning to France, would make her letters public and expose her, if not to Charles' displeasure, to the ridicule of her fellow-countrymen. Louis, however, realizing the importance of Louise to his schemes and not ungrateful for what he considered the good work she had done for France, forbade the Grand Prior to speak of his English love affair, and eventually the matter was forgotten.

That winter was the coldest for years. The Thames was so thick with ice that coaches were driven across it. A fair was set up on the ice which was firm enough to bear both booths and the weight of merrymakers. There was skating, sledging, and dancing on the frozen river.

London was now springing up, a gracious city, from the ruins of the great fire. The King's architect, Christopher Wren, had long consultations with His Majesty, who took a personal interest in most of the building.

On the Continent there were continual wars. Charles, absolute monarch, kept his country aloof. He had introduced, as far as he could, freedom of religion.

'I want everyone to live under his own vine and fig-tree,' he said. 'Give me my just prerogative and for subsidies I will never ask more unless I and the nation should be so unhappy as to have a war on our hands and that at most may be one summer's business at sea.'

And so his subjects, dancing on the ice at the blanket fair, blessed Good King Charles; and the King in his Palace, with his three chief mistresses beside him, was contented, for indeed, now that he was approaching fifty-five and suffered an odd twinge of the gout, he found these three enough. His Queen Catherine was a good woman; she was docile and gentle and never gave way to those fits of jealousy which had made such strife between them in the beginning. She was as much in love with him as she ever was. Poor Catherine! He feared her life had not been as happy as it might have been.

Nell was happy now, for Charles had given Lord Burford his dukedom and the boy was the Duke of St Albans, so that Nell could strut about the Court and city, talking constantly about my lord Duke.

Dear Nelly! She deserved her dukedom. He would have liked to have given her honours for herself. And why should he not? It was others who had withheld them. Why should not Nelly be a Countess? She was his good friend – perhaps the best he ever had.

Yes, Nelly should be a Countess; and there was only one thing he needed to make him feel perfectly content. He thought often of Jemmy in Holland. It was such a pity that he could not have every member of his handsome family about him. He was so proud of them all. He was even honouring Moll Davies' girl – the last of his children, for there had been none after that bout of the disease which had robbed him of his fertility.

Ah, it was indeed a great pity that Jemmy was not there in this happy circle.

Poor Jemmy! Mayhap he had been led astray. Mayhap by now he had learned his lesson.

*   *   *

Charles was in his Palace of Whitehall. It was a Sunday and he felt completely at peace.

In the gallery a young boy was singing French love songs. At a table, not far from where the King and his mistresses were sitting, some of the courtiers were playing basset.

On one side of the King sat Louise, on the other, Nell; and not far away was the lovely Hortense. And as Charles watched them all with the utmost affection, he was thinking that soon Jemmy would be home. It would be good to see the boy again. He could not let his resentment burn against him for ever.

He bent towards Nell and said: 'And how is His Grace the Duke of St Albans?'

Nell's face was animated as she talked of her son's latest words and actions. 'His Grace hopes Your Majesty will grant him a little time tomorrow. He says it is long since he saw his father.'

'Tell His Grace that we are at his disposal,' said Charles.

'The Duke will present himself at Whitehall tomorrow.'

'Nell,' said the King, 'methinks His Grace deserves a Countess for a mother.'

Nell opened her eyes very wide; then her face was screwed up with laughter. It was the laughter she had enjoyed when she sat on the cobbles of the Cole-yard with Rose, the laughter of happiness rather than amusement.

'Countess of Greenwich, I think,' said the King.

'You are good to me, Charles,' she said.

'Nay,' he answered. 'I would have the world know that I have both love and value for you.'

*   *   *

It was late that night. The King's page, Bruce – the son of Lord Bruce, whom Charles had taken into service, having a fondness for the boy, and had declared he would have him close to his person – helped him to undress and went before him with the candle to light him to his bed-chamber.

There was no wind in the long dark gallery, yet the flame was suddenly extinguished.

''Tis well we know our way in the dark, Bruce,' said Charles, laying his hand on the young boy's shoulder.

He chatted awhile with those few whose duty it was to assist at his retirement for the night. Bruce and Harry Killigrew, who shared the bedchamber, said afterwards that they slept little. A fire burned through the night, but the King's many dogs, which occupied his sleeping apartment, were restless; and the clocks, which struck every quarter, made continual clangour. Both Bruce and Killigrew noticed that, although the King slept, he turned repeatedly from side to side and murmured in his sleep.

In the morning it was seen that Charles was very pale. He had had a sore heel for some days, which had curtailed his usual walks in the park, and when the surgeon came to dress the sore place he did not speak to him in his usual jovial manner. He said something which no one heard, and it was as though he were addressing someone whom they could not see. One of the gentlemen bent to buckle his garter and said: 'Sir, are you unwell?'

The King did not answer him; he got up suddenly and went to his closet.

Bruce, terrified, asked Chaffinch to go to the closet and see what ailed the King, for he was sure that his behaviour was very strange and it was unlike him not to answer when spoken to.

Chaffinch went into the closet and found the King trying to find the drops which he himself had made and which he believed to be efficacious for many ailments.

Chaffinch found the drops and gave them to Charles, who took them and said he felt better. He came out of the closet and, seeing that his barber had arrived and that the chair by the window was ready for him, he made his way to it.

As the barber began to shave him, Charles slipped to one side and Bruce hurried forward to catch him. The King's face was distorted and there was foam on his lips as he slipped into unconsciousness.

Those present managed to get Charles to his bed, and one of the physicians hastily drew sixteen ounces of blood. Charles had begun to writhe and twitch, and it was necessary to pry open his jaws lest he should bite his tongue.

James, Duke of York, wearing one shoe and one slipper, hurried into the apartment. He was followed by gentlemen of the Court.

'What is happening?' demanded James.

'His Majesty is very ill, mayhap dying.'

'Let this news not go beyond the Palace,' said James.

He looked at his brother and tears filled his eyes. 'Oh, God,' he cried. 'Charles . . . Charles . . . what is happening, my dear brother?' He turned to the surgeons. 'Do something, I implore you. Use all your skill. The King's life must be saved.'

Those about the King now began to minister to him. Pans of hot coal and blisters were applied to every part of his body. Cupping glasses were brought and more blood was withdrawn. They were determined to try all cures in order to find the right one. Clysters were administered, emetics, purgatives, a hot cautery, and blistering agents were applied to the head, one after another.

In spite of these attentions Charles regained consciousness.

It was impossible to keep the news from leaking from the Palace. In the streets the people heard it in shocked silence. It could not be true. Such a little while ago they had seen him sauntering in the park with a mistress on either arm, his dogs at his heels. It could not have been more than a week ago. There had been no indication that he was near his end.

The Duke of York took charge and ordered that the news must be stopped at all ports. Monmouth must not hear what was happening at home.

The King smiled wanly at all those about his bed; he tried to speak to them, but could not.

The doctors would give him no rest. They began forcing more drugs down his throat; they gave him quinine which had served him well before; they set more hot irons on his head; they put spirit of sal ammoniac under his nose that he might sneeze violently. They proceeded with their cupping and blistering all through the day.

By nightfall he had lapsed into sleep and, mercifully, while he slept, those about him ceased their ministrations.

The next day he was weak but a little better. Still his physicians continued to plague him. He must drink broth containing cream of tartar; he must take a little light ale.

He must submit to more clysters, more purging, more blood-letting, more blisters. He gave himself into the hands of his torturers with that sweetness of temper and patience which he had shown throughout his life.

To add to his discomfort, all through the day crowds entered his bedchamber to look on his suffering. He lay very still, in great pain, trying to smile at them.

In the streets the citizens wept and asked what would become of them when he was no longer there. They remembered the Popish terror; they remembered that the heir presumptive was a Catholic and that across the water the Duke of Monmouth was waiting perhaps to claim the throne.

This King of theirs, this kind-hearted cynic, this tolerant libertine, had stood between them and revolution, they believed. Therefore they must wait in fear for what would happen were he taken from them.

In the churches special services were held. Prayers were delivered that this sickness might pass and that they might see their King sauntering in his park once more.

By Wednesday he seemed better, and the Privy Council issued a bulletin to this effect. In the streets the people cheered wildly; they embraced each other; they told each other that he was a man with the strength of two; he would recover to continue to reign over them.

Although he was in great pain and was allowed no rest from his physicians, Charles managed to appear cheerful. But soon after midday on Thursday it became clear that he could not recover.

He joked in his characteristic way. 'I am sorry, gentlemen,' he said, 'to be such an unconscionable time a-dying.'

They sought new remedies, and it was hard to find one which they had not tried upon him. They gave him black cherry water, flowers of lime and lilies of the valley, and white sugar candy. They administered a spirit distilled from human skulls.

He asked for his wife. She had come earlier, they said, and now so prostrate with grief was she that she was fainting on her bed.

She had sent a message to him, begging his forgiveness for any faults she may have committed.

And when they told him this, they saw the tears in his eyes. 'Alas, poor woman,' he said. 'She begs my pardon? I beg hers with all my heart. Go tell her that.'

*   *   *

Louise was waiting outside his apartments. The attitude towards her had changed subtly, and there were many to remind her that, since she was not the King's wife, she had no place in that chamber of death. She had hung over him when he was unconscious, but he had been unable to recognize her, and a great terror possessed Louise.

What will become of me now? she asked herself.

She was rich; she would return to France, to her duchy of Aubigny. But the King of France would no longer honour her, having no need of her services. He would remind her that she had failed in the one great task for which she had been sent to England. Charles had been paid vast sums of money to declare himself a Catholic at the appropriate time. Now he was dying and he had not done this. But he must do it. Louise must return to France victorious. She must say to Louis: 'I came to do this and, although it was delayed to that time when he was on his deathbed, still I did what I set out to do.'

She thought of Charles, only half conscious in his agony, made more acute by the attention of his doctors. It might well be that now was the time, when he could not be fully aware of what he did.

It must be done. Only thus could Louise serve the King to whose country she must soon return.

She sent for Barrillon.

'Monsieur L'Ambassadeur,' she said, 'I am now going to reveal a secret which could cost me my head. The King is at the bottom of his heart a Catholic. There is no one to administer to his need. I cannot in decency enter his room, for the Queen is there constantly. Go to the Duke of York and tell him of this. There is little time in which to save his brother's soul.'

Barrillon understood. He nodded admiringly. It was in the interests of France that the King should die a Catholic.

By great good fortune, when Bishop Ken had come to the King's bedside to administer the last rites of the Church of England, Charles had turned wearily away. He had submitted to too much. He had never been a good churchman and he was not the man to change on his deathbed. He had lived his life as he had meant to live it; he had declared that the true sins were malice and unkindness and, within his limits, he had done his best to avoid these sins. He had said that the God he visualized would not wish a gentleman to forgo his pleasures. He had meant that; and he was no coward to scuttle for safety at the last moment.

The Duke of York came into his bedroom. He knelt by the bed and whispered in his ear. 'For your soul's sake, Charles, you must die in the Catholic Faith. The Duchess of Portsmouth has told me of your secret belief. She will never forgive herself if it is denied to you.'

At the mention of Louise's name Charles tried to turn his glazed eyes to his brother, and a smile touched his lips. Then he said, half comprehending: 'James . . . do nothing that will bring harm to you.'

'I will do this,' said James, 'though it cost me my life. I will bring a priest to you.'

Into the chamber of death an altar was smuggled, and with it came a priest, Father Huddleston, a man who had helped to save Charles after Worcester and whom Charles had saved from death during the Popish troubles. In spite of his drugged and dazed state, Charles recognized him.

'Sir,' said James, 'here is a man whose life you saved and who is now come to save your soul.'

'He is welcome,' said Charles.

Huddleston knelt by the bed.

'Is it Your Majesty's wish to receive the final rites of the Catholic Church?'

The glazed eyes stared ahead. Charles was conscious of little but his pain-racked body. He thought it was Louise who was beside him. Louise making her demands on behalf of the King she was really serving.

316

'With all my heart,' he said wearily.

'Do you desire to die in that communion?'

Charles nodded.

He repeated all that Huddleston wished him to.

His lips moved. 'Mercy, sweet Jesu, mercy.'

Extreme unction was administered. Charles could scarcely see the cross which Huddleston held before his eyes. He was conscious for brief intervals before he swooned with the pain and the exhaustion which was in part due to the terrible ordeal through which his physicians had caused him to pass.

When the priest left, those who had been waiting outside burst into the room.

*　　*　　*

From her house in Pall Mall Nell looked out on the street. She saw the people silently standing about. London had changed. It was sombre out there in the streets.

She could not believe that she would never see him again. She thought of the first occasion she had seen him at the time of his Restoration, tall, lean and smiling, the most charming man in the world. She thought of the last time she had seen him when he had taken her hand and promised to make her a Countess that all might know what love and value he had for her.

And now . . . never to see him again! How could she picture her life without him?

She sat still while the tears slowly ran down her cheeks.

She thought, I shall never be happy again.

Her son came and threw himself into her arms. He was sobbing wildly.

He knew, for how could such things be kept from children?

She held him fast against her, for in those moments of desolate grief she could not bear to look into that face which was so like his father's.

She did not think of the future. What did the future matter? Life for her was blank since her King and her love would no longer be there.

*　　*　　*

317

Charles lay still, uncomplaining. He was aware that he was dying and that those who crowded into his apartment had come to take their last farewell.

They knelt about his bed, his beloved children, and he blessed them in turn. He looked in vain for one, for he had forgotten that his eldest son was still in exile.

He called his brother to him.

'James,' he said. 'James . . . I am going. . . . It will not be long now. Forgive me if I have been unkind. I was forced to it. James . . . may good luck attend you. Look to Louise. Look to my poor children. And, James, let not poor Nelly starve.'

He sank back then; he was conscious of those weeping about his bed. Scenes from his past life flitted before his eyes. He thought he was sore from riding so far to Boscobel and Whiteladies. He thought he was cramped because he was hiding in an oak while the Roundheads searched for him below.

But then he knew that he was in his bed and that soon this familiar room would be his no more.

'Open the curtains,' he said, 'that I may once more see the day.'

So they drew them back, and he stared at the window. He listened to the sounds of his city's waking to life, and he slipped into unconsciousness again.

He was breathing so painfully that his gasps mingled oddly with the ticking of the clocks. His dogs began to whimper. Then, just before noon, he fell back on his pillows and ceased to live.

Bruce, who had loved him dearly, said as the tears rolled down his cheeks: 'He is gone . . . my good and gracious master, the best that ever reigned over us. He has died in peace and glory, and may the Lord God have mercy on his soul.'

Other Pan books that may
interest you are listed overleaf

Susan Howatch
Cashelmara £3.95

Three generations of drama, passion and turmoil . . .

A glorious, full-blooded novel, brimming with memorable characters, which centres on Cashelmara, the coldly beautiful Georgian house in Galway, ancestral home of Edward de Salis.

Charged with emotion, the fast-moving plot follows the turbulent fortunes of an aristocratic Victorian family through half a century of furious encounters, ill-advised liaisons and bitter-sweet interludes of love.

Penmarric £3.95

The magnificent bestseller of the passionate loves and hatreds of a Cornish family.

'I was ten years old when I first saw the inheritance and twenty years old when I saw Janna Roslyn, but my reaction to both was identical. I wanted them.'

The inheritance is Penmarric, a huge gaunt house in Cornwall belonging to the tempestuous, hot-blooded Castallacks: Janna Roslyn is a beautiful village girl who becomes mistress of Laurance Castallack, wife to his son . . .